HERE AND THERE

SHORT STORIES

BY

W. SOMERSET MAUGHAM

THE REPRINT SOCIETY
LONDON

THIS EDITION PUBLISHED BY THE REPRINT SOCIETY LTD
BY ARRANGEMENT WITH WILLIAM HEINEMANN LTD
1948

PRINTED IN GREAT BRITAIN BY WILLIAM CLOWES AND SONS LTD
LONDON AND BECCLES

CONTENTS

THREE FAT WOMEN OF ANTIBES

ONE was called Mrs. Richman and she was a widow. The second was called Mrs. Sutcliffe; she was American and she had divorced two husbands. The third was called Miss Hickson and she was a spinster. They were all in the comfortable forties and they were all well off. Mrs. Sutcliffe had the odd first name of Arrow. When she was young and slender she had liked it well enough. It suited her and the jests it occasioned though too often repeated were very flattering; she was not disinclined to believe that it suited her character too: it suggested directness, speed and purpose. She liked it less now that her delicate features had grown muzzy with fat, that her arms and shoulders were so substantial and her hips so massive. It was increasingly difficult to find dresses to make her look as she liked to look. The jests her name gave rise to now were made behind her back and she very well knew that they were far from obliging. But she was by no means resigned to middle age. She still wore blue to bring out the colour of her eyes and, with the help of art, her fair hair had kept its lustre. What she liked about Beatrice Richman and Frances Hickson was that they were both so much fatter than she, it made her look quite slim; they were both of them older and much inclined to treat her as a little young thing. It was not disagreeable. They were good-natured women and they chaffed her pleasantly about her beaux; they had both given up the thought of that kind of nonsense, indeed Miss Hickson had never given it a moment's consideration, but they were sympathetic to her flirtations. It was understood that one of these days Arrow would make a third man happy.

"Only you mustn't get any heavier, darling," said Mrs. Richman.

"And for goodness' sake make certain of his bridge," said Miss Hickson.

They saw for her a man of about fifty, but well-preserved and of distinguished carriage, an admiral on the retired list and a good golfer, or a widower without encumbrances, but in any case with a substantial income. Arrow listened to them amiably, and kept to herself the fact that this was not at all her idea. It was true that she would have liked to marry again, but her fancy turned to a dark slim Italian with flashing eyes and a sonorous title or to a Spanish don of noble lineage; and not a day more than thirty. There were times when, looking at herself in her mirror, she was certain she did not look any more than that herself.

They were great friends, Miss Hickson, Mrs. Richman and Arrow Sutcliffe. It was their fat that had brought them together and bridge that had cemented their alliance. They had met first at Carlsbad where they were staying at the same hotel and were treated by the same doctor who used them with the same ruthlessness. Beatrice Richman was enormous. She was a handsome woman, with fine eyes, rouged cheeks and painted lips. She was very well content to be a widow with a handsome fortune. She adored her food. She liked bread and butter, cream, potatoes and suet puddings, and for eleven months of the year ate pretty well everything she had a mind to, and for one month went to Carlsbad to reduce. But every year she grew fatter. She upbraided the doctor, but got no sympathy from him. He pointed out to her various plain and simple facts.

"But if I'm never to eat a thing I like life isn't worth living," she expostulated.

He shrugged his disapproving shoulders. Afterwards she told Miss Hickson that she was beginning to suspect he wasn't so clever as she had thought. Miss Hickson gave a great guffaw. She was that sort of woman. She had a deep bass voice, a large flat sallow face from which twinkled little bright eyes; she walked with a slouch, her hands in her pockets, and when she could do so without exciting attention smoked a long cigar. She dressed as like a man as she could.

"What the deuce should I look like in frills and furbelows?" she said. "When you're as fat as I am you may just as well be comfortable."

She wore tweeds and heavy boots and whenever she could went about bareheaded. But she was as strong as an ox and boasted that few men could drive a longer ball than she. She was plain of speech, and she could swear more variously than a stevedore. Though her name was Frances she preferred to be called Frank. Masterful, but with tact, it was her jovial strength of character that held the three together. They drank their waters together, had their baths at the same hour, they took their strenuous walks together, pounded about the tennis court with a professional to make them run, and ate at the same table their sparse and regulated meals. Nothing impaired their good humour but the scales, and when one or other of them weighed as much on one day as she had the day before neither Frank's coarse jokes, the *bonhomie* of Beatrice nor Arrow's pretty kittenish ways sufficed to dispel the gloom. Then drastic measures were resorted to, the culprit went to bed for twenty-four hours and nothing passed her lips but the doctor's famous vegetable soup which tasted like hot water in which cabbage had been well rinsed.

Never were three women greater friends. They would have been independent of anyone else if they had not needed a fourth at bridge. They were fierce, enthusiastic players and the moment the day's cure was over they sat down at the bridge table. Arrow, feminine as she was, played the best game of the three, a hard, brilliant game, in which she showed no mercy and never conceded a point or failed to take advantage of a mistake. Beatrice was solid and reliable. Frank was dashing;

1*

she was a great theorist, and had all the authorities at the tip of
her tongue. They had long arguments over the rival systems.
They bombarded one another with Culbertson and Sims. It
was obvious that not one of them ever played a card without
fifteen good reasons, but it was also obvious from the sub-
sequent conversation that there were fifteen equally good
reasons why she should not have played it. Life would have
been perfect, even with the prospect of twenty-four hours of
that filthy soup when the doctor's rotten (Beatrice) bloody
(Frank) lousy (Arrow) scales pretended one hadn't lost an
ounce in two days, if only there had not been this constant
difficulty of finding someone to play with them who was in
their class.

It was for this reason that on the occasion with which this
narrative deals Frank invited Lena Finch to come and stay
with them at Antibes. They were spending some weeks there
on Frank's suggestion. It seemed absurd to her, with her
common sense, that immediately the cure was over Beatrice
who always lost twenty pounds should by giving way to her
ungovernable appetite put it all on again. Beatrice was weak.
She needed a person of strong will to watch her diet. She
proposed then that on leaving Carlsbad they should take a
house at Antibes where they could get plenty of exercise,
everyone knew that nothing slimmed you like swimming, and
as far as possible could go on with the cure. With a cook of
their own they could at least avoid things that were obviously
fattening. There was no reason why they should not all lose
several pounds more. It seemed a very good idea. Beatrice
knew what was good for her, and she could resist temptation
well enough if temptation was not put right under her nose.
Besides, she liked gambling, and a flutter at the Casino two or
three times a week would pass the time very pleasantly. Arrow
adored Antibes, and she would be looking her best after a
month at Carlsbad. She could just pick and choose among the

young Italians, the passionate Spaniards, the gallant Frenchmen, and the long-limbed English who sauntered about all day
in bathing trunks and gay-coloured dressing-gowns. The plan
worked very well. They had a grand time. Two days a week
they ate nothing but hard-boiled eggs and raw tomatoes and
they mounted the scales every morning with light hearts.
Arrow got down to eleven stone and felt just like a girl;
Beatrice and Frank by standing in a certain way just avoided
the thirteen. The machine they had bought registered kilo-
grammes, and they got extraordinarily clever at translating
these in the twinkling of an eye to pounds and ounces.

But the fourth at bridge continued to be the difficulty. This
person played like a fool, the other was so slow that it drove
you frantic, one was quarrelsome, another was a bad loser, a
third was next door to a crook. It was strange how hard it was
to find exactly the player you wanted.

One morning when they were sitting in pyjamas on the
terrace overlooking the sea, drinking their tea (without milk or
sugar) and eating a rusk prepared by Dr. Hudebert and guaran-
teed not to be fattening, Frank looked up from her letters.

"Lena Finch is coming down to the Riviera," she said.

"Who's she?" asked Arrow.

"She married a cousin of mine. He died a couple of months
ago and she's just recovering from a nervous breakdown.
What about asking her to come here for a fortnight?"

"Does she play bridge?" asked Beatrice.

"You bet your life she does," boomed Frank in her deep
voice. "And a damned good game too. We should be absolutely independent of outsiders."

"How old is she?" asked Arrow.

"Same age as I am."

"That sounds all right."

It was settled. Frank, with her usual decisiveness, stalked
out as soon as she had finished her breakfast to send a wire,

and three days later Lena Finch arrived. Frank met her at the station. She was in deep but not obtrusive mourning for the recent death of her husband. Frank had not seen her for two years. She kissed her warmly and took a good look at her.

"You're very thin, darling," she said.

Lena smiled bravely.

"I've been through a good deal lately. I've lost a lot of weight."

Frank sighed, but whether from sympathy with her cousin's sad loss, or from envy, was not obvious.

Lena was not however unduly depressed, and after a quick bath was quite ready to accompany Frank to Eden Roc. Frank introduced the stranger to her two friends and they sat down in what was known as the Monkey House. It was an enclosure covered with glass overlooking the sea, with a bar at the back, and it was crowded with chattering people in bathing costumes, pyjamas or dressing-gowns, who were seated at the tables having drinks. Beatrice's soft heart went out to the lorn widow and Arrow, seeing that she was pale, quite ordinary to look at and probably forty-eight, was prepared to like her very much. A waiter approached them.

"What will you have, Lena dear?" Frank asked.

"Oh, I don't know, what you all have, a dry Martini or a White Lady."

Arrow and Beatrice gave her a quick look. Everyone knows how fattening cocktails are.

"I daresay you're tired after your journey," said Frank kindly.

She ordered a dry Martini for Lena and a mixed lemon and orange juice for herself and her two friends.

"We find alcohol isn't very good in all this heat," she explained.

"Oh, it never affects me at all," Lena answered airily. "I like cocktails."

Arrow went very slightly pale under her rouge (neither she nor Beatrice ever wet their faces when they bathed and they thought it absurd of Frank, a woman of her size, to pretend she liked diving) but she said nothing. The conversation was gay and easy, they all said the obvious things with gusto, and presently they strolled back to the villa for luncheon.

In each napkin were two little antifat rusks. Lena gave a bright smile as she put them by the side of her plate.

"May I have some bread?" she asked.

The grossest indecency would not have fallen on the ears of those three women with such a shock. Not one of them had eaten bread for ten years. Even Beatrice, greedy as she was, drew the line there. Frank, the good hostess, recovered herself first.

"Of course, darling," she said and turning to the butler asked him to bring some.

"And some butter," said Lena in that pleasant easy way of hers.

There was a moment's embarrassed silence.

"I don't know if there's any in the house," said Frank, "but I'll enquire. There may be some in the kitchen."

"I adore bread and butter, don't you?" said Lena, turning to Beatrice.

Beatrice gave a sickly smile and an evasive reply. The butler brought a long crisp roll of French bread. Lena slit it in two and plastered it with the butter which was miraculously produced. A grilled sole was served.

"We eat very simply here," said Frank. "I hope you won't mind."

"Oh, no, I like my food very plain," said Lena as she took some butter and spread it over the fish. "As long as I can have bread and butter and potatoes and cream I'm quite happy."

The three friends exchanged a glance. Frank's great sallow face sagged a little and she looked with distaste at the dry, insipid sole on her plate. Beatrice came to the rescue.

"It's such a bore, we can't get cream here," she said. "It's one of the things one has to do without on the Riviera."

"What a pity," said Lena.

The rest of the luncheon consisted of lamb cutlets, with the fat carefully removed so that Beatrice should not be led astray, and spinach boiled in water, with stewed pears to end up with. Lena tasted her pears and gave the butler a look of enquiry. That resourceful man understood her at once and though powdered sugar had never been served at that table before handed her without a moment's hesitation a bowl of it. She helped herself liberally. The other three pretended not to notice. Coffee was served and Lena took three lumps of sugar in hers.

"You have a very sweet tooth," said Arrow in a tone which she struggled to keep friendly.

"We think saccharine so much more sweetening," said Frank, as she put a tiny tablet of it into her coffee.

"Disgusting stuff," said Lena.

Beatrice's mouth drooped at the corners, and she gave the lump sugar a yearning look.

"Beatrice," boomed Frank sternly.

Beatrice stifled a sigh, and reached for the saccharine.

Frank was relieved when they could sit down to the bridge table. It was plain to her that Arrow and Beatrice were upset. She wanted them to like Lena and she was anxious that Lena should enjoy her fortnight with them. For the first rubber Arrow cut with the newcomer.

"Do you play Vanderbilt or Culbertson?" she asked her.

"I have no conventions," Lena answered in a happy-go-lucky way, "I play by the light of nature."

"I play strict Culbertson," said Arrow acidly.

The three fat women braced themselves to the fray. No conventions indeed! They'd learn her. When it came to bridge even Frank's family feeling was forgotten and she settled down with the same determination as the others to trim the stranger in their midst. But the light of nature served Lena very well. She had a natural gift for the game and great experience. She played with imagination, quickly, boldly, and with assurance. The other players were in too high a class not to realise very soon that Lena knew what she was about, and since they were all thoroughly good-natured, generous women, they were gradually mollified. This was real bridge. They all enjoyed themselves. Arrow and Beatrice began to feel more kindly towards Lena, and Frank, noticing this, heaved a fat sigh of relief. It was going to be a success.

After a couple of hours they parted, Frank and Beatrice to have a round of golf, and Arrow to take a brisk walk with a young Prince Roccamare whose acquaintance she had lately made. He was very sweet and young and good-looking. Lena said she would rest.

They met again just before dinner.

"I hope you've been all right, Lena dear," said Frank. "I was rather conscience-stricken at leaving you with nothing to do all this time."

"Oh, don't apologise. I had a lovely sleep and then I went down to Juan and had a cocktail. And d'you know what I discovered? You'll be so pleased. I found a dear little tea-shop where they've got the most beautiful thick fresh cream. I've ordered half a pint to be sent every day. I thought it would be my little contribution to the household."

Her eyes were shining. She was evidently expecting them to be delighted.

"How very kind of you," said Frank, with a look that sought to quell the indignation that she saw on the faces of her two friends. "But we never eat cream. In this climate it makes one so bilious."

"I shall have to eat it all myself then," said Lena cheerfully.

"Don't you ever think of your figure?" Arrow asked with icy deliberation.

"The doctor said I must eat."

"Did he say you must eat bread and butter and potatoes and cream?"

"Yes. That's what I thought you meant when you said you had simple food."

"You'll get simply enormous," said Beatrice.

Lena laughed gaily.

"No, I shan't. You see, nothing ever makes me fat. I've always eaten everything I wanted to and it's never had the slightest effect on me."

The stony silence that followed this speech was only broken by the entrance of the butler.

"*Mademoiselle est servie*," he announced.

They talked the matter over late that night, after Lena had gone to bed, in Frank's room. During the evening they had been furiously cheerful, and they had chaffed one another with a friendliness that would have taken in the keenest observer. But now they dropped the mask. Beatrice was sullen, Arrow was spiteful and Frank was unmanned.

"It's not very nice for me to sit there and see her eat all the things I particularly like," said Beatrice plaintively.

"It's not very nice for any of us," Frank snapped back.

"You should never have asked her here," said Arrow.

"How was I to know?" cried Frank.

"I can't help thinking that if she really cared for her husband she would hardly eat so much," said Beatrice. "He's only been buried two months. I mean, I think you ought to show some respect for the dead."

"Why can't she eat the same as we do?" asked Arrow viciously. "She's a guest."

"Well, you heard what she said. The doctor told her she must eat."

"Then she ought to go to a sanatorium."

"It's more than flesh and blood can stand, Frank," moaned Beatrice.

"If I can stand it you can stand it."

"She's your cousin, she's not our cousin," said Arrow. "I'm not going to sit there for fourteen days and watch that woman make a hog of herself."

"It's so vulgar to attach all this importance to food," Frank boomed, and her voice was deeper than ever. "After all the only thing that counts really is spirit."

"Are you calling *me* vulgar, Frank?" asked Arrow with flashing eyes.

"No, of course she isn't," interrupted Beatrice.

"I wouldn't put it past you to go down in the kitchen when we're all in bed and have a good square meal on the sly."

Frank sprang to her feet.

"How dare you say that, Arrow! I'd never ask anybody to do what I'm not prepared to do myself. Have you known me all these years and do you think me capable of such a mean thing?"

"How is it you never take off any weight then?"

Frank gave a gasp and burst into a flood of tears.

"What a cruel thing to say! I've lost pounds and pounds."

She wept like a child. Her vast body shook and great tears splashed on her mountainous bosom.

"Darling, I didn't mean it," cried Arrow.

She threw herself on her knees and enveloped what she could of Frank in her own plump arms. She wept and the mascara ran down her cheeks.

"D'you mean to say I don't look thinner?" Frank sobbed. "After all I've gone through."

"Yes, dear, of course you do," cried Arrow through her tears. "Everybody's noticed it."

Beatrice, though naturally of a placid disposition, began to cry gently. It was very pathetic. Indeed, it would have been a hard heart that failed to be moved by the sight of Frank, that lion-hearted woman, crying her eyes out. Presently, however, they dried their tears and had a little brandy and water, which every doctor had told them was the least fattening thing they could drink, and then they felt much better. They decided that Lena should have the nourishing food that had been ordered her and they made a solemn resolution not to let it disturb their equanimity. She was certainly a first-rate bridge player and after all it was only for a fortnight. They would do whatever they could to make her stay enjoyable. They kissed one another warmly and separated for the night feeling strangely uplifted. Nothing should interfere with the wonderful friendship that had brought so much happiness into their three lives.

But human nature is weak. You must not ask too much of it. They ate grilled fish while Lena ate macaroni sizzling with cheese and butter, they ate grilled cutlets and boiled spinach while Lena ate *pâté de foie gras*; twice a week they ate hard-boiled eggs and raw tomatoes, while Lena ate peas swimming in cream and potatoes cooked in all sorts of delicious ways. The chef was a good chef and he leapt at the opportunity afforded him to send up one dish more rich, tasty and succulent than the other.

"Poor Jim," sighed Lena, thinking of her husband, "he loved French cooking."

The butler disclosed the fact that he could make half a dozen kinds of cocktail and Lena informed them that the doctor had recommended her to drink burgundy at luncheon and champagne at dinner. The three fat women persevered. They were gay, chatty and even hilarious (such is the natural gift that women have for deception) but Beatrice grew limp and forlorn, and Arrow's tender blue eyes acquired a steely glint. Frank's deep voice grew more raucous. It was when they played bridge that the strain showed itself. They had always been fond of talking over their hands, but their discussions had been friendly. Now a distinct bitterness crept in and sometimes one pointed out a mistake to another with quite unnecessary frankness. Discussion turned to argument and argument to altercation. Sometimes the session ended in angry silence. Once Frank accused Arrow of deliberately letting her down. Two or three times Beatrice, the softest of the three, was reduced to tears. On another occasion Arrow flung down her cards and swept out of the room in a pet. Their tempers were getting frayed. Lena was the peacemaker.

"I think it's such a pity to quarrel over bridge," she said. "After all, it's only a game."

It was all very well for her. She had had a square meal and half a bottle of champagne. Besides, she had phenomenal luck. She was winning all their money. The score was put down in a book after each session, and hers mounted up day after day with unfailing regularity. Was there no justice in the world? They began to hate one another. And though they hated her too they could not resist confiding in her. Each of them went to her separately and told her how detestable the others were. Arrow said she was sure it was bad for her to see so much of women so much older than herself. She had a good mind to sacrifice her share of the lease and go to Venice for the rest of the summer. Frank told Lena that with her masculine mind it was too much to expect that she could be satisfied with anyone so frivolous as Arrow and so frankly stupid as Beatrice.

"I must have intellectual conversation," she boomed. "When you have a brain like mine you've got to consort with your intellectual equals."

Beatrice only wanted peace and quiet.

"Really I hate women," she said. "They're so unreliable; they're so malicious."

By the time Lena's fortnight drew to its close the three fat women were barely on speaking terms. They kept up appearances before Lena, but when she was not there made no pretences. They had got past quarrelling. They ignored one another, and when this was not possible treated each other with icy politeness.

Lena was going to stay with friends on the Italian Riviera and Frank saw her off by the same train as that by which she had arrived. She was taking away with her a lot of their money.

"I don't know how to thank you," she said, as she got into the carriage. "I've had a wonderful visit."

If there was one thing that Frank Hickson prided herself on more than on being a match for any man it was that she was a gentlewoman, and her reply was perfect in its combination of majesty and graciousness.

"We've all enjoyed having you here, Lena," she said. "It's been a real treat."

But when she turned away from the departing train she heaved such a vast sigh of relief that the platform shook beneath her. She flung back her massive shoulders and strode home to the villa.

"Ouf!" she roared at intervals. "Ouf!"

She changed into her one-piece bathing-suit, put on her espadrilles and a man's dressing-gown (no nonsense about it) and went to Eden Roc. There was still time for a bathe before luncheon. She passed through the Monkey House, looking about her to say good morning to anyone she knew, for she felt on a sudden at peace with mankind, and then stopped dead still. She could not believe her eyes. Beatrice was sitting at one of the tables, by herself; she wore the pyjamas she had bought at Molyneux's a day or two before, she had a string of pearls round her neck, and Frank's quick eyes saw that she had just had her hair waved; her cheeks, her eyes, her lips were made up. Fat, nay vast, as she was none could deny that she was an extremely handsome woman. But what was she doing? With the slouching gait of the Neanderthal man which was Frank's characteristic walk she went up to Beatrice. In her black bathing-dress Frank looked like the huge cetacean which the Japanese catch in the Torres Straits and which the vulgar call a sea-cow.

"Beatrice, what are you doing?" she cried in her deep voice. It was like the roll of thunder in the distant mountains. Beatrice looked at her coolly.

"Eating," she answered.

"Damn it, I can see you're eating."

In front of Beatrice was a plate of *croissants* and a plate of butter, a pot of strawberry jam, coffee and a jug of cream. Beatrice was spreading butter thick on the delicious hot bread, covering this with jam, and then pouring the thick cream over all.

"You'll kill yourself," said Frank.

"I don't care," mumbled Beatrice with her mouth full.

"You'll put on pounds and pounds."

"Go to hell!"

She actually laughed in Frank's face. My God, how good those *croissants* smelt!

"I'm disappointed in you, Beatrice. I thought you had more character."

"It's your fault. That blasted woman. You would have her down. For a fortnight I've watched her gorge like a hog. It's more than flesh and blood can stand. I'm going to have one square meal if I bust."

The tears welled up to Frank's eyes. Suddenly she felt very weak and womanly. She would have liked a strong man to take her on his knee and pet her and cuddle her and call her little baby names. Speechless she sank down on a chair by Beatrice's side. A waiter came up. With a pathetic gesture she waved towards the coffee and *croissants*.

"I'll have the same," she sighed.

She listlessly reached out her hand to take a roll, but Beatrice snatched away the plate.

"No, you don't," she said. "You wait till you get your own."

Frank called her a name which ladies seldom apply to one another in affection. In a moment the waiter brought her *croissants*, butter, jam and coffee.

"Where's the cream, you fool?" she roared like a lioness at bay.

She began to eat. She ate gluttonously. The place was beginning to fill up with bathers coming to enjoy a cocktail or two after having done their duty by the sun and the sea. Presently Arrow strolled along with Prince Roccamare. She had on a beautiful silk wrap which she held tightly round her with one hand in order to look as slim as possible and she bore her head high so that he should not see her double chin. She was laughing gaily. She felt like a girl. He had just told her (in Italian) that her eyes made the blue of the Mediterranean look like pea-soup. He left her to go into the men's room to brush his sleek black hair and they arranged to meet in five minutes for a drink. Arrow walked on to the women's room to put a little more rouge on her cheeks and a little more red on her lips. On her way she caught sight of Frank and Beatrice. She stopped. She could hardly believe her eyes.

"My God!" she cried. "You beasts. You hogs." She seized a chair. "Waiter."

Her appointment went clean out of her head. In the twinkling of an eye the waiter was at her side.

"Bring me what these ladies are having," she ordered.

Frank lifted her great heavy head from her plate.

"Bring me some *pâté de foie gras*," she boomed.

"Frank," cried Beatrice.

"Shut up."

"All right. I'll have some too."

The coffee was brought and the hot rolls and cream and the *pâté de foie gras* and they set to. They spread the cream on the *pâté* and they ate it. They devoured great spoonfuls of jam. They crunched the delicious crisp bread voluptuously. What was love to Arrow then? Let the Prince keep his palace in Rome and his castle in the Apennines. They did not speak. What they were about was much too serious. They ate with solemn, ecstatic fervour.

"I haven't eaten potatoes for twenty-five years," said Frank in a far-off brooding tone.

"Waiter," cried Beatrice, "bring fried potatoes for three."

"*Très bien, Madame.*"

The potatoes were brought. Not all the perfumes of Arabia smelt so sweet. They ate them with their fingers.

"Bring me a dry Martini," said Arrow.

"You can't have a dry Martini in the middle of a meal, Arrow," said Frank.

"Can't I? You wait and see."

"All right then. Bring me a double dry Martini," said Frank.

"Bring three double dry Martinis," said Beatrice.

They were brought and drunk at a gulp. The women looked at one another and sighed. The misunderstandings of the last fortnight dissolved and the sincere affection each had for the other welled up again in their hearts. They could hardly believe that they had ever contemplated the possibility of severing a friendship that had brought them so much solid satisfaction. They finished the potatoes.

"I wonder if they've got any chocolate éclairs," said Beatrice.

"Of course they have."

And of course they had. Frank thrust one whole into her huge mouth, swallowed it and seized another, but before she ate it she looked at the other two and plunged a vindictive dagger into the heart of the monstrous Lena.

"You can say what you like, but the truth is she played a damned rotten game of bridge, really."

"Lousy," agreed Arrow.

But Beatrice suddenly thought she would like a meringue.

THE LOTUS EATER

MOST people, the vast majority in fact, lead the lives that circumstances have thrust upon them, and though some repine, looking upon themselves as round pegs in square holes, and think that if things had been different they might have made a much better showing, the greater part accept their lot, if not with serenity, at all events with resignation. They are like tramcars travelling for ever on the selfsame rails. They go backwards and forwards, backwards and forwards, inevitably, till they can go no longer and then are sold as scrap-iron. It is not often that you find a man who has boldly taken the course of his life into his own hands. When you do, it is worth while having a good look at him.

That is why I was curious to meet Thomas Wilson. It was an interesting and a bold thing he had done. Of course the end was not yet and until the experiment was concluded it was impossible to call it successful. But from what I had heard it seemed he must be an odd sort of fellow and I thought I should like to know him. I had been told he was reserved, but I had a notion that with patience and tact I could persuade him to confide in me. I wanted to hear the facts from his own lips. People exaggerate, they love to romanticise, and I was quite prepared to discover that his story was not nearly so singular as I had been led to believe.

And this impression was confirmed when at last I made his acquaintance. It was on the Piazza in Capri, where I was spending the month of August at a friend's villa, and a little before sunset, when most of the inhabitants, native and foreign, gather together to chat with their friends in the cool of the evening. There is a terrace that overlooks the bay of Naples, and when the sun sinks slowly into the sea the island of Ischia is silhouetted against a blaze of splendour. It is one of the most lovely sights in the world. I was standing there with my friend and host watching it, when suddenly he said:

"Look, there's Wilson."

"Where?"

"The man sitting on the parapet, with his back to us. He's got a blue shirt on."

I saw an undistinguished back and a small head of grey hair short and rather thin.

"I wish he'd turn round," I said.

"He will presently."

"Ask him to come and have a drink with us at Morgano's."

"All right."

The instant of overwhelming beauty had passed and the sun, like the top of an orange, was dipping into a wine-red sea. We turned round and leaning our backs against the parapet looked at the people who were sauntering to and fro. They were all talking their heads off and the cheerful noise was exhilarating. Then the church bell, rather cracked, but with a fine resonant note, began to ring. The Piazza at Capri, with its clock tower over the footpath that leads up from the harbour, with the church up a flight of steps, is a perfect setting for an opera by Donizetti, and you felt that the voluble crowd might at any moment break out into a rattling chorus. It was charming and unreal.

I was so intent on the scene that I had not noticed Wilson get off the parapet and come towards us. As he passed us my friend stopped him.

"Hulloa, Wilson, I haven't seen you bathing the last few days."

"I've been bathing on the other side for a change."

My friend then introduced me. Wilson shook hands with me politely, but with indifference; a great many strangers come to Capri for a few days, or a few weeks, and I had no doubt he was constantly meeting people who came and went; and then my friend asked him to come along and have a drink with us.

"I was just going back to supper," he said.

"Can't it wait?" I asked.

"I suppose it can," he smiled.

Though his teeth were not very good his smile was attractive. It was gentle and kindly. He was dressed in a blue cotton shirt and a pair of grey trousers, much creased and none too clean, of a thin canvas, and on his feet he wore a pair of very old espadrilles. The get-up was picturesque, and very suitable to the place and the weather, but it did not at all go with his face. It was a lined, long face, deeply sunburned, thin-lipped, with small grey eyes rather close together and tight, neat features. The grey hair was carefully brushed. It was not a plain face, indeed in his youth Wilson might have been good-looking, but a prim one. He wore the blue shirt, open at the neck, and the grey canvas trousers, not as though they belonged to him, but as though, shipwrecked in his pyjamas, he had been fitted out with odd garments by compassionate strangers. Notwithstanding this careless attire he looked like the manager of a branch office in an insurance company, who should by rights be wearing a black coat with pepper and salt trousers, a white collar and an unobjectionable tie. I could very well see myself going to him to claim the insurance money when I had lost a watch, and being rather disconcerted while I answered the questions he put to me by his obvious impression, for all his politeness, that people who made such claims were either fools or knaves.

Moving off, we strolled across the Piazza and down the street till we came to Morgano's. We sat in the garden. Around us people were talking in Russian, German, Italian and English. We ordered drinks. Donna Lucia, the host's wife, waddled up and in her low, sweet voice passed the time of day with us. Though middle-aged now and portly, she had still traces of the wonderful beauty that thirty years before had driven artists to paint so many bad portraits of her. Her eyes, large and liquid, were the eyes of Hera and her smile was affectionate and gracious. We three gossiped for a while, for there is always a scandal of one sort or another in Capri to make a topic of conversation, but nothing was said of particular interest and in a little while Wilson got up and left us. Soon afterwards we strolled up to my friend's villa to dine. On the way he asked me what I had thought of Wilson.

"Nothing," I said. "I don't believe there's a word of truth in your story."

"Why not?"

"He isn't the sort of man to do that sort of thing."

"How does anyone know what anyone is capable of?"

"I should put him down as an absolutely normal man of business who's retired on a comfortable income from gilt-edged securities. I think your story's just the ordinary Capri tittle-tattle."

"Have it your own way," said my friend.

We were in the habit of bathing at a beach called the Baths of Tiberius. We took a fly down the road to a certain point and then wandered through lemon groves and vineyards, noisy with cicadas and heavy with the hot smell of the sun, till we came to the top of the cliff down which a steep winding path led to the sea. A day or two later, just before we got down my friend said:

"Oh, there's Wilson back again."

We scrunched over the beach, the only drawback to the bathing-place being that it was shingle and not sand, and as we came along Wilson saw us and waved. He was standing up, a pipe in his mouth, and he wore nothing but a pair of trunks. His body was dark brown, thin but not emaciated, and, considering his wrinkled face and grey hair, youthful. Hot from our walk, we undressed quickly and plunged at once into the water. Six feet from the shore it was thirty feet deep, but so clear that you could see the bottom. It was warm, yet invigorating.

When I got out Wilson was lying on his belly, with a towel under him, reading a book. I lit a cigarette and went and sat down beside him.

"Had a nice swim?" he asked.

He put his pipe inside his book to mark the place and closing it put it down on the pebbles beside him. He was evidently willing to talk.

"Lovely," I said. "It's the best bathing in the world."

"Of course people think those were the Baths of Tiberius." He waved his hand towards a shapeless mass of masonry that stood half in the water and half out. "But that's all rot. It was just one of his villas, you know."

I did. But it is just as well to let people tell you things when they want to. It disposes them kindly towards you if you suffer them to impart information. Wilson gave a chuckle.

"Funny old fellow, Tiberius. Pity they're saying now there's not a word of truth in all those stories about him."

He began to tell me all about Tiberius. Well, I had read my Suetonius too and I had read histories of the Early Roman Empire, so there was nothing very new to me in what he said. But I observed that he was not ill-read. I remarked on it.

"Oh, well, when I settled down here I was naturally interested, and I have plenty of time for reading. When you live in a place like this, with all its associations, it seems to make history so actual. You might almost be living in historical times yourself."

I should remark here that this was in 1913. The world was an easy, comfortable place and no one could have imagined that anything might happen seriously to disturb the serenity of existence.

"How long have you been here?" I asked.

"Fifteen years." He gave the blue and placid sea a glance,

and a strangely tender smile hovered on his thin lips. "I fell in love with the place at first sight. You've heard, I dare say, of the mythical German who came here on the Naples boat just for lunch and a look at the Blue Grotto and stayed forty years; well, I can't say I exactly did that, but it's come to the same thing in the end. Only it won't be forty years in my case. Twenty-five. Still, that's better than a poke in the eye with a sharp stick."

I waited for him to go on. For what he had just said looked indeed as though there might be something after all in the singular story I had heard. But at that moment my friend came dripping out of the water very proud of himself because he had swum a mile, and the conversation turned to other things.

After that I met Wilson several times, either in the Piazza or on the beach. He was amiable and polite. He was always pleased to have a talk and I found out that he not only knew every inch of the island but also the adjacent mainland. He had read a great deal on all sorts of subjects, but his speciality was the history of Rome and on this he was very well informed. He seemed to have little imagination and to be of no more than average intelligence. He laughed a good deal, but with restraint, and his sense of humour was tickled by simple jokes. A commonplace man. I did not forget the odd remark he had made during the first short chat we had had by ourselves, but he never so much as approached the topic again. One day on our return from the beach, dismissing the cab at the Piazza, my friend and I told the driver to be ready to take us up to Anacapri at five. We were going to climb Monte Solaro, dine at a tavern we favoured, and walk down in the moonlight. For it was full moon and the views by night were lovely. Wilson was standing by while we gave the cabman instructions, for we had given him a lift to save him the hot dusty walk, and more from politeness than for any other reason I asked him if he would care to join us.

"It's my party," I said.

"I'll come with pleasure," he answered.

But when the time came to set out my friend was not feeling well, he thought he had stayed too long in the water, and would not face the long and tiring walk. So I went alone with Wilson. We climbed the mountain, admired the spacious view, and got back to the inn as night was falling, hot, hungry and thirsty. We had ordered our dinner beforehand. The food was good, for Antonio was an excellent cook, and the wine came from his own vineyard. It was so light that you felt you could drink it like water and we finished the first bottle with our macaroni. By the time we had finished the second we felt that there was nothing much wrong with life. We sat in a little garden under a great vine laden with grapes. The air was exquisitely soft. The night was still and we were alone. The maid brought us *bel paese* cheese and a plate of figs. I ordered coffee and strega, which is the best liqueur they make in Italy. Wilson would not have a cigar, but lit his pipe.

"We've got plenty of time before we need start," he said, "the moon won't be over the hill for another hour."

"Moon or no moon," I said briskly, "of course we've got plenty of time. That's one of the delights of Capri, that there's never any hurry."

"Leisure," he said. "If people only knew! It's the most priceless thing a man can have and they're such fools they don't even know it's something to aim at. Work? They work for work's sake. They haven't got the brains to realise that the only object of work is to obtain leisure."

Wine has the effect on some people of making them indulge in general reflections. These remarks were true, but no one could have claimed that they were original. I did not say anything, but struck a match to light my cigar.

"It was full moon the first time I came to Capri," he went on reflectively. "It might be the same moon as to-night."

"It was, you know," I smiled.

He grinned. The only light in the garden was what came from an oil lamp that hung over our heads. It had been scanty to eat by, but it was good now for confidences.

"I didn't mean that. I mean, it might be yesterday. Fifteen years it is, and when I look back it seems like a month. I'd never been to Italy before. I came for my summer holiday. I went to Naples by boat from Marseilles and I had a look round, Pompeii, you know, and Paestum and one or two places like that, then I came here for a week. I liked the look of the place right away, from the sea, I mean, as I watched it come closer and closer; and then when we got into the little boats from the steamer and landed at the quay, with all that crowd of jabbering people who wanted to take your luggage, and the hotel touts, and the tumbledown houses on the Marina and the walk up to the hotel, and dining on the terrace—well, it just got me. That's the truth. I didn't know if I was standing on my head or my heels. I'd never drunk Capri wine before, but I'd heard of it; I think I must have got a bit tight. I sat on that terrace after they'd all gone to bed and watched the moon over the sea, and there was Vesuvius with a great red plume of smoke rising up from it. Of course I know now that wine I drank was ink, Capri wine my eye, but I thought it all right then. But it wasn't the wine that made me drunk, it was the shape of the island and those jabbering people, the moon and the sea and the oleander in the hotel garden. I'd never seen an oleander before."

It was a long speech and it had made him thirsty. He took up his glass, but it was empty. I asked him if he would have another strega.

"It's sickly stuff. Let's have a bottle of wine. That's sound, that is, pure juice of the grape and can't hurt anyone."

I ordered more wine, and when it came filled the glasses. He took a long drink and after a sigh of pleasure went on.

"Next day I found my way to the bathing-place we go to.

Not bad bathing, I thought. Then I wandered about the island. As luck would have it, there was a festa up at the Punta di Timberio and I ran straight into the middle of it. An image of the Virgin and priests, acolytes swinging censers, and a whole crowd of jolly, laughing, excited people, a lot of them all dressed up. I ran across an Englishman there and asked him what it was all about. 'Oh, it's the feast of the Assumption,' he said, 'at least that's what the Catholic Church says it is, but that's just their hanky-panky. It's the festival of Venus. Pagan, you know. Aphrodite rising from the sea and all that.' It gave me quite a funny feeling to hear him. It seemed to take one a long way back, if you know what I mean. After that I went down one night to have a look at the Faraglioni by moonlight. If the fates had wanted me to go on being a bank manager they oughtn't to have let me take that walk."

"You were a bank manager, were you?" I asked.

I had been wrong about him, but not far wrong.

"Yes. I was manager of the Crawford Street branch of the York and City. It was convenient for me because I lived up Hendon way. I could get from door to door in thirty-seven minutes."

He puffed at his pipe and relit it.

"That was my last night, that was. I'd got to be back at the bank on Monday morning. When I looked at those two great rocks sticking out of the water, with the moon above them, and all the little lights of the fishermen in their boats catching cuttle-fish, all so peaceful and beautiful, I said to myself, well, after all, why should I go back? It wasn't as if I had anyone dependent on me. My wife had died of bronchial pneumonia four years before and the kid went to live with her grandmother, my wife's mother. She was an old fool, she didn't look after the kid properly and she got blood-poisoning, they amputated her leg, but they couldn't save her and she died, poor little thing."

2

"How terrible," I said.

"Yes, I was cut up at the time, though of course not so much as if the kid had been living with me, but I dare say it was a mercy. Not much chance for a girl with only one leg. I was sorry about my wife too. We got on very well together. Though I don't know if it would have continued. She was the sort of woman who was always bothering about what other people'd think. She didn't like travelling. Eastbourne was her idea of a holiday. D'you know, I'd never crossed the Channel till after her death."

"But I suppose you've got other relations, haven't you?"

"None. I was an only child. My father had a brother, but he went to Australia before I was born. I don't think anyone could easily be more alone in the world than I am. There wasn't any reason I could see why I shouldn't do exactly what I wanted. I was thirty-four at that time."

He had told me he had been on the island for fifteen years. That would make him forty-nine. Just about the age I should have given him.

"I'd been working since I was seventeen. All I had to look forward to was doing the same old thing day after day till I retired on my pension. I said to myself, is it worth it? What's wrong with chucking it all up and spending the rest of my life down here? It was the most beautiful place I'd ever seen. But I'd had a business training, I was cautious by nature. 'No,' I said, 'I won't be carried away like this, I'll go to-morrow like I said I would and think it over. Perhaps when I get back to London I'll think quite differently.' Damned fool, wasn't I? I lost a whole year that way."

"You didn't change your mind, then?"

"You bet I didn't. All the time I was working I kept thinking of the bathing here and the vineyards and the walks over the hills and the moon and the sea, and the Piazza in the evening when everyone walks about for a bit of a chat after the day's work is over. There was only one thing that bothered me; I wasn't sure if I was justified in not working like everybody else did. Then I read a sort of history book, by a man called Marion Crawford it was, and there was a story about Sybaris and Crotona. There were two cities; and in Sybaris they just enjoyed life and had a good time, and in Crotona they were hardy and industrious and all that. And one day the men of Crotona came over and wiped Sybaris out, and then after a while a lot of other fellows came over from somewhere else and wiped Crotona out. Nothing remains of Sybaris, not a stone, and all that's left of Crotona is just one column. That settled the matter for me."

"Oh?"

"It came to the same in the end, didn't it? And when you look back now, who were the mugs?"

I did not reply and he went on.

"The money was rather a bother. The bank didn't pension one off till after thirty years' service, but if you retired before that they gave you a gratuity. With that and what I'd got for the sale of my house and the little I'd managed to save, I just hadn't enough to buy an annuity to last the rest of my life. It would have been silly to sacrifice everything so as to lead a pleasant life and not have a sufficient income to make it pleasant. I wanted to have a little place of my own, a servant to look after me, enough to buy tobacco, decent food, books now and then, and something over for emergencies. I knew pretty well how much I needed. I found I had just enough to buy an annuity for twenty-five years."

"You were thirty-five at the time?"

"Yes. It would carry me on till I was sixty. After all, no one can be certain of living longer than that, a lot of men die in their fifties, and by the time a man's sixty he's had the best of life."

"On the other hand no one can be sure of dying at sixty," I said.

"Well, I don't know. It depends on himself, doesn't it?"

"In your place I should have stayed on at the bank till I was entitled to my pension."

"I should have been forty-seven then. I shouldn't have been too old to enjoy my life here, I'm older than that now and I enjoy it as much as I ever did, but I should have been too old to experience the particular pleasure of a young man. You know, you can have just as good a time at fifty as you can at thirty, but it's not the same sort of good time. I wanted to live the perfect life while I still had the energy and the spirit to make the most of it. Twenty-five years seemed a long time to me, and twenty-five years of happiness seemed worth paying something pretty substantial for. I'd made up my mind to wait a year and I waited a year. Then I sent in my resignation and as soon as they paid me my gratuity I bought the annuity and came on here."

"An annuity for twenty-five years?"

"That's right."

"Have you never regretted?"

"Never. I've had my money's worth already. And I've got ten years more. Don't you think after twenty-five years of perfect happiness one ought to be satisfied to call it a day?"

"Perhaps."

He did not say in so many words what he would do then, but his intention was clear. It was pretty much the story my friend had told me, but it sounded different when I heard it from his own lips. I stole a glance at him. There was nothing about him that was not ordinary. No one, looking at that neat, prim face, could have thought him capable of an unconventional action. I did not blame him. It was his own life that he had arranged in this strange manner, and I did not see why he should not do what he liked with it. Still, I could not prevent the little shiver that ran down my spine.

"Getting chilly?" he smiled. "We might as well start walking down. The moon'll be up by now."

Before we parted Wilson asked me if I would like to go and see his house one day; and two or three days later, finding out where he lived, I strolled up to see him. It was a peasant's cottage, well away from the town, in a vineyard, with a view of the sea. By the side of the door grew a great oleander in full flower. There were only two small rooms, a tiny kitchen and a lean-to in which firewood could be kept. The bedroom was furnished like a monk's cell, but the sitting-room, smelling agreeably of tobacco, was comfortable enough, with two large armchairs that he had brought from England, a large roll-top desk, a cottage piano and crowded bookshelves. On the walls were framed engravings of pictures by G. F. Watts and Lord Leighton. Wilson told me that the house belonged to the owner of the vineyard who lived in another cottage higher up the hill, and his wife came in every day to do the rooms and the cooking. He had found the place on his first visit to Capri, and taking it on his return for good had been there ever since. Seeing the piano and music open on it, I asked him if he would play.

"I'm no good, you know, but I've always been fond of music and I get a lot of fun out of strumming."

He sat down at the piano and played one of the movements from a Beethoven sonata. He did not play very well. I looked at his music, Schumann and Schubert, Beethoven, Bach and Chopin. On the table on which he had his meals was a greasy pack of cards. I asked him if he played patience.

"A lot."

From what I saw of him then and from what I heard from other people I made for myself what I think must have been a fairly accurate picture of the life he had led for the last fifteen years. It was certainly a very harmless one. He bathed; he walked a great deal, and he seemed never to lose his sense of the beauty of the island which he knew so intimately; he played the piano and he played patience; he read. When he was asked to a party he went and, though a trifle dull, was agreeable. He was not affronted if he was neglected. He liked people, but with an aloofness that prevented intimacy. He lived thriftily, but with sufficient comfort. He never owed a penny. I imagine he had never been a man whom sex had greatly troubled, and if in his younger days he had had now and then a passing affair with a visitor to the island whose head was turned by the atmosphere, his emotion, while it lasted, remained, I am pretty sure, well under his control. I think he was determined that nothing should interfere with his independence of spirit. His only passion was for the beauty of nature, and he sought felicity in the simple and natural things that life offers to everyone. You may say that it was a grossly selfish existence. It was. He was of no use to anybody, but on the other hand he did nobody any harm. His only object was his own happiness, and it looked as though he had attained it. Very few people know where to look for happiness; fewer still find it. I don't know whether he was a fool or a wise man. He was certainly a man who knew his own mind. The odd thing about him to me was that he was so immensely commonplace. I should never have given him a second thought but for what I knew, that on a certain day, ten years from then, unless a chance illness cut the thread before, he must deliberately take leave of the world he loved so well. I wondered whether it was the thought of this, never quite absent from his mind, that gave him the peculiar zest with which he enjoyed every moment of the day.

I should do him an injustice if I omitted to state that he was not at all in the habit of talking about himself. I think the friend I was staying with was the only person in whom he had confided. I believe he only told me the story because he suspected I already knew it, and on the evening on which he told it me he had drunk a good deal of wine.

My visit drew to a close and I left the island. The year after, war broke out. A number of things happened to me, so that the course of my life was greatly altered, and it was thirteen years before I went to Capri again. My friend had been back some time, but he was no longer so well off, and had moved into a house that had no room for me; so I was putting up at the hotel. He came to meet me at the boat and we dined together. During dinner I asked him where exactly his house was.

"You knew it," he answered. "It's the little place Wilson had. I've built on a room and made it quite nice."

With so many other things to occupy my mind I had not given Wilson a thought for years, but now, with a little shock, I remembered. The ten years he had before him when I made his acquaintance must have elapsed long ago.

"Did he commit suicide as he said he would?"

"It's rather a grim story."

Wilson's plan was all right. There was only one flaw in it and this, I suppose, he could not have foreseen. It had never occurred to him that after twenty-five years of complete happiness, in this quiet backwater, with nothing in the world to disturb his serenity, his character would gradually lose its strength. The will needs obstacles in order to exercise its power; when it is never thwarted, when no effort is needed to achieve one's desires, because one has placed one's desires only in the things that can be obtained by stretching out one's hand, the will grows impotent. If you walk on a level all the time the muscles you need to climb a mountain will atrophy. These observations are trite, but there they are. When Wilson's annuity expired he had no longer the resolution to make the end which was the price he had agreed to pay for that long period of happy tranquillity. I do not think, as far as I could gather, both from what my friend told me and afterwards from others, that he wanted courage. It was just that he couldn't make up his mind. He put it off from day to day.

He had lived on the island for so long and had always settled his accounts so punctually, that it was easy for him to get credit; never having borrowed money before, he found a number of people who were willing to lend him small sums when now he asked for them. He had paid his rent regularly for so many years that his landlord, whose wife Assunta still acted as his servant, was content to let things slide for several months. Everyone believed him when he said that a relative had died and that he was temporarily embarrassed because owing to legal formalities he could not for some time get the money that was due to him. He managed to hang on after this fashion for something over a year. Then he could get no more credit from the local tradesmen, and there was no one to lend him any more money. His landlord gave him notice to leave the house unless he paid up the arrears of rent before a certain date.

The day before this he went into his tiny bedroom, closed the door and the window, drew the curtain and lit a brazier of charcoal. Next morning when Assunta came to make his breakfast she found him insensible but still alive. The room was draughty, and though he had done this and that to keep out the fresh air he had not done it very thoroughly. It almost looked as though at the last moment, and desperate though his situation was, he had suffered from a certain infirmity of purpose. Wilson was taken to the hospital, and though very ill for some time he at last recovered. But as a result either of the charcoal poisoning or of the shock he was no longer in complete possession of his faculties. He was not insane, at all events not insane enough to be put in an asylum, but he was quite obviously no longer in his right mind.

"I went to see him," said my friend. "I tried to get him to talk, but he kept looking at me in a funny sort of way, as though he couldn't quite make out where he'd seen me before. He looked rather awful lying there in bed, with a week's growth of grey beard on his chin; but except for that funny look in his eyes he seemed quite normal."

"What funny look in his eyes?"

"I don't know exactly how to describe it. Puzzled. It's an absurd comparison, but suppose you threw a stone up into the air and it didn't come down but just stayed there . . ."

"It would be rather bewildering," I smiled.

"Well, that's the sort of look he had."

It was difficult to know what to do with him. He had no money and no means of getting any. His effects were sold, but for too little to pay what he owed. He was English, and the Italian authorities did not wish to make themselves responsible for him. The British Consul in Naples had no funds to deal with the case. He could of course be sent back to England, but no one seemed to know what could be done with him when he got there. Then Assunta, the servant, said that he had been a good master and a good tenant, and as long as he had the money had paid his way; he could sleep in the woodshed in the cottage in which she and her husband lived, and he could share their meals. This was suggested to him. It was difficult to know whether he understood or not. When Assunta came to take him from the hospital he went with her without remark. He seemed to have no longer a will of his own. She had been keeping him now for two years.

"It's not very comfortable, you know," said my friend. "They've rigged him up a ramshackle bed and given him a couple of blankets, but there's no window, and it's icy cold in winter and like an oven in summer. And the food's pretty rough. You know how these peasants eat: macaroni on Sundays and meat once in a blue moon."

"What does he do with himself all the time?"

"He wanders about the hills. I've tried to see him two or three times, but it's no good; when he sees you coming he runs like a hare. Assunta comes down to have a chat with me now

2*

and then and I give her a bit of money so that she can buy him tobacco, but God knows if he ever gets it."

"Do they treat him all right?" I asked.

"I'm sure Assunta's kind enough. She treats him like a child. I'm afraid her husband's not very nice to him. He grudges the cost of his keep. I don't believe he's cruel or anything like that, but I think he's a bit sharp with him. He makes him fetch water and clean the cowshed and that sort of thing."

"It sounds pretty rotten," I said.

"He brought it on himself. After all, he's only got what he deserved."

"I think on the whole we all get what we deserve," I said. "But that doesn't prevent its being rather horrible."

Two or three days later my friend and I were taking a walk. We were strolling along a narrow path through an olive grove.

"There's Wilson," said my friend suddenly. "Don't look, you'll only frighten him. Go straight on."

I walked with my eyes on the path, but out of the corners of them I saw a man hiding behind an olive tree. He did not move as we approached, but I felt that he was watching us. As soon as we had passed I heard a scamper. Wilson, like a hunted animal, had made for safety. That was the last I ever saw of him.

He died last year. He had endured that life for six years. He was found one morning on the mountainside lying quite peacefully as though he had died in his sleep. From where he lay he had been able to see those two great rocks called the Faraglioni which stand out of the sea. It was full moon and he must have gone to see them by moonlight. Perhaps he died of the beauty of that sight.

LORD MOUNTDRAGO

D R. AUDLIN looked at the clock on his desk. It was twenty minutes to six. He was surprised that his patient was late, for Lord Mountdrago prided himself on his punctuality, he had a sententious way of expressing himself which gave the air of an epigram to a commonplace remark, and he was in the habit of saying that punctuality is a compliment you pay to the intelligent and a rebuke you administer to the stupid. Lord Mountdrago's appointment was for five-thirty.

There was in Dr. Audlin's appearance nothing to attract attention. He was tall and spare, with narrow shoulders and something of a stoop; his hair was grey and thin; his long, sallow face deeply lined. He was not more than fifty, but he looked older. His eyes, pale-blue and rather large, were weary. When you had been with him for a while you noticed that they moved very little; they remained fixed on your face, but so empty of expression were they that it was no discomfort. They seldom lit up. They gave no clue to his thoughts nor changed with the words he spoke. If you were of an observant turn it might have struck you that he blinked much less often than most of us. His hands were on the large side, with long, tapering fingers; they were soft but firm, cool but not clammy. You could never have said what Dr. Audlin wore unless you had made a point of looking. His clothes were dark. His tie was black. His dress made his sallow lined face paler, and his pale eyes more wan. He gave you the impression of a very sick man.

Dr. Audlin was a psycho-analyst. He had adopted the profession by accident and practised it with misgiving. When the war broke out he had not been long qualified and was getting experience at various hospitals; he offered his services to the authorities, and after a time was sent out to France. It was then that he discovered his singular gift. He could allay certain pains by the touch of his cool, firm hands, and by talking to them often induce sleep in men who were suffering from sleeplessness. He spoke slowly. His voice had no particular colour, and its tone did not alter with the words he uttered, but it was musical, soft and lulling. He told the men that they must rest, that they mustn't worry, that they must sleep; and rest stole into their jaded bones, tranquillity pushed their anxieties away, like a man finding a place for himself on a crowded bench, and slumber fell on their tired eyelids like the light rain of spring upon the fresh-turned earth. Dr. Audlin found that by speaking to men with that low, monotonous voice of his, by looking at them with his pale, quiet eyes, by stroking their weary foreheads with his long firm hands, he could soothe their perturbations, resolve the conflicts that distracted them and banish the phobias that made their lives a torment. Sometimes he effected cures that seemed miraculous. He restored speech to a man who, after being buried under the earth by a bursting shell, had been struck dumb, and he gave back the use of his limbs to another who had been paralysed after a crash in a plane. He could not understand his powers; he was of a sceptical turn, and though they say that in circumstances of this kind the first thing is to believe in yourself, he never quite succeeded in doing that; and it was only the outcome of his activities, patent to the most incredulous observer, that obliged him to admit that he had some faculty, coming from he knew not where, obscure and uncertain, that enabled him to do things for which he could offer no explanation. When the war was over he went to Vienna and studied there, and afterwards to Zurich; and then settled down in London to practise the art he had so strangely acquired. He had been practising now for fifteen years, and had attained, in the speciality he followed, a distinguished reputation. People told one another of the amazing things he had done, and though his fees were high, he had as many patients as he had time to see. Dr. Audlin knew that he had achieved some very extraordinary results; he had saved men from suicide, others from the lunatic asylum, he had assuaged griefs that embittered useful lives, he had turned unhappy marriages into happy ones, he had eradicated abnormal instincts and thus delivered not a few from a hateful bondage, he had given health to the sick in spirit; he had done all this, and yet at the back of his mind remained the suspicion that he was little more than a quack.

It went against his grain to exercise a power that he could not understand, and it offended his honesty to trade on the faith of the people he treated when he had no faith in himself. He was rich enough now to live without working, and the work exhausted him; a dozen times he had been on the point of giving up practice. He knew all that Freud and Jung and the rest of them had written. He was not satisfied; he had an intimate conviction that all their theory was hocus-pocus, and yet there the results were, incomprehensible, but manifest. And what had he not seen of human nature during the fifteen years that patients had been coming to his dingy back room in Wimpole Street? The revelations that had been poured into his ears, sometimes only too willingly, sometimes with shame, with reservations, with anger, had long ceased to surprise him. Nothing could shock him any longer. He knew by now that men were liars, he knew how extravagant was their vanity; he knew far worse than that about them; but he knew that it was not for him to judge or to condemn. But year by year as these terrible confidences were imparted to him his face grew a little greyer, its lines a little more marked and his pale eyes more weary. He seldom laughed, but now and again when for relaxation he read a novel he smiled. Did their authors really think the men and women they wrote of were like that? If they only knew how much more complicated they were, how much

more unexpected, what irreconcilable elements coexisted
within their souls and what dark and sinister contentions
afflicted them!

It was a quarter to six. Of all the strange cases he had been
called upon to deal with Dr. Audlin could remember none
stranger than that of Lord Mountdrago. For one thing the
personality of his patient made it singular. Lord Mountdrago
was an able and a distinguished man. Appointed Secretary for
Foreign Affairs when still under forty, now after three years in
office he had seen his policy prevail. It was generally acknowledged that he was the ablest politician in the Conservative
Party, and only the fact that his father was a peer, on whose
death he would no longer be able to sit in the House of
Commons, made it impossible for him to aim at the premier-
ship. But if in these democratic times it is out of the question
for a Prime Minister of England to be in the House of Lords,
there was nothing to prevent Lord Mountdrago from continu-
ing to be Secretary for Foreign Affairs in successive Conservative administrations and so for long directing the foreign
policy of his country.

Lord Mountdrago had many good qualities. He had intelligence and industry. He was widely travelled, and spoke
several languages fluently. From early youth he had specialised
in foreign affairs, and had conscientiously made himself
acquainted with the political and economic circumstances of
other countries. He had courage, insight and determination.
He was a good speaker, both on the platform and in the House,
clear, precise and often witty. He was a brilliant debater and
his gift of repartee was celebrated. He had a fine presence: he
was a tall, handsome man, rather bald and somewhat too
stout, but this gave him solidity and an air of maturity that
were of service to him. As a young man he had been something
of an athlete and had rowed in the Oxford boat, and he was
known to be one of the best shots in England. At twenty-four

he had married a girl of eighteen whose father was a duke and her mother a great American heiress, so that she had both position and wealth, and by her he had had two sons. For several years they had lived privately apart, but in public united, so that appearances were saved, and no other attachment on either side had given the gossips occasion to whisper. Lord Mountdrago indeed was too ambitious, too hard-working, and it must be added too patriotic, to be tempted by any pleasures that might interfere with his career. He had, in short, a great deal to make him a popular and success-ful figure. He had unfortunately great defects.

He was a fearful snob. You would not have been surprised at this if his father had been the first holder of the title. That the son of an ennobled lawyer, a manufacturer or a distiller, should attach an inordinate importance to his rank is under-standable. The earldom held by Lord Mountdrago's father was created by Charles II, and the barony held by the first Earl dated from the Wars of the Roses. For three hundred years the successive holders of the title had allied themselves with the noblest families of England. But Lord Mountdrago was as conscious of his birth as a *nouveau riche* is conscious of his money. He never missed an opportunity of impressing it upon others. He had beautiful manners when he chose to display them, but this he did only with people whom he regarded as his equals. He was coldly insolent to those whom he looked upon as his social inferiors. He was rude to his servants and insulting to his secretaries. The subordinate officials in the government offices to which he had been successively attached feared and hated him. His arrogance was horrible. He knew that he was a great deal cleverer than most of the persons he had to do with, and never hesitated to apprise them of the fact. He had no patience with the infirmities of human nature. He felt himself born to command and was irritated with people who expected him to listen to their arguments or wished to hear the reasons for his decisions. He was immeasurably selfish. He looked upon any service that was rendered him as a right due to his rank and intelligence and therefore deserving of no gratitude. It never entered his head that he was called upon to do anything for others. He had many enemies: he despised them. He knew no one who merited his assistance, his sympathy or his compassion. He had no friends. He was distrusted by his chiefs, because they doubted his loyalty; he was unpopular with his party, because he was overbearing and discourteous; and yet his merit was so great, his patriotism so evident, his intelligence so solid and his management of affairs so brilliant, that they had to put up with him. And what made it possible to do this was that on occasion he could be enchanting: when he was with persons whom he considered his equals, or whom he wished to captivate, in the company of foreign dignitaries or women of distinction, he could be gay, witty and debonair; his manners then reminded you that in his veins ran the same blood as had run in the veins of Lord Chesterfield; he could tell a story with point, he could be natural, sensible and even profound. You were surprised at the extent of his knowledge and the sensitiveness of his taste. You thought him the best company in the world, you forgot that he had insulted you the day before and was quite capable of cutting you dead the next.

Lord Mountdrago almost failed to become Dr. Audlin's patient. A secretary rang up the doctor and told him that his lordship, wishing to consult him, would be glad if he would come to his house at ten o'clock on the following morning. Dr. Audlin answered that he was unable to go to Lord Mountdrago's house, but would be pleased to give him an appointment at his consulting-room at five o'clock on the next day but one. The secretary took the message and presently rang back to say that Lord Mountdrago insisted on seeing Dr. Audlin in his own house and the doctor could fix his own fee. Dr. Audlin replied that he only saw patients in his consulting-room and expressed his regret that unless Lord Mountdrago was prepared to come to him he could not give him his attention. In a quarter of an hour a brief message was delivered to him that his lordship would come not next day but one, but next day, at five.

When Lord Mountdrago was then shown in he did not come forward, but stood at the door and insolently looked the doctor up and down. Dr. Audlin perceived that he was in a rage; he gazed at him, silently, with still eyes. He saw a big heavy man, with greying hair, receding on the forehead so that it gave nobility to his brow, a puffy face with bold regular features and an expression of haughtiness. He had somewhat the look of one of the Bourbon sovereigns of the eighteenth century.

"It seems that it is as difficult to see you as a Prime Minister, Dr. Audlin. I'm an extremely busy man."

"Won't you sit down?" said the doctor.

His face showed no sign that Lord Mountdrago's speech in any way affected him. Dr. Audlin sat in his chair at the desk. Lord Mountdrago still stood and his frown darkened.

"I think I should tell you that I am His Majesty's Secretary for Foreign Affairs," he said acidly.

"Won't you sit down?" the doctor repeated.

Lord Mountdrago made a gesture, which might have suggested that he was about to turn on his heel and stalk out of the room, but if that was his intention he apparently thought better of it. He seated himself. Dr. Audlin opened a large book and took up his pen. He wrote without looking at his patient.

"How old are you?"

"Forty-two."

"Are you married?"

"Yes."

"How long have you been married?"

"Eighteen years."

"Have you any children?"

"I have two sons."

Dr. Audlin noted down the facts as Lord Mountdrago abruptly answered his questions. Then he leaned back in his chair and looked at him. He did not speak; he just looked, gravely, with pale eyes that did not move.

"Why have you come to see me?" he asked at length.

"I've heard about you. Lady Canute is a patient of yours, I understand. She tells me you've done her a certain amount of good."

Dr. Audlin did not reply. His eyes remained fixed on the other's face, but they were so empty of expression that you might have thought he did not even see him.

"I can't do miracles," he said at length. Not a smile, but the shadow of a smile flickered in his eyes. "The Royal College of Physicians would not approve of it if I did."

Lord Mountdrago gave a brief chuckle. It seemed to lessen his hostility. He spoke more amiably.

"You have a very remarkable reputation. People seem to believe in you."

"Why have you come to me?" repeated Dr. Audlin.

Now it was Lord Mountdrago's turn to be silent. It looked as though he found it hard to answer. Dr. Audlin waited. At last Lord Mountdrago seemed to make an effort. He spoke.

"I'm in perfect health. Just as a matter of routine I had myself examined by my own doctor the other day, Sir Augustus Fitzherbert, I dare say you've heard of him, and he tells me I have the physique of a man of thirty. I work hard, but I'm never tired, and I enjoy my work. I smoke very little and I'm an extremely moderate drinker. I take a sufficiency of exercise and I lead a regular life. I am a perfectly sound, normal, healthy man. I quite expect you to think it very silly and childish of me to consult you."

Dr. Audlin saw that he must help him.

"I don't know if I can do anything to help you. I'll try. You're distressed?"

Lord Mountdrago frowned.

"The work that I'm engaged in is important. The decisions I am called upon to make can easily affect the welfare of the country and even the peace of the world. It is essential that my judgment should be balanced and my brain clear. I look upon it as my duty to eliminate any cause of worry that may interfere with my usefulness."

Dr. Audlin had never taken his eyes off him. He saw a great deal. He saw behind his patient's pompous manner and arrogant pride an anxiety that he could not dispel.

"I asked you to be good enough to come here because I know by experience that it's easier for someone to speak openly in the dingy surroundings of a doctor's consulting-room than in his accustomed environment."

"They're certainly dingy," said Lord Mountdrago acidly. He paused. It was evident that this man who had so much self-assurance, so quick and decided a mind that he was never at a loss, at this moment was embarrassed. He smiled in order to show the doctor that he was at his ease, but his eyes betrayed his disquiet. When he spoke again it was with unnatural heartiness.

"The whole thing's so trivial that I can hardly bring myself to bother you with it. I'm afraid you'll just tell me not to be a fool and waste your valuable time."

"Even things that seem very trivial may have their importance. They can be a symptom of a deep-seated derangement. And my time is entirely at your disposal."

Dr. Audlin's voice was low and grave. The monotone in which he spoke was strangely soothing. Lord Mountdrago at length made up his mind to be frank.

"The fact is I've been having some very tiresome dreams

lately. I know it's silly to pay any attention to them, but—well, the honest truth is that I'm afraid they've got on my nerves."

"Can you describe any of them to me?"

Lord Mountdrago smiled, but the smile that tried to be careless was only rueful.

"They're so idiotic, I can hardly bring myself to narrate them."

"Never mind."

"Well, the first I had was about a month ago. I dreamt that I was at a party at Connemara House. It was an official party. The King and Queen were to be there and of course decorations were worn. I was wearing my ribbon and my star. I went into a sort of cloakroom they have to take off my coat. There was a little man there called Owen Griffiths, who's a Welsh Member of Parliament, and to tell you the truth, I was surprised to see him. He's very common, and I said to myself: 'Really, Lydia Connemara is going too far, whom will she ask next?' I thought he looked at me rather curiously, but I didn't take any notice of him; in fact I cut the little bounder and walked upstairs. I suppose you've never been there?"

"Never."

"No, it's not the sort of house you'd ever be likely to go to. It's a rather vulgar house, but it's got a very fine marble staircase, and the Connemaras were at the top receiving their guests. Lady Connemara gave me a look of surprise when I shook hands with her, and began to giggle; I didn't pay much attention, she's a very silly, ill-bred woman and her manners are no better than those of her ancestress whom King Charles II made a duchess. I must say the reception rooms at Connemara House are stately. I walked through, nodding to a number of people and shaking hands; then I saw the German Ambassador talking with one of the Austrian Archdukes. I particularly wanted to have a word with him, so I went up and held out my hand. The moment the Archduke saw me he burst into a roar of laughter. I was deeply affronted. I looked him up and down sternly, but he only laughed the more. I was about to speak to him rather sharply, when there was a sudden hush and I realised that the King and Queen had come. Turning my back on the Archduke, I stepped forward, and then, quite suddenly, I noticed that I hadn't got any trousers on. I was in short silk drawers, and I wore scarlet sock-suspenders. No wonder Lady Connemara had giggled; no wonder the Archduke had laughed! I can't tell you what that moment was. An agony of shame. I awoke in a cold sweat. Oh, you don't know the relief I felt to find it was only a dream."

"It's the kind of dream that's not so very uncommon," said Dr. Audlin.

"I dare say not. But an odd thing happened next day. I was in the lobby of the House of Commons, when that fellow Griffiths walked slowly past me. He deliberately looked down at my legs and then he looked me full in the face and I was almost certain he winked. A ridiculous thought came to me. He'd been there the night before and seen me make that ghastly exhibition of myself and was enjoying the joke. But of course I knew that was impossible because it was only a dream. I gave him an icy glare and he walked on. But he was grinning his head off."

Lord Mountdrago took his handkerchief out of his pocket and wiped the palms of his hands. He was making no attempt now to conceal his perturbation. Dr. Audlin never took his eyes off him.

"Tell me another dream."

"It was the night after, and it was even more absurd than the first one. I dreamt that I was in the House. There was a debate on foreign affairs which not only the country, but the world, had been looking forward to with the gravest concern. The government had decided on a change in their policy which vitally affected the future of the Empire. The occasion was historic. Of course the House was crowded. All the ambassadors were there. The galleries were packed. It fell to me to make the important speech of the evening. I had prepared it carefully. A man like me has enemies, there are a lot of people who resent my having achieved the position I have at an age when even the cleverest men are content with situations of relative obscurity, and I was determined that my speech should not only be worthy of the occasion, but should silence my detractors. It excited me to think that the whole world was hanging on my lips. I rose to my feet. If you've ever been in the House you'll know how members chat to one another during a debate, rustle papers and turn over reports. The silence was the silence of the grave when I began to speak. Suddenly I caught sight of that odious little bounder on one of the benches opposite, Griffiths the Welsh member; he put out his tongue at me. I don't know if you've ever heard a vulgar music-hall song called *A Bicycle Made for Two*. It was very popular a great many years ago. To show Griffiths how completely I despised him I began to sing it. I sang the first verse right through. There was a moment's surprise, and when I finished they cried 'Hear, hear', on the opposite benches. I put up my hand to silence them and sang the second verse. The House listened to me in stony silence and I felt the song wasn't going down very well. I was vexed, for I have a good baritone voice, and I was determined that they should do me justice. When I started the third verse the members began to laugh; in an instant the laughter spread; the ambassadors, the strangers in the Distinguished Strangers' Gallery, the ladies in the Ladies' Gallery, the reporters, they shook, they bellowed, they held their sides, they rolled in their seats; everyone was overcome with laughter except the ministers on the Front Bench immediately behind me. In that incredible, in that unprecedented uproar, they sat petrified. I gave them a glance, and suddenly the enormity of what I had done fell upon me. I had made myself the laughing-stock of the whole world. With misery I realised that I should have to resign. I woke and knew it was only a dream."

Lord Mountdrago's grand manner had deserted him as he narrated this, and now having finished he was pale and trembling. But with an effort he pulled himself together. He forced a laugh to his shaking lips.

"The whole thing was so fantastic that I couldn't help being amused. I didn't give it another thought, and when I went into the House on the following afternoon I was feeling in very good form. The debate was dull, but I had to be there, and I read some documents that required my attention. For some reason I chanced to look up and I saw that Griffiths was speaking. He has an unpleasant Welsh accent and an un-prepossessing appearance. I couldn't imagine that he had anything to say that it was worth my while to listen to, and I was about to return to my papers when he quoted two lines from *A Bicycle Made for Two*. I couldn't help glancing at him and I saw that his eyes were fixed on me with a grin of bitter mockery. I faintly shrugged my shoulders. It was comic that a scrubby little Welsh member should look at me like that. It was an odd coincidence that he should quote two lines from that disastrous song that I'd sung all through in my dream. I began to read my papers again, but I don't mind telling you that I found it difficult to concentrate on them. I was a little puzzled. Owen Griffiths had been in my first dream, the one at Connemara House, and I'd received a very definite impression afterwards that he knew the sorry figure I'd cut. Was it a mere coincidence that he had just quoted those two lines? I asked myself if it was possible that he was dreaming the same dreams as I was. But of course the idea was preposterous and I determined not to give it a second thought."

There was a silence. Dr. Audlin looked at Lord

Mountdrago and Lord Mountdrago looked at Dr. Audlin.

"Other people's dreams are very boring. My wife used to dream occasionally and insist on telling me her dreams next day with circumstantial detail. I found it maddening."

Dr. Audlin faintly smiled.

"You're not boring me."

"I'll tell you one more dream I had a few days later. I dreamt that I went into a public-house at Limehouse. I've never been to Limehouse in my life and I don't think I've ever been in a public-house since I was at Oxford, and yet I saw the street and the place I went into as exactly as if I were at home there. I went into a room, I don't know whether they call it the saloon bar or the private bar; there was a fireplace and a large leather armchair on one side of it, and on the other a small sofa; a bar ran the whole length of the room and over it you could see into the public bar. Near the door was a round marble-topped table and two armchairs beside it. It was a Saturday night and the place was packed. It was brightly lit, but the smoke was so thick that it made my eyes smart. I was dressed like a rough, with a cap on my head and a handkerchief round my neck. It seemed to me that most of the people there were drunk. I thought it rather amusing. There was a gramophone going, or the radio, I don't know which, and in front of the fireplace two women were doing a grotesque dance. There was a little crowd round them, laughing, cheering and singing. I went up to have a look and some man said to me: ' 'Ave a drink, Bill?' There were glasses on the table full of a dark liquid which I understand is called brown ale. He gave me a glass and not wishing to be conspicuous I drank it. One of the women who were dancing broke away from the other and took hold of the glass. ' 'Ere, what's the idea?' she said. 'That's my beer you're putting away.' 'Oh, I'm so sorry,' I said, 'this gentleman offered it me and I very naturally thought it was his to offer.' 'All right, mate,' she said, 'I don't mind. You come an' 'ave a dance with me.' Before I could protest she'd caught hold of me and we were dancing together. And then I found myself sitting in the armchair with the woman on my lap and we were sharing a glass of beer. I should tell you that sex has never played any great part in my life. I married young because in my position it was desirable that I should marry, but also in order to settle once and for all the question of sex. I had the two sons I had made up my mind to have, and then I put the whole matter on one side. I've always been too busy to give much thought to that kind of thing, and living so much in the public eye as I do it would have been madness to do anything that might give rise to scandal. The greatest asset a politician can have is a blameless record as far as women are concerned. I have no patience with the men who smash up their careers for women. I only despise them. The woman I had on my knees was drunk; she wasn't pretty and she wasn't young; in fact, she was just a blowsy old prostitute. She filled me with disgust, and yet when she put her mouth to mine and kissed me, though her breath stank of beer and her teeth were decayed, though I loathed myself, I wanted her—I wanted her with all my soul. Suddenly I heard a voice. 'That's right, old boy, have a good time.' I looked up and there was Owen Griffiths. I tried to spring out of the chair, but that horrible woman wouldn't let me. 'Don't you pay no attention to 'im,' she said, ' 'e's only one of them nosy-parkers.' 'You go to it,' he said. 'I know Moll. She'll give you your money's worth all right.' You know, I wasn't so much annoyed at his seeing me in that absurd situation as angry that he should address me as 'old boy'. I pushed the woman aside and stood up and faced him. 'I don't know you and I don't want to know you,' I said. 'I know you all right,' he said. 'And my advice to you, Molly, is, see that you get your money, he'll bilk you if he can.' There was a bottle of beer standing on the table close by. Without a word I seized it by the neck and hit him over the head with it as hard as I could. I made such a violent gesture that it woke me up."

"A dream of that sort is not incomprehensible," said Dr. Audlin. "It is the revenge nature takes on persons of unimpeachable character."

"The story's idiotic. I haven't told it you for its own sake. I've told it you for what happened next day. I wanted to look up something in a hurry and I went into the library of the House. I got the book and began reading. I hadn't noticed when I sat down that Griffiths was sitting in a chair close by me. Another of the Labour members came in and went up to him. 'Hullo, Owen,' he said to him, 'you're looking pretty dicky to-day.' 'I've got an awful headache,' he answered. 'I feel as if I'd been cracked over the head with a bottle.' "

Now Lord Mountdrago's face was grey with anguish.

"I knew then that the idea I'd had and dismissed as preposterous was true. I knew that Griffiths was dreaming my dreams and that he remembered them as well as I did."

"It may also have been a coincidence."

"When he spoke he didn't speak to his friend, he deliberately spoke to me. He looked at me with sullen resentment."

"Can you offer any suggestion why this same man should come into your dreams?"

"None."

Dr. Audlin's eyes had not left his patient's face and he saw that he lied. He had a pencil in his hand and he drew a straggling line or two on his blotting-paper. It often took a long time to get people to tell the truth, and yet they knew that unless they told it he could do nothing for them.

"The dream you've just described to me took place just over three weeks ago. Have you had any since?"

"Every night."

"And does this man Griffiths come into them all?"

"Yes."

The doctor drew more lines on his blotting-paper. He wanted the silence, the drabness, the dull light of that little room to have its effect on Lord Mountdrago's sensibility. Lord Mountdrago threw himself back in his chair and turned his head away so that he should not see the other's grave eyes.

"Dr. Audlin, you must do something for me. I'm at the end of my tether. I shall go mad if this goes on. I'm afraid to go to sleep. Two or three nights I haven't. I've sat up reading and when I felt drowsy put on my coat and walked till I was exhausted. But I must have sleep. With all the work I have to do I must be at concert pitch; I must be in complete control of all my faculties. I need rest; sleep brings me none. I no sooner fall asleep than my dreams begin, and he's always there, that vulgar little cad, grinning at me, mocking me, despising me. It's a monstrous persecution. I tell you, doctor, I'm not the man of my dreams; it's not fair to judge me by them. Ask anyone you like. I'm an honest, upright, decent man. No one can say anything against my moral character either private or public. My whole ambition is to serve my country and maintain its greatness. I have money, I have rank, I'm not exposed to many of the temptations of lesser men, so that it's no credit to me to be incorruptible; but this I can claim, that no honour, no personal advantage, no thought of self would induce me to swerve by a hair's breadth from my duty. I've sacrificed everything to become the man I am. Greatness is my aim. Greatness is within my reach and I'm losing my nerve. I'm not that mean, despicable, cowardly, lewd creature that horrible little man sees. I've told you three of my dreams; they're nothing; that man has seen me do things that are so beastly, so horrible, so shameful, that even if my life depended on it I wouldn't tell them. And he remembers them. I can hardly meet the derision and disgust I see in his eyes and I even hesitate to speak because I know my words can seem to him nothing but utter humbug. He's seen me do things that no man with any self-respect would do, things for which men are driven out of the society of their fellows and sentenced to long terms of imprisonment; he's heard the foulness of my speech; he's seen me not only ridiculous, but revolting. He despises me and he no longer pretends to conceal it. I tell you that if you can't do something to help me I shall either kill myself or kill him."

"I wouldn't kill him if I were you," said Dr. Audlin, coolly, in that soothing voice of his. "In this country the consequences of killing a fellow-creature are awkward."

"I shouldn't be hanged for it, if that's what you mean. Who would know that I'd killed him? That dream of mine has shown me how. I told you, the day after I'd hit him over the head with a beer-bottle he had such a headache that he couldn't see straight. He said so himself. That shows that he can feel with his waking body what happens to his body asleep. It's not with a bottle I shall hit him next time. One night, when I'm dreaming, I shall find myself with a knife in my hand or a revolver in my pocket, I must because I want to so intensely, and then I shall seize my opportunity. I'll stick him like a pig; I'll shoot him like a dog. In the heart. And then I shall be free of this fiendish persecution."

Some people might have thought that Lord Mountdrago was mad; after all the years during which Dr. Audlin had been treating the diseased souls of men he knew how thin a line divides those whom we call sane from those whom we call insane. He knew how often in men who to all appearance were healthy and normal, who were seemingly devoid of imagination, and who fulfilled the duties of common life with credit to themselves and with benefit to their fellows, when you gained their confidence, when you tore away the mask they wore to the world, you found not only hideous abnormality, but kinks so strange, mental extravagances so fantastic, that in that respect you could only call them lunatic. If you put them in an asylum not all the asylums in the world would be large enough. Anyhow, a man was not certifiable because he had strange dreams and they had shattered his nerve. The case was singular, but it was only an exaggeration of others that had come under Dr. Audlin's observation; he was doubtful, however, whether the methods of treatment that he had so often found efficacious would here avail.

"Have you consulted any other member of my profession?" he asked.

"Only Sir Augustus. I merely told him that I suffered from nightmares. He said I was overworked and recommended me to go for a cruise. That's absurd. I can't leave the Foreign Office just now when the international situation needs constant attention. I'm indispensable, and I know it. On my conduct at the present juncture my whole future depends. He gave me sedatives. They had no effect. He gave me tonics. They were worse than useless. He's an old fool."

"Can you give any reason why it should be this particular man who persists in coming into your dreams?"

"You asked me that question before. I answered it."

That was true. But Dr. Audlin had not been satisfied with the answer.

"Just now you talked of persecution. Why should Owen Griffiths want to persecute you?"

"I don't know."

Lord Mountdrago's eyes shifted a little. Dr. Audlin was sure that he was not speaking the truth.

"Have you ever done him an injury?"

"Never."

Lord Mountdrago made no movement, but Dr. Audlin had a queer feeling that he shrank into his skin. He saw before him a large, proud man who gave the impression that the questions put to him were an insolence, and yet for all that, behind that façade, was something shifting and startled that made you

think of a frightened animal in a trap. Dr. Audlin leaned
forward and by the power of his eyes forced Lord Mountdrago
to meet them.

"Are you quite sure?"

"Quite sure. You don't seem to understand that our ways
lead along different paths. I don't wish to harp on it, but I
must remind you that I am a Minister of the Crown and
Griffiths is an obscure member of the Labour Party. Naturally
there's no social connection between us; he's a man of very
humble origin, he's not the sort of person I should be likely to
meet at any of the houses I go to; and politically our respective
stations are so far separated that we could not possibly have
anything in common."

"I can do nothing for you unless you tell me the complete
truth."

Lord Mountdrago raised his eyebrows. His voice was
rasping.

"I'm not accustomed to having my word doubted, Dr.
Audlin. If you're going to do that I think to take up any more
of your time can only be a waste of mine. If you will kindly let
my secretary know what your fee is he will see that a cheque is
sent to you."

For all the expression that was to be seen on Dr. Audlin's
face you might have thought that he simply had not heard what
Lord Mountdrago said. He continued to look steadily into his
eyes and his voice was grave and low.

"Have you done anything to this man that *he* might look
upon as an injury?"

Lord Mountdrago hesitated. He looked away, and then, as
though there were in Dr. Audlin's eyes a compelling force that
he could not resist, looked back. He answered sulkily:

"Only if he was a dirty, second-rate little cad."

"But that is exactly what you've described him to be."

Lord Mountdrago sighed. He was beaten. Dr. Audlin

knew that the sigh meant he was going at last to say what he had till then held back. Now he had no longer to insist. He dropped his eyes and began again drawing vague geometrical figures on his blotting-paper. The silence lasted two or three minutes.

"I'm anxious to tell you everything that can be of any use to you. If I didn't mention this before, it's only because it was so unimportant that I didn't see how it could possibly have anything to do with the case. Griffiths won a seat at the last election and he began to make a nuisance of himself almost at once. His father's a miner, and he worked in a mine himself when he was a boy; he's been a schoolmaster in the board schools and a journalist. He's that half-baked, conceited intellectual, with inadequate knowledge, ill-considered ideas and impractical plans, that compulsory education has brought forth from the working-classes. He's a scrawny, grey-faced man, who looks half-starved, and he's always very slovenly in appearance; heaven knows members nowadays don't bother much about their dress, but his clothes are an outrage to the dignity of the House. They're ostentatiously shabby, his collar's never clean and his tie's never tied properly; he looks as if he hadn't had a bath for a month and his hands are filthy. The Labour Party have two or three fellows on the Front Bench who've got a certain ability, but the rest of them don't amount to much. In the kingdom of the blind the one-eyed man is king: because Griffiths is glib and has a lot of superficial information on a number of subjects, the Whips on his side began to put him up to speak whenever there was a chance. It appeared that he fancied himself on foreign affairs, and he was continually asking me silly, tiresome questions. I don't mind telling you that I made a point of snubbing him as soundly as I thought he deserved. From the beginning I hated the way he talked, his whining voice and his vulgar accent; he had nervous mannerisms that intensely irritated me. He talked rather shyly, hesitatingly, as though it were torture to him to speak and yet he was forced to by some inner passion, and often he used to say some very disconcerting things. I'll admit that now and again he had a sort of tub-thumping eloquence. It had a certain influence over the ill-regulated minds of the members of his party. They were impressed by his earnestnesss and they weren't, as I was, nauseated by his sentimentality. A certain sentimentality is the common coin of political debate. Nations are governed by self-interest, but they prefer to believe that their aims are altruistic, and the politician is justified if with fair words and fine phrases he can persuade the electorate that the hard bargain he is driving for his country's advantage tends to the good of humanity. The mistake people like Griffiths make is to take these fair words and fine phrases at their face value. He's a crank, and a noxious crank. He calls himself an idealist. He has at his tongue's end all the tedious blather that the intelligentsia have been boring us with for years. Non-resistance. The brotherhood of man. You know the hopeless rubbish. The worst of it was that it impressed not only his own party, it even shook some of the sillier, more sloppy-minded members of ours. I heard rumours that Griffiths was likely to get office when a Labour Government came in; I even heard it suggested that he might get the Foreign Office. The notion was grotesque but not impossible. One day I had occasion to wind up a debate on foreign affairs which Griffiths had opened. He'd spoken for an hour. I thought it a very good opportunity to cook his goose, and by God, sir, I cooked it. I tore his speech to pieces. I pointed out the faultiness of his reasoning and emphasised the deficiency of his knowledge. In the House of Commons the most devastating weapon is ridicule: I mocked him; I bantered him; I was in good form that day and the House rocked with laughter. Their laughter excited me and I excelled myself. The Opposition sat glum and silent, but even some of them couldn't help laughing once or twice;

it's not intolerable, you know, to see a colleague, perhaps a rival, made a fool of. And if ever a man was made a fool of I made a fool of Griffiths. He shrank down in his seat, I saw his face go white, and presently he buried it in his hands. When I sat down I'd killed him. I'd destroyed his prestige for ever; he had no more chance of getting office when a Labour Government came in than the policeman at the door. I heard afterwards that his father, the old miner, and his mother had come up from Wales, with various supporters of his in the constituency, to watch the triumph they expected him to have. They had seen only his utter humiliation. He'd won the constituency by the narrowest margin. An incident like that might very easily lose him his seat. But that was no business of mine."

"Should I be putting it too strongly if I said you had ruined his career?" asked Dr. Audlin.

"I don't suppose you would."

"That is a very serious injury you've done him."

"He brought it on himself."

"Have you never felt any qualms about it?"

"I think perhaps if I'd known that his father and mother were there I might have let him down a little more gently."

There was nothing further for Dr. Audlin to say, and he set about treating his patient in such a manner as he thought might avail. He sought by suggestion to make him forget his dreams when he awoke; he sought to make him sleep so deeply that he would not dream. He found Lord Mountdrago's resistance impossible to break down. At the end of an hour he dismissed him. Since then he had seen Lord Mountdrago half a dozen times. He had done him no good. The frightful dreams continued every night to harass the unfortunate man, and it was clear that his general condition was growing rapidly worse. He was worn out. His irritability was uncontrollable. Lord

3

Mountdrago was angry because he received no benefit from his treatment, and yet continued it, not only because it seemed his only hope, but because it was a relief to him to have someone with whom he could talk openly. Dr. Audlin came to the conclusion at last that there was only one way in which Lord Mountdrago could achieve deliverance, but he knew him well enough to be assured that of his own free will he would never, never take it. If Lord Mountdrago was to be saved from the breakdown that was threatening he must be induced to take a step that must be abhorrent to his pride of birth and his self-complacency. Dr. Audlin was convinced that to delay was impossible. He was treating his patient by suggestion, and after several visits found him more susceptible to it. At length he managed to get him into a condition of somnolence. With his low, soft, monotonous voice he soothed his tortured nerves. He repeated the same words over and over again. Lord Mountdrago lay quite still, his eyes closed; his breathing was regular, and his limbs were relaxed. Then Dr. Audlin in the same quiet tone spoke the words he had prepared.

"You will go to Owen Griffiths and say that you are sorry that you caused him that great injury. You will say that you will do whatever lies in your power to undo the harm that you have done him."

The words acted on Lord Mountdrago like the blow of a whip across his face. He shook himself out of his hypnotic state and sprang to his feet. His eyes blazed with passion and he poured forth upon Dr. Audlin a stream of angry vituperation such as even he had never heard. He swore at him. He cursed him. He used language of such obscenity that Dr. Audlin, who had heard every sort of foul word, sometimes from the lips of chaste and distinguished women, was surprised that he knew it.

"Apologise to that filthy little Welshman? I'd rather kill myself."

"I believe it to be the only way in which you can regain your balance."

Dr. Audlin had not often seen a man presumably sane in such a condition of uncontrollable fury. He grew red in the face and his eyes bulged out of his head. He did really foam at the mouth. Dr. Audlin watched him coolly, waiting for the storm to wear itself out, and presently he saw that Lord Mountdrago, weakened by the strain to which he had been subjected for so many weeks, was exhausted.

"Sit down," he said then, sharply.

Lord Mountdrago crumpled up into a chair.

"Christ, I feel all in. I must rest a minute and then I'll go."

For five minutes perhaps they sat in complete silence. Lord Mountdrago was a gross, blustering bully, but he was also a gentleman. When he broke the silence he had recovered his self-control.

"I'm afraid I've been very rude to you. I'm ashamed of the things I've said to you and I can only say you'd be justified if you refused to have anything more to do with me. I hope you won't do that. I feel that my visits to you do help me. I think you're my only chance."

"You mustn't give another thought to what you said. It was of no consequence."

"But there's one thing you mustn't ask me to do, and that is to make excuses to Griffiths."

"I've thought a great deal about your case. I don't pretend to understand it, but I believe that your only chance of release is to do what I proposed. I have a notion that we're none of us one self, but many, and one of the selves in you has risen up against the injury you did Griffiths and has taken on the form of Griffiths in your mind and is punishing you for what you cruelly did. If I were a priest I should tell you that it is your conscience that has adopted the shape and lineaments of this man to scourge you to repentance and persuade you to reparation."

"My conscience is clear. It's not my fault if I smashed the man's career. I crushed him like a slug in my garden. I regret nothing."

It was on these words that Lord Mountdrago had left him. Reading through his notes, while he waited, Dr. Audlin considered how best he could bring his patient to the state of mind that, now that his usual methods of treatment had failed, he thought alone could help him. He glanced at his clock. It was six. It was strange that Lord Mountdrago did not come. He knew he had intended to because a secretary had rung up that morning to say that he would be with him at the usual hour. He must have been detained by pressing work. This notion gave Dr. Audlin something else to think of: Lord Mountdrago was quite unfit to work and in no condition to deal with important matters of state. Dr. Audlin wondered whether it behoved him to get in touch with someone in authority, the Prime Minister or the Permanent Under Secretary for Foreign Affairs, and impart to him his conviction that Lord Mountdrago's mind was so unbalanced that it was dangerous to leave affairs of moment in his hands. It was a ticklish thing to do. He might cause needless trouble and get roundly snubbed for his pains. He shrugged his shoulders.

"After all," he reflected, "the politicians have made such a mess of the world during the last five-and-twenty years, I don't suppose it makes much odds if they're mad or sane."

He rang the bell.

"If Lord Mountdrago comes now will you tell him that I have another appointment at six-fifteen and so I'm afraid I can't see him."

"Very good, sir."

"Has the evening paper come yet?"

"I'll go and see."

In a moment the servant brought it in. A huge headline ran across the front page: Tragic Death of Foreign Minister.

"My God!" cried Dr. Audlin.

For once he was wrenched out of his wonted calm. He was shocked, horribly shocked, and yet he was not altogether surprised. The possibility that Lord Mountdrago might commit suicide had occurred to him several times, for that it was suicide he could not doubt. The paper said that Lord Mountdrago had been waiting in a tube station, standing on the edge of the platform, and as the train came in was seen to fall on the rail. It was supposed that he had had a sudden attack of faintness. The paper went on to say that Lord Mountdrago had been suffering for some weeks from the effects of overwork, but had felt it impossible to absent himself while the foreign situation demanded his unremitting attention. Lord Mountdrago was another victim of the strain that modern politics placed upon those who played the more important parts in it. There was a neat little piece about the talents and industry, the patriotism and vision, of the deceased statesman, followed by various surmises upon the Prime Minister's choice of his successor. Dr. Audlin read all this. He had not liked Lord Mountdrago. The chief emotion that his death caused in him was dissatisfaction with himself because he had been able to do nothing for him.

Perhaps he had done wrong in not getting into touch with Lord Mountdrago's doctor. He was discouraged, as always when failure frustrated his conscientious efforts, and repulsion seized him for the theory and practice of this empiric doctrine by which he earned his living. He was dealing with dark and mysterious forces that it was perhaps beyond the powers of the human mind to understand. He was like a man blindfold trying to feel his way to he knew not whither. Listlessly he turned the pages of the paper. Suddenly he gave a great start, and an exclamation once more was forced from his lips. His eyes had fallen on a small paragraph near the bottom of a column. Sudden Death of an M.P., he read. Mr. Owen

Griffiths, member for so-and-so, had been taken ill in Fleet Street that afternoon and when he was brought to Charing Cross Hospital life was found to be extinct. It was supposed that death was due to natural causes, but an inquest would be held. Dr. Audlin could hardly believe his eyes. Was it possible that the night before Lord Mountdrago had at last in his dream found himself possessed of the weapon, knife or gun, that he had wanted, and had killed his tormentor, and had that ghostly murder, in the same way as the blow with the bottle had given him a racking headache on the following day, taken effect a certain number of hours later on the waking man? Or was it, more mysterious and more frightful, that when Lord Mountdrago sought relief in death, the enemy he had so cruelly wronged, unappeased, escaping from his own mortality, had pursued him to some other sphere there to torment him still? It was strange. The sensible thing was to look upon it merely as an odd coincidence. Dr. Audlin rang the bell.

"Tell Mrs. Milton that I'm sorry I can't see her this evening. I'm not well."

It was true; he shivered as though of an ague. With some kind of spiritual sense he seemed to envisage a bleak, a horrible void. The dark night of the soul engulfed him, and he felt a strange, primeval terror of he knew not what.

GIGOLO AND GIGOLETTE

T HE bar was crowded. Sandy Westcott had had a couple of cocktails and he was beginning to feel hungry. He looked at his watch. He had been asked to dinner at half-past nine and it was nearly ten. Eva Barrett was always late and he would be lucky if he got anything to eat by ten-thirty. He turned to the barman to order another cocktail and caught sight of a man who at that moment came up to the bar.

"Hullo, Cotman," he said. "Have a drink?"

"I don't mind if I do, sir."

Cotman was a nice-looking fellow, of thirty perhaps, short, but with so good a figure that he did not look it, very smartly dressed in a double-breasted dinner jacket, a little too much waisted, and a butterfly tie a good deal too large. He had a thick mat of black, wavy hair, very sleek and shiny, brushed straight back from his forehead, and large flashing eyes. He spoke with great refinement, but with a Cockney accent.

"How's Stella?" asked Sandy.

"Oh, she's all right. Likes to have a lay-down before the show, you know. Steadies the old nerves, she says."

"I wouldn't do that stunt of hers for a thousand pounds."

"I don't suppose you would. No one can do it but her, not from that height, I mean, and only five foot of water."

"It's the most sick-making thing I've ever seen."

Cotman gave a little laugh. He took this as a compliment. Stella was his wife. Of course she did the trick and took the risk, but it was he who had thought of the flames, and it was the flames that had taken the public fancy and made the turn the huge success it was. Stella dived into a tank from the top of a ladder sixty feet high, and as he said, there were only five feet of water in the tank. Just before she dived they poured enough

65

petrol on to cover the surface and he set it alight; the flames soared up and she dived straight into them.

"Paco Espinel tells me it's the biggest draw the Casino has ever had," said Sandy.

"I know. He told me they'd served as many dinners in July as they generally do in August. And that's you, he says to me."

"Well, I hope you're making a packet."

"Well, I can't exactly say that. You see, we've got our contract and naturally we didn't know it was going to be a riot, but Mr. Espinel's talking of booking us for next month, and I don't mind telling you he's not going to get us on the same terms or anything like it. Why, I had a letter from an agent only this morning saying they wanted us to go to Deauville."

"Here are my people," said Sandy.

He nodded to Cotman and left him. Eva Barrett sailed in with the rest of her guests. She had gathered them together downstairs. It was a party of eight.

"I knew we should find you here, Sandy," she said. "I'm not late, am I?"

"Only half an hour."

"Ask them what cocktails they want and then we'll dine."

While they were standing at the bar, emptying now, for nearly everyone had gone down to the terrace for dinner, Paco Espinel passed through and stopped to shake hands with Eva Barrett. Paco Espinel was a young man who had run through his money and now made his living by arranging the turns with which the Casino sought to attract visitors. It was his duty to be civil to the rich and great. Mrs. Chaloner Barrett was an American widow of vast wealth; she not only entertained expensively, but also gambled. And after all, the dinners and suppers and the two cabaret shows that accompanied them were only provided to induce people to lose their money at the tables.

"Got a good table for me, Paco?" said Eva Barrett.

"The best." His eyes, fine, dark Argentine eyes, expressed his admiration of Mrs. Barrett's opulent, ageing charms. This also was business. "You've seen Stella?"

"Of course. Three times. It's the most terrifying thing I've ever seen."

"Sandy comes every night."

"I want to be in at the death. She's bound to kill herself one of these nights and I don't want to miss that if I can help it."

Paco laughed.

"She's been such a success, we're going to keep her on another month. All I ask is that she shouldn't kill herself till the end of August. After that she can do as she likes."

"Oh, God, have I got to go on eating trout and roast chicken every night till the end of August?" cried Sandy.

"You brute, Sandy," said Eva Barrett. "Come on, let's go in to dinner. I'm starving."

Paco Espinel asked the barman if he'd seen Cotman. The barman said he'd had a drink with Mr. Westcott.

"Oh, well, if he comes in here again, tell him I want a word with him."

Mrs. Barrett paused at the top of the steps that led down to the terrace long enough for the press representative, a little haggard woman with an untidy head, to come up with her note-book. Sandy whispered the names of the guests. It was a representative Riviera party. There was an English Lord and his Lady, long and lean both of them, who were prepared to dine with anyone who would give them a free meal. They were certain to be as tight as drums before midnight. There was a gaunt Scotch woman, with a face like a Peruvian mask that has been battered by the storms of ten centuries, and her English husband. Though a broker by profession, he was bluff, military and hearty. He gave you an impression of such integrity that you were almost more sorry for him than for

3*

yourself when the good thing he had put you on to as a special favour turned out to be a dud. There was an Italian countess who was neither Italian nor a countess, but played a beautiful game of bridge, and there was a Russian prince who was ready to make Mrs. Barrett a princess and in the meantime sold champagne, motor-cars and Old Masters on commission. A dance was in progress and Mrs. Barrett, waiting for it to end, surveyed with a look which her short upper lip made scornful the serried throng on the dance floor. It was a gala night and the dining tables were crowded together. Beyond the terrace the sea was calm and silent. The music stopped and the head waiter, affably smiling, came up to guide her to her table. She swept down the steps with majestic gait.

"We shall have quite a good view of the dive," she said as she sat down.

"I like to be next door to the tank," said Sandy, "so that I can see her face."

"Is she pretty?" asked the Countess.

"It's not that. It's the expression of her eyes. She's scared to death every time she does it."

"Oh, I don't believe that," said the City gentleman, Colonel Goodhart by name, though no one had ever discovered how he came by the title. "I mean, the whole bally stunt's only a trick. There's no danger really, I mean."

"You don't know what you're talking about. Diving from that height in as little water as that, she's got to turn like a flash the moment she touches the water. And if she doesn't do it right she's bound to bash her head against the bottom and break her back."

"That's just what I'm telling you, old boy," said the Colonel, "it's a trick. I mean, there's no argument."

"If there's no danger there's nothing to it, anyway," said Eva Barrett. "It's over in a minute. Unless she's risking her life it's the biggest fraud of modern times. Don't say we've come to see this over and over again and it's only a fake."

"Pretty well everything is. You can take my word for that."

"Well, you ought to know," said Sandy.

If it occurred to the Colonel that this might be a nasty dig he admirably concealed it. He laughed.

"I don't mind saying I know a thing or two," he admitted. "I mean, I've got my eyes peeled all right. You can't put much over on me."

The tank was on the far left of the terrace, and behind it, supported by stays, was an immensely tall ladder at the top of which was a tiny platform. After two or three dances more, when Eva Barrett's party were eating asparagus, the music stopped and the lights were lowered. A spot was turned on the tank. Cotman was visible in the brilliance. He ascended half a dozen steps so that he was on a level with the top of the tank.

"Ladies and gentlemen," he cried out, in a loud clear voice, "you are now going to see the most marvellous feat of the century. Madam Stella, the greatest diver in the world, is about to dive from a height of sixty feet into a lake of flames five foot deep. This is a feat that has never been performed before, and Madam Stella is prepared to give one hundred pounds to anyone who will attempt it. Ladies and gentlemen, I have the honour to present Madam Stella."

A little figure appeared at the top of the steps that led on to the terrace, ran quickly up to the tank, and bowed to the applauding audience. She wore a man's silk dressing-gown and on her head a bathing-cap. Her thin face was made up as if for the stage. The Italian countess looked at her through her *face-à-main*.

"Not pretty," she said.

"Good figure," said Eva Barrett. "You'll see."

Stella slipped out of her dressing-gown and gave it to Cotman. He went down the steps. She stood for a moment and looked at the crowd. They were in darkness and she could only see vague white faces and white shirt-fronts. She was small, beautifully made, with legs long for her body and slim hips. Her bathing costume was very scanty.

"You're quite right about the figure, Eva," said the Colonel. "Bit undeveloped, of course, but I know you girls think that's quite the thing."

Stella began to climb the ladder and the spot-light followed her. It seemed an incredible height. An attendant poured petrol on the surface of the water. Cotman was handed a flaming torch. He watched Stella reach the top of the ladder and settle herself on the platform.

"Ready?" he cried.

"Yes."

"Go," he shouted.

And as he shouted he seemed to plunge the burning torch into the water. The flames sprang up, leaping high, and really terrifying to look at. At the same moment Stella dived. She came down like a streak of lightning and plunged through the flames, which subsided a moment after she had reached the water. A second later she was at the surface and jumped out to a roar, a storm of applause. Cotman wrapped the dressing-gown round her. She bowed and bowed. The applause went on. Music struck up. With a final wave of the hand she ran down the steps and between the tables to the door. The lights went up and the waiters hurried along with their neglected service.

Sandy Westcott gave a sigh. He did not know whether he was disappointed or relieved.

"Top hole," said the English peer.

"It's a bally fake," said the Colonel, with his British pertinacity. "I bet you anything you like."

"It's over so quickly," said her English ladyship. "I mean, you don't get your money's worth really."

Anyhow it wasn't her money. That it never was. The

Italian countess leaned forward. She spoke fluent English, but with a strong accent.

"Eva, my darling, who are those extraordinary people at the table near the door under the balcony?"

"Packet of fun, aren't they?" said Sandy. "I simply haven't been able to take my eyes off them."

Eva Barrett glanced at the table the Countess indicated, and the Prince, who sat with his back to it, turned round to look.

"They can't be true," cried Eva. "I must ask Angelo who they are."

Mrs. Barrett was the sort of woman who knew the head waiters of all the principal restaurants in Europe by their first names. She told the waiter who was at that moment filling her glass to send Angelo to her.

It was certainly an odd pair. They were sitting by themselves at a small table. They were very old. The man was big and stout, with a mass of white hair, great bushy white eyebrows and an enormous white moustache. He looked like the late King Humbert of Italy, but much more like a king. He sat bolt upright. He wore full evening dress, with a white tie and a collar that has been out of fashion for hard on thirty years. His companion was a little old lady in a black satin ball dress, cut very low and tight at the waist. Round her neck were several chains of coloured beads. She wore what was obviously a wig, and a very ill-fitting one at that; it was very elaborate, all curls and sausages, and raven black. She was outrageously made-up, bright blue under the eyes and on the eyelids, the eyebrows heavily black, a great patch of very pink rouge on each cheek and the lips a livid scarlet. The skin hung loosely on her face in deep wrinkles. She had large bold eyes and they darted eagerly from table to table. She was taking everything in, and every other minute called the old man's attention to someone or other. The appearance of the couple was so fantastic in that fashionable crowd, the men in dinner jackets, the women in thin, pale-coloured frocks, that many eyes were turned on them. The staring did not seem to incommode the old lady. When she felt certain persons were looking at her she raised her eyebrows archly, smiled and rolled her eyes. She seemed on the point of acknowledging applause.

Angelo hurried up to the good customer that Eva Barrett was.

"You wished to see me, my lady?"

"Oh, Angelo, we're simply dying to know who those absolutely marvellous people are at the next table to the door."

Angelo gave a look and then assumed a deprecating air. The expression of his face, the movement of his shoulders, the turn of his spine, the gesture of his hands, probably even the twiddle of his toes, all indicated a half-humorous apology.

"You must overlook them, my lady." He knew of course that Mrs. Barrett had no right to be thus addressed, just as he knew that the Italian countess was neither Italian nor a countess and that the English lord never paid for a drink if anyone else would pay for it, but he also knew that to be thus addressed did not displease her. "They begged me to give them a table because they wanted to see Madame Stella do her dive. They were in the profession themselves once. I know they're not the sort of people one expects to see dining here, but they made such a point of it I simply hadn't the heart to refuse."

"But I think they're a perfect scream. I adore them."

"I've known them for many years. The man indeed is a compatriot of mine." The head waiter gave a condescending little laugh. "I told them I'd give them a table on the condition that they didn't dance. I wasn't taking any risks, my lady."

"Oh, but I should have loved to see them dance."

"One has to draw the line somewhere, my lady," said Angelo gravely.

He smiled, bowed again and withdrew.

"Look," cried Sandy, "they're going."

The funny old couple were paying their bill. The old man got up and put round his wife's neck a large white, but not too clean, feather boa. She rose. He gave her his arm, holding himself very erect, and she, small in comparison, tripped out beside him. Her black satin dress had a long train, and Eva Barrett (who was well over fifty) screamed with joy.

"Look, I remember my mother wearing a dress like that when I was in the school-room."

The comic pair walked, still arm in arm, through the spacious rooms of the Casino till they came to the door. The old man addressed a commissionaire.

"Be so good as to direct me to the artistes' dressing-rooms. We wish to pay our respects to Madame Stella."

The commissionaire gave them a look and summed them up. They were not people with whom it was necessary to be very polite.

"You won't find her there."

"She has not gone? I thought she gave a second performance at two."

"That's true. They might be in the bar."

"It won't 'urt us just to go an' 'ave a look, Carlo," said the old lady.

"Right-o, my love," he answered with a great roll of the R.

They walked slowly up the great stairs and entered the bar. It was empty but for the deputy-barman and a couple sitting in two armchairs in the corner. The old lady released her husband's arm and tripped up with outstretched hands.

" 'Ow are you, dear? I felt I just 'ad to come and congratulate you, bein' English same as you are. And in the profession meself. It's a grand turn, my dear, it deserves to be a success." She turned to Cotman. "And is this your 'usband?"

Stella got out of her armchair and a shy smile broke on her

lips as she listened with some confusion to the voluble old lady.

"Yes, that's Syd."

"Pleased to meet you," he said.

"And this is mine," said the old lady, with a little dig of the elbow in the direction of the tall, white-haired man. "Mr. Penezzi. 'E's a count really, and I'm the Countess Penezzi by rights, but when we retired from the profession we dropped the title."

"Will you have a drink?" said Cotman.

"No, you 'ave one with us," said Mrs. Penezzi, sinking into an armchair. "Carlo, you order."

The barman came, and after some discussion three bottles of beer were ordered. Stella would not have anything.

"She never has anything till after the second show," explained Cotman.

Stella was slight and small, about twenty-six, with light brown hair, cut short and waved, and grey eyes. She had reddened her lips, but wore little rouge on her face. Her skin was pale. She was not very pretty, but she had a neat little face. She wore a very simple evening frock of white silk. The beer was brought and Mr. Penezzi, evidently not very talkative, took a long swig.

"What was your line?" asked Syd Cotman, politely.

Mrs. Penezzi gave him a rolling glance of her flashing, made-up eyes and turned to her husband.

"Tell 'em who I am, Carlo," she said.

"The 'uman cannon-ball," he announced.

Mrs. Penezzi smiled brightly and with a quick, birdlike glance looked from one to the other. They stared at her in dismay.

"Flora," she said. "The 'uman cannon-ball."

She so obviously expected them to be impressed that they did not quite know what to do. Stella gave her Syd a puzzled look. He came to the rescue.

"It must have been before our time."

"Naturally it was before your time. Why, we retired from the profession definitely the year poor Queen Victoria died. It made quite a sensation when we did too. But you've 'eard of me of course." She saw the blank look on their faces; her tone changed a little. "But I was the biggest draw in London. At the Old Aquarium, that was. All the swells came to see me. The Prince of Wales and I don't know who all. I was the talk of the town. Isn't that true, Carlo?"

"She crowded the Aquarium for a year."

"It was the most spectacular turn they'd ever 'ad there. Why, only a few years ago I went up and introduced meself to Lady de Bathe. Lily Langtry, you know. She used to live down 'ere. She remembered me perfectly. She told me she'd seen me ten times."

"What did you do?" asked Stella.

"I was fired out of a cannon. Believe me, it was a sensation. And after London I went all over the world with it. Yes, my dear, I'm an old woman now and I won't deny it. Seventy-eight Mr. Penezzi is and I shall never see seventy again, but I've 'ad me portrait on every 'oardin' in London. Lady de Bathe said to me: my dear, you was as celebrated as I was. But you know what the public is, give 'em a good thing and they go mad over it, only they want change; 'owever good it is, they get sick of it and then they won't go and see it any more. It'll 'appen to you, my dear, same as it 'appened to me. It comes to all of us. But Mr. Penezzi always 'ad 'is 'ead screwed on 'is shoulders the right way. Been in the business since 'e was so 'igh. Circus, you know. Ringmaster. That's 'ow I first knew 'im. I was in a troupe of acrobacks. Trapeze act, you know. 'E's a fine-lookin' man now, but you should 'ave seen 'im then, in 'is Russian boots, and ridin' breeches, and a tight-fittin' coat with frogs all down the front of it, crackin' 'is long whip as 'is 'orses galloped round the ring, the 'andsomest man I ever see in my life."

Mr. Penezzi did not make any remark, but thoughtfully twisted his immense white moustache.

"Well, as I was tellin' you, 'e was never one to throw money about and when the agents couldn't get us bookin's any more 'e said, let's retire. An 'e was quite right, after 'avin' been the biggest star in London, we couldn't go back to circus work any more, I mean, Mr. Penezzi bein' a count really, 'e 'ad 'is dignity to think of, so we come down 'ere and we bought a 'ouse and started a pension. It always 'ad been Mr. Penezzi's ambition to do something like that. Thirty-five years we been 'ere now. We 'aven't done so badly, not until the last two or three years, and the slump came, though visitors are very different from what they was when we first started, the things they want, electric light and runnin' water in their bedrooms and I don't know what all. Give them a card, Carlo. Mr. Penezzi does the cookin' 'imself, and if ever you want a real 'ome from 'ome, you'll know where to find it. I like professional people and we'd 'ave a rare lot to talk about, you and me, dearie. Once a professional always a professional, I say."

At that moment the head barman came back from his supper. He caught sight of Syd.

"Oh, Mr. Cotman, Mr. Espinel was looking for you, wants to see you particularly."

"Oh, where is he?"

"You'll find him around somewhere."

"We'll be going," said Mrs. Penezzi, getting up. "Come and 'ave lunch with us one day, will you? I'd like to show you my old photographs and me press cuttin's. Fancy you not 'avin' 'eard of the 'uman cannon-ball. Why, I was as well known as the Tower of London."

Mrs. Penezzi was not vexed at finding that these young people had never even heard of her. She was simply amused.

They bade one another good-bye, and Stella sank back again into her chair.

"I'll just finish my beer," said Syd, "and then I'll go and see what Paco wants. Will you stay here, ducky, or would you like to go to your dressing-room?"

Stella's hands were tightly clenched. She did not answer. Syd gave her a look and then quickly glanced away.

"Perfect riot, that old girl," he went on, in his hearty way. "Real figure of fun. I suppose it's true what she said. It's difficult to believe, I must say. Fancy 'er drawing all London, what, forty years ago? And the funny thing is, her thinking anybody remembered. Seemed as though she simply couldn't understand us not having heard of her even."

He gave Stella another glance, from the corner of his eye so that she should not see he was looking at her, and he saw she was crying. He faltered. The tears were rolling down her pale face. She made no sound.

"What's the matter, darling?"

"Syd, I can't do it again to-night," she sobbed.

"Why on earth not?"

"I'm afraid."

He took her hand.

"I know you better than that," he said. "You're the bravest little woman in the world. Have a brandy, that'll pull you together."

"No, that'd only make it worse."

"You can't disappoint your public like that."

"That filthy public. Swine who eat too much and drink too much. A pack of chattering fools with more money than they know what to do with. I can't stick them. What do they care if I risk my life?"

"Of course it's the thrill they come for, there's no denying that," he replied uneasily. "But you know and I know, there's no risk, not if you keep your nerve."

"But I've lost my nerve, Syd. I shall kill myself."

She had raised her voice a little, and he looked round

quickly at the barman. But the barman was reading the *Eclaireur de Nice* and paying no attention.

"You don't know what it looks like from up there, the top of the ladder, when I look down at the tank. I give you my word, to-night I thought I was going to faint. I tell you I can't do it again to-night, you've got to get me out of it, Syd."

"If you funk it to-night it'll be worse to-morrow."

"No, it won't. It's having to do it twice kills me. The long wait and all that. You go and see Mr. Espinel and tell him I can't give two shows a night. It's more than my nerves'll stand."

"He'll never stand for that. The whole supper trade depends on you. It's only to see you they come in then at all."

"I can't help it, I tell you I can't go on."

He was silent for a moment. The tears still streamed down her pale little face, and he saw that she was quickly losing control of herself. He had felt for some days that something was up and he had been anxious. He had tried not to give her an opportunity to talk. He knew obscurely that it was better for her not to put into words what she felt. But he had been worried. For he loved her.

"Anyhow Espinel wants to see me," he said.

"What about?"

"I don't know. I'll tell him you can't give the show more than once a night and see what he says. Will you wait here?"

"No, I'll go along to the dressing-room."

Ten minutes later he found her there. He was in great spirits and his step was jaunty. He burst open the door.

"I've got grand news for you, honey. They're keeping us on next month at twice the money."

He sprang forward to take her in his arms and kiss her, but she pushed him away.

"Have I got to go on again to-night?"

"I'm afraid you must. I tried to make it only one show a

night, but he wouldn't hear of it. He says it's quite essential you should do the supper turn. And after all, for double the money, it's worth it."

She flung herself down on the floor and this time burst into a storm of tears.

"I can't, Syd, I can't. I shall kill myself."

He sat down on the floor and raised her head and took her in his arms and petted her.

"Buck up, darling. You can't refuse a sum like that. Why, it'll keep us all the winter and we shan't have to do a thing. After all there are only four more days to the end of July and then it's only August."

"No, no, no. I'm frightened. I don't want to die, Syd. I love you."

"I know you do, darling, and I love you. Why, since we married I've never looked at another woman. We've never had money like this before and we shall never get it again. You know what these things are, we're a riot now, but we can't expect it to go on for ever. We've got to strike while the iron's hot."

"D'you want me to die, Syd?"

"Don't talk so silly. Why, where should I be without you? You mustn't give way like this. You've got your self-respect to think of. You're famous all over the world."

"Like the human cannon-ball was," she cried with a laugh of fury.

"That damned old woman," he thought.

He knew that was the last straw. Bad luck, Stella taking it like that.

"That was an eye-opener to me," she went on. "What do they come and see me over and over again for? On the chance they'll see me kill myself. And a week after I'm dead they'll have forgotten even my name. That's what the public is. When I looked at that painted old hag I saw it all. Oh, Syd,

I'm so miserable." She threw her arms round his neck and pressed her face to his. "Syd, it's no good, I can't do it again."

"To-night, d'you mean? If you really feel like that about it, I'll tell Espinel you've had a fainting fit. I dare say it'll be all right just for once."

"I don't mean to-night, I mean never."

She felt him stiffen a little.

"Syd dear, don't think I'm being silly. It's not just to-day, it's been growing on me. I can't sleep at night thinking of it, and when I do drop off I see myself standing at the top of the ladder and looking down. To-night I could hardly get up it, I was trembling so, and when you lit the flames and said go, something seemed to be holding me back. I didn't even know I'd jumped. My mind was a blank till I found myself on the platform and heard them clapping. Syd, if you loved me you wouldn't want me to go through such torture."

He sighed. His own eyes were wet with tears. For he loved her devotedly.

"You know what it means," he said. "The old life. Marathons and all."

"Anything's better than this."

The old life. They both remembered it. Syd had been a dancing gigolo since he was eighteen, he was very good-looking in his dark Spanish way and full of life, old women and middle-aged women were glad to pay to dance with him, and he was never out of work. He had drifted from England to the Continent and there he had stayed, going from hotel to hotel, to the Riviera in the winter, to watering-places in France in the summer. It wasn't a bad life they led, there were generally two or three of them together, the men, and they shared a room in cheap lodgings. They didn't have to get up till late, and they only dressed in time to go to the hotel at twelve to dance with stout women who wanted to get their weight down. Then they were free till five, when they went to the hotel again and sat at a table, the three of them together, keeping a sharp eye open for anyone who looked a likely client. They had their regular customers. At night they went to the restaurant and the house provided them with quite a decent meal. Between the courses they danced. It was good money. They generally got fifty or a hundred francs from anyone they danced with. Sometimes a rich woman, after dancing a good deal with one of them for two or three nights, would give him as much as a thousand francs. Sometimes a middle-aged woman would ask one to spend a night with her, and he would get two hundred and fifty francs for that. There was always the chance of a silly old fool losing her head, and then there were platinum and sapphire rings, cigarette-cases, clothes and a wrist-watch to be got. One of Syd's friends had married one of them, who was old enough to be his mother, but she gave him a car and money to gamble with, and they lived in a beautiful villa at Biarritz. Those were the good days when everybody had money to burn. The slump came and hit the gigolos hard. The hotels were empty, and the clients didn't seem to want to pay for the pleasure of dancing with a nice-looking young fellow. Often and often Syd passed a whole day without earning the price of a drink, and more than once a fat old girl who weighed a ton had had the nerve to give him ten francs. His expenses didn't go down, for he had to be smartly dressed or the manager of the hotel made remarks, washing cost a packet, and you'd be surprised the amount of linen he needed; then shoes, those floors were terribly hard on shoes, and they had to look new. He had his room to pay for and his lunch.

It was then he met Stella. It was at Evian, and the season was disastrous. She was a swimming instructress. She was Australian, and a beautiful diver. She gave exhibitions every morning and afternoon. At night she was engaged to dance at the hotel. They dined together at a little table in the restaurant apart from the guests, and when the band began to play they danced together to induce the customers to come on to the floor. But often no one followed them and they danced by themselves. Neither of them got anything much in the way of paying partners. They fell in love with one another, and at the end of the season got married.

They had never regretted it. They had gone through hard times. Even though for business reasons (elderly ladies didn't so much like the idea of dancing with a married man when his wife was there) they concealed their marriage, it was not so easy to get an hotel job for the pair of them and Syd was far from being able to earn enough to keep Stella, even in the most modest pension, without working. The gigolo business had gone to pot. They went to Paris and learnt a dancing act, but the competition was fearful and cabaret engagements were very hard to get. Stella was a good ballroom dancer, but the rage was for acrobatics, and however much they practised she never managed to do anything startling. The public was sick of the apache turn. They were out of a job for weeks at a time. Syd's wrist-watch, his gold cigarette-case, his platinum ring, all went up the spout. At last they found themselves in Nice reduced to such straits that Syd had to pawn his evening clothes. It was a catastrophe. They were forced to enter for the Marathon that an enterprising manager was starting. Twenty-four hours a day they danced, resting every hour for fifteen minutes. It was frightful. Their legs ached, their feet were numb. For long periods they were unconscious of what they were doing. They just kept time to the music, exerting themselves as little as possible. They made a little money, people gave them sums of a hundred francs, or two hundred, to encourage them, and sometimes to attract attention they roused themselves to give an exhibition dance. If the public was in a good humour this might bring in a decent sum. They grew terribly tired. On the eleventh day Stella fainted and had to give up. Syd went on by himself, moving, moving without pause, grotesquely, without a partner. That was the worst time they had ever had. It was the final degradation. It had left with them a recollection of horror and misery.

But it was then that Syd had his inspiration. It had come to him while he was slowly going round the hall by himself. Stella always said she could dive in a saucer. It was just a trick.

"Funny how ideas come," he said afterwards. "Like a flash of lightning."

He suddenly remembered having seen a boy set fire to some petrol that had been spilt on the pavement, and the sudden blaze-up. For of course it was the flames on the water and the spectacular dive into them that had caught the public fancy. He stopped dancing there and then; he was too excited to go on. He talked it over with Stella, and she was enthusiastic. He wrote to an agent who was a friend of his; everyone liked Syd, he was a nice little man, and the agent put up the money for the apparatus. He got them an engagement at a circus in Paris, and the turn was a success. They were made. Engagements followed here and there, Syd bought himself an entire outfit of new clothes, and the climax came when they got a booking for the summer casino on the coast. It was no exaggeration of Syd's when he said that Stella was a riot.

"All our troubles are over, old girl," he said fondly. "We can put a bit by now for a rainy day, and when the public's sick of this I'll just think of something else."

And now, without warning, at the top of their boom, Stella wanted to chuck it. He didn't know what to say to her. It broke his heart to see her so unhappy. He loved her more now even than when he had married her. He loved her because of all they'd gone through together; after all for five days once they'd had nothing to eat but a hunk of bread each and a glass of milk, and he loved her because she'd taken him out of all that; he had good clothes to wear again and his three meals a day. He couldn't look at her, the anguish in her dear grey eyes was more than he could bear. Timidly she stretched out her hand and touched his. He gave a deep sigh.

"You know what it means, honey. Our connection in the hotels has gone west, and the business is finished, anyway. What there is'll go to people younger than us. You know what these old women are as well as I do; it's a boy they want, and besides, I'm not tall enough really. It didn't matter so much when I was a kid. It's no good saying I don't look my age because I do."

"Perhaps we can get into pictures."

He shrugged his shoulders. They'd tried that before when they were down and out.

"I wouldn't mind what I did. I'd serve in a shop."

"D'you think jobs can be had for the asking?"

She began to cry again.

"Don't, honey. It breaks my heart."

"We've got a bit put by."

"I know we have. Enough to last us six months. And then it'll mean starvation. First popping the bits and pieces, and then the clothes'll have to go, same as they did before. And then dancing in low-down joints for our supper and fifty francs a night. Out of a job for weeks together. And Marathons whenever we hear of one. And how long will the public stand for them?"

"I know you think I'm unreasonable, Syd."

He turned and looked at her now. There were tears in her eyes. He smiled, and the smile he gave her was charming and tender.

"No, I don't, ducky. I want to make you happy. After all, you're all I've got. I love you."

He took her in his arms and held her. He could feel the beating of her heart. If Stella felt like that about it, well, he must just make the best of it. After all, supposing she were killed? No, no, let her chuck it and be damned to the money. She made a little movement.

"What is it, honey?"

She released herself and stood up. She went over to the dressing-table.

"I expect it's about time for me to be getting ready," she said.

He started to his feet.

"You're not going to do a show to-night?"

"To-night, and every night till I kill myself. What else is there? I know you're right, Syd. I can't go back to all that other, stinking rooms in fifth-rate hotels and not enough to eat. Oh, that Marathon. Why did you bring that up? Being tired and dirty for days at a time and then having to give up because flesh and blood just couldn't stand it. Perhaps I can go on another month and then there'll be enough to give you a chance of looking round."

"No, darling, I can't stand for that. Chuck it. We'll manage somehow. We starved before, we can starve again."

She slipped out of her clothes, and for a moment stood naked but for her stockings, looking at herself in the glass. She gave her reflection a hard smile.

"I mustn't disappoint my public," she sniggered.

AN OFFICIAL POSITION

HE was a sturdy broad-shouldered fellow, of the middle
height; though his bones were well covered as became his
age, which was fifty, he was not fat; he had a ruddy complexion which neither the heat of the sun nor the unwhole-
someness of the climate had affected. It was good rich blood
that ran through his veins. His hair was brown and thick, and
only at the temples touched with grey; he was very proud of his
fair, handsome moustache and he kept it carefully brushed.
There was a pleasant twinkle in his blue eyes. You would have
said that this was a man whom life had treated well. There
was in his appearance an air of good nature and in his vigour a
glow of health that gave you confidence. He reminded you of
one of those well-fed, rubicund burghers in an old Dutch
picture, with their pink-cheeked wives, who made money and
enjoyed the good things with which their industry provided
them. He was, however, a widower. His name was Louis
Remire, and his number 68763. He was serving a twelve-year
sentence at St. Laurent de Maroni, the great penal settlement of
French Guiana, for killing his wife, but partly because he had
served in the police force at Lyons, his native town, and partly
on account of his good character, he had been given an official
position. He had been chosen among nearly two hundred
applicants to be the public executioner.

That was why he was allowed to sport the handsome
moustache of which he took so much care. He was the only
convict who wore one. It was in a manner of speaking his
badge of office. That also was why he was allowed to wear his
own clothes. The convicts wear pyjamas in pink and white
stripes, round straw hats and clumsy boots with wooden soles
and leather tops. Louis Remire wore espadrilles on his bare

feet, blue cotton trousers, and a khaki shirt the open neck of which exposed to view his hairy and virile chest. When you saw him strolling about the public garden, with a kindly eye looking at the children, black or half-caste, who played there, you would have taken him for a respectable shopkeeper who was enjoying an hour's leisure. He had his own house. That was not only one of the perquisites of his office, but it was a necessity, since if he had lodged in the prison camp the convicts would have made short work of him. One morning he would have been found with his belly ripped open. It was true that the house was small, it was just a wooden shack of one room, with a lean-to that served as a kitchen; but it was surrounded by a tiny garden, within a palisade, and in the garden grew bananas, papaias and such vegetables as the climate allowed him to raise. The garden faced the sea and was surrounded by a coconut grove. The situation was charming. It was only a quarter of a mile from the prison, which was convenient for his rations. They were fetched by his assistant who lived with him. The assistant, a tall, gawky ungainly fellow, with deep-set, staring eyes and cavernous jaws, was serving a life sentence for rape and murder; he was not very intelligent, but in civil life he had been a cook and it was wonderful what, with the help of the vegetables they grew and such condiments as Louis Remire could afford to buy at the Chinese grocer's, he managed to do with the soup, potatoes and cabbage, and eternal beef, beef for three hundred and sixty-five days of the year, which the prison kitchens provided. It was on this account that Louis Remire had pressed his claim on the commandant when it had been found necessary to get a new assistant. The last one's nerves had given way and, absurdly enough, thought Louis Remire with a good-natured laugh, he had developed scruples about capital punishment; now, suffering from neurasthenia, he was on the Ile St. Joseph, where the insane were confined.

His present assistant happened to be ill. He had high fever, and looked very much as if he were going to die. It had been necessary to send him to hospital. Louis Remire was sorry; he would not easily find so good a cook again. It was bad luck that this should have happened just now, for next day there was a job of work to be done. Six men were to be executed. Two were Algerians, one was a Pole, another a Spaniard from the mainland, and only two were French. They had escaped from prison in a band and gone up the river. For nearly twelve months, stealing, raping and killing, they had spread terror through the colony. People scarcely dared move from their homesteads. Recaptured at last, they had all been sentenced to death, but the sentence had to be confirmed by the Minister of the Colonies, and the confirmation had only just arrived. Louis Remire could not manage without help, and besides there was a lot to arrange beforehand; it was particularly unfortunate that on this occasion of all others he should have to depend on an inexperienced man. The commandant had assigned to him one of the turnkeys. The turnkeys are convicts like the others, but they have been given their places for good behaviour and they live in separate quarters. They are on the side of the authorities and so are disliked by the other prisoners. Louis Remire was a conscientious fellow, and he was anxious that everything next day should go without a hitch. He arranged that his temporary assistant should come that afternoon to the place where the guillotine was kept so that he might explain to him thoroughly how it worked and show him exactly what he would have to do.

The guillotine, when not in use, stood in a small room which was part of the prison building, but which was entered by a separate door from the outside. When he sauntered along there at the appointed hour he found the man already waiting. He was a large-limbed, coarse-faced fellow. He was dressed in the pink and white stripes of the prison garb, but as turnkey he wore a felt hat instead of the straw of common convicts.

"What are you here for?"

The man shrugged his shoulders.

"I killed a farmer and his wife."

"H'm. How long have you got?"

"Life."

He looked a brute, but you could never be sure of people. He had himself seen a warder, a big, powerful man, faint dead away at an execution. He did not want his assistant to have an attack of nerves at the wrong moment. He gave him a friendly smile, and with his thumb pointed to the closed door behind which stood the guillotine.

"This is another sort of job," he said. "There are six of them, you know. They're a bad lot. The sooner they're out of the way the better."

"Oh, that's all right. After what I've seen in this place I'm scared of nothing. It means no more to me than cutting the head off a chicken."

Louis Remire unlocked the door and walked in. His assistant followed him. The guillotine in that small room, hardly larger than a cell, seemed to take up a great deal of space. It stood grim and sinister. Louis Remire heard a slight gasp and turning round saw that the turnkey was staring at the instrument with terrified eyes. His face was sallow and drawn from the fever and the hookworm from which all the convicts intermittently suffered, but now its pallor was ghastly. The executioner smiled good-naturedly.

"Gives you a turn, does it? Have you never seen it before?"

"Never."

Louis Remire gave a little throaty chuckle.

"If you had, I suppose you wouldn't have survived to tell the tale. How did you escape it?"

"I was starving when I did my job. I'd asked for something to eat and they set the dogs on me. I was condemned to death. My lawyer went to Paris and he got the President to reprieve me."

"It's better to be alive than dead, there's no denying that," said Louis Remire, with that agreeable twinkle in his eyes.

He always kept his guillotine in perfect order. The wood, a dark hard native wood somewhat like mahogany, was highly polished; but there was a certain amount of brass, and it was Louis Remire's pride that this should be as bright and clean as the brass-work on a yacht. The knife shone as though it had just come out of the workshop. It was necessary not only to see that everything functioned properly, but to show his assistant how it functioned. It was part of the assistant's duty to refix the rope when the knife had dropped, and to do this he had to climb a short ladder.

It was with the satisfaction of a competent workman who knows his job from A to Z that Remire entered upon the necessary explanations. It gave him a certain quiet pleasure to point out the ingenuity of the apparatus. The condemned man was strapped to the bascule, a sort of shelf, and this by a simple mechanism was precipitated down and forwards so that the man's neck was conveniently under the knife. The conscientious fellow had brought with him a banana stem, about five feet long, and the turnkey had wondered why. He was now to learn. The stem was of about the same circumference and consistency as the human neck, so that it afforded a very good way, not only of showing a novice how the apparatus worked, but of making sure beforehand that it was in perfect order. Louis Remire placed the banana stem in position. He released the knife. It fell with incredible speed and with a great bang. From the time the man was attached to the bascule to the time his head was off only thirty seconds elapsed. The head fell in the basket. The executioner took it up by the ears and exhibited it to those whose duty it was to watch the execution. He uttered the solemn words:

"*Au nom du peuple français justice est faite.* In the name of the French people justice is done."

Then he dropped the head back into the basket. To-morrow, with six to be dispatched, the trunk would have to be unstrapped from the bascule and placed with the head on a stretcher, and the next man brought forward. They were taken in the order of their guilt. The least guilty, executed first, were spared the horror of seeing the death of their mates.

"We shall have to be careful that the right head goes with the right body," said Louis Remire, in that rather jovial manner of his, "or there may be no end of confusion at the Resurrection."

He let down the knife two or three times in order to make quite sure that the assistant understood how to fix it, and then getting his cleaning-materials from the shelf on which he kept them set him to work on the brass. Though it was spotless he thought that a final polish would do no harm. He leaned against the wall and idly smoked cigarettes.

Finally everything was in order and Louis Remire dismissed the assistant till midnight. At midnight they were moving the guillotine from the room in which it stood to the prison yard. It was always a bit of a job to set it up again, but it had to be in place an hour before dawn, at which time the execution took place. Louis Remire strolled slowly home to his shack. The afternoon was drawing to its close, and as he walked along he passed a working party who were returning to the prison. They spoke to one another in undertones and he guessed that they spoke of him; some looked down, two or three threw him a glance of hatred and one spat on the ground. Louis Remire, the end of a cigarette sticking to his lip, looked at them with irony. He was indifferent to the loathing, mingled with fear, with which they regarded him. It did not matter to him that not one of them would speak to him, and it only amused him to think that there was hardly one who would not gladly have thrust a knife into his guts. He had a supreme contempt for them all. He could take care of himself. He could use a knife as well as any of them, and he had confidence in his strength.

4

The convicts knew that men were to be executed next day, and as always before an execution they were depressed and nervous. They went about their work in sullen silence, and the warders had to be more than usually on the alert.

"They'll settle down when it's all over," said Louis Remire as he let himself into his little compound.

The dogs barked as he came along, and brave though he was, he listened to their uproar with satisfaction. With his own assistant ill, so that he was alone in the house, he was not sorry that he had the protection of those two savage mongrels. They prowled about the coconut grove outside his compound all night and they would give him good warning if anyone lurked there. They could be relied on to spring at the throat of any stranger who ventured too near. If his predecessor had had these dogs he wouldn't have come to his end.

The man who had been executioner before Louis Remire had only held the job a couple of years when one day he disappeared. The authorities thought he had run away; he was known to have a bit of money, and it was very probable that he had managed to make arrangements with the captain of a schooner to take him to Brazil. His nerves had given way. He had gone two or three times to the governor of the prison and told him that he feared for his life. He was convinced that the convicts were out to kill him. The governor felt pretty sure that his fears were groundless and paid no attention, but when the man was nowhere to be found he concluded that his terror had got the better of him and he had preferred to run the danger of escape, and the danger of being recaptured and put back into prison, rather than face the risk of an avenging convict's knife. About three weeks later the warder in charge of a working party in the jungle noticed a great flock of vultures clustered round a tree. These vultures, called urubus, are large black birds, of a horrible aspect, and they fly about the market-place of St. Laurent, picking up the offal that is left there by the starving liberated convicts, and flit heavily from tree to tree in the neat, well-kept streets of the town. They fly in the prison yard to remind the convicts that if they attempt an escape into the jungle their end, ten to one, will be to have their bones picked clean by these loathsome creatures. They were fighting and screaming in such a mass round the tree that the warder thought there was something strange there. He reported it and the commandant sent a party to see. They found a man hanging by the neck from one of the branches, and when they cut him down discovered that he was the executioner. It was given out that he had committed suicide, but there was a knife-thrust in his back, and the convicts knew that he had been stabbed and then, still alive, taken to the jungle and hanged.

Louis Remire had no fear that anything of that sort would happen to him. He knew how his predecessor had been caught. The job had not been done by the convicts. By the French law when a man is sentenced to hard labour for a certain number of years he has at the expiration of his sentence to remain in the colony for the same number of years. He is free, but he may not stir from the spot that is assigned to him as a residence. In certain circumstances he can get a concession and if he works hard he manages to scrape a bare living from it, but after a long term of penal servitude, during which he has lost all power of initiative, what with the debilitating effect of fever, hookworm and so on, he is unfit for heavy and continuous labour, and so most of the liberated men subsist on begging, larceny, smuggling tobacco or money to the prisoners, and loading and unloading cargoes when two or three times a month a steamer comes into the harbour. It was the wife of one of these freed men that had been the means of the undoing of Louis Remire's predecessor. She was a coloured woman, young and pretty, with a neat little figure and mischievous eyes. The plot was well-considered. The executioner was a burly, sanguine man, of ardent passions. She had thrown herself in his way, and when she caught his approving glance, had cast him a saucy look. He saw her a day or two later in the public garden. He did not venture to speak to her (no one, man, woman or child, would be seen speaking to him), but when he winked at her she smiled. One evening he met her walking through the coconut grove that surrounded his compound. No one was about. He got into conversation with her. They only exchanged a few words, for she was evidently terrified of being seen with him. But she came again to the coconut grove. She played him carefully till his suspicions were allayed; she teased his desires; she made him give her little presents, and at last on the promise of what was for both of them quite a sum of money she agreed to come one dark night to the compound. A ship had just come in and her husband would be working till dawn. It was when he opened the door for her and she hesitated to come in as though at the last moment she could not make up her mind, that he stepped outside to draw her in, and fell to the ground with the violence of the knife-thrust in his back.

"The fool," muttered Louis Remire. "He only got what he deserved. He should have smelt a rat. The eternal vanity of man."

For his part he was through with women. It was on account of women that he found himself in the situation he was in now, at least on account of one woman; and besides, at his time of life, his passions were assuaged. There were other things in life and after a certain age a man, if he was sensible, turned his attention to them. He had always been a great fisherman. In the old days, at home in France before he had had his misfortune, as soon as he came off duty, he took his rod and line and went down to the Rhone. He got a lot of fishing now. Every morning, till the sun grew hot, he sat on his favourite rock and generally managed to get enough for the prison governor's table. The governor's wife knew the value of things and beat him down on the price he asked, but he did not blame her for that; she knew that he had to take what she was prepared to give and it would have been stupid of her to pay a penny more than she had to. In any case it brought in a little money useful for tobacco and rum and other odds and ends. But this evening he was going to fish for himself. He got his bait from the lean-to, and his rod, and settled down on his rock. No fish was so good as the fish you caught yourself, and by now he knew which were those that were good to eat and which were so tough and flavourless that you could only throw them back into the sea. There was one sort that, fried in real olive oil, was as good as mullet. He had not been sitting there five minutes when his float gave a sudden jerk, and when he pulled up his line, there, like an answer to prayer, was one of those very fish wriggling on the hook. He took it off, banged its head on the rock, and putting it down, replaced his bait. Four of them would make a good supper, the best a man could have, and with a night's hard work before him he needed a hearty meal. He would not have time to fish to-morrow morning. First of all the scaffold would have to be taken down and the pieces brought back to the room in which it was kept, and there would be a lot of cleaning to do. It was a bloody business; last time he had had his pants so soaked that he had been able to do nothing with them and had had to throw them away. The brass would have to be polished, the knife would have to be honed. He was not a man to leave a job half finished, and by the time it was through he would be pretty peckish. It would be worth while to catch a few more fish and put them in a cool place so that he could have a substantial breakfast. A cup of coffee, a couple of eggs and a bit of fried fish; he could do with that. Then he would have a good sleep; after a night on his feet, the anxiety of an inexperienced assistant, and the clearing away of all the mess, God knew he would deserve it.

In front of him was spread the bay in a noble sweep, and in

the distance was a little island green with trees. The afternoon was exquisitely still. Peace descended on the fisherman's soul. He watched his float idly. When you came to think of it, he reflected, he might be a great deal worse off; some of them, the convicts he meant, the convicts who swarmed in the prison a few hundred yards away from him, some of them had such a nostalgia for France that they went mad with melancholy; but he was a bit of a philosopher, so long as he could fish he was content; and did it really matter if he watched his float on the southern sea or in the Rhone? His thoughts wandered back to the past. His wife was an intolerable woman and he did not regret that he had killed her. He had never meant to marry her. She was a dressmaker, and he had taken a fancy to her because she was always neatly and smartly dressed. She seemed respectable and ladylike. He would not have been surprised if she had looked upon herself as a cut above a policeman. But he had a way with him. She soon gave him to understand that she was no snob, and when he made the customary advances he discovered to his relief, for he was not a man who considered that resistance added a flavour to conquest, that she was no prude. He liked to be seen with her when he took her out to dinner. She talked intelligently, and she was economical. She knew where they could dine well at the cheapest price. His situation was enviable. It added to his satisfaction that he could gratify the sexual desires natural to his healthy temperament at so moderate an expense. When she came to him and said she was going to have a baby it seemed natural enough that they should get married. He was earning good wages, and it was time that he should settle down. He often grew tired of eating, *en pension*, at a restaurant, and he looked forward to having his own home and home cooking. Well, it turned out that it had been a mistake about the baby, but Louis Remire was a good-natured fellow, and he didn't hold it up against Adèle. But he found, as many men have found before, that the wife was a very different woman from the mistress. She was jealous and possessive. She seemed to think that on a Sunday afternoon he ought to take her for a walk instead of going out fishing, and she made it a grievance that, on coming off duty, he would go to the café. There was one café he frequented where other fishermen went and where he met men with whom he had a lot in common. He found it much pleasanter to spend his free evenings there over a glass or two of beer, whiling away the time with a game of cards, than to sit at home with his wife. She began to make scenes. Though sociable and jovial by nature he had a quick temper. There was a rough crowd at Lyons, and sometimes you could not manage them unless you were prepared to show a certain amount of firmness. When his wife began to make a nuisance of herself it never occurred to him that there was any other way of dealing with her than that he adopted. He let her know the strength of his hand. If she had been a sensible woman she would have learnt her lesson, but she was not a sensible woman. He found occasion more and more often to apply a necessary correction; she revenged herself by screaming the place down and by telling the neighbours—they lived in a two-roomed apartment on the fifth floor of a big house—what a brute he was. She told them that she was sure he would kill her one day. And yet never was there a more good-natured man than Louis Remire; she blamed him for the money he spent at the café, she accused him of wasting it on other women; well, in his position he had opportunities now and then, and as any man would he took them, and he was easy with his money, he never minded paying a round of drinks for his friends, and when a girl who had been nice to him wanted a new hat or a pair of silk stockings he wasn't the man to say no. His wife looked upon money that he did not spend on her as money stolen from her; she tried to make him account for every penny he spent, and when in his jovial way he told her he had

thrown it out of the window, she was infuriated. Her tongue
grew bitter and her voice was rasping. She was in a sullen
rage with him all the time. She could not speak without saying
something disagreeable. They led a cat-and-dog life. Louis
Remire used to tell his friends what a harridan she was, he
used to tell them that he wished ten times a day that he had
never married her, and sometimes he would add that if an
epidemic of influenza did not carry her off he would really have
to kill her.

It was these remarks, made merely in jest, and the fact that
she had so often told the neighbours that she knew he would
murder her, that had sent him to St. Laurent de Maroni with a
twelve-year sentence. Otherwise he might very well have got
off with three or four years in a French prison. The end had
come one hot summer's day. He was, which was rare for him,
in a bad temper. There was a strike in progress and the strikers
had been violent. The police had had to make a good many
arrests and the men had not submitted to this peaceably.
Louis Remire had got a nasty blow on the jaw and he had had
to make free use of his truncheon. To get the arrested men to
the station had been a hot and tiring job. On coming off duty
he had gone home to get out of his uniform and was intending
to go to the café and have a glass of beer and a pleasant game
of cards. His jaw was hurting him. His wife chose that
moment to ask him for money and when he told her that he had
none to give her she made a scene. He had plenty of money to
go to the café, but none for her to buy a scrap of food with, she
could starve for all he cared. He told her to shut up, and then
the row began. She got in front of the door and swore that he
should not pass till he gave her money. He told her to get out
of the way and took a step towards her. She whipped out his
service revolver which he had taken off when he removed his
uniform and threatened that she would shoot him if he moved a
step. He was used to dealing with dangerous criminals, and the

words were hardly out of her mouth before he had sprung upon her and snatched the revolver out of her hand. She screamed and hit him in the face. She hit him exactly where his jaw most hurt him. Blind with rage and mad with pain, he fired, he fired twice and she fell to the floor. For a moment he stood and stared at her. He was dazed. She looked as if she were dead. His first feeling was one of indescribable relief. He listened. No one seemed to have heard the sound of the shot. The neighbours must be out. That was a bit of luck, for it gave him time to do what he had to do in his own way. He changed back into his uniform, went out, locking the door behind him and putting the key in his pocket; he stopped for five minutes at his familiar café to have a glass of beer and then returned to the police station he had lately left. On account of the day's disturbances the chief inspector was still there. Louis Remire went to his room and told him what had happened. He spent the night in a cell adjoining those of the strikers he had so recently himself arrested. Even at that tragic moment he was struck by the irony of the situation.

Louis Remire had on frequent occasions appeared as a police witness in criminal cases and he knew how eager are a man's companions to give any information that may damage him when he gets into trouble. It had caused him a certain grim amusement to realise how often it happened that a conviction was obtained only by the testimony of a prisoner's best friends. But notwithstanding his experience he was amazed, when his own case came up for trial, to listen to the evidence given by the proprietor of the little café he had so much frequented, and to that of the men who for years had fished with him, played cards with him and drunk with him. They seemed to have treasured every careless word he had ever uttered, the complaints he had made about his wife and the joking threats he had from time to time made that he would get even with her. He knew that at the time they had taken them no more seriously than he meant

4*

them. If he was able to do them a small service, and a man in the force often has it in his power to do one, he never hesitated. He had never been ungenerous with his money. You would have thought as you listened to them in the witness-box that it gave them the most intense satisfaction to disclose every trivial detail that could damage him.

From what appeared at the trial you would have thought that he was a bad man, dissolute, of violent temper, extravagant, idle and corrupt. He knew that he was nothing of the kind. He was just an ordinary, good-natured, easy-going fellow, who was willing to let you go your way if you would let him go his. It was true that he liked his game of cards and his glass of beer, it was true that he liked a pretty girl, but what of it? When he looked at the jury he wondered how many of them would come out of it any better than he if all their errors, all their rash words, all their follies, were thus laid bare. He did not resent the long term of penal servitude to which he was sentenced. He was an officer of the law; he had committed a crime and it was right that he should be punished. But he was not a criminal; he was the victim of an unfortunate accident.

At St. Laurent de Maroni, in the prison camp, wearing the pink and white stripe of the prison garb and the ugly straw hat, he remembered still that he had been a policeman and that the convicts with whom he must now consort had always been his natural enemies. He despised and disliked them. He had as little to do with them as he could. And he was not frightened of them. He knew them too well. Like all the rest he had a knife and he showed that he was prepared to use it. He did not want to interfere with anybody, but he was not going to allow anyone to interfere with him.

The chief of the Lyons police had liked him, his character while in the force had been exemplary, and the *fiche* which accompanied every prisoner spoke well of him. He knew that what officials like is a prisoner who gives no trouble, who accepts his position with cheerfulness and who is willing. He got a soft job; very soon he got a cell of his own and so escaped the horrible promiscuity of the dormitories; he got on well with the warders, they were decent chaps, most of them, and knowing that he had formerly been in the police they treated him more as a comrade than as a convict. The commandant of the prison trusted him. Presently he got the job of servant to one of the prison officials. He slept in the prison, but otherwise enjoyed complete freedom. He took the children of his master to school every day and fetched them at the end of their school hours. He made toys for them. He accompanied his mistress to market and carried back the provisions she bought. He spent long hours gossiping with her. The family liked him. They liked his chaffing manner and his good-natured smile. He was industrious and trustworthy. Life once more was tolerable.

But after three years his master was transferred to Cayenne. It was a blow. But it happened just then that the post of executioner fell free and he obtained it. Now once more he was in the service of the state. He was an official. However humble his residence it was his own. He need no longer wear the prison uniform. He could grow his hair and his moustache. He cared little if the convicts looked upon him with horror and contempt. That was how he looked upon them. Scum. When he took the bleeding head of an executed man from the basket and holding it by the ears pronounced those solemn words: *Au nom du peuple français justice est faite*, he felt that he did represent the republic. He stood for law and order. He was the protector of society against that vast horde of ruthless criminals.

He got a hundred francs for each execution. That and what the governor's wife paid him for his fish provided him with many a pleasant comfort and not a few luxuries. And now as he sat on his rock in the peace of eventide he considered what he would do with the money he would earn next day. Occasionally he got a bite, now and then a fish; he drew it out of the water, took it off the hook and put on fresh bait, but he did this mechanically, and it did not disturb the current of his thoughts. Six hundred francs. It was a respectable sum. He scarcely knew what to do with it. He had everything he wanted in his little house, he had a good store of groceries, and plenty of rum for one who was as little of a drinker as he was; he needed no fishing tackle; his clothes were good enough. The only thing was to put it aside. He already had a tidy little sum hidden in the ground at the root of a papaia tree. He chuckled when he thought how Adèle would have stared had she known that he was actually saving. It would have been balm to her avaricious soul. He was saving up gradually for when he was released. That was the difficult moment for the convicts. So long as they were in prison they had a roof over their heads and food to eat, but when they were released, with the obligation of staying for so many years more in the colony, they had to shift for themselves. They all said the same thing: it was at the expiration of their term that their real punishment began. They could not get work. Employers mistrusted them. Contractors would not engage them because the prison authorities hired out convict labour at a price that defied competition. They slept in the open, in the market-place, and for food were often glad to go to the Salvation Army. But the Salvation Army made them work hard for what they gave and besides forced them to listen to their services. Sometimes they committed a violent crime merely to get back to the safety of prison. Louis Remire was not going to take any risks. He meant to amass a sufficient capital to start in business. He ought to be able to get permission to settle in Cayenne, and there he might open a bar. People might hesitate to come at first because he had been the executioner, but if he provided good liquor they would get over their prejudice, and with his jovial manner, with his experience in keeping order, he ought to be able to make a go of it.

Visitors came to Cayenne now and then and they would come out of curiosity. It would be something interesting to tell their friends when they got home that the best rum punch they had had in Cayenne was at the executioner's. But he had a good many years to go yet, and if there really was something he needed there was no reason why he shouldn't get it. He racked his brains. No, there wasn't a thing in the world he wanted. He was surprised. He allowed his eyes to wander from his float. The sea was wonderfully calm and now it was rich with all the colour of the setting sun. In the sky already a solitary star twinkled. A thought came to him that filled him with an extraordinary sensation.

"But if there's nothing in the world you want, surely that's happiness." He stroked his handsome moustache and his blue eyes shone softly. "There are no two ways about it, I'm a happy man and till this moment I never knew it."

The notion was so unexpected that he did not know what to make of it. It was certainly a very odd one. But there it was, as obvious to anyone with a logical mind as a proposition of Euclid.

"Happy, that's what I am. How many men can say the same? In St. Laurent de Maroni of all places, and for the first time in my life."

The sun was setting. He had caught enough fish for his supper and enough for his breakfast. He drew in his line, gathered up his fish, and went back to his house. It stood but a few yards from the sea. It did not take him long to light his fire and in a little while he had four little fish cheerfully frizzling in a pan. He was always very particular about the oil he used. The best olive oil was expensive, but it was worth the money. The prison bread was good, and after he had fried his fish, he fried a couple of pieces of bread in the rest of the oil. He sniffed the savoury smell with satisfaction. He lit a lamp, washed a lettuce grown in his own garden, and mixed himself a salad. He had a notion that no one in the world could mix a salad better than he. He drank a glass of rum and ate his supper with appetite. He gave a few odds and ends to the two mongrel dogs who were lying at his feet, and then, having washed up, for he was by nature a tidy man, and when he came in to breakfast next morning did not want to find things in a mess, let the dogs out of the compound to wander about the coconut grove. He took the lamp into the house, made himself comfortable in his deck-chair, and smoking a cigar smuggled in from the neighbouring Dutch Colony settled down to read one of the French papers that had arrived by the last mail. Replete, his mind at ease, he could not but feel that life, with all its disadvantages, was good to live. He was still affected by the amused surprise that had overcome him when it suddenly occurred to him that he was a happy man. When you considered that men spent their lives seeking for happiness, it seemed hardly believable that he had found it. Yet the fact stared him in the face. A man who has everything he wants is happy, he had everything he wanted, therefore he was happy. He chuckled as a new thought crossed his mind.

"There's no denying it, I owe it to Adèle."

Old Adèle. What a foul woman!

Presently he decided that he had better have a nap; he set his alarm clock for a quarter to twelve and lying down on his bed in a few minutes was fast asleep. He slept soundly and no dreams troubled him. He woke with a start when the alarm sounded, but in a moment remembered why he had set it. He yawned and stretched himself lazily.

"Ah, well, I suppose I must get to work. Every job has its inconveniences."

He slipped from under his mosquito-net and relit his lamp. To freshen himself he washed his hands and face, and then as a protection against the night air drank a glass of rum. He thought for a moment of his inexperienced assistant and wondered whether it would be wise to take some rum in a flask with him.

"It would be a pretty business if his nerves went back on him."

It was unfortunate that so many as six men had to be executed. If there had been only one, it wouldn't have mattered so much his assistant being new to the game; but with five others waiting there, it would be awkward if there were a hitch. He shrugged his shoulders. They would just have to do the best they could. He passed a comb through his tousled hair and carefully brushed his handsome moustache. He lit a cigarette. He walked through his compound, unlocked the door in the stout palisade that surrounded it, and locked it again behind him. There was no moon. He whistled for his dogs. He was surprised that they did not come. He whistled again. The brutes. They'd probably caught a rat and were fighting over it. He'd give them a good hiding for that; he'd teach them not to come when he whistled. He set out to walk in the direction of the prison. It was dark under the coconut trees and he would just as soon have had the dogs with him. Still there were only fifty yards to go and then he would be out in the open. There were lights in the governor's house, and it gave him confidence to see them. He smiled, for he guessed what those lights at that late hour meant; the governor, with the execution before him at dawn, was finding it hard to sleep. The anxiety, the malaise, that affected convicts and ex-convicts alike on the eve of an execution, had got on his nerves. It was true that there was always the chance of an outbreak then, and the warders went around with their eyes skinned and their hands ready to draw their guns at a suspicious movement.

Louis Remire whistled for his dogs once more, but they did not come. He could not understand it. It was a trifle disquieting. He was a man who habitually walked slowly, strolling along with a sort of roll, but now he hastened his pace. He spat

the cigarette out of his mouth. It had struck him that it was
prudent not to betray his whereabouts by the light it gave.
Suddenly he stumbled against something. He stopped dead.
He was a brave man, with nerves of steel, but on a sudden he
felt sick with terror. It was something soft and rather large that
he had stumbled against, and he was pretty sure what it was.
He wore espadrilles, and with one foot he cautiously felt the
object on the ground before him. Yes, he was right. It was one
of his dogs. It was dead. He took a step backwards and drew
his knife. He knew it was no good to shout. The only house in
the neighbourhood was the prison governor's, it faced the
clearing just beyond the coconut grove; but they would not
hear him, or if they did would not stir. St. Laurent de Maroni
was not a place where you went out in the dead of night when
you heard a man calling for help. If next day one of the freed
convicts was found lying dead, well, it was no great loss. Louis
Remire saw in a flash what had happened.

He thought rapidly. They had killed his dogs while he was
sleeping. They must have got them when he had put them out
of his compound after supper. They must have thrown them
some poisoned meat and the brutes had snatched at it. If the
one he had stumbled over was near his house it was because it
tried to crawl home to die. Louis Remire strained his eyes.
He could see nothing. The night was pitch black. He could
hardly see the trunks of the coconut trees a yard away from
him. His first thought was to make a rush for his shack. If he
got back to the safety of that he could wait till the prison
people, wondering why he did not come, sent to fetch him. But
he knew he could never get back. He knew they were there in
the darkness, the men who had killed his dogs; he would have
to fumble with the key to find the lock and before he found it
he would have a knife plunged in his back. He listened intently.
There was not a sound. And yet he felt that there were men
there, lurking behind the trees, and they were there to kill him.

They would kill him as they had killed his dogs. And he would die like a dog. There was more than one certainly. He knew them, there were three or four of them at least, there might be more, convicts in service in private houses who were not obliged to get back to the camp till a late hour, or desperate and starving freed men who had nothing to lose. For a moment he hesitated what to do. He dared not make a run for it, they might easily have put a rope across the pathway that led from his house to the open, and if he tripped he was done for. The coconut trees were loosely planted and among them his enemies would see him as little as he saw them. He stepped over the dead dog and plunged into the grove. He stood with his back to a tree to decide how he should proceed. The silence was terrifying. Suddenly he heard a whisper and the horror of it was frightful. Again a dead silence. He felt he must move on, but his feet seemed rooted to the ground. He felt that they were peering at him out of the darkness and it seemed to him that he was as visible to them as though he stood in the broad light of day. Then from the other side was a little cough. It came as such a shock that Louis Remire nearly screamed. He was conscious now that they were all round him. He could expect no mercy from those robbers and murderers. He remembered the other executioner, his predecessor, whom they had carried still alive into the jungle, whose eyes they had gouged out, and whom they had left hanging for the vultures to devour. His knees began to tremble. What a fool he had been to take on the job! There were soft jobs he could have found in which you ran no risk. It was too late to think of that. He pulled himself together. He had no chance of getting out of the coconut grove alive, he knew that; he wanted to be sure that he would be dead. He tightened his grip on his knife. The awful part was that he could hear no one, he could see no one, and yet he knew that they were lurking there waiting to strike. For one moment he had a mad idea, he would throw his knife away and shout out to them that he was unarmed and they could come and kill him in safety. But he knew them; they would never be satisfied merely to kill him. Rage seized him. He was not the man to surrender tamely to a pack of criminals. He was an honest man and an official of the state; it was his duty to defend himself. He could not stay there all night. It was better to get it over quickly. Yet that tree at his back seemed to offer a sort of security, he could not bring himself to move. He stared at the trunk of a tree in front of him and suddenly it moved and he realised with horror that it was a man. That made up his mind for him and with a huge effort he stepped forwards. He advanced slowly and cautiously. He could hear nothing, he could see nothing. But he knew that as he advanced they advanced too. It was as though he were accompanied by an invisible bodyguard. He thought he could hear the sound of their naked feet on the ground. His fear had left him. He walked on, keeping as close to the trees as he could, so that they should have less chance of attacking him from behind; a wild hope sprang up in his breast that they would be afraid to strike, they knew him, they all knew him, and whoever struck the first blow would be lucky if he escaped a knife in his own guts; he had only another thirty yards to go, and once in the open, able to see, he could make a fight for it. A few yards more and then he would run for his life. Suddenly something happened that made him start out of his skin, and he stopped dead. A light was flashed and in that heavy darkness the sudden glare was terrifying. It was an electric torch. Instinctively he sprang to a tree and stood with his back to it. He could not see who held the light. He was blinded by it. He did not speak. He held his knife low, he knew that when they struck it was in the belly, and if someone flung himself at him he was prepared to strike back. He was going to sell his life dearly. For half a minute perhaps the light shone on his face, but it seemed to him an eternity. He thought now that he discerned dimly the faces of men. Then a word broke the horrible silence.

"Throw."

At the same instant a knife came flying through the air and struck him on the breast-bone. He threw up his hands and as he did so someone sprang at him and with a great sweep of the knife ripped up his belly. The light was switched off. Louis Remire sank to the ground with a groan, a terrible groan of pain. Five, six men gathered out of the gloom and stood over him. With his fall the knife that had stuck in his breast-bone was dislodged. It lay on the ground. A quick flash of the torch showed where it was. One of the men took it and with a single, swift motion cut Remire's throat from ear to ear.

"*Au nom du peuple français justice est faite*," he said.

They vanished into the darkness and in the coconut grove was the immense silence of death.

IT was Henry Garnet's habit on leaving the city of an afternoon to drop in at his club and play bridge before going home to dinner. He was a pleasant man to play with. He knew the game well and you could be sure that he would make the best of his cards. He was a good loser; and when he won was more inclined to ascribe his success to his luck than to his skill. He was indulgent, and if his partner made a mistake could be trusted to find an excuse for him. It was surprising then on this occasion to hear him telling his partner with unnecessary sharpness that he had never seen a hand worse played; and it was more surprising still to see him not only make a grave error himself, an error of which you would never have thought him capable, but when his partner, not unwilling to get a little of his own back, pointed it out, insist against all reason and with considerable heat that he was perfectly right. But they were all old friends, the men he was playing with, and none of them took his ill humour very seriously. Henry Garnet was a broker, a partner in a firm of repute, and it occurred to one of them that something had gone wrong with some stock he was interested in.

"How's the market to-day?" he asked.

"Booming. Even the suckers are making money."

It was evident that stocks and shares had nothing to do with Henry Garnet's vexation; but something was the matter; that was evident too. He was a hearty fellow, who enjoyed excellent health; he had plenty of money; he was fond of his wife and devoted to his children. As a rule he had high spirits, and he laughed easily at the nonsense they were apt to talk while they played; but to-day he sat glum and silent. His brows were crossly puckered and there was a sulky look about his mouth.

Presently, to ease the tension, one of the others mentioned a subject upon which they all knew Henry Garnet was glad to speak.

"How's your boy, Henry? I see he's done pretty well in the tournament."

Henry Garnet's frown grew darker.

"He's done no better than I expected him to."

"When does he come back from Monte?"

"He got back last night."

"Did he enjoy himself?"

"I suppose so; all I know is that he made a damned fool of himself."

"Oh. How?"

"I'd rather not talk about it if you don't mind."

The three men looked at him with curiosity. Henry Garnet scowled at the green baize.

"Sorry, old boy. Your call."

The game proceeded in a strained silence. Garnet got his bid, and when he played his cards so badly that he went three down not a word was said. Another rubber was begun and in the second game Garnet denied a suit.

"Having none?" his partner asked him.

Garnet's irritability was such that he did not even reply, and when at the end of the hand it appeared that he had revoked, and that his revoke cost the rubber, it was not to be expected that his partner should let his carelessness go without remark.

"What the devil's the matter with you, Henry?" he said. "You're playing like a fool."

Garnet was disconcerted. He did not so much mind losing a big rubber himself, but he was sore that his inattention should have made his partner lose too. He pulled himself together.

"I'd better not play any more. I thought a few rubbers would calm me, but the fact is I can't give my mind to the game. To tell you the truth I'm in a hell of a temper."

They all burst out laughing.

"You don't have to tell us that, old boy. It's obvious."

Garnet gave them a rueful smile.

"Well, I bet you'd be in a temper if what's happened to me had happened to you. As a matter of fact I'm in a damned awkward situation, and if any of you fellows can give me any advice how to deal with it I'd be grateful."

"Let's have a drink and you tell us all about it. With a K.C., a Home Office official and an eminent surgeon—if we can't tell you how to deal with a situation, nobody can."

The K.C. got up and rang the bell for a waiter.

"It's about that damned boy of mine," said Henry Garnet.

Drinks were ordered and brought. And this is the story that Henry Garnet told them.

The boy of whom he spoke was his only son. His name was Nicholas and of course he was called Nicky. He was eighteen. The Garnets had two daughters besides, one of sixteen and the other of twelve, but however unreasonable it seemed, for a father is generally supposed to like his daughters best, and though he did all he could not to show his preference, there was no doubt that the greater share of Henry Garnet's affection was given to his son. He was kind, in a chaffing, casual way, to his daughters, and gave them handsome presents on their birthdays and at Christmas; but he doted on Nicky. Nothing was too good for him. He thought the world of him. He could hardly take his eyes off him. You could not blame him, for Nicky was a son that any parent might have been proud of. He was six foot two, lithe but muscular, with broad shoulders and a slim waist, and he held himself gallantly erect; he had a charming head, well placed on the shoulders, with pale brown hair that waved slightly, blue eyes with long dark lashes under well-marked eyebrows, a full red mouth and a tanned, clean skin. When he smiled he showed very regular and very white teeth. He was not shy, but there was a modesty in his demeanour that was attractive. In social intercourse he was easy, polite and quietly gay. He was the offspring of nice, healthy, decent parents, he had been well brought up in a good home, he had been sent to a good school, and the general result was as engaging a specimen of young manhood as you were likely to find in a long time. You felt that he was as honest, open and virtuous as he looked. He had never given his parents a moment's uneasiness. As a child he was seldom ill and never naughty. As a boy he did everything that was expected of him. His school reports were excellent. He was wonderfully popular, and he ended his career, with a creditable number of prizes, as head of the school and captain of the football team. But this was not all. At the age of fourteen Nicky had developed an unexpected gift for lawn tennis. This was a game that his father not only was fond of, but played very well, and when he discerned in the boy the promise of a tennis-player he fostered it. During the holidays he had him taught by the best professionals and by the time he was sixteen he had won a number of tournaments for boys of his age. He could beat his father so badly that only parental affection reconciled the older player to the poor show he put up. At eighteen Nicky went to Cambridge and Henry Garnet conceived the ambition that before he was through with the university he should play for it. Nicky had all the qualifications for becoming a great tennis-player. He was tall, he had a long reach, he was quick on his feet and his timing was perfect. He realised instinctively where the ball was coming and, seemingly without hurry, was there to take it. He had a powerful serve, with a nasty break that made it difficult to return, and his forehand drive, low, long and accurate, was deadly. He was not so good on the back-hand and his volleying was wild, but all through the summer before he went to Cambridge Henry Garnet made him work on these points under the best teacher in England. At the back of his mind, though he did not even mention it to Nicky, he cherished a further ambition, to see his son play at Wimbledon, and who could tell, perhaps be chosen to represent his country in the Davis Cup. A great lump came into Henry Garnet's throat as he saw in fancy his son leap over the net to shake hands with the American champion whom he had just defeated, and walk off the court to the deafening plaudits of the multitude.

As an assiduous frequenter of Wimbledon Henry Garnet had a good many friends in the tennis world, and one evening he found himself at a City dinner sitting next to one of them, a Colonel Brabazon, and in due course began talking to him of Nicky and what chance there might be of his being chosen to play for his university during the following season.

"Why don't you let him go down to Monte Carlo and play in the spring tournament there?" said the Colonel suddenly.

"Oh, I don't think he's good enough for that. He's not nineteen yet, he only went up to Cambridge last October; he wouldn't stand a chance against all those cracks."

"Of course, Austin and von Cramm and so on would knock spots off him, but he might snatch a game or two; and if he got up against some of the smaller fry there's no reason why he shouldn't win two or three matches. He's never been up against any of the first-rate players and it would be wonderful practice for him. He'll learn a lot more than he'll ever learn in the seaside tournaments you enter him for."

"I wouldn't dream of it. I'm not going to let him leave Cambridge in the middle of a term. I've always impressed upon him that tennis is only a game and it mustn't interfere with work."

Colonel Brabazon asked Garnet when the term ended.

"That's all right. He'd only have to cut about three days. Surely that could be arranged. You see, two of the men we were depending on have let us down, and we're in a hole. We want to send as good a team as we can. The Germans are sending their best players and so are the Americans."

"Nothing doing, old boy. In the first place Nicky's not good enough, and secondly, I don't fancy the idea of sending a kid like that to Monte Carlo without anyone to look after him. If I could get away myself I might think of it, but that's out of the question."

"I shall be there. I'm going as the non-playing captain of the English team. I'll keep an eye on him."

"You'll be busy, and besides, it's not a responsibility I'd like to ask you to take. He's never been abroad in his life, and to tell you the truth, I shouldn't have a moment's peace all the time he was there."

They left it at that and presently Henry Garnet went home. He was so flattered by Colonel Brabazon's suggestion that he could not help telling his wife.

"Fancy his thinking Nicky's as good as that. He told me he'd seen him play and his style was fine. He only wants more practice to get into the first flight. We shall see the kid playing in the semi-finals at Wimbledon yet, old girl."

To his surprise Mrs. Garnet was not so much opposed to the notion as he would have expected.

"After all the boy's eighteen. Nicky's never got into mischief yet and there's no reason to suppose he will now."

"There's his work to be considered; don't forget that. I think it would be a very bad precedent to let him cut the end of term."

"But what can three days matter? It seems a shame to rob him of a chance like that. I'm sure he'd jump at it if you asked him."

"Well, I'm not going to. I haven't sent him to Cambridge just to play tennis. I know he's steady, but it's silly to put temptation in his way. He's much too young to go to Monte Carlo by himself."

"You say he won't have a chance against these crack players, but you can't tell."

Henry Garnet sighed a little. On the way home in the car it had struck him that Austin's health was uncertain and that von Cramm had his off-days. Supposing, just for the sake of argument, that Nicky had a bit of luck like that—then there would be no doubt that he would be chosen to play for Cambridge. But of course that was all nonsense.

"Nothing doing, my dear. I've made up my mind and I'm not going to change it."

Mrs. Garnet held her peace. But next day she wrote to Nicky, telling him what had happened, and suggested to him what she would do in his place if, wanting to go, he wished to get his father's consent. A day or two later Henry Garnet received a letter from his son. He was bubbling over with excitement. He had seen his tutor, who was a tennis-player himself, and the Provost of his college, who happened to know Colonel Brabazon, and no objection would be made to his leaving before the end of term; they both thought it an opportunity that shouldn't be missed. He didn't see what harm he could come to, and if only, just this once, his father would stretch a point, well, next term, he promised faithfully, he'd work like blazes. It was a very pretty letter. Mrs. Garnet watched her husband read it at the breakfast table; she was undisturbed by the frown on his face. He threw it over to her.

"I don't know why you thought it necessary to tell Nicky something I told you in confidence. It's too bad of you. Now you've thoroughly unsettled him."

"I'm so sorry. I thought it would please him to know that Colonel Brabazon had such a high opinion of him. I don't see why one should only tell people the disagreeable things that are said about them. Of course I made it quite clear that there could be no question of his going."

"You've put me in an odious position. If there's anything I

hate it's for the boy to look upon me as a spoil-sport and a tyrant."

"Oh, he'll never do that. He may think you rather silly and unreasonable, but I'm sure he'll understand that it's only for his own good that you're being so unkind."

"Christ," said Henry Garnet.

His wife had a great inclination to laugh. She knew the battle was won. Dear, oh dear, how easy it was to get men to do what you wanted. For appearance sake Henry Garnet held out for forty-eight hours, but then he yielded, and a fortnight later Nicky came to London. He was to start for Monte Carlo next morning, and after dinner, when Mrs. Garnet and her elder daughter had left them, Henry took the opportunity to give his son some good advice.

"I don't feel quite comfortable about letting you go off to a place like Monte Carlo at your age practically by yourself," he finished, "but there it is and I can only hope you'll be sensible. I don't want to play the heavy father, but there are three things especially that I want to warn you against: one is gambling, don't gamble; the second is money, don't lend anyone money, and the third is women, don't have anything to do with women. If you don't do any of those three things you can't come to much harm, so remember them well."

"All right, father," Nicky smiled.

"That's my last word to you. I know the world pretty well and believe me, my advice is sound."

"I won't forget it. I promise you."

"That's a good chap. Now let's go up and join the ladies."

Nicky beat neither Austin nor von Cramm in the Monte Carlo tournament, but he did not disgrace himself. He snatched an unexpected victory over a Spanish player and gave one of the Austrians a closer match than anyone had thought possible. In the mixed doubles he got into the semi-finals. His charm conquered everyone and he vastly enjoyed himself. It was generally allowed that he showed promise, and Colonel Brabazon told him that when he was a little older and had had more practice with first-class players he would be a credit to his father. The tournament came to an end and the day following he was to fly back to London. Anxious to play his best he had lived very carefully, smoking little and drinking nothing, and going to bed early; but on his last evening he thought he would like to see something of the life in Monte Carlo of which he had heard so much. An official dinner was given to the tennis-players and after dinner with the rest of them he went into the Sporting Club. It was the first time he had been there. Monte Carlo was very full and the rooms were crowded. Nicky had never before seen roulette played except in the pictures; in a maze he stopped at the first table he came to; chips of different sizes were scattered over the green cloth in what looked like a hopeless muddle; the croupier gave the wheel a sharp turn and with a flick threw in the little white ball. After what seemed an endless time the ball stopped and another croupier with a broad, indifferent gesture raked in the chips of those who had lost.

Presently Nicky wandered over to where they were playing *trente et quarante*, but he couldn't understand what it was all about and he thought it dull. He saw a crowd in another room and sauntered in. A big game of baccara was in progress and he was immediately conscious of the tension. The players were protected from the thronging bystanders by a brass rail; they sat round the table, nine on each side, with the dealer in the middle and the croupier facing him. Big money was changing hands. The dealer was a member of the Greek Syndicate. Nicky looked at his impassive face. His eyes were watchful, but his expression never changed whether he won or lost. It was a terrifying, strangely impressive sight. It gave Nicky, who had been thriftily brought up, a peculiar thrill to see someone risk a thousand pounds on the turn of a card and when he lost make a little joke and laugh. It was all terribly exciting. An acquaintance came up to him.

"Been doing any good?" he asked.

"I haven't been playing."

"Wise of you. Rotten game. Come and have a drink."

"All right."

While they were having it Nicky told his friend that this was the first time he had ever been in the rooms.

"Oh, but you must have one little flutter before you go. It's idiotic to leave Monte without having tried your luck. After all it won't hurt you to lose a hundred francs or so."

"I don't suppose it will, but my father wasn't any too keen on my coming at all and one of the three things he particularly advised me not to do was to gamble."

But when Nicky left his companion he strolled back to one of the tables where they were playing roulette. He stood for a while looking at the losers' money being raked in by the croupier and the money that was won paid out to the winners. It was impossible to deny that it was thrilling. His friend was right, it did seem silly to leave Monte without putting something on the table just once. It would be an experience, and at his age you had to have all the experience you could get. He reflected that he hadn't promised his father not to gamble, he'd promised him not to forget his advice. It wasn't quite the same, was it? He took a hundred-franc note out of his pocket and rather shyly put it on number eighteen. He chose it because that was his age. With a wildly beating heart he watched the wheel turn; the little white ball whizzed about like a small demon of mischief; the wheel went round more slowly, the little white ball hesitated, it seemed about to stop, it went on again; Nicky could hardly believe his eyes when it fell into number eighteen. A lot of chips were passed over to him and his hands trembled as he took them. It seemed to amount to a lot of money. He was so confused that he never thought of putting anything on the following round; in fact he had no intention of playing any more, once was enough; and he was surprised when eighteen again came up. There was only one chip on it.

"By George, you've won again," said a man who was standing near to him.

"Me? I hadn't got anything on."

"Yes, you had. Your original stake. They always leave it on unless you ask for it back. Didn't you know?"

Another packet of chips was handed over to him. Nicky's head reeled. He counted his gains: seven thousand francs. A queer sense of power seized him; he felt wonderfully clever. This was the easiest way of making money that he had ever heard of. His frank, charming face was wreathed in smiles. His bright eyes met those of a woman standing by his side. She smiled.

"You're in luck," she said.

She spoke English, but with a foreign accent.

"I can hardly believe it. It's the first time I've ever played."

"That explains it. Lend me a thousand francs, will you? I've lost everything I've got. I'll give it you back in half an hour."

"All right."

She took a large red chip from his pile and with a word of thanks disappeared. The man who had spoken to him before grunted.

"You'll never see that again."

Nicky was dashed. His father had particularly advised him not to lend anyone money. What a silly thing to do! And to somebody he'd never seen in his life. But the fact was, he felt at that moment such a love for the human race that it had never occurred to him to refuse. And that big red chip, it was almost impossible to realise that it had any value. Oh well, it didn't matter, he still had six thousand francs, he'd just try his luck once or twice more and if he didn't win he'd go home. He put a chip on sixteen, which was his elder sister's age, but it didn't come up; then on twelve, which was his younger sister's and that didn't come up either; he tried various numbers at random, but without success. It was funny, he seemed to have lost his knack. He thought he would try just once more and then stop; he won. He had made up all his losses and had something over. At the end of an hour, after various ups and downs, having experienced such thrills as he had never known in his life, he found himself with so many chips that they would hardly go in his pockets. He decided to go. He went to the changers' office and he gasped when twenty thousand-franc notes were spread out before him. He had never had so much money in his life. He put it in his pocket and was turning away when the woman to whom he had lent the thousand francs came up to him.

"I've been looking for you everywhere," she said. "I was afraid you'd gone. I was in a fever, I didn't know what you'd think of me. Here's your thousand francs and thank you so much for the loan."

Nicky, blushing scarlet, stared at her with amazement. How he had misjudged her! His father had said, don't gamble; well, he had, and he'd made twenty thousand francs; and his father had said, don't lend anyone money; well, he had, he'd lent quite a lot to a total stranger, and she'd returned it. The fact was that he wasn't nearly such a fool as his father thought: he'd had an instinct that he could lend her the money with safety, and you see, his instinct was right. But he was so obviously taken aback that the little lady was forced to laugh.

"What is the matter with you?" she asked.

"To tell you the truth I never expected to see the money back."

"What did you take me for? Did you think I was a—cocotte?"

Nicky reddened to the roots of his wavy hair.

"No, of course not."

"Do I look like one?"

"Not a bit."

She was dressed very quietly, in black, with a string of gold beads round her neck; her simple frock showed off a neat, slight figure; she had a pretty little face and a trim head. She was made up, but not excessively, and Nicky supposed that she was not more than three or four years older than himself. She gave him a friendly smile.

"My husband is in the administration in Morocco, and I've come to Monte Carlo for a few weeks because he thought I wanted a change."

"I was just going," said Nicky because he couldn't think of anything else to say.

"Already!"

"Well, I've got to get up early to-morrow. I'm going back to London by air."

"Of course. The tournament ended to-day, didn't it? I saw you play, you know, two or three times."

"Did you? I don't know why you should have noticed me."

"You've got a beautiful style. And you looked very sweet in your shorts."

Nicky was not an immodest youth, but it did cross his mind that perhaps she had borrowed that thousand francs in order to scrape acquaintance with him.

"Do you ever go to the Knickerbocker?" she asked.

"No. I never have."

"Oh, but you mustn't leave Monte without having been there. Why don't you come and dance a little? To tell you the truth, I'm starving with hunger and I should adore some bacon and eggs."

Nicky remembered his father's advice not to have anything to do with women, but this was different; you had only to look at the pretty little thing to know at once that she was perfectly respectable. Her husband was in what corresponded he supposed to the Civil Service. His father and mother had friends who were Civil Servants and they and their wives sometimes came to dinner. It was true that the wives were neither so young nor so pretty as this one, but she was just as ladylike as they were. And after winning twenty thousand francs he thought it wouldn't be a bad idea to have a little fun.

"I'd love to go with you," he said. "But you won't mind if I don't stay very long. I've left instructions at my hotel that I'm to be called at seven."

"We'll leave as soon as ever you like."

Nicky found it very pleasant at the Knickerbocker. He ate his bacon and eggs with appetite. They shared a bottle of champagne. They danced, and the little lady told him he danced beautifully. He knew he danced pretty well, and of course she was easy to dance with. As light as a feather. She laid her cheek against his and when their eyes met there was in hers a smile that made his heart go pit-a-pat. A coloured woman sang in a throaty, sensual voice. The floor was crowded.

"Have you ever been told that you're very good-looking?" she asked.

"I don't think so," he laughed. "Gosh," he thought, "I believe she's fallen for me."

Nicky was not such a fool as to be unaware that women often liked him, and when she made that remark he pressed her to him a little more closely. She closed her eyes and a faint sigh escaped her lips.

"I suppose it wouldn't be quite nice if I kissed you before all these people," he said.

"What do you think they would take me for?"

It began to grow late and Nicky said that really he thought he ought to be going.

5

"I shall go too," she said. "Will you drop me at my hotel on your way?"

Nicky paid the bill. He was rather surprised at its amount, but with all that money he had in his pocket he could afford not to care, and they got into a taxi. She snuggled up to him and he kissed her. She seemed to like it.

"By Jove," he thought, "I wonder if there's anything doing."

It was true that she was a married woman, but her husband was in Morocco, and it certainly did look as if she'd fallen for him. Good and proper. It was true also that his father had warned him to have nothing to do with women, but, he reflected again, he hadn't actually promised he wouldn't, he'd only promised not to forget his advice. Well, he hadn't; he was bearing it in mind that very minute. But circumstances alter cases. She was a sweet little thing; it seemed silly to miss the chance of an adventure when it was handed to you like that on a tray. When they reached the hotel he paid off the taxi.

"I'll walk home," he said. "The air will do me good after the stuffy atmosphere of that place."

"Come up a moment," she said. "I'd like to show you the photo of my little boy."

"Oh, have you got a little boy?" he exclaimed, a trifle dashed.

"Yes, a sweet little boy."

He walked upstairs after her. He didn't in the least want to see the photograph of her little boy, but he thought it only civil to pretend he did. He was afraid he'd made a fool of himself; it occurred to him that she was taking him up to look at the photograph in order to show him in a nice way that he'd made a mistake. He'd told her he was eighteen.

"I suppose she thinks I'm just a kid."

He began to wish he hadn't spent all that money on champagne at the night-club.

But she didn't show him the photograph of her little boy

after all. They had no sooner got into her room than she turned to him, flung her arms round his neck, and kissed him full on the lips. He had never in all his life been kissed so passionately.

"Darling," she said.

For a brief moment his father's advice once more crossed Nicky's mind and then he forgot it.

Nicky was a light sleeper and the least sound was apt to wake him. Two or three hours later he awoke and for a moment could not imagine where he was. The room was not quite dark, for the door of the bathroom was ajar, and the light in it had been left on. Suddenly he was conscious that someone was moving about the room. Then he remembered. He saw that it was his little friend, and he was on the point of speaking when something in the way she was behaving stopped him. She was walking very cautiously, as though she were afraid of waking him; she stopped once or twice and looked over at the bed. He wondered what she was after. He soon saw. She went over to the chair on which he had placed his clothes and once more looked in his direction. She waited for what seemed to him an interminable time. The silence was so intense that Nicky thought he could hear his own heart beating. Then, very slowly, very quietly, she took up his coat, slipped her hand into the inside pocket and drew out all those beautiful thousand-franc notes that Nicky had been so proud to win. She put the coat back and placed some other clothes on it so that it should look as though it had not been disturbed, then, with the bundle of notes in her hand, for an appreciable time stood once more stock-still. Nicky had repressed an instinctive impulse to jump up and grab her, it was partly surprise that had kept him quiet, partly the notion that he was in a strange hotel, in a foreign country, and if he made a row he didn't know what might happen. She looked at him. His eyes were partly closed and he was sure that she thought he was asleep. In the silence she could hardly fail to hear his regular breathing. When she had reassured herself that her movements had not disturbed him she stepped, with infinite caution, across the room. On a small table in the window a cineraria was growing in a pot. Nicky watched her now with his eyes wide open. The plant was evidently placed quite loosely in the pot, for taking it by the stalks she lifted it out; she put the bank-notes in the bottom of the pot and replaced the plant. It was an excellent hiding-place. No one could have guessed that anything was concealed under that richly-flowering plant. She pressed the earth down with her fingers and then, very slowly, taking care not to make the smallest noise, crept across the room, and slipped back into bed.

"Chéri," she said, in a caressing voice.

Nicky breathed steadily, like a man immersed in deep sleep. The little lady turned over on her side and disposed herself to slumber. But though Nicky lay so still his thoughts worked busily. He was extremely indignant at the scene he had just witnessed, and to himself he spoke his thoughts with vigour.

"She's nothing but a damned tart. She and her dear little boy and her husband in Morocco. My eye! She's a rotten thief, that's what she is. Took me for a mug. If she thinks she's going to get away with anything like that, she's mistaken."

He had already made up his mind what he was going to do with the money he had so cleverly won. He had long wanted a car of his own, and had thought it rather mean of his father not to have given him one. After all, a feller doesn't always want to drive about in the family bus. Well, he'd just teach the old man a lesson and buy one himself. For twenty thousand francs, two hundred pounds roughly, he could get a very decent second-hand car. He meant to get the money back, but just then he didn't quite know how. He didn't like the idea of kicking up a row, he was a stranger, in an hotel he knew nothing of; it might very well be that the beastly woman had friends there, he didn't mind facing anyone in a fair fight, but he'd look pretty foolish if someone pulled a gun on him. He reflected besides, very sensibly, that he had no proof the money was his. If it came to a show-down and she swore it was hers, he might very easily find himself hauled off to a police station. He really didn't know what to do. Presently by her regular breathing he knew that the little lady was asleep. She must have fallen asleep with an easy mind, for she had done her job without a hitch. It infuriated Nicky that she should rest so peacefully while he lay awake worried to death. Suddenly an idea occurred to him. It was such a good one that it was only by the exercise of all his self-control that he prevented himself from jumping out of bed and carrying it out at once. Two could play at her game. She'd stolen his money; well, he'd steal it back again, and they'd be all square. He made up his mind to wait quite quietly until he was sure that deceitful woman was sound asleep. He waited for what seemed to him a very long time. She did not stir. Her breathing was as regular as a child's.

"Darling," he said at last.

No answer. No movement. She was dead to the world. Very slowly, pausing after every movement, very silently, he slipped out of bed. He stood still for a while, looking at her to see whether he had disturbed her. Her breathing was as regular as before. During the time he was waiting he had taken note carefully of the furniture in the room so that in crossing it he should not knock against a chair or a table and make a noise. He took a couple of steps and waited, he took a couple of steps more; he was very light on his feet and made no sound as he walked; he took fully five minutes to get to the window, and here he waited again. He started, for the bed slightly creaked, but it was only because the sleeper turned in her sleep. He forced himself to wait till he had counted one hundred. She was sleeping like a log. With infinite care he seized the cineraria by the stalks and gently pulled it out of the pot; he put his other hand in, his heart beat nineteen to the dozen as his fingers touched the notes, his hand closed on them and he slowly drew them out. He replaced the plant and in his turn carefully pressed down the earth. While he was doing all this he had kept one eye on the form lying in the bed. It remained still. After another pause he crept softly to the chair on which his clothes were lying. He first put the bundle of notes in his coat pocket and then proceeded to dress. It took him a good quarter of an hour, because he could afford to make no sound. He had been wearing a soft shirt with his dinner jacket, and he congratulated himself on this, because it was easier to put on silently than a stiff one. He had some difficulty in tying his tie without a looking-glass, but he very wisely reflected that it didn't really matter if it wasn't tied very well. His spirits were rising. The whole thing now began to seem rather a lark. At length he was completely dressed except for his shoes, which he took in his hand; he thought he would put them on when he got into the passage. Now he had to cross the room to get to the door. He reached it so quietly that he could not have disturbed the lightest sleeper. But the door had to be unlocked. He turned the key very slowly; it creaked.

"Who's that?"

The little woman suddenly sat up in bed. Nicky's heart jumped to his mouth. He made a great effort to keep his head.

"It's only me. It's six o'clock and I've got to go. I was trying not to wake you."

"Oh, I forgot."

She sank back on to the pillow.

"Now that you're awake I'll put on my shoes."

He sat down on the edge of the bed and did this.

"Don't make a noise when you go out. The hotel people don't like it. Oh, I'm so sleepy."

"You go right off to sleep again."

"Kiss me before you go." He bent down and kissed her. "You're a sweet boy and a wonderful lover. *Bon voyage.*"

Nicky did not feel quite safe till he got out of the hotel. The dawn had broken. The sky was unclouded, and in the harbour the yachts and the fishing-boats lay motionless on the still water. On the quay fishermen were getting ready to start on their day's work. The streets were deserted. Nicky took a long breath of the sweet morning air. He felt alert and well. He also felt as pleased as Punch. With a swinging stride, his shoulders well thrown back, he walked up the hill and along the gardens in front of the Casino—the flowers in that clear light had a dewy brilliance that was delicious—till he came to his hotel. Here the day had already begun. In the hall porters with mufflers round their necks and berets on their heads were busy sweeping. Nicky went up to his room and had a hot bath. He lay in it and thought with satisfaction that he was not such a mug as some people might think. After his bath he did his exercises, dressed, packed and went down to breakfast. He had a grand appetite. No continental breakfast for him! He had grape-fruit, porridge, bacon and eggs, rolls fresh from the oven, so crisp and delicious they melted in your mouth, marmalade and three cups of coffee. Though feeling perfectly well before, he felt better after that. He lit the pipe he had recently learnt to smoke, paid the bill and stepped into the car that was waiting to take him to the aerodrome on the other side of Cannes. The road as far as Nice ran over the hills and below him was the blue sea and the coast-line. He couldn't help thinking it damned pretty. They passed through Nice, so gay and friendly in the early morning, and presently they came to a long stretch of straight road that ran by the sea. Nicky had paid his bill, not with the money he had won the night before, but with the money his father had given him; he had changed a thousand francs to pay for supper at the Knickerbocker, but that deceitful little woman had returned him the thousand francs he had lent her, so that he still had twenty thousand-franc notes in his pocket. He thought he would like to have a look at them. He had so nearly lost them that they had a double value for him. He took them out of his hip-pocket into which for safety's sake he had stuffed them when he put on the suit he was travelling in, and counted them one by one. Something very strange had happened to them. Instead of there being twenty notes as there should have been there were twenty-six. He couldn't understand it at all. He counted them twice more. There was no doubt about it; somehow or other he had twenty-six thousand francs instead of the twenty he should have had. He couldn't make it out. He asked himself if it was possible that he had won more at the Sporting Club than he had realised. But no, that was out of the question; he distinctly remembered the man at the desk laying the notes out in four rows of five, and he had counted them himself. Suddenly the explanation occurred to him; when he had put his hand into the flower-pot, after taking out the cineraria, he had grabbed everything he felt there. The flower-pot was the little hussy's money-box and he had taken out not only his own money, but her savings as well. Nicky leant back in the car and burst into a roar of laughter. It was the funniest thing he had ever heard in his life. And when he thought of her going to the flower-pot some time later in the morning when she awoke, expecting to find the money she had so cleverly got away with, and finding, not only that it wasn't there, but that her own had gone too, he laughed more than ever. And so far as he was concerned there was nothing to do about it; he neither knew her name, nor the name of the hotel to which she had taken him. He couldn't return her money even if he wanted to.

"It serves her damned well right," he said.

This then was the story that Henry Garnet told his friends over the bridge-table, for the night before, after dinner when his wife and daughter had left them to their port, Nicky had narrated it in full.

"And you know what infuriated me is that he's so damned pleased with himself. Talk of a cat swallowing a canary. And d'you know what he said to me when he'd finished? He looked at me with those innocent eyes of his and said: 'You know, father, I can't help thinking there was something wrong about the advice you gave me. You said, don't gamble; well, I did, and I made a packet; you said, don't lend money; well, I did, and I got it back; and you said, don't have anything to do with women; well, I did, and I made six thousand francs on the deal.'"

It didn't make it any better for Henry Garnet that his three companions burst out laughing.

"It's all very well for you fellows to laugh, but you know, I'm in a damned awkward position. The boy looked up to me, he respected me, he took whatever I said as gospel truth, and now, I saw it in his eyes, he just looks upon me as a drivelling old fool. It's no good my saying one swallow doesn't make a summer; he doesn't see that it was just a fluke, he thinks the whole thing was due to his own cleverness. It may ruin him."

"You do look a bit of a damned fool, old man," said one of the others. "There's no denying that, is there?"

"I know I do, and I don't like it. It's so dashed unfair. Fate has no right to play one tricks like that. After all, you must admit that my advice was good."

"Very good."

"And the wretched boy ought to have burnt his fingers. Well, he hasn't. You're all men of the world, you tell me how I'm to deal with the situation now."

But they none of them could.

"Well, Henry, if I were you I wouldn't worry," said the lawyer. "My belief is that your boy's born lucky, and in the long run that's better than to be born clever or rich."

5*

WINTER CRUISE

CAPTAIN ERDMANN knew Miss Reid very little till the *Friedrich Weber* reached Haiti. She came on board at Plymouth, but by then he had taken on a number of passengers, French, Belgian and Haitian, many of whom had travelled with him before, and she was placed at the chief engineer's table. The *Friedrich Weber* was a freighter sailing regularly from Hamburg to Cartagena on the Columbian coast and on the way touching at a number of islands in the West Indies. She carried phosphates and cement from Germany and took back coffee and timber; but her owners, the Brothers Weber, were always willing to send her out of her route if a cargo of any sort made it worth their while. The *Friedrich Weber* was prepared to take cattle, mules, potatoes or anything else that offered the chance of earning an honest penny. She carried passengers. There were six cabins on the upper deck and six below. The accommodation was not luxurious, but the food was good, plain and abundant, and the fares were cheap. The round trip took nine weeks and was not costing Miss Reid more than forty-five pounds. She looked forward not only to seeing many interesting places, with historical associations, but also to acquiring a great deal of information that would enrich her mind.

The agent had warned her that till the ship reached Port au Prince in Haiti she would have to share a cabin with another woman. Miss Reid did not mind that, she liked company, and when the steward told her that her companion was Madame Bollin she thought at once that it would be a very good opportunity to rub up her French. She was only very slightly disconcerted when she found that Madame Bollin was coal-black. She told herself that one had to accept the rough with the smooth and that it takes all sorts to make a world. Miss

Reid was a good sailor, as indeed was only to be expected since her grandfather had been a naval officer, but after a couple of roughish days the weather was fine and in a very short while she knew all her fellow-passengers. She was a good mixer. That was one of the reasons why she had made a success of her business; she owned a tea-room at a celebrated beauty spot in the west of England and she always had a smile and a pleasant word for every customer who came in; she closed down in the winter and for the last four years had taken a cruise. You met such interesting people, she said, and you always learnt something. It was true that the passengers on the *Friedrich Weber* weren't of quite so good a class as those she had met the year before on her Mediterranean cruise, but Miss Reid was not a snob, and though the table manners of some of them shocked her somewhat, determined to look upon the bright side of things she decided to make the best of them. She was a great reader and she was glad, on looking at the ship's library, to find that there were a lot of books by Phillips Oppenheim, Edgar Wallace and Agatha Christie; but with so many people to talk to she had no time for reading and she made up her mind to leave them till the ship emptied herself at Haiti.

"After all," she said, "human nature is more important than literature."

Miss Reid had always had the reputation of being a good talker and she flattered herself that not once during the many days they were at sea had she allowed the conversation at table to languish. She knew how to draw people out, and whenever a topic seemed to be exhausted she had a remark ready to revive it or another topic waiting on the tip of her tongue to set the conversation off again. Her friend Miss Price, daughter of the late Vicar of Campden, who had come to see her off at Plymouth, for she lived there, had often said to her:

"You know, Venetia, you have a mind like a man. You're never at a loss for something to say."

"Well, I think if you're interested in everyone, everyone will be interested in you," Miss Reid answered modestly. "Practice makes perfect, and I have the infinite capacity for taking pains which Dickens said was genius."

Miss Reid was not really called Venetia, her name was Alice, but disliking it she had, when still a girl, adopted the poetic name which she felt so much better suited to her personality.

Miss Reid had a great many interesting talks with her fellow-passengers and she was really sorry when the ship at length reached Port au Prince and the last of them disembarked. The *Friedrich Weber* stopped two days there, during which she visited the town and the neighbourhood. When they sailed she was the only passenger. The ship was skirting the coast of the island stopping off at a variety of ports to discharge or to take on cargo.

"I hope you will not feel embarrassed alone with so many men, Miss Reid," said the captain heartily as they sat down to midday dinner.

She was placed on his right hand and at table besides sat the first mate, the chief engineer and the doctor.

"I'm a woman of the world, Captain. I always think if a lady is a lady gentlemen will be gentlemen."

"We're only rough sailor men, madam, you mustn't expect too much."

"Kind hearts are more than coronets and simple faith than Norman blood, Captain," answered Miss Reid.

He was a short, thick-set man, with a clean-shaven head and a red, clean-shaven face. He wore a white stingah-shifter, but except at meal-times unbuttoned at the neck and showing his hairy chest. He was a jovial fellow. He could not speak without bellowing. Miss Reid thought him quite an eccentric, but she had a keen sense of humour and was prepared to make allowances for that. She took the conversation in hand. She had learnt a great deal about Haiti on the voyage out and more during the two days she had spent there, but she knew that men liked to talk rather than to listen, so she put them a number of questions to which she already knew the answers; oddly enough they didn't. In the end she found herself obliged to give quite a little lecture and before dinner was over, *Mittag Essen* they called it in their funny way, she had imparted to them a great deal of interesting information about the history and economic situation of the Republic, the problems that confronted it and its prospects for the future. She talked rather slowly, in a refined voice, and her vocabulary was extensive.

At nightfall they put in at a small port where they were to load three hundred bags of coffee, and the agent came on board. The captain asked him to stay to supper and ordered cocktails. As the steward brought them Miss Reid swam into the saloon. Her movements were deliberate, elegant and self-assured. She always said that you could tell at once by the way she walked if a woman was a lady. The captain introduced the agent to her and she sat down.

"What is that you men are drinking?" she asked.

"A cocktail. Will you have one, Miss Reid?"

"I don't mind if I do."

She drank it and the captain somewhat doubtfully asked her if she would have another.

"Another? Well, just to be matey."

The agent, much whiter than some, but a good deal darker than many, was the son of a former minister of Haiti to the German court, and having lived for many years in Berlin spoke good German. It was indeed on this account that he had got a job with a German shipping firm. On the strength of this Miss Reid, during supper, told them all about a trip down the Rhine that she had once taken. Afterwards she and the agent, the skipper, the doctor and the mate, sat round a table and drank beer. Miss Reid made it her business to draw the agent out.

The fact that they were loading coffee suggested to her that he would be interested in learning how they grew tea in Ceylon, yes, she had been to Ceylon on a cruise, and the fact that his father was a diplomat made it certain that he would be interested in the royal family of England. She had a very pleasant evening. When she at last retired to rest, for she would never have thought of saying she was going to bed, she said to herself:

"There's no doubt that travel is a great education."

It was really an experience to find herself alone with all those men. How they would laugh when she told them all about it when she got home! They would say that things like that only happened to Venetia. She smiled when she heard the captain on deck singing with that great booming voice of his. Germans were so musical. He had a funny way of strutting up and down on his short legs singing Wagner tunes to words of his own invention. It was *Tannhaüser* he was singing now (that lovely thing about the evening star) but knowing no German Miss Reid could only wonder what absurd words he was putting to it. It was as well.

"Oh, what a bore that woman is, I shall certainly kill her if she goes on much longer." Then he broke into Siegfried's martial strain. "She's a bore, she's a bore, she's a bore. I shall throw her into the sea."

And that of course is what Miss Reid was. She was a crashing, she was a stupendous, she was an excruciating bore. She talked in a steady monotone, and it was no use to interrupt her because then she started again from the beginning. She had an insatiable thirst for information and no casual remark could be thrown across the table without her asking innumerable questions about it. She was a great dreamer and she narrated her dreams at intolerable length. There was no subject upon which she had not something prosy to say. She had a truism for every occasion. She hit on the commonplace like a hammer

driving a nail into the wall. She plunged into the obvious like a
clown in a circus jumping through a hoop. Silence did not
abash her. Those poor men far away from their homes and
the patter of little feet, and with Christmas coming on, no
wonder they felt low; she redoubled her efforts to interest and
amuse them. She was determined to bring a little gaiety into
their dull lives. For that was the awful part of it: Miss Reid
meant well. She was not only having a good time herself, but
she was trying to give all of them a good time. She was convinced that they liked her as much as she liked them. She felt
that she was doing her bit to make the party a success and she
was naïvely happy to think that she was succeeding. She told
them all about her friend Miss Price and how often she had
said to her: Venetia, no one ever has a dull moment in your
company. It was the captain's duty to be polite to a passenger,
and however much he would have liked to tell her to hold her
silly tongue he could not, but even if he had been free to say
what he liked, he knew that he could not have brought himself
to hurt her feelings. Nothing stemmed the torrent of her
loquacity. It was as irresistible as a force of nature. Once in
desperation they began talking German, but Miss Reid stopped
this at once.

"Now I won't have you saying things I don't understand.
You ought all to make the most of your good luck in having me
all to yourselves and practise your English."

"We were talking of technical matters that would only bore
you, Miss Reid," said the captain.

"I'm never bored. That's why, if you won't think me
a wee bit conceited to say so, I'm never boring. You see,
I like to know things. Everything interests me and you
never know when a bit of information won't come in useful."

The doctor smiled drily.

"The captain was only saying that because he was

embarrassed. In point of fact he was telling a story that was
not fit for the ears of a maiden lady."

"I may be a maiden lady but I'm also a woman of the world,
I don't expect sailors to be saints. You need never be afraid of
what you say before me, Captain, I shan't be shocked. I should
love to hear your story."

The doctor was a man of sixty with thin grey hair, a grey
moustache and small bright blue eyes. He was a silent, bitter
man, and however hard Miss Reid tried to bring him into the
conversation it was almost impossible to get a word out of him.
But she wasn't a woman who would give in without a struggle,
and one morning when they were at sea and she saw him sitting
on deck with a book, she brought her chair next to his and sat
down beside him.

"Are you fond of reading, Doctor?" she said brightly.

"Yes."

"So am I. And I suppose like all Germans you're musical."

"I'm fond of music."

"So am I. The moment I saw you I thought you looked
clever."

He gave her a brief look and pursing his lips went on reading.
Miss Reid was not disconcerted.

"But of course one can always read. I always prefer a good
talk to a good book. Don't you?"

"No."

"How very interesting. Now do tell me why?"

"I can't give you a reason."

"That's very strange, isn't it? But then I always think
human nature is strange. I'm terribly interested in people, you
know. I always like doctors, they know so much about human
nature, but I could tell you some things that would surprise
even you. You learn a great deal about people if you run a tea-
shop like I do, that's to say if you keep your eyes open."

The doctor got up.

"I must ask you to excuse me, Miss Reid. I have to go and see a patient."

"Anyhow I've broken the ice now," she thought, as he walked away. "I think he was only shy."

But a day or two later the doctor was not feeling at all well. He had an internal malady that troubled him now and then, but he was used to it and disinclined to talk about it. When he had one of his attacks he only wanted to be left alone. His cabin was small and stuffy, so he settled himself on a long chair on deck and lay with his eyes closed. Miss Reid was walking up and down to get the half-hour's exercise she took morning and evening. He thought that if he pretended to be asleep she would not disturb him. But when she had passed him half a dozen times she stopped in front of him and stood quite still. Though he kept his eyes closed he knew that she was looking at him.

"Is there anything I can do, Doctor?" she said.

He started.

"Why, what should there be?"

He gave her a glance and saw that her eyes were deeply troubled.

"You look dreadfully ill," she said.

"I'm in great pain."

"I know. I can see that. Can't something be done?"

"No, it'll pass off presently."

She hesitated for a moment then went away. Presently she returned.

"You look so uncomfortable with no cushions or anything. I've brought you my own pillow that I always travel with. Do let me put it behind your head."

He felt at that moment too ill to remonstrate. She lifted his head gently and put the soft pillow behind it. It really did make him feel more comfortable. She passed her hand across his forehead and it was cool and soft.

"Poor dear," she said. "I know what doctors are. They haven't the first idea how to take care of themselves."

She left him, but in a minute or two returned with a chair and a bag. The doctor when he saw her gave a twitch of anguish.

"Now I'm not going to let you talk, I'm just going to sit beside you and knit. I always think it's a comfort when one isn't feeling very well to have someone near."

She sat down and taking an unfinished muffler out of her bag began busily to ply her needles. She never said a word. And strangely enough the doctor found her company a solace. No one else on board had even noticed that he was ill, he had felt lonely, and the sympathy of that crashing bore was grateful to him. It soothed him to see her silently working and presently he fell asleep. When he awoke she was still working. She gave him a little smile, but did not speak. His pain had left him and he felt much better.

He did not go into the saloon till late in the afternoon. He found the captain and Hans Krause, the mate, having a glass of beer together.

"Sit down, Doctor," said the captain. "We're holding a council of war. You know that the day after to-morrow is Sylvester Abend."

"Of course."

Sylvester Abend, New Year's Eve, is an occasion that means a great deal to a German and they had all been looking forward to it. They had brought a Christmas tree all the way from Germany with them.

"At dinner to-day Miss Reid was more talkative than ever. Hans and I have decided that something must be done about it."

"She sat with me for two hours this morning in silence. I suppose she was making up for lost time."

"It's bad enough to be away from one's home and family just now anyway and all we can do is to make the best of a bad job.

We want to enjoy our Sylvester Abend, and unless something is done about Miss Reid we haven't a chance."

"We can't have a good time if she's with us," said the mate. "She'll spoil it as sure as eggs is eggs."

"How do you propose to get rid of her, short of throwing her overboard?" smiled the doctor. "She's not a bad old soul; all she wants is a lover."

"At her age?" cried Hans Krause.

"Especially at her age. That inordinate loquacity, that passion for information, the innumerable questions she asks, her prosiness, the way she goes on and on—it is all a sign of her clamouring virginity. A lover would bring her peace. Those jangled nerves of hers would relax. At least for an hour she would have lived. The deep satisfaction which her being demands would travel through those exacerbated centres of speed, and we should have quiet."

It was always a little difficult to know how much the doctor meant what he said and when he was having a joke at your expense. The captain's blue eyes, however, twinkled mischievously.

"Well, Doctor, I have great confidence in your powers of diagnosis. The remedy you suggest is evidently worth trying, and since you are a bachelor it is clear that it is up to you to apply it."

"Pardon me, Captain, it is my professional duty to prescribe remedies for the patients under my charge in this ship, but not to administer them personally. Besides, I am sixty."

"I am a married man with grown-up children," said the captain. "I am old and fat and asthmatic, it is obvious that I cannot be expected to undertake a task of this kind. Nature cut me out for the role of a husband and father, not for that of a lover."

"Youth in these matters is essential and good looks are advantageous," said the doctor gravely.

The captain gave a great bang on the table with his fist.

"You are thinking of Hans. You're quite right. Hans must do it."

The mate sprang to his feet.

"Me? Never."

"Hans, you are tall, handsome, strong as a lion, brave and young. We have twenty-three days more at sea before we reach Hamburg, you wouldn't desert your trusted old captain in an emergency or let down your good friend the doctor?"

"No, Captain, it's asking too much of me. I have been married less than a year and I love my wife. I can hardly wait to get back to Hamburg. She is yearning for me as I am yearning for her. I will not be unfaithful to her, especially with Miss Reid."

"Miss Reid's not so bad," said the doctor.

"Some people might call her even nice-looking," said the captain.

And indeed when you took Miss Reid feature by feature she was not in fact a plain woman. True, she had a long, stupid face, but her brown eyes were large and she had very thick lashes; her brown hair was cut short and curled rather prettily over her neck; she hadn't a bad skin, and she was neither too fat nor too thin. She was not old as people go nowadays, and if she had told you that she was forty you would have been quite willing to believe it. The only thing against her was that she was drab and dull.

"Must I then for twenty-three mortal days endure the prolixity of that tedious woman? Must I for twenty-three mortal days answer her inane questions and listen to her fatuous remarks? Must I, an old man, have my Sylvester Abend, the jolly evening I was looking forward to, ruined by the unwelcome company of that intolerable virgin? And all because no one can be found to show a little gallantry, a little human kindness, a spark of charity to a lonely woman. I shall wreck the ship."

"There's always the radio-operator," said Hans.

The captain gave a loud shout.

"Hans, let the ten thousand virgins of Cologne arise and call you blessed. Steward," he bellowed, "tell the radio-operator that I want him."

The radio-operator came into the saloon and smartly clicked his heels together. The three men looked at him in silence. He wondered uneasily whether he had done something for which he was to be hauled over the coals. He was above the middle height, with square shoulders and narrow hips, erect and slender, his tanned, smooth skin looked as though a razor had never touched it, he had large eyes of a startling blue and a mane of curling golden hair. He was a perfect specimen of young Teutonic manhood. He was so healthy, so vigorous, so much alive that even when he stood some way from you, you felt the glow of his vitality.

"Aryan, all right," said the captain. "No doubt about that. How old are you, my boy?"

"Twenty-one, sir."

"Married?"

"No, sir."

"Engaged?"

The radio-operator chuckled. There was an engaging boyishness in his laugh.

"No, sir."

"You know that we have a female passenger on board?"

"Yes, sir."

"Do you know her?"

"I've said good morning to her when I've seen her on deck."

The captain assumed his most official manner. His eyes, which generally twinkled with fun, were stern and he got a sort of bark into his rich, fruity voice.

"Although this is a cargo-boat and we carry valuable freight, we also take such passengers as we can get, and this is a branch of our business that the company is anxious to encourage. My instructions are to do everything possible to promote the happiness and comfort of the passengers. Miss Reid needs a lover. The doctor and I have come to the conclusion that you are well suited to satisfy Miss Reid's requirements."

"Me, sir?"

The radio-operator blushed scarlet and then began to giggle, but quickly composed himself when he saw the set faces of the three men who confronted him.

"But she's old enough to be my mother."

"That at your age is a matter of no consequence. She is a woman of the highest distinction and allied to all the great families of England. If she were German she would be at least a countess. That you should have been chosen for this responsible position is an honour that you should greatly appreciate. Furthermore, your English is halting and this will give you an excellent opportunity to improve it."

"That of course is something to be thought of," said the radio-operator. "I know that I want practice."

"It is not often in this life that it is possible to combine pleasure with intellectual improvement, and you must congratulate yourself on your good fortune."

"But if I may be allowed to put the question, sir, why does Miss Reid want a lover?"

"It appears to be an old English custom for unmarried women of exalted rank to submit themselves to the embraces of a lover at this time of year. The company is anxious that Miss Reid should be treated exactly as she would be on an English ship, and we trust that if she is satisfied, with her aristocratic connections she will be able to persuade many of her friends to take cruises in the line's ships."

"Sir, I must ask to be excused."

"It is not a request that I am making, it is an order. You

will present yourself to Miss Reid, in her cabin, at eleven o'clock to-night."

"What shall I do when I get there?"

"Do?" thundered the captain. "Do? Act naturally."

With a wave of the hand he dismissed him. The radio-operator clicked his heels, saluted and went out.

"Now let us have another glass of beer," said the captain.

At supper that evening Miss Reid was at her best. She was verbose. She was playful. She was refined. There was not a truism that she failed to utter. There was not a commonplace that she forbore to express. She bombarded them with foolish questions. The captain's face grew redder and redder as he sought to contain his fury; he felt that he could not go on being polite to her any longer and if the doctor's remedy did not help, one day he would forget himself and give her, not a piece, but the whole of his mind.

"I shall lose my job," he thought, "but I'm not sure that it wouldn't be worth it."

Next day they were already sitting at table when she came in to dinner.

"Sylvester Abend to-morrow," she said, brightly. That was the sort of thing she would say. She went on: "Well, what have you all been up to this morning?"

Since they did exactly the same thing every day, and she knew very well what that was, the question was enraging. The captain's heart sank. He briefly told the doctor what he thought of him.

"Now, no German, please," said Miss Reid archly. "You know I don't allow that, and why, Captain, did you give the poor doctor that sour look? It's Christmas time, you know; peace and goodwill to all men. I'm so excited about to-morrow evening, and will there be candles on the Christmas tree?"

"Naturally."

"How thrilling! I always think a Christmas tree without candles isn't a Christmas tree. Oh, d'you know, I had such a funny experience last night. I can't understand it at all."

A startled pause. They all looked intently at Miss Reid. For once, they hung on her lips.

"Yes," she went on in that monotonous, rather finicking way of hers, "I was just getting into bed last night when there was a knock at my door. 'Who is it?' I said. 'It's the radio-operator,' was the answer. 'What is it?' I said. 'Can I speak to you?' he said."

They listened with rapt attention.

" 'Well, I'll just pop on a dressing-gown,' I said, 'and open the door.' So I popped on a dressing-gown and opened the door. The radio-operator said: 'Excuse me, miss, but do you want to send a radio?' Well, I did think it was funny his coming at that hour to ask me if I wanted to send a radio, I just laughed in his face, it appealed to my sense of humour if you understand what I mean, but I didn't want to hurt his feelings so I said: 'Thank you so much, but I don't think I want to send a radio.' He stood there, looking so funny, as if he was quite embarrassed, so I said: 'Thank you all the same for asking me,' and then I said 'Good night, pleasant dreams' and shut the door."

"The damned fool," cried the captain.

"He's young, Miss Reid," the doctor put in. "It was excess of zeal. I suppose he thought you would want to send a New Year's greeting to your friends and he wished you to get the advantage of the special rate."

"Oh, I don't mind at all. I like these queer little things that happen to one when one's travelling. I just get a good laugh out of them."

As soon as dinner was over and Miss Reid had left them the captain sent for the radio-operator.

"You idiot, what in heaven's name made you ask Miss

Reid last night whether she wanted to send a radio?"

"Sir, you told me to act naturally. I am a radio-operator. I thought it natural to ask her if she wanted to send a radio. I didn't know what else to say."

"God in heaven," shouted the captain, "when Siegfried saw Brünhilde lying on her rock and cried: *Das ist kein Mann*" (the captain sang the words, and being pleased with the sound of his voice, repeated the phrase two or three times before he continued), "did Siegfried when she awoke ask her if she wished to send a radio, to announce to her papa, I suppose, that she was sitting up after her long sleep and taking notice?"

"I beg most respectfully to draw your attention to the fact that Brünhilde was Siegfried's aunt. Miss Reid is a total stranger to me."

"He did not reflect that she was his aunt. He knew only that she was a beautiful and defenceless woman of obviously good family and he acted as any gentleman would have done. You are young, handsome, Aryan to the tips of your fingers, the honour of Germany is in your hands."

"Very good, sir. I will do my best."

That night there was another knock on Miss Reid's door.

"Who is it?"

"The radio-operator. I have a radio for you, Miss Reid."

"For me." She was surprised, but it at once occurred to her that one of her fellow passengers who had got off at Haiti had sent her New Year's greetings. "How very kind people are," she thought. "I'm in bed. Leave it outside the door."

"It needs an answer. Ten words prepaid."

Then it couldn't be a New Year's greeting. Her heart stopped beating. It could only mean one thing; her shop had been burned to the ground. She jumped out of bed.

"Slip it under the door and I'll write the answer and slip it back to you."

The envelope was pushed under the door and as it appeared

on the carpet it had really a sinister look. Miss Reid snatched it up and tore the envelope open. The words swam before her eyes and she couldn't for a moment find her spectacles. This is what she read:

"Happy New Year. Stop. Peace and goodwill to all men. Stop. You are very beautiful. Stop. I love you. Stop. I must speak to you. Stop. Signed: Radio Operator."

Miss Reid read this through twice. Then she slowly took off her spectacles and hid them under a scarf. She opened the door.

"Come in," she said.

Next day was New Year's Eve. The officers were cheerful and a little sentimental when they sat down to dinner. The stewards had decorated the saloon with tropical creepers to make up for holly and mistletoe, and the Christmas tree stood on a table with the candles ready to be lit at supper time. Miss Reid did not come in till the officers were seated, and when they bade her good-morning she did not speak but merely bowed. They looked at her curiously. She ate a good dinner, but uttered never a word. Her silence was uncanny. At last the captain could stand it no longer, and he said:

"You're very quiet to-day, Miss Reid."

"I'm thinking," she remarked.

"And will you not tell us your thoughts, Miss Reid?" the doctor asked playfully.

She gave him a cool, you might almost have called it a supercilious look.

"I prefer to keep them to myself, Doctor. I will have a little more of that hash, I've got a very good appetite."

They finished the meal in a blessed silence. The captain heaved a sigh of relief. That was what meal-time was for, to eat, not to chatter. When they had finished he went up to the doctor and wrung his hand.

"Something has happened, Doctor."

"It has happened. She's a changed woman."

"But will it last?"

"One can only hope for the best."

Miss Reid put on an evening dress for the evening's cele-
bration, a very quiet black dress, with artificial roses at her
bosom and a long string of imitation jade round her neck.
The lights were dimmed and the candles on the Christmas
tree were lit. It felt a little like being in church. The junior
officers were supping in the saloon that evening and they
looked very smart in their white uniforms. Champagne was
served at the company's expense and after supper they had a
Maibowle. They pulled crackers. They sang songs to the
gramophone, *Deutschland, Deutschland über Alles, Heidelberg*
and *Auld Lang Syne.* They shouted out the tunes lustily, the
captain's voice rising loud above the others, and Miss Reid
joining in with a pleasing contralto. The doctor noticed
that Miss Reid's eyes from time to time rested on the radio-
operator, and in them he read an expression of some bewilder-
ment.

"He's a good-looking fellow, isn't he?" said the doctor.

Miss Reid turned round and looked at the doctor coolly.

"Who?"

"The radio-operator. I thought you were looking at him."

"Which is he?"

"The duplicity of women," the doctor muttered, but with
a smile he answered: "He's sitting next to the chief engineer."

"Oh, of course, I recognise him now. You know, I never
think it matters what a man looks like. I'm so much more
interested in a man's brains than in his looks."

"Ah," said the doctor.

They all got a little tight, including Miss Reid, but she did
not lose her dignity and when she bade them good-night it was
in her best manner.

"I've had a very delightful evening. I shall never forget my New Year's Eve on a German boat. It's been very interesting. Quite an experience."

She walked steadily to the door, and this was something of a triumph, for she had drunk drink for drink with the rest of them through the evening.

They were all somewhat jaded next day. When the captain, the mate, the doctor and the chief engineer came down to dinner they found Miss Reid already seated. Before each place was a small parcel tied up in pink ribbon. On each was written: Happy New Year. They gave Miss Reid a questioning glance.

"You've all been so very kind to me I thought I'd like to give each of you a little present. There wasn't much choice at Port au Prince, so you mustn't expect too much."

There was a pair of briar pipes for the captain, half a dozen silk handkerchiefs for the doctor, a cigar-case for the mate and a couple of ties for the chief engineer. They had dinner and Miss Reid retired to her cabin to rest. The officers looked at one another uncomfortably. The mate fiddled with the cigar-case she had given him.

"I'm a little ashamed of myself," he said at last.

The captain was pensive and it was plain that he too was a trifle uneasy.

"I wonder if we ought to have played that trick on Miss Reid," he said. "She's a good old soul and she's not rich; she's a woman who earns her own living. She must have spent the best part of a hundred marks on these presents. I almost wish we'd left her alone."

The doctor shrugged his shoulders.

"You wanted her silenced and I've silenced her."

"When all's said and done, it wouldn't have hurt us to listen to her chatter for three weeks more," said the mate.

"I'm not happy about her," added the captain. "I feel there's something ominous in her quietness."

She had spoken hardly a word during the meal they had just shared with her. She seemed hardly to listen to what they said.

"Don't you think you ought to ask her if she's feeling quite well, Doctor?" suggested the captain.

"Of course she's feeling quite well. She's eating like a wolf. If you want inquiries made you'd much better make them of the radio-operator."

"You may not be aware of it, Doctor, but I am a man of great delicacy."

"I am a man of heart myself," said the doctor.

For the rest of the journey those men spoilt Miss Reid outrageously. They treated her with the consideration they would have shown to someone who was convalescent after a long and dangerous illness. Though her appetite was excellent they sought to tempt her with new dishes. The doctor ordered wine and insisted on her sharing his bottle with him. They played dominoes with her. They played chess with her. They played bridge with her. They engaged her in conversation. But there was no doubt about it, though she responded to their advances with politeness, she kept herself to herself. She seemed to regard them with something very like disdain; you might almost have thought that she looked upon those men and their efforts to be amiable as pleasantly ridiculous. She seldom spoke unless spoken to. She read detective stories and at night sat on deck looking at the stars. She lived a life of her own.

At last the journey drew to its close. They sailed up the English Channel on a still grey day; they sighted land. Miss Reid packed her trunk. At two o'clock in the afternoon they docked at Plymouth. The captain, the mate and the doctor came along to say good-bye to her.

"Well, Miss Reid," said the captain in his jovial way, "we're sorry to lose you, but I suppose you're glad to be getting home."

"You've been very kind to me, you've all been very kind to me, I don't know what I've done to deserve it. I've been very happy with you. I shall never forget you."

She spoke rather shakily, she tried to smile, but her lips quivered, and tears ran down her cheeks. The captain got very red. He smiled awkwardly.

"May I kiss you, Miss Reid?"

She was taller than he by half a head. She bent down and he planted a fat kiss on one wet cheek and a fat kiss on the other. She turned to the mate and the doctor. They both kissed her.

"What an old fool I am," she said. "Everybody's so good."

She dried her eyes and slowly, in her graceful, rather absurd way, walked down the companion. The captain's eyes were wet. When she reached the quay she looked up and waved to someone on the boat deck.

"Who's she waving to?" asked the captain.

"The radio-operator."

Miss Price was waiting on the quay to welcome her. When they had passed the customs and got rid of Miss Reid's heavy luggage they went to Miss Price's house and had an early cup of tea. Miss Reid's train did not start till five. Miss Price had much to tell Miss Reid.

"But it's too bad of me to go on like this when you've just come home. I've been looking forward to hearing all about your journey."

"I'm afraid there's not very much to tell."

"I can't believe that. Your trip was a success, wasn't it?"

"A distinct success. It was very nice."

"And you didn't mind being with all those Germans?"

"Of course they're not like English people. One has to get

used to their ways. They sometimes do things that—well, that English people wouldn't do, you know. But I always think that one has to take things as they come."

"What sort of things do you mean?"

Miss Reid looked at her friend calmly. Her long, stupid face had a placid look, and Miss Price never noticed that in the eyes was a strangely mischievous twinkle.

"Things of no importance really. Just funny, unexpected, rather nice things. There's no doubt that travel is a wonderful education."

FLOTSAM AND JETSAM

NORMAN GRANGE was a rubber-planter. He was up before day-break to take the roll-call of his labour and then walked over the estate to see that the tapping was properly done. This duty performed, he came home, bathed and changed, and now with his wife opposite him he was eating the substantial meal, half breakfast and half luncheon, which in Borneo is called brunch. He read as he ate. The dining-room was dingy. The worn electro-plate, the shabby cruet, the chipped dishes betokened poverty, but a poverty accepted with apathy. A few flowers would have brightened the table, but there was apparently no one to care how things looked. When Grange had finished he belched, filled his pipe and lit it, rose from the table and went out on to the veranda. He took no more notice of his wife than if she had not been there. He lay down in a long rattan chair and went on reading. Mrs. Grange reached over for a tin of cigarettes and smoked while she sipped her tea. Suddenly she looked out, for the houseboy came up the steps and accompanied by two men went up to her husband. One was a Dyak and the other Chinese. Strangers seldom came and she could not imagine what they wanted. She got up and went to the door to listen. Though she had lived in Borneo for so many years she knew no more Malay than was necessary to get along with the boys, and she only vaguely understood what was said. She gathered from her husband's tone that something had happened to annoy him. He seemed to be asking questions first of the Chink and then of the Dyak; it looked as though they were pressing him to do something he didn't want to do; at length, however, with a frown on his face he raised himself from his chair and followed by the men walked down the steps. Curious to see where he was going she slipped out on to the veranda. He had taken the path that led down to the river. She shrugged her thin shoulders and went to her room. Presently she gave a violent start, for she heard her husband call her.

"Vesta."

She came out.

"Get a bed ready. There's a white man in a prahu at the landing-stage. He's damned ill."

"Who is he?"

"How the hell should I know? They're just bringing him up."

"We can't have anyone to stay here."

"Shut up and do as I tell you."

He left her on that and again went down to the river. Mrs. Grange called the boy and told him to put sheets on the bed in the spare room. Then she stood at the top of the steps and waited. In a little while she saw her husband coming back and behind him a huddle of Dyaks carrying a man on a mattress. She stood aside to let them pass and caught a glimpse of a white face.

"What shall I do?" she asked her husband.

"Get out and keep quiet."

"Polite, aren't you?"

The sick man was taken into the room, and in two or three minutes the Dyaks and Grange came out.

"I'm going to see about his kit. I'll have it brought up. His boy's looking after him and there's no cause for you to butt in!"

"What's the matter with him?"

"Malaria. His boatmen are afraid he's going to die and won't take him on. His name's Skelton."

"He isn't going to die, is he?"

"If he does we'll bury him."

But Skelton didn't die. He woke next morning to find
6

himself in a room, in bed and under a mosquito-net. He couldn't think where he was. It was a cheap iron bed and the mattress was hard, but to lie on it was a relief after the discomfort of the prahu. He could see nothing of the room but a chest of drawers, roughly made by a native carpenter, and a wooden chair. Opposite was a doorway, with a blind down, and this he guessed led on to a veranda.

"Kong," he called.

The blind was drawn aside and his boy came in. The Chinaman's face broke into a grin when he saw that his master was free from fever.

"You more better, Tuan. Velly glad."

"Where the devil am I?"

Kong explained.

"Luggage all right?" asked Skelton.

"Yes, him all right."

"What's the name of this fellow—the tuan whose house this is?"

"Mr. Norman Glange."

To confirm what he said he showed Skelton a little book in which the owner's name was written. It was Grange. Skelton noticed that the book was Bacon's *Essays*. It was curious to find it in a planter's house away up a river in Borneo.

"Tell him I'd be glad to see him."

"Tuan out. Him come presently."

"What about my having a wash? And by God, I want a shave."

He tried to get out of bed, but his head swam and with a bewildered cry he sank back. But Kong shaved and washed him, and changed the shorts and singlet in which he had been lying ever since he fell ill for a sarong and a baju. After that he was glad to lie still. But presently Kong came in and said that the tuan of the house was back. There was a knock on the door and a large stoutish man stepped in.

"I hear you're better," he said.

"Oh, much. It's terribly kind of you to have taken me in like this. It seemed awful, planting myself on you."

Grange answered a trifle harshly.

"That's all right. You were pretty bad, you know. No wonder those Dyaks wanted to get rid of you."

"I don't want to impose myself on you longer than I need. If I could hire a launch here, or a prahu, I could get off this afternoon."

"There's no launch to hire. You'd better stay a bit. You must be as weak as a rat."

"I'm afraid I shall be a frightful bother."

"I don't see why. You've got your own boy and he'll look after you."

Grange had just come in from his round of the estate and wore dirty shorts, a khaki shirt open at the neck and an old, battered terai hat. He looked as shabby as a beachcomber. He took off his hat to wipe his sweating brow; he had close-cropped grey hair; his face was red, a broad, fleshy face, with a large mouth under a stubble of grey moustache, a short, pugnacious nose and small, mean eyes.

"I wonder if you could let me have something to read," said Skelton.

"What sort of thing?"

"I don't mind so long as it's lightish."

"I'm not much of a novel reader myself, but I'll send you in two or three books. My wife can provide you with novels. They'll be trash, because that's all she reads. But it may suit you."

With a nod he withdrew. Not a very likeable man. But he was obviously very poor, the room in which Skelton lay, something in Grange's appearance, indicated that; he was probably manager of an estate on a cut salary, and it was not unlikely that the expense of a guest and his servant was unwelcome. Living in that remote spot, and so seeing white men but seldom, it might be that he was ill at ease with strangers. Some people improve unbelievably on acquaintance. But his hard, shifty little eyes were disconcerting; they gave the lie to the red face and the massive frame which otherwise might have persuaded you that this was a jolly sort of fellow with whom you could quickly make friends.

After a while the houseboy came in with a parcel of books. There were half a dozen novels by authors he had never heard of, and a glance told him they were slop; these must be Mrs. Grange's; and then there was a Boswell's *Johnson*, Borrow's *Lavengro* and Lamb's *Essays*. It was an odd choice. They were not the books you would have expected to find in a planter's house. In most planters' houses there is not more than a shelf or two of books and for the most part they're detective stories. Skelton had a disinterested curiosity in human creatures, and he amused himself now by trying to make out from the books Norman Grange had sent, from the look of him and from the few words they had exchanged, what sort of a man he could be. Skelton was a little surprised that his host did not come to see him again that day; it looked as though he were going to content himself with giving his uninvited guest board and lodging, but were not sufficiently interested in him to seek his company. Next morning he felt well enough to get up, and with Kong's help settled himself in a long chair on the veranda. It badly needed a coat of paint. The bungalow stood on the brow of a hill, about fifty yards from the river; and on the opposite bank, looking very small across that great stretch of water, you could see native houses on piles nestling among the greenery. Skelton had not yet the activity of mind to read steadily, and after a page or two, his thoughts wandering, he found himself content to watch idly the sluggish flow of the turbid stream. Suddenly he heard a step. He saw a little elderly woman come towards him, and knowing that this must be Mrs. Grange tried to get up.

"Don't move," she said. "I only came to see if you had everything you wanted."

She wore a blue cotton dress, simple enough, but more suited to a young girl than to a woman of her age; her short hair was tousled, as though on getting out of bed she had scarcely troubled to pass a comb through it, and dyed a vivid yellow, but badly, and the roots showed white. Her skin was raddled and dry, and there was a great dab of rouge on each cheekbone, put on however so clumsily that you could not for a moment take it for a natural colour, and a smear of lipstick on her mouth. But the strangest thing about her was a tic she had that made her jerk her head as though she were beckoning you to an inner room. It seemed to come at regular intervals, perhaps three times a minute, and her left hand was in almost constant movement; it was not quite a tremble, it was a rapid twirl as though she wanted to draw your attention to something behind her back. Skelton was startled by her appearance and embarrassed by her tic.

"I hope I'm not making myself too great a nuisance," he said. "I think I shall be well enough to make a move to-morrow or the day after."

"It's not often we see anybody in a place like this, you know. It's a treat to have someone to talk to."

"Won't you sit down? I'll tell my boy to bring you a chair."

"Norman said I was to leave you alone."

"I haven't spoken to a white person for two years. I've been longing for a good old talk."

Her head twitched violently, more quickly than usual, and her hand gave that queer spasmodic gesture.

"He won't be back for another hour. I'll get a chair."

Skelton told her who he was and what he had been doing, but he discovered that she had questioned his boy and already knew all about him.

"You must be crazy to get back to England?" she asked.

"I shan't be sorry."

Suddenly Mrs. Grange seemed to be attacked by what one could only describe as a nerve storm. Her head twitched so madly, her hand shook with such fury, that it was disconcerting. You could only look away.

"I haven't been to England for sixteen years," she said.

"You don't mean that? Why, I thought all you planters went home every five years at the longest."

"We can't afford it; we're broke to the wide. Norman put all the money he had into this plantation, and it hasn't really paid for years. It only just brings in enough to keep us from starvation. Of course it doesn't matter to Norman. He isn't English really."

"He looks English enough."

"He was born in Sarawak. His father was in the government service. If he's anything he's a native of Borneo."

Then, without warning, she began to cry. It was horribly painful to see the tears running down the raddled, painted cheeks of that woman with the constant tic. Skelton knew neither what to say nor what to do. He did what was probably the best thing, he kept silent. She dried her eyes.

"You must think me a silly old fool. I sometimes wonder that after all these years I can still cry. I suppose it's in my nature. I always could cry very easy when I was on the stage."

"Oh, were you on the stage?"

"Yes, before I married. That's how I met Norman. We were playing in Singapore and he was there on holiday. I don't suppose I shall ever see England any more. I shall stay here till I die and every day of my life I shall look at that beastly river. I shall never get away now. Never."

"How did you happen to find yourself in Singapore?"

"Well, it was soon after the war, I couldn't get anything to suit me in London, I'd been on the stage a good many years and

I was fed up with playing small parts; the agents told me a fellow called Victor Palace was taking a company out East. His wife was playing lead, but I could play seconds. They'd got half a dozen plays, comedies, you know, and farces. The salary wasn't much, but they were going to Egypt and India, the Malay States and China and then down to Australia. It was a chance to see the world and I accepted. We didn't do badly in Cairo and I think we made money in India, but Burma wasn't much good, and Siam was worse; Penang was a disaster and so were the rest of the Malay States. Well, one day Victor called us together and said he was bust, he hadn't got the money for our fares on to Hong Kong, and the tour was a wash-out and he was very sorry but we'd have to get back home as best we could. Of course we told him he couldn't do that to us. You never heard such a row. Well, the long and short of it was that he said we could have the scenery and the props if we thought they was any good to us, but as to money it was no use asking for it because he damned well hadn't got it. And next day we found out that him and his wife, without saying a word to anybody, had got on a French boat and skipped. I was in a rare state, I can tell you. I had a few pounds I'd saved out of me salary, and that was all; somebody told me if we was absolutely stranded the government would have to send us home, but only steerage, and I didn't much fancy that. We got the Press to put our plight before the public and someone came along with the proposition that we should give a benefit performance. Well, we did, but it wasn't much without Victor or his wife, and by the time we'd paid the expenses we weren't any better off than we'd been before. I was at my wits' end, I don't mind telling you. It was then that Norman proposed to me. The funny thing is that I hardly knew him. He'd taken me for a drive round the island and we'd had tea two or three times at the Europe and danced. Men don't often do things for you without wanting something in return, and I thought he expected to get a little bit of fun, but I'd had a good deal of experience and I thought he'd be clever if he got round me. But when he asked me to marry him, well, I was so surprised, I couldn't hardly believe me own ears. He said he'd got his own estate in Borneo and it only wanted a little patience and he'd make a packet. And it was on the banks of a fine river and all round was the jungle. He made it sound very romantic. I was getting on, you know, I was thirty, it wasn't going to be any easier to get work as time went on, and it was tempting to have a house of me own and all that. Never to have to hang around agents' offices no more. Never to have to lay awake no more and wonder how you was going to pay next week's rent. He wasn't a bad-looking chap in those days, brown and big and virile. No one could say I was willing to marry anybody just to . . ." Suddenly she stopped. "There he is. Don't say you've seen me."

She picked up the chair she had been sitting in and quickly slipped away with it into the house. Skelton was bewildered. Her grotesque appearance, the painful tears, her story told with that incessant twitching; and then her obvious fear when she heard her husband's voice in the compound, and her hurried escape; he could make nothing of it.

In a few minutes Norman Grange stumped along the veranda.

"I hear you're better," he said.

"Much, thanks."

"If you care to join us at brunch I'll have a place laid for you."

"I'd like it very much."

"All right. I'm just going to have a bath and a change."

He walked away. Presently a boy came along and told Skelton his tuan was waiting for him. Skelton followed him into a small sitting-room, with the jalousies drawn to keep out the heat, an uncomfortable, overcrowded room with a medley of furniture, English and Chinese, and occasional tables littered with worthless junk. It was neither cosy nor cool. Grange had changed into a sarong and baju and in the native dress looked coarse but powerful. He introduced Skelton to his wife. She shook hands with him as though she had never seen him before and uttered a few polite words of greeting. The boy announced that their meal was ready and they went into the dining-room.

"I hear that you've been in this bloody country for some time," said Grange.

"Two years. I'm an anthropologist and I wanted to study the manners and customs of tribes that haven't had any contact with civilisation."

Skelton felt that he should tell his host how it had come about that he had been forced to accept a hospitality which he could not but feel was grudgingly offered. After leaving the village that had been his headquarters he had journeyed by land for ten days till he reached the river. There he had engaged a couple of prahus, one for himself and his luggage and the other for Kong, his Chinese servant, and the camp equipment, to take him to the coast. The long trek across country had been hard going and he found it very comfortable to lie on a mattress under an awning of rattan matting and take his ease. All the time he had been away Skelton had been in perfect health, and as he travelled down the river he could not but think that he was very lucky; but even as the thought passed through his mind, it occurred to him that if he happened just then to congratulate himself on his good fortune in this respect, it was because he did not feel quite so well as usual. It was true that he had been forced to drink a great deal of arak the night before at the longhouse where he had put up, but he was used to it and that hardly accounted for his headache. He had a general sense of malaise. He was wearing nothing but shorts and a singlet, and he felt chilly; it was curious because the

6*

sun was shining fiercely and when he put his hand on the gunwale of the prahu the heat was hardly bearable. If he had had a coat handy he would have put it on. He grew colder and colder and presently his teeth began to chatter; he huddled up on his mattress, shivering all over in a desperate effort to get warm. He could not fail to guess what was the matter.

"Christ," he groaned. "Malaria."

He called the headman who was steering the prahu.

"Get Kong."

The headman shouted to the second prahu and ordered his own paddlers to stop. In a moment the two boats were side by side and Kong stepped in.

"I've got a fever, Kong," gasped Skelton. "Get me the medicine chest and, for God's sake, blankets. I'm freezing to death."

Kong gave his master a big dose of quinine and piled on him what coverings they had. They started off again.

Skelton was too ill to be taken ashore when they tied up for the night and so passed it in the prahu. All next day and the day after he was very ill. Sometimes one or other of the crew came and looked at him, and often the headman stayed for quite a long while staring at him thoughtfully.

"How many days to the coast?" Skelton asked the boy.

"Four, five." He paused for a minute. "Headman, he no go coast. He say, he wantchee go home."

"Tell him to go to hell."

"Headman say, you velly sick, you die. If you die and he go coast he catchee trouble."

"I'm not thinking of dying," said Skelton. "I shall be all right. It's just an ordinary go of malaria."

Kong did not answer. The silence irritated Skelton. He knew that the Chinese had something in mind that he did not like to say.

"Spit it out, you fool," he cried.

Skelton's heart sank when Kong told him the truth. When they reached their resting-place that night the headman was going to demand his money and slip away with the two prahus before dawn. He was too frightened to carry a dying man farther. Skelton had no strength to take the determined attitude that might have availed him; he could only hope by the offer of more money to persuade the headman to carry out his agreement. The day passed in long arguments between Kong and the headman, but when they tied up for the night the headman came to Skelton and told him sulkily that he would go no farther. There was a longhouse nearby where he might get lodging till he grew better. He began to unload the baggage. Skelton refused to move. He got Kong to give him his revolver and swore to shoot anyone who came near him.

Kong, the crew and the headman went up to the longhouse and Skelton was left alone. Hour after hour he lay there, the fever burning his body and his mouth parched while muddled thoughts hammered away in his brain. Then there were lights and the sound of men talking. The Chinese boy came with the headman and another man, whom Skelton had not yet seen, from the neighbouring longhouse. He did his best to understand what Kong was telling him. It appeared that a few hours down-stream there lived a white man, and to his house, if that would satisfy Skelton, the headman was willing to take him.

"More better you say yes," said Kong. "Maybe white man has launch then we go down to coast chop-chop."

"Who is he?"

"Planter," said Kong. "This fellow say, him have rubber estate."

Skelton was too tired to argue further. All he wanted just then was to sleep. He accepted the compromise.

"To tell you the truth," he finished, "I don't remember much more till I woke up yesterday morning to find myself an uninvited guest in your house."

"I don't blame those Dyaks, you know," said Grange. "When I came down to the prahu and saw you, I thought you were for it."

Mrs. Grange sat silent while Skelton told his story, her head and her hand twitching regularly, as though by the action of some invisible clockwork, but when her husband addressed her, asking for the Worcester sauce, and that was the only time he spoke to her, she was seized with such a paroxysm of involuntary movement that it was horrible to see. She passed him what he asked for without a word. Skelton got an uncomfortable impression that she was terrified of Grange. It was odd, because to all appearance he was not a bad sort. He was knowledgeable and far from stupid; and though you could not have said that his manner was cordial, it was plain that he was ready to be of what service he could.

They finished their meal and separated to rest through the heat of the day.

"See you again at six for a sun-downer," said Grange.

When Skelton had had a good sleep, a bath and a read, he went out on to the veranda. Mrs. Grange came up to him. It looked as though she had been waiting.

"He's back from the office. Don't think it's funny if I don't speak to you. If he thought I liked having you here he'd turn you out to-morrow."

She said these words in a whisper and slipped back into the house. Skelton was startled. It was a strange house he had come into in a strange manner. He went into the overcrowded sitting-room and there found his host. He had been worried by the evident poverty of the establishment and he felt that the Granges could ill afford even the small expense he must be putting them to. But he had already formed the impression that Grange was a quick-tempered, susceptible man and he did not know how he would take an offer to help. He made up his mind to risk it.

"Look here," he said to him, "it looks as though I might have to inflict myself on you for several days, I'd be so much more comfortable if you'd let me pay for my board and lodging."

"Oh, that's all right, your lodging costs nothing, the house belongs to the mortgagees, and your board doesn't come to much."

"Well, there are drinks anyway and I've had to come down on your stores of tobacco and cigarettes."

"It's not more than once a year that anyone comes up here, and then it's only the D.O. or someone like that—besides, when one's as broke as I am nothing matters much."

"Well, then, will you take my camp equipment? I shan't be wanting it any more, and if you'd like one of my guns, I'd be only too glad to leave it with you."

Grange hesitated. There was a glimmer of cupidity in those small, cunning eyes of his.

"If you'd let me have one of your guns you'd pay for your board and lodging over and over again."

"That's settled then."

They began to talk over the whisky and sparkler with which, following the Eastern habit, they celebrated the setting of the sun. Discovering that they both played chess they had a game. Mrs. Grange did not join them till dinner. The meal was dull. An insipid soup, a tasteless river fish, a tough piece of steak and a caramel pudding. Norman Grange and Skelton drank beer; Mrs. Grange water. She never of her own will uttered a word. Skelton had again the uncomfortable impression that she was scared to death of her husband. Once or twice, Skelton from common politeness sought to bring her into the conversation, addressing himself to her, telling her a story or asking her a question, but it evidently distressed her so much, her head twitched so violently, her hand was agitated by gestures so spasmodic that he thought it kinder not to insist. When the meal was over she got up.

"I'll leave you gentlemen to your port," she said.

Both the men got up as she left the room. It was rather absurd, and somehow sinister, to see this social pretence in those poverty-stricken surroundings on a Borneo river.

"I may add that there is no port. There might be a little Benedictine left."

"Oh, don't bother."

They talked for a while and Grange began to yawn. He got up every morning before sunrise and by nine o'clock at night could hardly keep his eyes open.

"Well, I'm going to turn in," he said.

He nodded to Skelton and without further ceremony left him. Skelton went to bed, but he could not sleep. Though the heat was oppressive, it was not the heat that kept him awake. There was something horrible about that house and those two people who lived in it. He didn't know what it was that affected him with this peculiar uneasiness, but this he knew, that he would be heartily thankful to be out of it and away from them. Grange had talked a good deal about himself, but he knew no more of him than he had learned at the first glance. To all appearances he was just the commonplace planter who had fallen upon evil days. He had bought his land immediately after the war and had planted trees; but by the time they were bearing the slump had come and since then it had been a constant struggle to keep going. The estate and the house were heavily mortgaged, and now that rubber was once more selling profitably all he made went to the mortgagees. That was an old story in Malaya. What made Grange somewhat unusual was that he was a man without a country. Born in Borneo, he had lived there with his parents till he was old enough to go to school in England; at seventeen he had come back and had never left it since except to go to Mesopotamia during the war. England meant nothing to him. He had neither relations nor friends there. Most planters, like civil servants, have come from England, go back on leave now and then, and look forward to settling down there when they retire. But what had England to offer Norman Grange?

"I was born here," he said, "and I shall die here. I'm a stranger in England. I don't like their ways over there and I don't understand the things they talk about. And yet I'm a stranger here too. To the Malays and the Chinese I'm a white man, though I speak Malay as well as they do, and a white man I shall always be." Then he said a significant thing. "Of course if I'd had any sense I'd have married a Malay girl and had half a dozen half-caste kids. That's the only solution really for us chaps who were born and bred here."

Grange's bitterness was greater than could be explained by his financial embarrassment. He had little good to say of any of the white men in the colony. He seemed to think that they despised him because he was native born. He was a sour, disappointed fellow, and a conceited one. He had shown Skelton his books. There were not many of them, but they were the best on the whole that English literature can show; he had read them over and over again; but it looked as though he had learnt from them neither charity nor loving kindness, it looked as though their beauty had left him unmoved; and to know them so well had only made him self-complacent. His exterior, which was so hearty and English, seemed to have little relation to the man within; you could not resist the suspicion that it masked a very sinister being.

Early next morning, to enjoy the cool of the day, Skelton, with his pipe and a book, was sitting on the veranda outside his room. He was still very weak, but felt much better. In a little while Mrs. Grange joined him. She held in her hand a large album.

"I thought I'd like to show you some of me old photos and

me notices. You mustn't think I always looked like what I do now. He's off on his round and he won't be back for two or three hours yet."

Mrs. Grange, in the same blue dress she had worn the day before, her hair as untidy, appeared strangely excited.

"It's all I have to remind me of the past. Sometimes when I can't bear life any more I look at my album."

She sat by Skelton's side as he turned the pages. The notices were from provincial papers and the references to Mrs. Grange, whose stage name had been apparently Vesta Blaise, were carefully underlined. From the photographs you could see that she had been pretty enough in an undistinguished way. She had acted in musical comedy and revue, in farce and comedy, and taking the photographs and the notices together it was easy to tell that here had been the common, dreary, rather vulgar career of the girl with no particular talent who has taken to the stage on the strength of a pretty face and a good figure. Her head twitching, her hand shaking, Mrs. Grange looked at the photographs and read the notices with as much interest as if she had never seen them before.

"You've got to have influence on the stage, and I never had any," she said. "If I'd only had my chance I know I'd have made good. I had bad luck, there's no doubt about that."

It was all sordid and somewhat pathetic.

"I daresay you're better off as you are," said Skelton.

She snatched the book from him and shut it with a bang. She had a paroxysm so violent that it was really frightening to look at her.

"What d'you mean by that? What d'you know about the life I lead here? I'd have killed myself years ago only I know he wants me to die. That's the only way I can get back on him, by living, and I'm going to live; I'm going to live as long as he does. Oh, I hate him. I've often thought I'd poison him, but I was afraid. I didn't know how to do it really, and if he died the

Chinks would foreclose and I'd be turned out. And where should I go then? I haven't a friend in the world."

Skelton was aghast. It flashed through his mind that she was crazy. He hadn't a notion what to say. She gave him a keen look.

"I suppose it surprises you to hear me talk like that. I mean it, you know, every word of it. He'd like to kill me too, but he daren't either. And he knows how to do it all right. He knows how the Malays kill people. He was born here. There's nothing he doesn't know about the country."

Skelton forced himself to speak.

"You know, Mrs. Grange, I'm a total stranger. Don't you think it's rather unwise to tell me all sorts of things there's no need for me to know? After all, you live a very solitary life. I daresay you get on one another's nerves. Now that things are looking up perhaps you'll be able to take a trip to England."

"I don't want to go to England. I'd be ashamed to let them see me like I am now. D'you know how old I am? Forty-six. I look sixty and I know it. That's why I showed you those photos, so as you might see I wasn't always like what I am now. Oh, my God, how I've wasted my life! They talk of the romance of the East. They can have it. I'd rather be a dresser in a provincial theatre, I'd rather be one of the sweepers that keep it clean, than what I am now. Until I came here I'd never been alone in me life, I'd always lived in a crowd; you don't know what it is to have nobody to talk to from year's end to year's end. To have to keep it all bottled up. How would you like to see no one, week in and week out, day after day for sixteen years, except the man you hate most in the world? How would you like to live for sixteen years with a man who hates you so he can't bear to look at you?"

"Oh, come, it can't be as bad as that."

"I'm telling you the truth. Why should I tell you a lie? I shall never see you again; what do I care what you think of me? And if you tell then what I've said when you get down to the coast, what's the odds? They'll say: 'God, you don't mean to say you stayed with those people? I pity you. He's an outsider and she's crazy; got a tic; they say it looks as if she was always trying to wipe the blood off her dress. They were mixed up in a damned funny business, but no one ever really knew the ins and outs of it; it all happened a long time ago and the country was pretty wild in those days.' A damned funny business and no mistake. I'd tell you for two pins. That would be a bit of dirt for them at the club. You wouldn't have to pay for a drink for days. Damn them. Oh, Christ, how I hate this country. I hate that river. I hate this house. I hate that damned rubber. I loathe the filthy natives. And that's all I've got to look forward to till I die—till I die without a doctor to take care of me, without a friend to hold me hand."

She began to cry hysterically. Mrs. Grange had spoken with a dramatic intensity of which Skelton would never have thought her capable. Her coarse irony was as painful as her anguish. Skelton was young, he was not yet thirty, and he did not know how to deal with the difficult situation. But he could not keep silent.

"I'm terribly sorry, Mrs. Grange. I wish I could do something to help you."

"I'm not asking for your help. No one can help me."

Skelton was distressed. From what she said he could not but suspect that she had been concerned in a mysterious and perhaps dreadful occurrence, and it might be that to tell him about it without fear of the consequences was just the relief she needed.

"I don't want to butt into what's no business of mine, but, Mrs. Grange, if you think it would ease your mind to tell me— what you were referring to just now, I mean what you said was a damned funny business, I promise you on my word of honour that I'll never repeat it to a living soul."

She stopped crying quite suddenly and gave him a long, intent look. She hesitated. He had an impression that the desire to speak was almost irresistible. But she shook her head and sighed.

"It wouldn't do any good. Nothing can do me any good."

She got up and abruptly left him.

The two men sat down to brunch by themselves.

"My wife asks you to excuse her," said Grange. "She's got one of her sick headaches and she's staying in bed to-day."

"Oh, I'm sorry."

Skelton had a notion that in the searching look that Grange gave him was mistrust and animosity. It flashed through his mind that somehow he had discovered that Mrs. Grange had been talking to him and perhaps had said things that should have been left unsaid. Skelton made an effort at conversation, but his host was taciturn, and they ended the meal in a silence that was only broken by Grange when he got up.

"You seem pretty fit to-day and I don't suppose you want to stay in this God-forsaken place longer than you must. I've sent over the river to arrange for a couple of prahus to take you down to the coast. They'll be here at six to-morrow morning."

Skelton felt sure then that he was right; Grange knew or guessed that his wife had spoken too freely, and he wanted to be rid as soon as possible of the dangerous visitor.

"That's terribly kind of you," Skelton answered, smiling. "I'm as fit as a fiddle."

But in Grange's eyes was no answering smile. They were coldly hostile.

"We might have another game of chess later on," said he.

"All right. When d'you get back from your office?"

"I haven't got much to do there to-day. I shall be about the house."

Skelton wondered if it were only his fancy that there was something very like a threat in the tone in which Grange uttered these words. It looked as though he were going to make sure that his wife and Skelton should not again be left alone. Mrs. Grange did not come to dinner. They drank their coffee and smoked their cheroots. Then Grange, pushing back his chair, said:

"You've got to make an early start to-morrow. I daresay you'd like to turn in. I shall have started out on my round by the time you go, so I'll say good-bye to you now."

"Let me get my guns. I want you to take the one you like best."

"I'll tell the boy to fetch them."

The guns were brought and Grange made his choice. He gave no sign that he was pleased with the handsome gift.

"You quite understand that this gun's worth a damned sight more than what your food and drink and smoke have run me into?" he said.

"For all I know you saved my life. I don't think an old gun is an over-generous return for that."

"Oh, well, if you like to look at it that way, I suppose it's your own business. Thank you very much all the same."

They shook hands and parted.

Next morning, while the baggage was being stowed away in the prahus, Skelton asked the houseboy whether, before starting, he could say good-bye to Mrs. Grange. The houseboy said he would go and see. He waited a little while. Mrs. Grange came out of her room on to the veranda. She was wearing a pink dressing-gown, shabby, rumpled and none too clean, of Japanese silk, heavily trimmed with cheap lace. The powder was thick on her face, her cheeks were rouged and her lips scarlet with lipstick. Her head seemed to twitch more violently than usual and her hand was agitated by that strange gesture. When first Skelton saw it he had thought that it suggested a wish to call attention to something behind her back, but now, after what she had told him yesterday, it did indeed look as though she were constantly trying to brush something off her dress. Blood, she had said.

"I didn't want to go without thanking you for all your kindness to me," he said.

"Oh, that's all right."

"Well, good-bye."

"I'll walk down with you to the landing-stage."

They hadn't far to go. The boatmen were still arranging the luggage. Skelton looked across the river where you could see some native houses.

"I suppose these men come from over there. It looks quite a village."

"No, only those few houses. There used to be a rubber estate there, but the company went broke and it was abandoned."

"D'you ever go over there?"

"Me?" cried Mrs. Grange. Her voice rose shrill and her head, her hand, were on a sudden convulsed by a paroxysm of involuntary movement. "No. Why should I?"

Skelton could not imagine why that simple question, asked merely for something to say, should so greatly upset her. But by now all was in order and he shook hands with her. He stepped into the boat and comfortably settled down. They pushed off. He waved to Mrs. Grange. As the boat slid into the current she cried out with a harsh, strident scream:

"Give my regards to Leicester Square."

Skelton heaved a great sigh of relief as with their powerful strokes the paddlers took him farther and farther away from that dreadful house and from those two unhappy and yet repellent people. He was glad now that Mrs. Grange had not told him the story that was on the tip of her tongue to tell. He did not want some tragic tale of sin or folly to connect him with them in a recollection that he could not escape. He wanted to forget them as one forgets a bad dream.

But Mrs. Grange watched the two prahus till a bend of the river took them out of sight. She walked slowly up to the house and went into her bedroom. The light was dim because the blinds were drawn to keep out the heat, but she sat down at her dressing-table and stared at herself in the glass. Norman had had the dressing-table made for her soon after they were married. It had been made by a native carpenter, of course, and they had had the mirror sent from Singapore, but it was made to her own design, of the exact size and shape she wanted, with plenty of room for all her toilet things and her make-up. It was the dressing-table she had hankered after for donkey's years and had never had. She remembered still how pleased she was when first she had it. She threw her arms round her husband's neck and kissed him.

"Oh, Norman, you are good to me," she said. "I'm a lucky little girl to have caught a chap like you, aren't I?"

But then everything delighted her. She was amused by the river life and the life of the jungle, the teeming growth of the forest, the birds with their gay plumage and the brilliant butterflies. She set about giving the house a woman's touch; she put out all her own photographs and she got vases to put flowers in; she routed around and got a lot of knick-knacks to place here and there. "They make a room look homey," she said. She wasn't in love with Norman, but she liked him all right; and it was lovely to be married; it was lovely to have nothing to do from morning till night, except play the gramophone, or patience, and read novels. It was lovely to think one hadn't got to bother about one's future. Of course it was a bit lonely sometimes, but Norman said she'd get used to that, and he'd promised that in a year, or two at the outside, he'd take her to England for three months. It would be a lark to show him off to her friends. She felt that what had caught him was the glamour of the stage and she'd made herself out a good deal more successful than she really had been. She wanted him to realise that she'd made a sacrifice when she'd thrown up her career to become a planter's wife. She'd claimed acquaintance with a good many stars that in point of fact she'd never even spoken to. That would need a bit of handling when they went home, but she'd manage it; after all, poor Norman knew no more about the stage than a babe unborn, if she couldn't cod a simple fellow like that, after twelve years on the stage, well, she'd wasted her time, that's all she could say. Things went all right the first year. At one moment she thought she was going to have a baby. They were both disappointed when it turned out not to be true. Then she began to grow bored. It seemed to her that she'd done the same damned thing day after day for ever and it frightened her to think that she'd have to go on doing the same damned thing day after day for ever more. Norman said he couldn't leave the plantation that year. They had a bit of a scene. It was then that he'd said something that scared her.

"I hate England," he said. "If I had my way I'd never set foot in the damned country again."

Living this lonely life Mrs. Grange got into the habit of talking out loud to herself. Shut up in her room she could be heard chattering away hour after hour; and now, dipping the puff in her powder and plastering her face with it, she addressed her reflection in the mirror exactly as though she were talking to another person.

"That ought to have warned me. I should have insisted on going by myself, and who knows, I might have got a job when I got to London. With all the experience I had and everything. Then I'd have written to him and said I wasn't coming back." Her thoughts turned to Skelton. "Pity I didn't tell him," she continued. "I had half a mind to. P'raps he was right, p'raps it would have eased me mind. I wonder what he'd have said." She imitated his Oxford accent. "I'm so terribly sorry, Mrs. Grange. I wish I could help you." She gave a chuckle which was almost a sob. "I'd have liked to tell him about Jack. Oh, Jack."

It was when they had been married for two years that they got a neighbour. The price of rubber at that time was so high that new estates were being put under cultivation and one of the big companies had bought a great tract of land on the opposite bank of the river. It was a rich company and everything was done on a lavish scale. The manager they had put in had a launch at his disposal so that it was no trouble for him to pop over and have a drink whenever he felt inclined. Jack Carr his name was. He was quite a different sort of chap from Norman; for one thing he was a gentleman, he'd been to a public school and a university; he was about thirty-five, tall, not beefy like Norman, but slight, he had the sort of figure that looked lovely in evening dress; and he had crisply curling hair and a laughing look in his eyes. Just her type. She took to him at once. It was a treat, having someone you could talk about London to, and the theatre. He was gay and easy. He made the sort of jokes you could understand. In a week or two she felt more at home with him than she did with her husband after two years. There had always been something about Norman that she hadn't quite been able to get to the bottom of. He was crazy about her, of course, and he'd told her a lot about himself, but she had a funny feeling that there was something he kept from her, not because he wanted to, but— well, you couldn't hardly explain it, because it was so alien, you might say, that he couldn't put it into words. Later, when she knew Jack better, she mentioned it to him, and Jack said it was because he was country-born; even though he hadn't a drop of native blood in his veins, something of the country had gone to the making of him so that he wasn't white really; he had an Eastern streak in him. However hard he tried he could never be quite English.

She chattered away aloud, in that empty house, for the two boys, the cook and the houseboy, were in their own quarters and the sound of her voice, ringing along the wooden floors, piercing the wooden walls, was like the uncanny, unhuman gibber of new wine fermenting in a vat. She spoke just as though Skelton were there, but so incoherently that if he had been, he would have had difficulty in following the story she told. It did not take her long to discover that Jack Carr wanted her. She was excited. She'd never been promiscuous, but in all those years she'd been on the stage naturally there'd been episodes. You couldn't hardly have put up with being on tour month after month if you didn't have a bit of fun sometimes. Of course now she wasn't going to give in too easily, she didn't want to make herself cheap, but what with the life she led, she'd be a fool if she missed the chance; and as far as Norman was concerned, well, what the eye didn't see the heart didn't grieve over. They understood one another all right, Jack and her; they knew it was bound to happen sooner or later, it was only a matter of waiting for the opportunity; and the opportunity came. But then something happened that they hadn't bargained for; they fell madly in love with one another. If Mrs. Grange really had been telling the story to Skelton it might have seemed as unlikely to him as it did to them. They were two very ordinary people, he a jolly, good-natured, commonplace planter, and she a small-part actress far from clever, not even very young, with nothing to recommend her but a neat figure and a prettyish face. What started as a casual affair turned without warning into a devastating passion, and neither of them was of a texture to sustain its exorbitant compulsion. They longed to be with one another; they were restless and miserable apart. She'd been finding Norman a bore for some time, but she'd put up with him because he was her husband; now he irritated her to frenzy because he stood between her and Jack. There was no question of their going off together, Jack Carr had nothing but his salary, and he couldn't throw up a job he'd been only too glad to get. It was difficult for them to meet. They had to run awful risks. Perhaps the chances they had to take, the obstacles they had to surmount, were fuel to their love; a year passed and it was as overwhelming as at the beginning; it was a year of agony and bliss, of fear and thrill. Then she discovered that she was pregnant. She had no doubt that Jack Carr was the father and she was wildly happy. It was true life was difficult, so difficult sometimes that she felt she just couldn't cope with it, but there'd be a baby, his baby, and that would make everything easy. She was going to Kuching for her confinement. It happened about then that Jack Carr had to go to Singapore on business and was to be away for several weeks; but he promised to get back before she left and he said he'd send word by a native the moment he arrived. When at last the message came she felt sick with the anguish of her joy. She had never wanted him so badly.

"I hear that Jack is back," she told her husband at dinner. "I shall go over to-morrow morning and get the things he promised to bring me."

"I wouldn't do that. He's pretty sure to drop in towards sundown and he'll bring them himself."

"I can't wait. I'm crazy to have them."

"All right. Have it your own way."

She couldn't help talking about him. For some time now they had seemed to have little to say to one another, Norman and she, but that night, in high spirits, she chattered away as she had done during the first months of their marriage. She always rose early, at six, and next morning she went down to the river and had a bathe. There was a little dent in the bank just there, with a tiny sandy beach, and it was delicious to splash about in the cool, transparent water. A kingfisher stood on the branch of a tree overhanging the pool and its reflection was brilliantly blue in the water. Lovely. She had a cup of tea and then stepped into a dug-out. A boy paddled her across the river. It took a good half-hour. As they got near she scanned the bank; Jack knew she would come at the earliest opportunity; he must be on the look out. Ah, there he was. The delicious pain in her heart was almost unbearable. He came down to the landing-stage and helped her to get out of the boat. They walked hand in hand up the pathway and when they were out of sight of the boy who had paddled her over and of prying eyes from the house, they stopped. He put his arms round her and she yielded with ecstasy to his embrace. She clung to him. His mouth sought hers. In that kiss was all the agony of their separation and all the bliss of their reunion. The miracle of love transfused them so that they were unconscious of time and place. They were not human any more, but two spirits united by a divine fire. No thought passed through their minds. No words issued from their lips. Suddenly there was a brutal shock, like a blow, and immediately, almost simultaneously, a deafening noise. Horrified, not understanding, she clung to Jack more tightly and his grip on her was spasmodic, so that she gasped; then she felt that he was bearing her over.

"Jack."

She tried to hold him up. His weight was too great for her and as he fell to the ground she fell with him. Then she gave a great cry, for she felt a gush of heat, and his blood sputtered over her. She began to scream. A rough hand seized her and dragged her to her feet. It was Norman. She was distraught. She could not understand.

"Norman, what have you done?"

"I've killed him."

She stared at him stupidly. She pushed him aside.

"Jack. Jack."

"Shut up. I'll go and get help. It was an accident."

He walked quickly up the pathway. She fell to her knees and took Jack's head in her arms.

"Darling," she moaned. "Oh, my darling."

Norman came back with some coolies and they carried him

up to the house. That night she had a miscarriage and was so ill that for days it looked as if she would die. When she recovered she had the nervous tic that she'd had ever since. She expected that Norman would send her away; but he didn't, he had to keep her to allay suspicion. There was some talk among the natives, and after a while the District Officer came up and asked a lot of questions; but the natives were frightened of Norman, and the D.O. could get nothing out of them. The Dyak boy who paddled her over had vanished. Norman said something had gone wrong with his gun and Jack was looking at it to see what was the matter and it went off. They bury people quickly in that country and by the time they might have dug him up there wouldn't have been much left to show that Norman's story wasn't true. The D.O. hadn't been satisfied.

"It all looks damned fishy to me," he said, "but in the absence of any evidence, I suppose I must accept your version."

She would have given anything to get away, but with that nervous affliction she had no ghost of a chance any longer of earning a living. She had to stay—or starve; and Norman had to keep her—or hang. Nothing had happened since then and now nothing ever would happen. The endless years one after another dragged out their weary length.

Mrs. Grange on a sudden stopped talking. Her sharp ears had caught the sound of a footstep on the path and she knew that Norman was back from his round. Her head twitching furiously, her hand agitated by that sinister, uncontrollable gesture, she looked in the untidy mess of her dressing-table for her precious lipstick. She smeared it on her lips, and then, she didn't know why, on a freakish impulse daubed it all over her nose till she looked like a red-nose comedian in a music-hall. She looked at herself in the glass and burst out laughing.

"To hell with life!" she shouted.

SANATORIUM

FOR the first six weeks that Ashenden was at the sanatorium he stayed in bed. He saw nobody but the doctor who visited him morning and evening, the nurses who looked after him and the maid who brought him his meals. He had contracted tuberculosis of the lungs and since at the time there were reasons that made it difficult for him to go to Switzerland the specialist he saw in London had sent him up to a sanatorium in the north of Scotland. At last the day came that he had been patiently looking forward to when the doctor told him he could get up; and in the afternoon his nurse, having helped him to dress, took him down to the veranda, placed cushions behind him, wrapped him up in rugs and left him to enjoy the sun that was streaming down from a cloudless sky. It was midwinter. The sanatorium stood on the top of a hill and from it you had a spacious view of the snow-clad country. There were people lying all along the veranda in deck-chairs, some chatting with their neighbours and some reading. Every now and then one would have a fit of coughing and you noticed that at the end of it he looked anxiously at his handkerchief. Before the nurse left Ashenden she turned with a kind of professional briskness to the man who was lying in the next chair.

"I want to introduce Mr. Ashenden to you," she said. And then to Ashenden: "This is Mr. McLeod. He and Mr. Campbell have been here longer than anyone else."

On the other side of Ashenden was lying a pretty girl, with red hair and bright blue eyes; she had on no make-up, but her lips were very red and the colour on her cheeks was high. It emphasised the astonishing whiteness of her skin. It was lovely even when you realised that its delicate texture was due to illness. She wore a fur coat and was wrapped up in rugs, so

183

that you could see nothing of her body, but her face was extremely thin, so thin that it made her nose, which wasn't really large, look a trifle prominent. She gave Ashenden a friendly look, but did not speak, and Ashenden, feeling rather shy among all those strange people, wanted to be spoken to.

"First time they've let you get up, is it?" said McLeod.

"Yes."

"Where's your room?"

Ashenden told him.

"Small. I know every room in the place. I've been here for seventeen years. I've got the best room here and so I damned well ought to have. Campbell's been trying to get me out of it, he wants it himself, but I'm not going to budge; I've got a right to it, I came here six months before he did."

McLeod, lying there, gave you the impression that he was immensely tall; his skin was stretched tight over his bones, his cheeks and temples hollow, so that you could see the formation of his skull under it; and in that emaciated face, with its great bony nose, the eyes were preternaturally large.

"Seventeen years is a long time," said Ashenden, because he could think of nothing else to say.

"Time passes very quickly. I like it here. At first, after a year or two, I went away in the summer, but I don't any more. It's my home now. I've got a brother and two sisters; but they're married and now they've got families; they don't want me. When you've been here a few years and you go back to ordinary life, you feel a bit out of it, you know. Your pals have gone their own ways and you've got nothing in common with them any more. It all seems an awful rush. Much ado about nothing, that's what it is. It's noisy and stuffy. No, one's better off here. I shan't stir again till they carry me out feet first in my coffin."

The specialist had told Ashenden that if he took care of

himself for a reasonable time he would get well, and he looked at McLeod with curiosity.

"What do you do with yourself all day long?" he asked.

"Do? Having T.B. is a whole-time job, my boy. There's my temperature to take and then I weigh myself. I don't hurry over my dressing. I have breakfast, I read the papers and go for a walk. Then I have my rest. I lunch and play bridge. I have another rest and then I dine. I play a bit more bridge and I go to bed. They've got quite a decent library here, we get all the new books, but I don't really have much time for reading. I talk to people. You meet all sorts here, you know. They come and they go. Sometimes they go because they think they're cured, but a lot of them come back, and sometimes they go because they die. I've seen a lot of people out and before I go I expect to see a lot more."

The girl sitting on Ashenden's other side suddenly spoke.

"I should tell you that few persons can get a heartier laugh out of a hearse than Mr. McLeod," she said.

McLeod chuckled.

"I don't know about that, but it wouldn't be human nature if I didn't say to myself: Well, I'm just as glad it's him and not me they're taking for a ride."

It occurred to him that Ashenden didn't know the pretty girl, so he introduced him.

"By the way, I don't think you've met Mr. Ashenden—Miss Bishop. She's English, but not a bad girl."

"How long have you been here?" asked Ashenden.

"Only two years. This is my last winter. Dr. Lennox says I shall be all right in a few months and there's no reason why I shouldn't go home."

"Silly, I call it," said McLeod. "Stay where you're well off, that's what I say."

At that moment a man, leaning on a stick, came walking slowly along the veranda.

"Oh, look, there's Major Templeton," said Miss Bishop, a smile lighting up her blue eyes; and then, as he came up: "I'm glad to see you up again."

"Oh, it was nothing. Only a bit of a cold. I'm quite all right now."

The words were hardly out of his mouth when he began to cough. He leaned heavily on his stick. But when the attack was over he smiled gaily.

"Can't get rid of this dammed cough," he said. "Smoking too much. Dr. Lennox says I ought to give it up, but it's no good—I can't."

He was a tall fellow, good-looking in a slightly theatrical way, with a dusky, sallow face, fine very dark eyes and a neat black moustache. He was wearing a fur coat with an Astrakhan collar. His appearance was smart and perhaps a trifle showy. Miss Bishop made Ashenden known to him. Major Templeton said a few civil words in an easy, cordial way, and then asked the girl to go for a stroll with him; he had been ordered to walk to a certain place in the wood behind the sanatorium and back again. McLeod watched them as they sauntered off.

"I wonder if there's anything between those two," he said. "They do say Templeton was a devil with the girls before he got ill."

"He doesn't look up to much in that line just now," said Ashenden.

"You never can tell. I've seen a lot of rum things here in my day. I could tell you no end of stories if I wanted to."

"You evidently do, so why don't you?"

McLeod grinned.

"Well, I'll tell you one. Three or four years ago there was a woman here who was pretty hot stuff. Her husband used to come and see her every other week-end, he was crazy about her, used to fly up from London; but Dr. Lennox was pretty sure she was carrying on with somebody here, but he couldn't find out who. So one night when we'd all gone to bed he had a thin coat of paint put down just outside her room and next day he had everyone's slippers examined. Neat, wasn't it? The fellow whose slippers had paint on them got the push. Dr. Lennox has to be particular, you know. He doesn't want the place to get a bad name."

"How long has Templeton been here?"

"Three or four months. He's been in bed most of the time. He's for it all right. Ivy Bishop'll be a damned fool if she gets stuck on him. She's got a good chance of getting well. I've seen so many of them, you know, I can tell. When I look at a fellow I make up my mind at once whether he'll get well or whether he won't, and if he won't I can make a pretty shrewd guess how long he'll last. I'm very seldom mistaken. I give Templeton about two years myself."

McLeod gave Ashenden a speculative look and Ashenden, knowing what he was thinking, though he tried to be amused, could not help feeling somewhat concerned. There was a twinkle in McLeod's eyes. He plainly knew what was passing through Ashenden's mind.

"You'll get all right. I wouldn't have mentioned it if I hadn't been pretty sure of that. I don't want Dr. Lennox to hoof me out for putting the fear of God into his bloody patients."

Then Ashenden's nurse came to take him back to bed. Even though he had only sat out for an hour, he was tired, and was glad to find himself once more between the sheets. Dr. Lennox came in to see him in the course of the evening. He looked at his temperature chart.

"That's not so bad," he said.

Dr. Lennox was small, brisk and genial. He was a good enough doctor, an excellent business man, and an enthusiastic fisherman. When the fishing season began he was inclined to leave the care of his patients to his assistants; the patients grumbled a little, but were glad enough to eat the young salmon

7

he brought back to vary their meals. He was fond of talking, and now, standing at the end of Ashenden's bed, he asked him, in his broad Scots, whether he had got into conversation with any of the patients that afternoon. Ashenden told him the nurse had introduced him to McLeod. Dr. Lennox laughed.

"The oldest living inhabitant. He knows more about the sanatorium and its inmates than I do. How he gets his information I haven't an idea, but there's not a thing about the private lives of anyone under this roof that he doesn't know. There's not an old maid in the place with a keener nose for a bit of scandal. Did he tell you about Campbell?"

"He mentioned him."

"He hates Campbell, and Campbell hates him. Funny, when you come to think of it, those two men, they've been here for seventeen years and they've got about one sound lung between them. They loathe the sight of one another. I've had to refuse to listen to the complaints about one another that they come to me with. Campbell's room is just below McLeod's and Campbell plays the fiddle. It drives McLeod wild. He says he's been listening to the same tunes for fifteen years, but Campbell says McLeod doesn't know one tune from another. McLeod wants me to stop Campbell playing, but I can't do that, he's got a perfect right to play so long as he doesn't play in the silence hours. I've offered to change McLeod's room, but he won't do that. He says Campbell only plays to drive him out of the room because it's the best in the house, and he's damned if he's going to have it. It's queer, isn't it, that two middle-aged men should think it worth while to make life hell for one another. Neither can leave the other alone. They have their meals at the same table, they play bridge together; and not a day passes without a row. Sometimes I've threatened to turn them both out if they don't behave like sensible fellows. That keeps them quiet for a bit. They don't want to go. They've been here so long, they've got no one any more who gives a damn for them, and they can't cope with the world outside. Campbell went away for a couple of months' holiday some years ago. He came back after a week: he said he couldn't stand the racket, and the sight of so many people in the streets scared him."

It was a strange world into which Ashenden found himself thrown when, his health gradually improving, he was able to mix with his fellow patients. One morning Dr. Lennox told him he could thenceforward lunch in the dining-room. This was a large, low room, with great window space; the windows were always wide open and on fine days the sun streamed in. There seemed to be a great many people and it took him some time to sort them out. They were of all kinds, young, middle-aged and old. There were some, like McLeod and Campbell, who had been at the sanatorium for years and expected to die there. Others had only been there for a few months. There was one middle-aged spinster called Miss Atkin who had been coming every winter for a long time and in the summer went to stay with friends and relations. She had nothing much the matter with her any more, and might just as well have stayed away altogether, but she liked the life. Her long residence had given her a sort of position, she was honorary librarian and hand in glove with the matron. She was always ready to gossip with you, but you were soon warned that everything you said was passed on. It was useful to Dr. Lennox to know that his patients were getting on well together and were happy, that they did nothing imprudent and followed his instructions. Little escaped Miss Atkin's sharp eyes, and from her it went to the matron and so to Dr. Lennox. Because she had been coming for so many years, she sat at the same table as McLeod and Campbell, together with an old general who had been put there on account of his rank. The table was in no way different from any other, and it was not more advantageously placed, but because the oldest residents sat there it was looked upon as the most desirable place to sit, and several elderly women were bitterly resentful because Miss Atkin, who went away for four or five months every summer, should be given a place there while they who spent the whole year in the sanatorium sat at other tables. There was an old Indian civilian who had been at the sanatorium longer than anyone but McLeod and Campbell; he was a man who in his day had ruled a province, and he was waiting irascibly for either McLeod or Campbell to die so that he might take his place at the first table. Ashenden made the acquaintance of Campbell. He was a long, big-boned fellow with a bald head, so thin that you wondered how his limbs held together; and when he sat crumpled in an arm-chair he gave you the uncanny impression of a mannikin in a puppet-show. He was brusque, touchy and bad-tempered. The first thing he asked Ashenden was:

"Are you fond of music?"

"Yes."

"No one here cares a damn for it. I play the violin. But if you like it, come to my room one day and I'll play to you."

"Don't you go," said McLeod, who heard him. "It's torture."

"How can you be so rude?" cried Miss Atkin. "Mr. Campbell plays very nicely."

"There's no one in this beastly place that knows one note from another," said Campbell.

With a derisive chuckle McLeod walked off. Miss Atkin tried to smooth things down.

"You musn't mind what Mr. McLeod said."

"Oh, I don't. I'll get back on him all right."

He played the same tune over and over again all that afternoon. McLeod banged on the floor, but Campbell went on. He sent a message by a maid to say that he had a headache and would Mr. Campbell mind not playing; Campbell replied that he had a perfect right to play and if Mr. McLeod didn't like it he could lump it. When next day they met high words passed.

Ashenden was put at a table with the pretty Miss Bishop, with Templeton, and with a London man, an accountant, called Henry Chester. He was a stocky, broad-shouldered, wiry little fellow, and the last person you would ever have thought would be attacked by T.B. It had come upon him as a sudden and unexpected blow. He was a perfectly ordinary man, somewhere between thirty and forty, married, with two children. He lived in a decent suburb. He went up to the City every morning and read the morning paper; he came down from the city every evening and read the evening paper. He had no interests except his business and his family. He liked his work; he made enough money to live in comfort, he put by a reasonable sum every year, he played golf on Saturday afternoon and on Sunday, he went every August for a three weeks' holiday to the same place on the east coast; his children would grow up and marry, then he would turn his business over to his son and retire with his wife to a little house in the country where he could potter about till death claimed him at a ripe old age. He asked nothing more from life than that, and it was a life that thousands upon thousands of his fellow men lived with satisfaction. He was the average citizen. Then this thing happened. He had caught cold playing golf, it had gone to his chest, and he had had a cough that he couldn't shake off. He had always been strong and healthy, and had no opinion of doctors; but at last at his wife's persuasion he had consented to see one. It was a shock to him, a fearful shock, to learn that there was tubercle in both his lungs and that his only chance of life was to go immediately to a sanatorium. The specialist he saw then told him that he might be able to go back to work in a couple of years, but two years had passed and Dr. Lennox advised him not to think of it for at least a year more. He showed him the bacilli in his sputum, and in an X-ray photograph the actively-diseased patches in his lungs. He lost heart.

It seemed to him a cruel and unjust trick that fate had played upon him. He could have understood it if he had led a wild life, if he had drunk too much, played around with women or kept late hours. He would have deserved it then. But he had done none of these things. It was monstrously unfair. Having no resources in himself, no interest in books, he had nothing to do but think of his health. It became an obsession. He watched his symptoms anxiously. They had to deprive him of a thermometer because he took his temperature a dozen times a day. He got it into his head that the doctors were taking his case too indifferently, and in order to force their attention used every method he could devise to make the thermometer register a temperature that would alarm; and when his tricks were foiled he grew sulky and querulous. But he was by nature a jovial, friendly creature, and when he forgot himself he talked and laughed gaily; then on a sudden he remembered that he was a sick man and you would see in his eyes the fear of death.

At the end of every month his wife came up to spend a day or two in a lodging-house nearby. Dr. Lennox did not much like the visits that relatives paid the patients, it excited and unsettled them. It was moving to see the eagerness with which Henry Chester looked forward to his wife's arrival; but it was strange to notice that once she had come he seemed less pleased than one would have expected. Mrs. Chester was a pleasant, cheerful little woman, not pretty, but neat, as commonplace as her husband, and you only had to look at her to know that she was a good wife and mother, a careful housekeeper, a nice, quiet body who did her duty and interfered with nobody. She had been quite happy in the dull, domestic life they had led for so many years, her only dissipation a visit to the pictures, her great thrill the sales in the big London shops; and it had never occurred to her that it was monotonous. It completely satisfied her. Ashenden liked her. He listened with interest while she prattled about her children and her house in the suburbs, her neighbours and her trivial occupations. On one occasion he met her in the road. Chester for some reason connected with his treatment had stayed in and she was alone. Ashenden suggested that they should walk together. They talked for a little of indifferent things. Then she suddenly asked him how he thought her husband was.

"I think he seems to be getting on all right."

"I'm so terribly worried."

"You must remember it's a slow, long business. One has to have patience."

They walked on a little and then he saw she was crying.

"You mustn't be unhappy about him," said Ashenden gently.

"Oh, you don't know what I have to put up with when I come here. I know I ought not to speak about it, but I must. I can trust you, can't I?"

"Of course."

"I love him. I'm devoted to him. I'd do anything in the world I could for him. We've never quarrelled, we've never even differed about a single thing. He's beginning to hate me and it breaks my heart."

"Oh, I can't believe that. Why, when you're not here he talks of you all the time. He couldn't talk more nicely. He's devoted to you."

"Yes, that's when I'm not here. It's when I'm here, when he sees me well and strong, that it comes over him. You see, he resents it so terribly that he's ill and I'm well. He's afraid he's going to die and he hates me because I'm going to live. I have to be on my guard all the time; almost everything I say, if I speak of the children, if I speak of the future, exasperates him, and he says bitter, wounding things. When I speak of something I've had to do to the house or a servant I've had to change it irritates him beyond endurance. He complains that I treat him as if he didn't count any more. We used to be so united, and now I feel there's a great wall of antagonism between us. I know I shouldn't blame him, I know it's only his illness, he's a dear good man really, and kindness itself, normally he's the easiest man in the world to get on with; and now I simply dread coming here and I go with relief. He'd be terribly sorry if I had T.B. but I know that in his heart of hearts it would be a relief. He could forgive me, he could forgive fate, if he thought I was going to die too. Sometimes he tortures me by talking about what I shall do when he's dead, and when I get hysterical and cry out to him to stop, he says I needn't grudge him a little pleasure when he'll be dead so soon and I can go on living for years and years and have a good time. Oh, it's so frightful to think that this love we've had for one another all these years should die in this sordid, miserable way."

Mrs. Chester sat down on a stone by the roadside and gave way to passionate weeping. Ashenden looked at her with pity, but could find nothing to say that might comfort her. What she had told him did not come quite as a surprise.

"Give me a cigarette," she said at last. "I mustn't let my eyes get all red and swollen, or Henry'll know I've been crying and he'll think I've had bad news about him. Is death so horrible? Do we all fear death like that?"

"I don't know," said Ashenden.

"When my mother was dying she didn't seem to mind a bit. She knew it was coming and she even made little jokes about it. But she was an old woman."

Mrs. Chester pulled herself together and they set off again. They walked for a while in silence.

"You won't think any the worse of Henry for what I've told you?" she said at last.

"Of course not."

"He's been a good husband and a good father. I've never known a better man in my life. Until this illness I don't think an unkind or ungenerous thought ever passed through his head."

The conversation left Ashenden pensive. People often said he had a low opinion of human nature. It was because he did not always judge his fellows by the usual standards. He accepted with a smile, a tear or a shrug of the shoulders, much that filled others with dismay. It was true that you would never have expected that good-natured, commonplace little chap to harbour such bitter and unworthy thoughts; but who has ever been able to tell to what depths man may fall or to what heights rise? The fault lay in the poverty of his ideals. Henry Chester was born and bred to lead an average life, exposed to the normal vicissitudes of existence, and when an unforeseeable accident befell him he had no means of coping with it. He was like a brick made to take its place with a million others in a huge factory, but by chance with a flaw in it so that it is inadequate to its purpose. And the brick too, if it had a mind, might cry: What have I done that I cannot fulfil my modest end, but must be taken away from all these other bricks that support me and thrown on the dust-heap? It was no fault of Henry Chester's that he was incapable of the conceptions that might have enabled him to bear his calamity with resignation. It is not everyone who can find solace in art or thought. It is the tragedy of our day that these humble souls have lost their faith in God, in whom lay hope, and their belief in a resurrection that might bring them the happiness that has been denied them on earth; and have found nothing to put in their place.

There are people who say that suffering ennobles. It is not true. As a general rule it makes man petty, querulous and selfish; but here in this sanatorium there was not much suffering. In certain stages of tuberculosis the slight fever that accompanies it excites rather than depresses, so that the patient feels alert and, upborne by hope, faces the future blithely; but for all that the idea of death haunts the subconscious. It is a sardonic theme song that runs through a sprightly operetta. Now and again the gay, melodious arias, the dance measures,

7*

deviate strangely into tragic strains that throb menacingly down the nerves; the petty interests of every day, the small jealousies and trivial concerns are as nothing; pity and terror make the heart on a sudden stand still and the awfulness of death broods as the silence that precedes a tropical storm broods over the tropical jungle. After Ashenden had been for some time at the sanatorium there came a boy of twenty. He was in the navy, a sub-lieutenant in a submarine, and he had what they used to call in novels galloping consumption. He was a tall, good-looking youth, with curly brown hair, blue eyes and a very sweet smile. Ashenden saw him two or three times lying on the terrace in the sun and passed the time of day with him. He was a cheerful lad. He talked of musical shows and film stars; and he read the paper for the football results and the boxing news. Then he was put to bed and Ashenden saw him no more. His relations were sent for and in two months he was dead. He died uncomplaining. He understood what was happening to him as little as an animal. For a day or two there was the same malaise in the sanatorium as there is in a prison when a man has been hanged; and then, as though by universal consent, in obedience to an instinct of self-preservation, the boy was put out of mind; life, with its three meals a day, its golf on the miniature course, its regulated exercise, its pre-scribed rests, its quarrels and jealousies, its scandal-mongering and petty vexations, went on as before. Campbell, to the exasperation of McLeod, continued to play the prize-song and "Annie Laurie" on his fiddle. McLeod continued to boast of his bridge and gossip about other people's health and morals. Miss Atkin continued to backbite. Henry Chester continued to complain that the doctors gave him insufficient attention and railed against fate because, after the model life he had led, it had played him such a dirty trick. Ashenden continued to read and with amused tolerance to watch the vagaries of his fellow creatures.

He became intimate with Major Templeton. Templeton was perhaps a little more than forty years of age. He had been in the Grenadier Guards, but had resigned his commission after the war. A man of ample means, he had since then devoted himself entirely to pleasure. He raced in the racing season, shot in the shooting season and hunted in the hunting season. When this was over he went to Monte Carlo. He told Ashenden of the large sums he had made and lost at baccarat. He was very fond of women and if his stories could be believed they were very fond of him. He loved good food and good drink. He knew by their first names the head waiters of every restaurant in London where you ate well. He belonged to half a dozen clubs. He had led for years a useless, selfish, worthless life, the sort of life which maybe it will be impossible for anyone to live in the future, but he had lived it without misgiving and had enjoyed it. Ashenden asked him once what he would do if he had his time over again and he answered that he would do exactly what he had done. He was an amusing talker, gay and pleasantly ironic, and he dealt with the surface of things, which was all he knew, with a light, easy and assured touch. He always had a pleasant word for the dowdy spinsters in the sanatorium and a joking one for the peppery old gentlemen, for he combined good manners with a natural kindliness. He knew his way about the superficial world of the people who have more money than they know what to do with as well as he knew his way about Mayfair. He was the kind of man who would always have been willing to take a bet, to help a friend and to give a tenner to a rogue. If he had never done much good in the world he had never done much harm. He amounted to nothing. But he was a more agreeable companion than many of more sterling character and of more admirable qualities. He was very ill now. He was dying and he knew it. He took it with the same easy, laughing nonchalance as he had taken all the rest. He'd had a thundering good time, he regretted nothing, it was rotten tough luck getting T.B., but to hell with it, no one can live for ever, and when you came to think of it, he might have been killed in the war or broken his bloody neck in a point to point. His principle all through life had been, when you've made a bad bet, pay up and forget about it. He'd had a good run for his money and he was ready to call it a day. It had been a damned good party while it lasted, but every party's got to come to an end, and next day it doesn't matter much if you went home with the milk or if you left while the fun was in full swing.

Of all those people in the sanatorium he was probably from the moral standpoint the least worthy, but he was the only one who genuinely accepted the inevitable with unconcern. He snapped his fingers in the face of death, and you could choose whether to call his levity unbecoming or his insouciance gallant.

The last thing that ever occurred to him when he came to the sanatorium was that he might fall more deeply in love there than he had ever done before. His amours had been numerous, but they had been light; he had been content with the politely mercenary love of chorus girls and with ephemeral unions with women of easy virtue whom he met at house parties. He had always taken care to avoid any attachment that might endanger his freedom. His only aim in life had been to get as much fun out of it as possible, and where sex was concerned he found every advantage and no inconvenience in ceaseless variety. But he liked women. Even when they were quite old he could not talk to them without a caress in his eyes and a tenderness in his voice. He was prepared to do anything to please them. They were conscious of his interest in them and were agreeably flattered, and they felt, quite mistakenly, that they could trust him never to let them down. He once said a thing that Ashenden thought showed insight.

"You know, any man can get any woman he wants if he

tries hard enough, there's nothing in that, but once he's got her, only a man who thinks the world of women can get rid of her without humiliating her."

It was simply from habit that he began to make love to Ivy Bishop. She was the prettiest and the youngest girl in the sanatorium. She was in point of fact not so young as Ashenden had first thought her, she was twenty-nine, but for the last eight years she had been wandering from one sanatorium to another, in Switzerland, England and Scotland, and the sheltered invalid life had preserved her youthful appearance so that you might easily have taken her for twenty. All she knew of the world she had learnt in these establishments, so that she combined rather curiously extreme innocence with extreme sophistication. She had seen a number of love affairs run their course. A good many men, of various nationalities, had made love to her; she accepted their attentions with self-possession and humour, but she had at her disposal plenty of firmness when they showed an inclination to go too far. She had a force of character unexpected in anyone who looked so flower-like and when it came to a show-down knew how to express her meaning in plain, cool and decisive words. She was quite ready to have a flirtation with George Templeton. It was a game she understood, and though always charming to him, it was with a bantering lightness that showed quite clearly that she had summed him up and had no mind to take the affair more seriously than he did. Like Ashenden, Templeton went to bed every evening at six and dined in his room, so that he saw Ivy only by day. They went for little walks together, but otherwise were seldom alone. At lunch the conversation between the four of them, Ivy, Templeton, Henry Chester and Ashenden, was general, but it was obvious that it was for neither of the two men that Templeton took so much trouble to be entertaining. It seemed to Ashenden that he was ceasing to flirt with Ivy to pass the time, and that his feeling for her was growing deeper and more sincere; but he could not tell whether she was conscious of it nor whether it meant anything to her. Whenever Templeton hazarded a remark that was more intimate than the occasion warranted she countered it with an ironic one that made them all laugh. But Templeton's laugh was rueful. He was no longer content to have her take him as a play-boy. The more Ashenden knew Ivy Bishop the more he liked her. There was something pathetic in her sick beauty, with that lovely transparent skin, the thin face in which the eyes were so large and so wonderfully blue; and there was something pathetic in her plight, for like so many others in the sanatorium she seemed to be alone in the world. Her mother led a busy social life, her sisters were married; they took but a perfunctory interest in the young woman from whom they had been separated now for eight years. They corresponded, they came to see her occasionally, but there was no longer very much between them. She accepted the situation without bitterness. She was friendly with everyone and prepared always to listen with sympathy to the complaints and the distress of all and sundry. She went out of her way to be nice to Henry Chester and did what she could to cheer him.

"Well, Mr. Chester," she said to him one day at lunch, "it's the end of the month, your wife will be coming to-morrow. That's something to look forward to."

"No, she's not coming this month," he said quietly, looking down at his plate.

"Oh, I am sorry. Why not? The children are all right, aren't they?"

"Dr. Lennox thinks it's better for me that she shouldn't come."

There was a silence. Ivy looked at him with troubled eyes.

"That's tough luck, old man," said Templeton in his hearty way. "Why didn't you tell Lennox to go to hell?"

"He must know best," said Chester.

Ivy gave him another look and began to talk of something else.

Looking back, Ashenden realised that she had at once suspected the truth. For next day he happened to walk with Chester.

"I'm awfully sorry your wife isn't coming," he said. "You'll miss her visit dreadfully."

"Dreadfully."

He gave Ashenden a sidelong glance. Ashenden felt that he had something he wanted to say, but could not bring himself to say it. He gave his shoulders an angry shrug.

"It's my fault if she's not coming. I asked Lennox to write and tell her not to. I couldn't stick it any more. I spend the whole month looking forward to her coming and then when she's here I hate her. You see, I resent so awfully having this filthy disease. She's strong and well and full of beans. It maddens me when I see the pain in her eyes. What does it matter to her really? Who cares if you're ill? They pretend to care, but they're jolly glad it's you and not them. I'm a swine, aren't I?"

Ashenden remembered how Mrs. Chester had sat on a stone by the side of the road and wept.

"Aren't you afraid you'll make her very unhappy, not letting her come?"

"She must put up with that. I've got enough with my own unhappiness without bothering with hers."

Ashenden did not know what to say and they walked on in silence. Suddenly Chester broke out irritably.

"It's all very well for you to be disinterested and unselfish, you're going to live. I'm going to die, and God damn it, I don't want to die. Why should I? It's not fair."

Time passed. In a place like the sanatorium where there was little to occupy the mind it was inevitable that soon everyone should know that George Templeton was in love with Ivy

Bishop. But it was not so easy to tell what her feelings were. It was plain that she liked his company, but she did not seek it, and indeed it looked as though she took pains not to be alone with him. One or two of the middle-aged ladies tried to trap her into some compromising admission, but ingenuous as she was, she was easily a match for them. She ignored their hints and met their straight questions with incredulous laughter. She succeeded in exasperating them.

"She can't be so stupid as not to see that he's mad about her."

"She has no right to play with him like that."

"I believe she's just as much in love with him as he is with her."

"Dr. Lennox ought to tell her mother."

No one was more incensed than McLeod.

"Too ridiculous. After all, nothing can come of it. He's riddled with T.B. and she's not much better."

Campbell on the other hand was sardonic and gross.

"I'm all for their having a good time while they can. I bet there's a bit of hanky-panky going on if one only knew, and I don't blame 'em."

"You cad," said McLeod.

"Oh, come off it. Templeton isn't the sort of chap to play bumble-puppy bridge with a girl like that unless he's getting something out of it, and she knows a thing or two, I bet."

Ashenden, who saw most of them, knew them better than any of the others. Templeton at last had taken him into his confidence. He was rather amused at himself.

"Rum thing at my time of life, falling in love with a decent girl. Last thing I'd ever expected of myself. And it's no good denying it, I'm in it up to the neck; if I were a well man I'd ask her to marry me to-morrow. I never knew a girl could be as nice as that. I've always thought girls, decent girls, I mean, damned bores. But she isn't a bore, she's as clever as she can stick. And pretty too. My God, what a skin! And that hair:

but it isn't any of that that's bowled me over like a row of pins. D'you know what's got me? Damned ridiculous when you come to think of it. An old rip like me. Virtue. Makes me laugh like a hyena. Last thing I've ever wanted in a woman, but there it is, no getting away from it, she's good, and it makes me feel like a worm. Surprises you, I suppose?"

"Not a bit," said Ashenden. "You're not the first rake who's fallen to innocence. It's merely the sentimentality of middle age."

"Dirty dog," laughed Templeton.

"What does she say to it?"

"Good God, you don't suppose I've told her. I've never said a word to her that I wouldn't have said before anyone else. I may be dead in six months, and besides, what have I got to offer a girl like that?"

Ashenden by now was pretty sure that she was just as much in love with Templeton as he was with her. He had seen the flush that coloured her cheeks when Templeton came into the dining-room and he had noticed the soft glance she gave him now and then when he was not looking at her. There was a peculiar sweetness in her smile when she listened to him telling some of his old experiences. Ashenden had the impression that she basked comfortably in his love as the patients on the terrace, facing the snow, basked in the hot sunshine; but it might very well be that she was content to leave it at that, and it was certainly no business of his to tell Templeton what perhaps she had no wish that he should know.

Then an incident occurred to disturb the monotony of life. Though McLeod and Campbell were always at odds they played bridge together because, till Templeton came, they were the best players in the sanatorium. They bickered incessantly, their post-mortems were endless, but after so many years each knew the other's game perfectly and they took a keen delight in scoring off one another. As a rule Templeton refused to play

with them; though a fine player he preferred to play with Ivy
Bishop, and McLeod and Campbell were agreed on this, that
she ruined the game. She was the kind of player who, having
made a mistake that lost the rubber, would laugh and say:
Well, it only made the difference of a trick. But one afternoon,
since Ivy was staying in her room with a headache, Templeton
consented to play with Campbell and McLeod. Ashenden was
the fourth. Though it was the end of March there had been
heavy snow for several days, and they played, in a veranda
open on three sides to the wintry air, in fur coats and caps,
with mittens on their hands. The stakes were too small for a
gambler like Templeton to take the game seriously and his
bidding was overbold, but he played so much better than the
other three that he generally managed to make his contract
or at least to come near it. But there was much doubling and
redoubling. The cards ran high, so that an inordinate number
of small slams were bid; it was a tempestuous game, and
McLeod and Campbell lashed one another with their tongues.
Half-past five arrived and the last rubber was started, for at six
the bell rang to send everyone to rest. It was a hard-fought
rubber, with sets on both sides, for McLeod and Campbell
were opponents and each was determined that the other should
not win. At ten minutes to six it was game all and the last hand
was dealt. Templeton was McLeod's partner and Ashenden
Campbell's. The bidding started with two clubs from McLeod;
Ashenden said nothing; Templeton showed that he had
substantial help, and finally McLeod called a grand slam.
Campbell doubled and McLeod redoubled. Hearing this, the
players at other tables who had broken off gathered round and
the hands were played in deadly silence .o a little crowd of
onlookers. McLeod's face was white with excitement and there
were beads of sweat on his brow. His hands trembled. Campbell was very grim. McLeod had to take two finesses and they
both came off. He finished with a squeeze and got the last of

the thirteen tricks. There was a burst of applause from the onlookers. McLeod, arrogant in victory, sprang to his feet. He shook his clenched fist at Campbell.

"Play that off on your blasted fiddle," he shouted. "Grand slam doubled and redoubled. I've wanted to get it all my life and now I've got it. By God. By God."

He gasped. He staggered forward and fell across the table. A stream of blood poured from his mouth. The doctor was sent for. Attendants came. He was dead.

He was buried two days later, early in the morning so that the patients should not be disturbed by the sight of a funeral. A relation in black came from Glasgow to attend it. No one had liked him. No one regretted him. At the end of a week so far as one could tell, he was forgotten. The Indian civilian took his place at the principal table and Campbell moved into the room he had so long wanted.

"Now we shall have peace," said Dr. Lennox to Ashenden. "When you think that I've had to put up with the quarrels and complaints of those two men for years and years. . . . Believe me, one has to have patience to run a sanatorium. And to think that after all the trouble he's given me he had to end up like that and scare all those people out of their wits."

"It was a bit of a shock, you know," said Ashenden.

"He was a worthless fellow, and yet some of the women have been quite upset about it. Poor little Miss Bishop cried her eyes out."

"I suspect that she was the only one who cried for him and not for herself."

But presently it appeared that there was one person who had not forgotten him. Campbell went about like a lost dog. He wouldn't play bridge. He wouldn't talk. There was no doubt about it, he was moping for McLeod. For several days he remained in his room, having his meals brought to him, and then went to Dr. Lennox and said he didn't like it as well as his old one and wanted to be moved back. Dr. Lennox lost his temper, which he rarely did, and told him he had been pestering him to give him that room for years and now he could stay there or get out of the sanatorium. He returned to it and sat gloomily brooding.

"Why don't you play your violin?" the matron asked him at length. "I haven't heard you play for a fortnight."

"I haven't."

"Why not?"

"It's no fun any more. I used to get a kick out of playing because I knew it maddened McLeod. But now nobody cares if I play or not. I shall never play again."

Nor did he for all the rest of the time that Ashenden was at the sanatorium. It was strange, now that McLeod was dead life had lost its savour for him. With no one to quarrel with, no one to infuriate, he had lost his incentive and it was plain that it would not be long before he followed his enemy to the grave.

But on Templeton McLeod's death had another effect, and one which was soon to have unexpected consequences. He talked to Ashenden about it in his cool, detached way.

"Grand, passing out like that in his moment of triumph. I can't make out why everyone got in such a state about it. He'd been here for years, hadn't he?"

"Eighteen, I believe."

"I wonder if it's worth it. I wonder if it's not better to have one's fling and take the consequences."

"I suppose it depends on how much you value life."

"But is this life?"

Ashenden had no answer. In a few months he could count on being well, but you only had to look at Templeton to know that he was not going to recover. The death-look was on his face.

"D'you know what I've done?" asked Templeton. "I've asked Ivy to marry me."

Ashenden was startled.

"What did she say?"

"Bless her little heart, she said it was the most ridiculous idea she'd ever heard in her life and I was crazy to think of such a thing."

"You must admit she was right."

"Quite. But she's going to marry me."

"It's madness."

"I daresay it is; but anyhow, we're going to see Lennox and ask him what he thinks about it."

The winter had broken at last; there was still snow on the hills, but in the valleys it was melted and on the lower slopes the birch trees were in bud all ready to burst into delicate leaf. The enchantment of spring was in the air. The sun was hot. Everyone felt alert and some felt happy. The old stagers who came only for the winter were making their plans to go south. Templeton and Ivy went to see Dr. Lennox together. They told him what they had in mind. He examined them; they were X-rayed and various tests were taken. Dr. Lennox fixed a day when he would tell them the results and in light of this discuss their proposal. Ashenden saw them just before they went to keep the appointment. They were anxious, but did their best to make a joke of it. Dr. Lennox showed them the results of his examinations and explained to them in plain language what their condition was.

"All that's very fine and large," said Templeton then, "but what we want to know is whether we can get married."

"It would be highly imprudent."

"We know that, but does it matter?"

"And criminal if you had a child."

"We weren't thinking of having one," said Ivy.

"Well, then I'll tell you in very few words how the matter stands. Then you must decide for yourselves."

Templeton gave Ivy a little smile and took her hand. The doctor went on.

"I don't think Miss Bishop will ever be strong enough to lead a normal life, but if she continues to live as she has been doing for the last eight years . . ."

"In sanatoriums?"

"Yes. There's no reason why she shouldn't live very comfortably, if not to a ripe old age, as long as any sensible person wants to live. The disease is quiescent. If she marries, if she attempts to live an ordinary life, the foci of infection may very well light up again, and what the results of that may be no one can foretell. So far as you are concerned, Templeton, I can put it even more shortly. You've seen the X-ray photos yourself. Your lungs are riddled with tubercle. If you marry you'll be dead in six months."

"And if I don't how long can I live?"

The doctor hesitated.

"Don't be afraid. You can tell me the truth."

"Two or three years."

"Thank you, that's all we wanted to know."

They went as they had come, hand in hand; Ivy was crying softly. No one knew what they said to one another; but when they came into luncheon they were radiant. They told Ashenden and Chester that they were going to be married as soon as they could get a licence. Then Ivy turned to Chester.

"I should so much like your wife to come up for my wedding. D'you think she would?"

"You're not going to be married here?"

"Yes. Our respective relations will only disapprove, so we're not going to tell them until it's all over. We shall ask Dr. Lennox to give me away."

She looked mildly at Chester, waiting for him to speak, for he had not answered her. The other two men watched him. His voice shook a little when he spoke.

"It's very kind of you to want her. I'll write and ask her."

When the news spread among the patients, though everyone congratulated them, most of them privately told one another that it was very injudicious; but when they learnt, as sooner or later everything that happened in the sanatorium was learnt, that Dr. Lennox had told Templeton that if he married he would be dead in six months, they were awed to silence. Even the dullest were moved at the thought of these two persons who loved one another so much that they were prepared to sacrifice their lives. A spirit of kindliness and goodwill descended on the sanatorium: people who hadn't been speaking spoke to one another again; others forgot for a brief space their own anxieties. Everyone seemed to share in the happiness of the happy pair. And it was not only the spring that filled those sick hearts with new hope, the great love that had taken possession of the man and the girl seemed to spread its effulgence on all that came near them. Ivy was quietly blissful; the excitement became her and she looked younger and prettier. Templeton seemed to walk on air. He laughed and joked as if he hadn't a care in the world. You would have said that he looked forward to long years of uninterrupted felicity. But one day he confided in Ashenden.

"This isn't a bad place, you know," he said. "Ivy's promised me that when I hand in my checks she'll come back here. She knows the people and she won't be so lonely."

"Doctors are often mistaken," said Ashenden. "If you live reasonably I don't see why you shouldn't go on for a long time yet."

"I'm only asking for three months. If I can only have that it'll be worth it."

Mrs. Chester came up two days before the wedding. She had not seen her husband for several months and they were shy with one another. It was easy to guess that when they were alone they felt awkward and constrained. Yet Chester did his best to shake off the depression that was now habitual and at all events at meal-times showed himself the jolly, hearty little fellow that he must have been before he fell ill. On the eve of the wedding day they all dined together, Templeton and Ashenden both sitting up for dinner; they drank champagne and stayed up till ten joking, laughing and enjoying themselves. The wedding took place next morning in the kirk. Ashenden was best man. Everyone in the sanatorium who could stand on his feet attended it. The newly married couple were setting out by car immediately after lunch. Patients, doctors and nurses assembled to see them off. Someone had tied an old shoe on the back of the car, and as Templeton and his wife came out of the door of the sanatorium rice was flung over them. A cheer was raised as they drove away, as they drove away to love and death. The crowd separated slowly. Chester and his wife went silently side by side. After they had gone a little way he shyly took her hand. Her heart seemed to miss a beat. With a sidelong glance she saw that his eyes were wet with tears.

"Forgive me, dear," he said. "I've been very unkind to you."

"I knew you didn't mean it," she faltered.

"Yes, I did. I wanted you to suffer because I was suffering. But not any more. All this about Templeton and Ivy Bishop—I don't know how to put it, it's made me see everything differently. I don't mind dying any more. I don't think death's very important, not so important as love. And I want you to live and be happy. I don't grudge you anything any more and I don't resent anything. I'm glad now it's me that must die and not you. I wish for you everything that's good in the world. I love you."

EPISODE

IT was quite a small party, because our hostess liked general conversation; we never sat down to dinner more than eight, and generally only six, and after dinner when we went up to the drawing-room the chairs were so arranged that it was impossible for two persons to go into a huddle in a corner and so break things up. I was glad on arriving to find that I knew everyone. There were two nice clever women besides our hostess and two men besides myself. One was my friend Ned Preston. Our hostess made it a point never to ask wives with their husbands, because she said each cramped the other's style and if they didn't like to come separately they needn't come at all. But since her food and her wine were good and the talk almost always entertaining they generally came. People sometimes accused her of asking husbands more often than wives, but she defended herself by saying that she couldn't possibly help it because more men were husbands than women were wives.

Ned Preston was a Scot, a good-humoured, merry soul, with a gift for telling a story, sometimes too lengthily, for he was uncommonly loquacious, but with dramatic intensity. He was a bachelor with a small income which sufficed for his modest needs, and in this he was lucky since he suffered from that form of chronic tuberculosis which may last for years without killing you, but which prevents you from working for your living. Now and then he would be ill enough to stay in bed for two or three weeks, but then he would get better and be as gay, cheerful and talkative as ever. I doubt whether he had enough money to live in an expensive sanatorium and he certainly hadn't the temperament to suit himself to its life. He was worldly. When he was well he liked to go out, out to lunch, out to dinner, and he liked to sit up late into the night smoking his pipe and drinking a good deal of whisky. If he had been content to live the life of an invalid he might have been alive now, but he wasn't; and who can blame him? He died at the age of fifty-five of a hæmorrhage which he had one night after coming home from some house where, he may well have flattered himself, he was the success of the party.

He had that febrile vitality that some consumptives have, and was always looking for an occupation to satisfy his desire for activity. I don't know how he heard that at Wormwood Scrubs they were in want of prison visitors, but the idea took his fancy, so he went to the Home Office and saw the official in charge of prisons to offer his services. The job is unpaid, and though a number of persons are willing to undertake it, either from compassion or curiosity, they are apt to grow tired of it, or find it takes up too much time, and the prisoners whose problems, interests and future they have been concerned with are left somewhat in the lurch. The Home Office people consequently are wary of taking on anyone who does not look as if he would persevere, and they make careful inquiries into the applicant's antecedents, character and general suitability. Then he is given a trial, is discreetly watched, and if the impression is unfavourable is politely thanked and told that his services are no longer required. But Ned Preston satisfied the dour and shrewd official who interviewed him that he was in every way reliable, and from the beginning he got on well with the governor, the warders and the prisoners. He was entirely lacking in class consciousness, so prisoners, whatever their station in life, felt at ease with him. He neither preached nor moralised. He had never done a criminal, or even a mean, thing in his life, but he treated the crime of the prisoners he had to deal with as though it were an illness like his own tuberculosis which was a nuisance you had to put up with, but which it did no good to talk about.

Wormwood Scrubs is a first offenders' prison and it is a building, grim and cold, of forbidding appearance. Ned took me over it once and I had goose-flesh as the gates were unlocked for us and we went in. We passed through the halls in which the men were working.

"If you see any pals of yours take no notice of them," Ned said to me. "They don't like it."

"Am I likely to see any pals of mine?" I asked drily.

"You never can tell. I shouldn't be surprised if you had had friends who'd passed bad cheques once too often or were caught in a compromising situation in one of the parks. You'd be surprised how often I run across chaps I've met out at dinner."

One of Ned's duties was to see prisoners through the first difficult days of their confinement. They were often badly shaken by their trial and sentence; and when, after the preliminary proceedings they had to go through on entering the jail, the stripping, the bath, the medical examination and the questioning, the getting into prison clothes, they were led into a cell and locked up, they were apt to break down. Sometimes they cried hysterically; sometimes they could neither eat nor sleep. Ned's business then was to cheer them, and his breezy manner, his natural kindliness, often worked wonders. If they were anxious about their wives and children he would go to see them and if they were destitute provide them with money. He brought them news so that they might get over the awful feeling that they were shut away from the common interests of their fellow men. He read the sporting papers to be able to tell them what horse had won an important race or whether the champion had won his fight. He would advise them about their future, and when the time approached for their release see what jobs they were fitted for and then persuade employers to give them a chance to make good.

Since everyone is interested in crime it was inevitable that sooner or later, with Ned there, the conversation should turn upon it. It was after dinner and we were sitting comfortably in the drawing-room with drinks in our hands.

"Had any interesting cases at the Scrubs lately, Ned?" I asked him.

"No, nothing much."

He had a high, rasping voice and his laugh was a raucous cackle. He broke into it now.

"I went to see an old girl to-day who was a packet of fun. Her husband's a burglar. The police have known about him for years, but they've never been able to get him till just now. Before he did a job he and his wife concocted an alibi, and though he's been arrested three or four times and sent up for trial, the police have never been able to break it and he's always got off. Well, he was arrested again a little while ago, but he wasn't upset, the alibi he and his wife had made up was perfect and he expected to be acquitted as he'd been before. His wife went into the witness-box and to his utter amazement she didn't give the alibi and he was convicted. I went to see him. He wasn't so much worried at being in jail as puzzled by his wife not having spoken up, and he asked me to go and see her and ask what the game was. Well, I went, and d'you know what she said to me? She said: 'Well, sir, it's like this; it was such a beautiful alibi I just couldn't bear to waste it.' "

Of course we all laughed. The story-teller likes an appreciative audience, and Ned Preston was never disinclined to hold the floor. He narrated two or three more anecdotes. They tended to prove a point he was fond of making, that in what till we all got democratic in England were called the lower orders there was more passion, more romance, more disregard of consequences than could ever be found in the well-to-do and presumably educated classes, whom prudence has made timid and convention inhibited.

"Because the working man doesn't read much," he said, "because he has no great gift for expressing himself, you think he has no imagination. You're wrong. He's extravagantly imaginative. Because he's a great husky brute you think he has no nerves. You're wrong again. He's a bundle of nerves."

Then he told us a story which I shall tell as best I can in my own words.

Fred Manson was a good-looking fellow, tall, well-made, with blue eyes, good features and a friendly, agreeable smile, but what made him remarkable so that people turned round in the streets to stare at him was that he had a thick head of hair, with a great wave in it, of a deep rich red. It was really a great beauty. Perhaps it was this that gave him so sensual a look. His maleness was like a heady perfume. His eyebrows were thick, only a little lighter than his hair, and he was lucky enough not to have the ugly skin that so often disfigures red-heads. His was a smooth olive. His eyes were bold, and when he smiled or laughed, which in the healthy vitality of his youth he did constantly, his expression was wonderfully alluring. He was twenty-two and he gave you the rather pleasant impression of just loving to be alive. It was inevitable that with such looks and above all with that troubling sexuality he should have success with women. He was charming, tender and passionate, but immensely promiscuous. He was not exactly callous or brazen, he had a kindly nature, but somehow or other he made it quite clear to the objects of his passing fancy that all he wanted was a little bit of fun and that it was impossible for him to remain faithful to anyone.

Fred was a postman. He worked in Brixton. It is a densely populated part of London, and has the curious reputation of harbouring more criminals than any other suburb because trams run to it from across the river all night long, so that when a man has done a job of housebreaking in the West End he can be sure of getting home without difficulty. Fred liked his job. Brixton is a district of innumerable streets lined with little houses inhabited by the people who work in the neighbourhood and also by clerks, shop-assistants, skilled workers of one sort or another whose jobs take them every day across the river. He was strong and healthy and it was a pleasure to him to walk from street to street delivering the letters. Sometimes there would be a postal packet to hand in or a registered letter that had to be signed for, and then he would have the opportunity of seeing people. He was a sociable creature. It was never long before he was well known on whatever round he was assigned to. After a time his job was changed. His duty then was to go to the red pillar-boxes into which the letters were put, empty them, and take the contents to the main post office of the district. His bag would be pretty heavy sometimes by the time he was through, but he was proud of his strength and the weight only made him laugh.

One day he was emptying a box in one of the better streets, a street of semi-detached houses, and had just closed his bag when a girl came running along.

"Postman," she cried, "take this letter, will you. I want it to go by this post most particularly."

He gave her his good-natured smile.

"I never mind obliging a lady," he said, putting down his bag and opening it.

"I wouldn't trouble you, only it's urgent," she said as she handed him the letter she had in her hand.

"Who is it to—a feller?" he grinned.

"None of your business."

"All right, be haughty. But I tell you this, he's no good. Don't you trust him."

"You've got a nerve," she said.

"So they tell me."

He took off his cap and ran his hand through his mop of curling red hair. The sight of it made her gasp.

"Where d'you get your perm?" she asked with a giggle.

"I'll show you one of these days if you like."

He was looking down at her with his amused eyes, and there was something about him that gave her a funny little feeling in the pit of her stomach.

"Well, I must be on my way," he said. "If I don't get on with the job pretty damn quick I don't know what'll happen to the country."

"I'm not detaining you," she said coolly.

"That's where you make a mistake," he answered.

He gave her a look that made her heart beat nineteen to the dozen and she felt herself blushing all over. She turned away and ran back to the house. Fred noticed it was four doors away from the pillar-box. He had to pass it and as he did so he looked up. He saw the net curtains twitch and knew she was watching. He felt pleased with himself. During the next few days he looked at the house whenever he passed it, but never caught a glimpse of the girl. One afternoon he ran across her by chance just as he was entering the street in which she lived.

"Hulloa," he said, stopping.

"Hulloa."

She blushed scarlet.

"Haven't seen you about lately."

"You haven't missed much."

"That's what you think."

She was prettier than he remembered, dark-haired, dark-eyed, rather tall, slight, with a good figure, a pale skin and very white teeth.

"What about coming to the pictures with me one evening?"

"Taking a lot for granted, aren't you?"

"It pays," he said with his impudent, charming grin.

She couldn't help laughing.

"Not with me, it doesn't."

"Oh, come on. One's only young once."

There was something so attractive in him that she couldn't bring herself to give him a saucy answer.

"I couldn't really. My people wouldn't like me going out with a fellow I don't know. You see, I'm the only one they have and they think a rare lot of me. Why, I don't even know your name."

"Well, I can tell you, can't I? Fred. Fred Manson. Can't you say you're going to the pictures with a girl friend?"

She had never felt before what she was feeling then. She didn't know if it was pain or pleasure. She was strangely breathless.

"I suppose I could do that."

They fixed the night, the time and the place. Fred was waiting for her and they went in, but when the picture started and he put his arm round her waist, without a word, her eyes fixed on the screen, she quietly took it away. He took hold of her hand, but she withdrew it. He was surprised. That wasn't the way girls usually behaved. He didn't know what one went to the pictures for if it wasn't to have a bit of a cuddle. He walked home with her after the show. She told him her name. Grace Carter. Her father had a shop of his own in the Brixton Road, he was a draper and he had four assistants.

"He must be doing well," said Fred.

"He doesn't complain."

Gracie was a student at London University. When she got her degree she was going to be a school teacher.

"What d'you want to do that for when there's a good business waiting for you?"

"Pa doesn't want me to have anything to do with the shop—not after the education he's given me. He wants me to better myself, if you know what I mean."

Her father had started life as an errand boy, then become a draper's assistant and because he was hard-working, honest and intelligent was now owner of a prosperous little business. Success had given him grand ideas for his only child. He didn't want her to have anything to do with trade. He hoped she'd marry a professional man perhaps, or at least someone in the City. Then he'd sell the business and retire, and Gracie would be quite the lady.

When they reached the corner of her street Gracie held out her hand.

"You'd better not come to the door," she said.

"Aren't you going to kiss me good-night?"

"I am not."

"Why?"

"Because I don't want to."

"You'll come to the pictures again, won't you?"

"I think I'd better not."

"Oh, come on."

There was such a warm urgency in his voice that she felt as though her knees would give way.

"Will you behave if I do?" He nodded. "Promise?"

"Swop me bob."

He scratched his head when he left her. Funny girl. He'd never met anyone quite like her. Superior, there was no doubt about that. There was something in her voice that got you. It was warm and soft. He tried to think what it was like. It was like as if the words kissed you. Sounded silly, that did, but that's just what it was like.

From then on they went to the pictures once or twice a week. After a while she allowed him to put his arm round her waist and to hold her hand, but she never let him go farther than that.

"Have you ever been kissed by a fellow?" he asked her once.

"No, I haven't," she said simply. "My ma's funny, she says you've got to keep a man's respect."

"I'd give anything in the world just to kiss you, Gracie."

"Don't be so silly."

"Won't you let me just once?" She shook her head. "Why not?"

8

"Because I like you too much," she said hoarsely, and then walked quickly away from him.

It gave him quite a turn. He wanted her as he'd never wanted a woman before. What she'd said finished him. He'd been thinking of her a lot, and he'd looked forward to the evenings they spent together as he'd never looked forward to anything in his life. For the first time he was uncertain of himself. She was above him in every way, what with her father making money hand over fist and her education and everything, and him only a postman. They had made a date for the following Friday night and he was in a fever of anxiety lest she shouldn't come. He repeated to himself over and over again what she'd said: perhaps it meant that she'd made up her mind to drop him. When at last he saw her walking along the street he almost sobbed with relief. That evening he neither put his arm round her nor took her hand and when he walked her home he never said a word.

"You're very quiet to-night, Fred," she said at last. "What's the matter with you?"

He walked a few steps before he answered.

"I don't like to tell you."

She stopped suddenly and looked up at him. There was terror on her face.

"Tell me whatever it is," she said unsteadily.

"I'm gone, I can't help myself, I'm so stuck on you I can't see straight. I didn't know what it was to love like I love you."

"Oh, is that all? You gave me such a fright. I thought you were going to say you were going to be married."

"Me? Who d'you take me for? It's you I want to marry."

"Well, what's to prevent you, silly?"

"Gracie! D'you mean it?"

He flung his arms round her and kissed her full on the mouth. She didn't resist. She returned his kiss and he felt in her a passion as eager as his own.

They arranged that Gracie should tell her parents that she was engaged to him and that on the Sunday he should come and be introduced to them. Since the shop stayed open late on Saturday and by the time Mr. Carter got home he was tired out, it was not till after dinner on Sunday that Gracie broke her news. George Carter was a brisk, not very tall man, but sturdy, with a high colour, who with increasing prosperity had put on weight. He was more than rather bald and he had a bristle of grey moustache. Like many another employer who has risen from the working class he was a slave-driver and he got as much work out of his assistants for as little money as was possible. He had an eye for everything and he wouldn't put up with any nonsense, but he was reasonable and even kindly, so that they did not dislike him. Mrs. Carter was a quiet, nice woman, with a pleasant face and the remains of good looks. They were both in the early fifties, for they had married late after "walking out" for nearly ten years.

They were very much surprised when Gracie told them what she had to tell, but not displeased.

"You are a sly one," said her father. "Why, I never suspected for a minute you'd taken up with anyone. Well, I suppose it had to come sooner or later. What's his name?"

"Fred Manson."

"A fellow you met at college?"

"No. You must have seen him about. He clears our pillar-box. He's a postman."

"Oh, Gracie," cried Mrs. Carter, "you can't mean it. You can't marry a common postman, not after all the education we've given you."

For an instant Mr. Carter was speechless. He got redder in the face than ever.

"Your ma's right, my girl," he burst out now. "You can't throw yourself away like that. Why, it's ridiculous."

"I'm not throwing myself away. You wait till you see him."

Mrs. Carter began to cry.

"It's such a come-down. It's such a humiliation. I shall never be able to hold up my head again."

"Oh, Ma, don't talk like that. He's a nice fellow and he's got a good job."

"You don't understand," she moaned.

"How d'you get to know him?" Mr. Carter interrupted. "What sort of a family's he got?"

"His pa drives one of the post-office vans," Gracie answered defiantly.

"Working-class people."

"Well, what of it? His pa's worked twenty-four years for the post office and they think a lot of him."

Mrs. Carter was biting the corner of her handkerchief.

"Gracie, I want to tell you something. Before your pa and me got married I was in domestic service. He wouldn't ever let me tell you because he didn't want you to be ashamed of me. That's why we was engaged all those years. The lady I was with said she'd leave me something in her will if I stayed with her till she passed away."

"It was that money that gave me my start," Mr. Carter broke in. "Except for that I'd never have been where I am to-day. And I don't mind telling you your ma's the best wife a man ever had."

"I never had a proper education," Mrs. Carter went on, "but I always was ambitious. The proudest moment of my life was when your pa said we could afford a girl to help me and he said then: 'The time'll come when you have a cook *and* a house-maid,' and he's been as good as his word, and now you're going back to what I come from. I'd set my heart on your marrying a gentleman."

She began crying again. Gracie loved her parents and couldn't bear to see them so distressed.

"I'm sorry, Ma, I knew it would be a disappointment to you,

but I can't help it, I can't really. I love him so, I love him so terribly. I'm sure you'll like him when you see him. We're going for a walk on the Common this afternoon. Can't I bring him back to supper?"

Mrs. Carter gave her husband a harassed look. He sighed.

"I don't like it and it's no good pretending I do, but I suppose we'd better have a look at him."

Supper passed off better than might have been expected. Fred wasn't shy, and he talked to Gracie's parents as though he had known them all his life. If to be waited on by a maid, if to sup in a dining-room furnished in solid mahogany and afterwards to sit in a drawing-room that had a grand piano in it was new to him, he showed no embarrassment. After he had gone and they were alone in their bedroom Mr. and Mrs. Carter talked him over.

"He is handsome, you can't deny that," she said.

"Handsome is as handsome does. D'you think he's after her money?"

"Well, he must know that you've got a tidy little bit tucked away somewhere, but he's in love with her all right."

"Oh, what makes you think that?"

"Why, you've only got to see the way he looks at her."

"Well, that's something at all events."

In the end the Carters withdrew their opposition on the condition that the young things shouldn't marry until Gracie had taken her degree. That would give them a year, and at the back of their minds was the hope that by then she would have changed her mind. They saw a good deal of Fred after that. He spent every Sunday with them. Little by little they began quite to like him. He was so easy, so gay, so full of high spirits, and above all so obviously head over ears in love with Gracie, that Mrs. Carter soon succumbed to his charm, and after a while even Mr. Carter was prepared to admit that he didn't seem a bad fellow. Fred and Gracie were happy. She went to London every day to attend lectures and worked hard. They spent blissful evenings together. He gave her a very nice engagement ring and often took her out to dinner in the West End and to a play. On fine Sundays he drove her out into the country in a car that he said a friend had lent him. When she asked him if he could afford all the money he spent on her he laughed, and said a chap had given him a tip on an outsider and he'd made a packet. They talked interminably of the little flat they would have when they were married and the fun it would be to furnish it. They were more in love with one another than ever.

Then the blow fell. Fred was arrested for stealing money from the letters he collected. Many people, to save themselves the trouble of buying postal orders, put notes in their envelopes, and it wasn't difficult to tell that they were there. Fred went up for trial, pleaded guilty, and was sentenced to two years' hard labour. Gracie went to the trial. Up to the last moment she had hoped that he would be able to prove his innocence. It was a dreadful shock to her when he pleaded guilty. She was not allowed to see him. He went straight from the dock to the prison van. She went home, and locking herself up in her bedroom, threw herself on the bed and wept. When Mr. Carter came back from the shop Gracie's mother went up to her room.

"Gracie, you're to come downstairs," she said. "Your father wants to speak to you."

Gracie got up and went down. She did not trouble to dry her eyes.

"Seen the paper?" he said, holding out to her the *Evening News*.

She didn't answer.

"Well, that's the end of that young man," he went on harshly.

They too, Gracie's parents, had been shocked when Fred was arrested, but she was so distressed, she was so convinced that everything could be explained, that they hadn't had the heart to tell her that she must have nothing more to do with him. But now they felt it time to have things out with her.

"So that's where the money came from for those dinners and theatres. And the car. I thought it funny he should have a friend who'd lend him a car on Sundays when he'd be wanting it himself. He hired it, didn't he?"

"I suppose so," she answered miserably. "I just believed what he told me."

"You've had a lucky escape, my girl, that's all I can say."

"He only did it because he wanted to give me a good time. He didn't want me to think I couldn't have everything as nice when I was with him as what I've been used to at home."

"You're not going to make excuses for him, I hope. He's a thief, that's what he is."

"I don't care," she said sullenly.

"You don't care? What d'you mean by that?"

"Exactly what I say. I'm going to wait for him and the moment he comes out I'm going to marry him."

Mrs. Carter gave a gasp of horror.

"Gracie, you can't do a thing like that," she cried. "Think of the disgrace. And what about us? We've always held our heads high. He's a thief, and once a thief always a thief."

"Don't go on calling him a thief," Gracie shrieked, stamping her foot with rage. "What he did he did just because he loved me. I don't care if he is a thief. I love him more than ever I loved him. You don't know what love is. You waited ten years to marry Pa just so as an old woman should leave you some money. D'you call that love?"

"You leave your ma out of this," Mr. Carter shouted. Then an idea occurred to him and he gave her a piercing glance. "Have you *got* to marry the feller?"

Gracie blushed furiously.

"No. There's never been anything of that sort. And not

through any fault of mine either. He loved me too much. He didn't want to do anything perhaps he'd regret afterwards."

Often on summer evenings in the country when they'd been lying in a field in one another's arms, mouth to mouth, her desire had been as intense as his. She knew how much he wanted her and she was ready to give him what he asked. But when things got too desperate he'd suddenly jump up and say:

"Come on, let's walk."

He'd drag her to her feet. She knew what was in his mind. He wanted to wait till they were married. His love had given him a delicacy of sentiment that he'd never known before. He couldn't make it out himself, but he had a funny sort of feeling about her, he felt that if he had her before marriage it would spoil things. Because she guessed what was in his heart she loved him all the more.

"I don't know what's come over you," moaned Mrs. Carter. "You was always such a good girl. You've never given us a day's uneasiness."

"Stop it, Ma," said Mr. Carter violently. "We've got to get this straight once and for all. You've got to give up this man, see? I've got me own position to think of and if you think I'm going to have a jail-bird for a son-in-law you'd better think again. I've had enough of this nonsense. You've got to promise me that you'll have nothing more to do with the feller ever."

"D'you think I'm going to give him up now? How often d'you want me to tell you I'm going to marry him the moment he gets out?"

"All right, then you can get out of my house and get out pretty damn quick. And stay out."

"Pa!" cried Mrs. Carter.

"Shut up."

"I'll be glad to go," said Gracie.

"Oh, will you? And how d'you think you're going to live?"

"I can work, can't I? I can get a job at Payne & Perkins. They'll be glad to have me."

"Oh, Gracie, you couldn't go and work in a shop. You can't demean yourself like that," said Mrs. Carter.

"Will you shut up, Ma," shouted Mr. Carter, beside himself now with rage. "Work, will you? You that's never done a stroke of work in your life except that tomfoolery at the college. Bright idea it was of your ma's to give you an education. Fat lot of good it'll be to you when you've got to stand on your feet for hours and got to be civil and pleasant to a lot of old trouts who just try and give you all the trouble they can just to show how superior they are. I bet you'll like it when you're bawled out by the manageress because you're not bright and snappy. All right, marry your jail-bird. I suppose you know you'll have to keep him too. You don't think anyone's going to give him a job, do you, not with his record. Get out, get out, get out."

He had worked himself up to such a pitch of fury that he sank panting into a chair. Mrs. Carter, frightened, poured out a glass of water and gave him some to drink. Gracie slipped out of the room.

Next day, when her father had gone to work, and her mother was out shopping, she left the house with such effects as she could get into a suitcase. Payne & Perkins was a large department store in the Brixton Road, and with her good appearance and pleasant manner she found no difficulty in getting taken on. She was put in the ladies' lingerie. For a few days she stayed at the Y.W.C.A. and then arranged to share a room with one of the girls who worked with her.

Ned Preston saw Fred in the evening of the day he went to jail. He found him shattered, but only because of Gracie. He took his thieving very lightly.

"I had to do the right thing by her, didn't I? Her people, they didn't think I was good enough for her; I wanted to show them I was just as good as they were. When we went up to the

8*

West End I couldn't give her a sandwich and half of bitter in a pub, why, she's never been in a pub in her life, I *had* to take her to a restaurant. If people are such fools as to put money in letters, well, they're just asking for it."

But he was frightened. He wasn't sure that Gracie would see it like that.

"I've got to know what she's going to do. If she chucks me now—well, it's the end of everything for me, see? I'll find some way of doing meself in, I swear to God I will."

He told Ned the whole story of his love for Gracie.

"I could have had her over and over again if I'd wanted to. And I did want to and so did she. I knew that. But I respected her, see? She's not like other girls. She's one in a thousand, I tell you."

He talked and talked. He stormed, he wept. From that confused torrent of words emerged one thing very clearly. A passionate, a frenzied love. Ned promised that he would see the girl.

"Tell her I love her, tell her that what I did I just did because I wanted her to have the best of everything, and tell her I just can't live without her."

As soon as he could find time Ned Preston went to the Carters' house, but when he asked for Gracie the maid who opened the door told him that she didn't live there any more. Then he asked to see her mother.

"I'll go and see if she's in."

He gave the maid his card, thinking the name of his club engraved in the corner would impress Mrs. Carter enough to make her willing to see him. The maid left him at the door, but in a minute or two asked him to come in. He was shown into the stiff and little-used sitting-room. Mrs. Carter kept him waiting for some time and when she came in, holding his card in the tips of her fingers, he guessed it was because she had thought fit to change her dress. The black silk she wore was

evidently a dress for occasions. He told her his connection
with Wormwood Scrubs, and said that he had to do with a
man named Frederick Manson. The moment he mentioned
the name Mrs. Carter assumed a hostile attitude.

"Don't speak to me of that man," she cried. "A thief, that's
what he is. The trouble he's caused us. They ought to have
given him five years, they ought."

"I'm sorry he's caused you trouble," said Ned mildly.
"Perhaps if you'd give me a few facts I might help to straighten
things out."

Ned Preston certainly had a way with him. Perhaps Mrs.
Carter was impressed because he was a gentleman. "Class he
is," she probably said to herself. Anyhow it was not long
before she was telling him the whole story. She grew upset as
she told it and began to cry.

"And now she's gone and left us. Run away. I don't know
how she could bring herself to do a thing like that. God knows,
we love her. She's all we've got and we done everything in the
world for her. Her pa never meant it when he told her to get
out of the house. Only she was so obstinate. He got in a
temper, he always was a quick-tempered man, he was just as
upset as I was when we found she'd gone. And d'you know
what she's been and gone and done? Got herself a job at Payne
& Perkins. Mr. Carter can't abide them. Cutting prices all the
time they are. Unfair competition, he calls it. And to think of
our Gracie working with a lot of shop-girls—oh, it's so
humiliating."

Ned made a mental note of the store's name. He hadn't been
at all sure of getting Gracie's address out of Mrs. Carter.

"Have you seen her since she left you?" he asked.

"Of course I have. I knew they'd jump at her at Payne &
Perkins, a superior girl like that, and I went there, and there
she was sure enough—in the ladies' lingerie. I waited outside
till closing time and then I spoke to her. I asked her to come

home. I said her pa was willing to let bygones be bygones. And d'you know what she said? She said she'd come home if we never said a word against Fred and if we was prepared to have her marry him as soon as ever he got out. Of course I had to tell her pa. I never saw him in such a state, I thought he was going to have a fit, he said he'd rather see her dead at his feet than married to that jail-bird."

Mrs. Carter again burst into tears and as soon as he could Ned Preston left her. He went to the department store, up to the ladies' lingerie, and asked for Grace Carter. She was pointed out to him and he went up to her.

"Can I speak to you for a minute? I've come from Fred Manson."

She went deathly white. For a moment it seemed that she could not utter a word.

"Follow me, please."

She took him into a passage smelling of disinfectants which seemed to lead to the lavatories. They were alone. She stared at him anxiously.

"He sends you his love. He's worried about you. He's afraid you're awfully unhappy. What he wants to know really is if you're going to chuck him."

"Me?" Her eyes filled with tears, but on her face was a look of ecstasy. "Tell him that nothing matters to me as long as he loves me. Tell him I'd wait twenty years for him if I had to. Tell him I'm counting the days till he gets out so as we can get married."

For fear of the manageress she couldn't stay away from her work for more than a minute or two. She gave Ned all the loving messages she could get into the time to give Fred Manson. Ned didn't get to the Scrubs till nearly six. The prisoners are allowed to put down their tools at five-thirty and Fred had just put his down. When Ned entered the cell he turned pale and sank on to the bed as though his anxiety was such that he didn't trust his legs. But when Ned told him his news he gave a gasp of relief. For a while he couldn't trust himself to speak.

"I knew you'd seen her the moment you came in. I smelt her."

He sniffed as though the smell of her body were strong in his nostrils, and his face was as it were a mask of desire. His features on a sudden seemed strangely blurred.

"You know, it made me feel quite uncomfortable so that I had to look the other way," said Ned Preston when he told us this, with a cackle of his shrill laughter. "It was sex in its nakedness all right."

Fred was an exemplary prisoner. He worked well, he gave no trouble. Ned suggested books for him to read and he took them out of the library, but that was about as far as he got.

"I can't get on well with them somehow," he said. "I start reading and then I begin thinking of Gracie. You know, when she kisses you ordinary like—oh, it's so sweet, but when she kisses you really, my God, it's lovely."

Fred was allowed to see Gracie once a month, but their meetings, with a glass screen between, under the eyes of a warder, were so painful that after several visits they agreed it would be better if she didn't come any more. A year passed. Owing to his good behaviour he could count on a remittance of his sentence and so would be free in another six months. Gracie had saved every penny she could out of her wages and now as the time approached for Fred's release she set about getting a home ready for him. She took two rooms in a house and furnished them on the hire-purchase system. One room of course was to be their bedroom and the other the living-room and kitchen. There was an old-fashioned range in it and this she had taken out and replaced by a gas-stove. She wanted everything to be nice and new and clean and comfortable. She took pains to make the two little rooms bright and pretty.

To do all this she had to go without all but the barest necessities of existence and she grew thin and pale. Ned suspected that she was starving herself and when he went to see her took a box of chocolates or a cake so that she should have at least something to eat. He brought the prisoner news of what Gracie was doing and she made him promise to give him accurate accounts of every article she bought. He took fond, more than fond, passionate messages from one to the other. He was convinced that Fred would go straight in future and he got him a job as commissionaire from a firm that had a chain of restaurants in London. The wages were good and by calling taxis or fetching cars he would be able to make money on the side. He was to start work as soon as he came out of jail. Gracie took the necessary steps so that they could get married at once. The eighteen months of Fred's imprisonment were drawing to an end. Gracie was in a fever of excitement.

It happened then that Ned Preston had one of his periodical bouts of illness and was unable to go to the prison for three weeks. It bothered him, for he didn't like to abandon his prisoners, so as soon as he could get out of bed he went to the Scrubs. The chief warder told him that Manson had been asking for him.

"I think you'd better go and see him. I don't know what's the matter with him. He's been acting rather funny since you've been away."

It was just a fortnight before Fred was due to be released. Ned Preston went to his cell.

"Well, Fred, how are you?" he asked. "Sorry I haven't been able to come and see you. I've been ill, and I haven't been able to see Gracie either. She must be all of a dither by now."

"Well, I want you to go and see her."

His manner was so surly that Ned was taken aback. It was unlike him to be anything but pleasant and civil.

"Of course I will."

"I want you to tell her that I'm not going to marry her."

Ned was so astounded that for a minute he could only stare blankly at Fred Manson.

"What on earth d'you mean?"

"Exactly what I say."

"You can't let her down now. Her people have thrown her out. She's been working all this time to get a home ready for you. She's got the licence and everything."

"I don't care. I'm not going to marry her."

"But why, why, why?"

Ned was flabbergasted. Fred Manson was silent for a bit. His face was dark and sullen.

"I'll tell you. I've thought about her night and day for eighteen months and now I'm sick to death of her."

When Ned Preston reached this point of his story our hostess and our fellow guests broke into loud laughter. He was plainly taken aback. There was some little talk after that and the party broke up. Ned and I, having to go in the same direction, walked along Piccadilly together. For a time we walked in silence.

"I noticed you didn't laugh with the others," he said abruptly.

"I didn't think it funny."

"What d'you make of it?"

"Well, I can see his point, you know. Imagination's an odd thing, it dries up; I suppose, thinking of her incessantly all that time he'd exhausted every emotion she could give him, and I think it was quite literally true, he'd just got sick to death of her. He'd squeezed the lemon dry and there was nothing to do but throw away the rind."

"I didn't think it funny either. That's why I didn't tell them the rest of the story. I wouldn't accept it at first. I thought it was just hysteria or something. I went to see him two or three days running. I argued with him. I really did my damnedest.

I thought if he'd only see her it would be all right, but he wouldn't even do that. He said he hated the sight of her. I couldn't move him. At last I had to go and tell her."

We walked on a little longer in silence.

"I saw her in that beastly, stinking corridor. She saw at once there was something the matter and she went awfully white. She wasn't a girl to show much emotion. There was something gracious and rather noble about her face. Tranquil. Her lips quivered a bit when I told her and she didn't say anything for a minute. When she spoke it was quite calmly, as though—well, as though she'd just missed a bus and would have to wait for another. As though it was a nuisance, you know, but nothing to make a song and dance about. 'There's nothing for me to do now but put my head in the gas-oven,' she said.

"And she did."

APPEARANCE AND REALITY

I DO not vouch for the truth of this story, but it was told me by a professor of French literature at an English university, and he was a man of too high a character, I think, to have told it to me unless it were true. His practice was to draw the attention of his students to three French writers who in his opinion combined the qualities that are the mainsprings of the French character. By reading them, he said, you could learn so much about the French people that, if he had the power, he would not trust such of our rulers as have to deal with the French nation to enter upon their offices till they had passed a pretty stiff examination on their works. They are Rabelais, with his *gauloiserie*, which may be described as the ribaldry that likes to call a spade something more than a bloody shovel; La Fontaine, with his *bon sens*, which is just horse sense; and finally Corneille with his *panache*. This is translated in the dictionaries as the plume, the plume the knight at arms wore on his helmet, but metaphorically it seems to signify dignity and bravado, display and heroism, vainglory and pride. It was *le panache* that made the French gentlemen at Fontenoy say to the officers of King George II, fire first, gentlemen; it was *le panache* that wrung from Cambronne's bawdy lips at Waterloo the phrase: the guard dies but never surrenders; and it is *le panache* that urges an indigent French poet awarded the Nobel prize, with a splendid gesture to give it all away. My professor was not a frivolous man and to his mind the story I am about to tell brought out so distinctly the three master qualities of the French that it had a high educational value.

I have called it *Appearance and Reality*. This is the title of what I suppose may be looked upon as the most important philosophical work that my country (right or wrong) produced in the nineteenth century. It is stiff, but stimulating reading, it is written in excellent English, with considerable humour, and even though the lay reader is unlikely to follow with understanding some of its very subtle arguments he has nevertheless the thrilling sensation of walking a spiritual tight-rope over a metaphysical abyss, and he ends the book with a comfortable feeling that nothing matters a hang anyway. There is no excuse for my making use of the title of so celebrated a book except that it so admirably suits my story. Though Lisette was a philosopher only in the sense in which we are all philosophers, that she exercised thought in dealing with the problems of existence, her feeling for reality was so strong and her sympathy for appearance so genuine that she might almost claim to have established that reconciliation of irreconcilables at which the philosophers have for so many centuries been aiming. Lisette was French, and she passed several hours of every working day dressing and undressing herself at one of the most expensive and fashionable establishments in Paris. A pleasant occupation for a young woman who was well aware that she had a lovely figure. She was in short a mannequin. She was tall enough to be able to wear a train with elegance and her hips were so slim that in sports clothes she could bring the scent of heather to your nostrils. Her long legs enabled her to wear pyjamas with distinction, and her slim waist, her little breasts, made the simplest bathing dress a ravishment. She could wear anything. She had a way of huddling herself in a chinchilla coat that made the most sensible persons admit that chinchilla was worth all the money it cost. Fat women, gross women, stumpy women, bony women, shapeless women, old women, plain women, sat in the spacious armchairs and because Lisette looked so sweet bought the clothes that so admirably suited her. She had large brown eyes, a large red mouth and a very clear but slightly freckled skin. It was difficult for her to preserve that haughty, sullen and coldly indifferent demeanour that appears to be essential to the mannequin as she sails in with deliberate steps, turns round slowly, and with an air of contempt for the universe equalled only by the camel's, sails out. There was the suspicion of a twinkle in Lisette's large brown eyes and her red lips seemed to tremble as though on the smallest provocation they would break into a smile. It was the twinkle that attracted the attention of Monsieur Raymond Le Sueur.

He was sitting in a spurious Louis XVI chair by the side of his wife (in another) who had induced him to come with her to see the private view of the spring fashions. This was a proof of Monsieur Le Sueur's amiable disposition, for he was an extremely busy man who, one would have thought, had many more important things to do than to sit for an hour and watch a dozen beautiful young women parade themselves in a bewildering variety of costumes. He could not have thought that any of them could possibly make his wife other than she was, and she was a tall, angular woman of fifty, with features considerably larger than life-size. He had not indeed married her for her looks, and she had never, even in the first delirious days of their honeymoon, imagined that he had. He had married her in order to combine the flourishing steel works of which she was the heiress with his equally flourishing manufactory of locomotives. The marriage had been a success. She had provided him with a son who could play tennis nearly as well as a professional, dance quite as well as a gigolo, and hold his own at bridge with any of the experts; and a daughter whom he had been able to dower sufficiently to marry to a very nearly authentic prince. He had reason to be proud of his children. By perseverance and a reasonable integrity he had prospered sufficiently to gain the controlling interest in a sugar refinery, a movie company, a firm that built motor-cars, and a newspaper; and finally he had been able to spend enough money to persuade the free and independent electorate of a certain district to send him to the Senate. He was a man of a dignified presence, a pleasing corpulence and a sanguine complexion, with a neat grey beard cut square, a bald head and a roll of fat at the back of his neck. You had no need to look at the red button that adorned his black coat to surmise that he was a person of consequence. He was a man who made up his mind quickly and when his wife left the dressmaker's to go and play bridge he parted from her saying that for the sake of exercise he would walk to the Senate where his duty to his country called him. He did not however go as far as this, but contented himself with taking his exercise up and down a back street into which he rightly surmised the young ladies of the dressmaker's establishment would emerge at the close of business hours. He had barely waited for a quarter of an hour when the appearance of a number of women in groups, some young and pretty, some not so young and far from pretty, apprised him that the moment for which he had been waiting was come, and in two or three minutes Lisette tripped into the street. The Senator was well aware that his appearance and his age made it unlikely that young women would find him attractive at first sight, but he had found that his wealth and his position counterbalanced these disadvantages. Lisette had a companion with her, which would possibly have embarrassed a man of less importance, but did not cause the Senator to hesitate for an instant; he went up to her, raising his hat politely but not so much as to show how bald he was, and bade her good evening.

"*Bon soir, Mademoiselle,*" he said with an ingratiating smile.

She gave him the shortest possible look and, her full red lips just trembling with a smile, stiffened; she turned her head away and breaking into conversation with her friend, walked on with a very good assumption of supreme indifference. Far from disconcerted, the Senator turned round and followed the two girls at a distance of a few yards. They walked along the little back street, turned into the boulevard and at the Place de la

Madeleine took a bus. The Senator was well satisfied. He had drawn a number of correct conclusions. The fact that she was obviously going home with a girl friend proved that she had no accredited admirer. The fact that she had turned away when he had accosted her showed that she was discreet and modest and well behaved, which he liked young women to be when they were pretty; and her coat and skirt, the plain black hat and the rayon stockings proclaimed that she was poor and therefore virtuous. In those clothes she looked just as attractive as in the splendid garments he had seen her wearing before. He had a funny little feeling in his heart. He had not had that peculiar sensation, pleasurable and yet oddly painful, for several years, but he recognised it at once.

"It's love, by blue," he muttered.

He had never expected to feel it again, and squaring his shoulders he walked on with a confident step. He walked to the offices of a private detective and there left instructions that inquiries should be made about a young person called Lisette, who worked as a mannequin at such and such an address; and then, remembering that at the Senate they were discussing the American Debt, took a cab to the impressive building, entered the library where there was an armchair he very much liked, and had a pleasant nap. The information he had asked for reached him three days later. It was cheap at the price. Mademoiselle Lisette Larion lived with a widowed aunt in a two-room apartment in the district of Paris known as the Batignolles. Her father, a wounded hero of the great war, had a *bureau de tabac* in a small country town in the south-west of France. The rent of the flat was two thousand francs. She led a regular life, but was fond of going to the pictures, was not known to have a lover, and was nineteen years old. She was well spoken of by the concierge of the apartments and well liked by her companions at the shop. Obviously she was a very respectable young woman and the Senator could not but think that she was eminently suited to solace the leisure moments of a man who wanted relaxation from the cares of state and the exacting pressure of Big Business.

It is unnecessary to relate in detail the steps that Monsieur Le Sueur took to achieve the end he had in view. He was too important and too busy to occupy himself with the matter personally, but he had a confidential secretary who was very clever at dealing with electors who had not made up their minds how to vote, and who certainly knew how to put before a young woman who was honest but poor the advantages that might ensue if she were lucky enough to secure the friendship of such a man as his employer. The confidential secretary paid the widowed aunt, Madame Saladin by name, a visit and told her that Monsieur Le Sueur, always abreast of the time, had lately begun to take an interest in films and was indeed about to engage in the production of a picture. (This shows how much a clever brain can make use of a fact that an ordinary person would have passed over as insignificant.) Monsieur Le Sueur had been struck by the appearance of Mademoiselle Lisette at the dressmaker's and the brilliant way she wore her clothes, and it had occurred to him that she might very well suit a part he had it in mind for her to play. (Like all intelligent people the Senator always stuck as close to the truth as he could.) The confidential secretary then invited Madame Saladin and her niece to a dinner where they could make one another's further acquaintance and the Senator could judge whether Mademoiselle Lisette had the aptitude for the screen that he suspected. Madame Saladin said she would ask her niece, but for her part seemed to think the suggestion quite reasonable.

When Madame Saladin put the proposition before Lisette and explained the rank, dignity and importance of their generous host, that young person shrugged her pretty shoulders disdainfully.

"*Cette vieille carpe*," she said, of which the not quite literal translation is: that old trout.

"What does it matter if he's an old trout if he gives you a part?" said Madame Saladin.

"*Et ta sœur*," said Lisette.

This phrase, which of course means: and your sister, and sounds harmless enough, and even pointless, is a trifle vulgar and is used by well-brought-up young women, I think, only if they want to shock. It expresses the most forcible unbelief, and the only correct translation into the vernacular is too coarse for my chaste pen.

"Anyhow we should get a slap-up dinner," said Madame Saladin. "After all, you're not a child any more."

"Where did he say we should dine?"

"The Château de Madrid. Everyone knows it's the most expensive restaurant in the world."

There is no reason why it should not be. The food is very good, the cellar is famous, and its situation makes it on a fine evening of early summer an enchanting place to eat at. A very pretty dimple appeared on Lisette's cheek, and a smile on her large red mouth. She had perfect teeth.

"I can borrow a dress from the shop," she murmured.

A few days later the Senator's confidential secretary fetched them in a taxi and drove Madame Saladin and her engaging niece to the Bois de Boulogne. Lisette looked ravishing in one of the firm's most successful models and Madame Saladin extremely respectable in her own black satin and a hat that Lisette had made for the occasion. The secretary introduced the ladies to Monsieur Le Sueur who greeted them with the benign dignity of the politician who is behaving graciously to the wife and daughter of a valued constituent; and this is exactly what in his astute way he thought people at adjacent tables who knew him would imagine his guests to be. The dinner passed off very agreeably, and less than a month later

Lisette moved into a charming little flat at a convenient distance both from her place of business and from the Senate. It was decorated in the modern style by a fashionable upholsterer. Monsieur Le Sueur wished Lisette to continue to work. It suited him very well that she should have something to do during the hours that he was obliged to devote to affairs, for it would keep her out of mischief, and he very well knew that a woman who has nothing to do all day spends much more money than one who has an occupation. An intelligent man thinks of these things.

But extravagance was a vice to which Lisette was strange. The Senator was fond and generous. It was a source of satisfaction to him that Lisette began very soon to save money. She ran her apartment with thrift and bought her clothes at trade prices, and every month sent a certain sum home to her heroic father who purchased little plots of land with it. She continued to lead a quiet and modest life and Monsieur Le Sueur was pleased to learn from the concierge, who had a son she wanted to place in a government office, that Lisette's only visitors were her aunt and one or two girls from the shop.

The Senator had never been happier in his life. It was very satisfactory to him to think that even in this world a good action had its reward, for was it not from pure kindness that he had accompanied his wife to the dressmaker's on that afternoon when they were discussing the American Debt at the Senate and thus seen for the first time the charming Lisette? The more he knew her the more he doted on her. She was a delightful companion. She was gay and debonair. Her intelligence was respectable and she could listen cleverly when he discussed business matters or affairs of state with her. She rested him when he was weary and cheered him when he was depressed. She was glad to see him when he came, and he came frequently, generally from five till seven, and sorry when he went away. She gave him the impression that he was not only her lover but her friend. Sometimes they dined together in her apartment, and the well-appointed meal, the genial comfort, gave him a keen appreciation of the charm of domesticity. His friends told the Senator he looked twenty years younger. He felt it. He was conscious of his good fortune. He could not but feel, however, that after a life of honest toil and public service it was only his due.

It was thus a shock to him, after things had been proceeding so happily for nearly two years, on coming back to Paris early one Sunday morning unexpectedly after a visit to his constituency which was to last over the week-end, when he let himself into the apartment with his latchkey, thinking since it was the day of rest to find Lisette in bed, to discover her having breakfast in her bedroom *tête-à-tête* with a young gentleman he had never seen before who was wearing his (the Senator's) brand new pyjamas. Lisette was surprised to see him. Indeed she gave a distinct start.

"*Tiens*," she said. "Where have you sprung from? I didn't expect you till to-morrow."

"The Ministry has fallen," he answered mechanically. "I have been sent for. I am to be offered the Ministry of the Interior." But that was not what he wanted to say at all. He gave the gentleman who was wearing his pyjamas a furious look. "Who is that young man?" he cried.

Lisette's large red mouth broke into a most alluring smile.

"My lover," she answered.

"Do you think I'm a fool?" shouted the Senator. "I know he's your lover."

"Why do you ask then?"

Monsieur Le Sueur was a man of action. He went straight up to Lisette and smacked her hard on her right cheek with his left hand and then smacked her hard on the left cheek with his right hand.

"Brute," screamed Lisette.

He turned to the young man who had watched this scene of violence with some embarrassment and, drawing himself to his full height, flung out his arm and with a dramatic finger pointed to the door.

"Get out," he cried. "Get out."

One would have thought, such was the commanding aspect of a man who was accustomed to sway a crowd of angry tax-payers and who could dominate with his frown an annual meeting of disappointed shareholders, that the young man would have made a bolt for the door; but he stood his ground, irresolutely it is true, but he stood his ground; he gave Lisette an appealing look and slightly shrugged his shoulders.

"What are you waiting for?" shouted the Senator. "Do you want me to use force?"

"He can't go out in his pyjamas," said Lisette.

"They're not his pyjamas, they're my pyjamas."

"He's waiting for his clothes."

Monsieur Le Sueur looked round and on the chair behind him, flung down in a disorderly fashion, was a variety of masculine garments. The Senator gave the young man a look of contempt.

"You may take your clothes, Monsieur," he said with cold disdain.

The young man picked them up in his arms, gathered up the shoes that were lying about the floor, and quickly left the room. Monsieur Le Sueur had a considerable gift of oratory. Never had he made better use of it than now. He told Lisette what he thought of her. It was not flattering. He painted her in-gratitude in the blackest colours. He ransacked an extensive vocabulary in order to find opprobrious names to call her. He called all the powers of heaven to witness that never had a woman repaid with such gross deception an honest man's belief in her. In short he said everything that anger, wounded vanity and disappointment suggested to him. Lisette did not seek to defend herself. She listened in silence, looking down and mechanically crumbling the roll which the Senator's appearance had prevented her from finishing. He flung an irritated glance at her plate.

"I was so anxious that you should be the first to hear my great news that I came straight here from the station. I was expecting to have my *pétit dejeuner* with you, sitting at the end of your bed."

"My poor dear, haven't you had your breakfast? I'll order some for you at once."

"I don't want any."

"Nonsense. With the great responsibility you are about to assume you must keep up your strength."

She rang and when the maid came told her to bring in hot coffee. It was brought and Lisette poured it out. He would not touch it. She buttered a roll. He shrugged his shoulders and began to eat. Meanwhile he uttered a few remarks on the perfidy of women. She remained silent.

"At all events it is something," he said, "that you have not the effrontery to attempt to excuse yourself. You know that I am not a man who can be ill-used with impunity. The soul of generosity when people behave well to me I am pitiless when they behave badly. The very moment I have drunk my coffee I shall leave this apartment for ever."

Lisette sighed.

"I will tell you now that I had prepared a surprise for you. I had made up my mind to celebrate the second anniversary of our union by settling a sum of money on you sufficient to give you a modest independence if anything happened to me."

"How much?" asked Lisette sombrely.

"A million francs."

She sighed again. Suddenly something soft hit the Senator on the back of the head and he gave a start.

"What is that?" he cried.

"He's returning your pyjamas."

The young man had opened the door, flung the pyjamas at the Senator's head, and quickly closed it again. The Senator disengaged himself from the silk trousers that clung round his neck.

"What a way to return them! It is obvious that your friend has no education."

"Of course he has not your distinction," murmured Lisette.

"And has he my intelligence?"

"Oh, no."

"Is he rich?"

"Penniless."

"Then, name of a name, what is it you see in him?"

"He's young," smiled Lisette.

The Senator looked down at his plate and a tear rose in his eyes and rolled down his cheek into the coffee. Lisette gave him a kindly look.

"My poor friend, one can't have everything in this life," she said.

"I knew I was not young. But my situation, my fortune, my vitality. I thought it made up. There are women who only like men of a certain age. There are celebrated actresses who look upon it as an honour to be the little friend of a Minister. I am too well brought up to throw your origins in your face, but the fact remains that you are a mannequin and I took you out of an apartment of which the rent is only two thousand francs a year. It was a step up for you."

"The daughter of poor but honest parents, I have no reason to be ashamed of my origins, and it is not because I have earned my living in a humble sphere that you have the right to reproach me."

"Do you love this boy?"

"Yes."

"And not me?"

"You too. I love you both, but I love you differently. I love you because you are so distinguished and your conversation is instructive and interesting. I love you because you are kind and generous. I love him because his eyes are so big and his hair waves and he dances divinely. It's very natural."

"You know that in my position I cannot take you to places where they dance and I daresay when he's as old as I am he'll have no more hair than I have."

"That may well be true," Lisette agreed, but she did not think it much mattered.

"What will your aunt, the respectable Madame Saladin, say to you when she hears what you have done?"

"It will not be exactly a surprise to her."

"Do you mean to say that worthy woman countenances your conduct? *O tempora, o mores!* How long then has this been going on?"

"Since I first went to the shop. He travels for a big silk firm in Lyons. He came in one day with his samples. We liked the look of one another."

"But your aunt was there to defend you from the temptations to which a young girl is exposed in Paris. She should never have allowed you to have anything to do with this young man."

"I did not ask her permission."

"It is enough to bring the grey hairs of your poor father to the grave. Had you no thought of that wounded hero whose services to his country have been rewarded with a licence to sell tobacco? Do you forget that as Minister of the Interior the department is under my control? I should be within my rights if I revoked the licence on account of your flagrant immorality."

"I know you are too great a gentleman to do a dastardly thing like that."

He waved his hand in an impressive, though perhaps too dramatic a manner.

"Don't be afraid, I will never stoop so low as to revenge

myself on one who has deserved well of his country for the misdeeds of a creature my sense of dignity forces me to despise."

He went on with his interrupted breakfast. Lisette did not speak and there was silence between them. But his appetite satisfied, his mood changed; he began to feel sorry for himself rather than angry with her, and with a strange ignorance of woman's heart he thought to arouse Lisette's remorse by exhibiting himself as an object of pity.

"It is hard to break a habit to which one has grown accustomed. It was a relief and a solace to me to come here when I could snatch a moment from my many occupations. Will you regret me a little, Lisette?"

"Of course."

He gave a deep sigh.

"I should never have thought you capable of so much deception."

"It is the deception that rankles," she murmured thoughtfully. "Men are funny in that way. They cannot forgive being made fools of. It is because they are so vain. They attach importance to things that are of no consequence."

"Do you call it a matter of no consequence that I should find you having breakfast with a young man wearing my pyjamas?"

"If he were my husband and you were my lover you would think it perfectly natural."

"Obviously. For then I should be deceiving him and my honour would be secure."

"In short I have only to marry him to make the situation perfectly regular."

For a moment he did not understand. Then her meaning flashed across his clever brain and he gave her a quick look. Her lovely eyes had the twinkle he always found so alluring and on her large red mouth was the suspicion of a roguish smile.

"Do not forget that as a member of the Senate I am by all the traditions of the Republic the authorised mainstay of morality and good behaviour."

"Does that weigh very heavily with you?"

He stroked his handsome square beard with a composed and dignified gesture.

"Not a row of beans," he replied, but the expression he used had a Gallic breadth that would perhaps have given his more conservative supporters something of a shock.

"Would he marry you?" he asked.

"He adores me. Of course he would marry me. If I told him I had a *dot* of a million francs he would ask nothing better."

Monsieur Le Sueur gave her another look. When in a moment of anger he told her it had been his intention to settle a million francs on her he had exaggerated a good deal in the desire to make her see how much her treachery was costing her. But he was not the man to draw back when his dignity was concerned.

"It is much more than a young man in his position of life could aspire to. But if he adores you he would be always at your side."

"Didn't I tell you that he was a commercial traveller? He can only come to Paris for the week-end."

"That of course is a horse of another colour," said the Senator. "It would naturally be a satisfaction to him to know that during his absence I should be there to keep an eye on you."

"A considerable satisfaction," said Lisette.

To facilitate the conversation she rose from her seat and made herself comfortable on the Senator's knees. He pressed her hand tenderly.

"I am very fond of you, Lisette," he said. "I should not like you to make a mistake. Are you sure he will make you happy?"

"I think so."

"I will have proper enquiries made. I would never consent to

your marrying anyone not of exemplary character and unimpeachable morality. For all our sakes we must make quite
sure about this young man whom we are preparing to bring
into our lives."

Lisette raised no objection. She was aware that the Senator
liked to do things with order and method. He now prepared to
leave her. He wanted to break his important news to Madame
Le Sueur, and he had to get in touch with various persons in the
parliamentary group to which he belonged.

"There is only one more thing," he said, as he bade Lisette
an affectionate farewell, "if you marry I must insist on your
giving up your work. The place of a wife is the home, and it is
against all my principles that a married woman should take the
bread out of a man's mouth."

Lisette reflected that a strapping young man would look
rather funny walking round the room, with his hips swaying,
to show off the latest models, but she respected the Senator's
principles.

"It shall be as you wish, darling," she said.

The enquiries he made were satisfactory and the marriage
took place on a Saturday morning as soon as the legal formalities were completed. Monsieur Le Sueur, Minister of the
Interior, and Madame Saladin were witnesses. The bridegroom
was a slim young man with a straight nose, fine eyes and black
waving hair brushed straight back from his forehead. He
looked more like a tennis-player than a traveller in silk. The
Mayor, impressed by the august presence of the Minister of the
Interior, made according to French practice a speech which he
sought to render eloquent. He began by telling the married
couple what presumably they knew already. He informed the
bridegroom that he was the son of worthy parents and was
engaged in an honourable profession. He congratulated him on
entering the bonds of matrimony at an age when many young
men thought only of their pleasures. He reminded the bride

that her father was a hero of the great war, whose glorious wounds had been rewarded by a concession to sell tobacco, and he told her that she had earned a decent living since her arrival in Paris in an establishment that was one of the glories of French taste and luxury. The Mayor was of a literary turn and he briefly mentioned various celebrated lovers of fiction. Romeo and Juliet whose short but legitimate union had been interrupted by a regrettable misunderstanding, Paul and Virginia who had met her death at sea rather than sacrifice her modesty by taking off her clothes, and finally Daphnis and Chloe who had not consummated their marriage till it was sanctioned by the legitimate authority. He was so moving that Lisette shed a few tears. He paid a compliment to Madame Saladin whose example and precept had preserved her young and beautiful niece from the dangers that are likely to befall a young girl alone in a great city, and finally he congratulated the happy pair on the honour that the Minister of the Interior had done them in consenting to be a witness at the ceremony. It was a testimony to their own probity that this captain of industry and eminent statesman should find time to perform a humble office to persons in their modest sphere, and it proved not only the excellence of his heart but his lively sense of duty. His action showed that he appreciated the importance of early marriage, affirmed the security of the family and emphasised the desirability of producing offspring to increase the power, influence and consequence of the fair land of France. A very good speech indeed.

The wedding breakfast was held at the Château de Madrid which had sentimental associations for Monsieur Le Sueur. It has been mentioned already that among his many interests the Minister (as we must now call him) was interested in a firm of motor-cars. His wedding present to the bridegroom was a very nice two-seater of his own manufacture, and in this, when lunch was over, the young couple started off for their honeymoon.

9

This could only last over the week-end since the young man had to get back to his work which would take him to Marseilles, Toulon and Nice. Lisette kissed her aunt and she kissed Le Sueur.

"I shall expect you at five on Monday," she whispered to him.

"I shall be there," he answered.

They drove away and for a moment Monsieur Le Sueur and Madame Saladin looked at the smart yellow roadster.

"As long as he makes her happy," sighed Madame Saladin, who was not used to champagne at lunch and felt unreasonably melancholy.

"If he does not make her happy he will have me to count with," said Monsieur Le Sueur impressively.

His car drove up.

"*Au revoir, chère Madame.* You will get a bus at the Avenue de Neuilly."

He stepped into his car and as he thought of the affairs of state that awaited his attention he sighed with content. It was evidently much more fitting to his situation that his mistress should be, not just a little mannequin in a dressmaker's shop, but a respectable married woman.

THE UNCONQUERED

HE came back into the kitchen. The man was still on the floor, lying where he had hit him, and his face was bloody. He was moaning. The woman had backed against the wall and was staring with terrified eyes at Willi, his friend, and when he came in she gave a gasp and broke into loud sobbing. Willi was sitting at the table, his revolver in his hand, with a half empty glass of wine beside him. Hans went up to the table, filled his glass and emptied it at a gulp.

"You look as though you'd had trouble, young fellow," said Willi with a grin.

Hans's face was blood-stained and you could see the gashes of five sharp finger-nails. He put his hand gingerly to his cheek.

"She'd have scratched my eyes out if she could, the bitch. I shall have to put some iodine on. But she's all right now. You go along."

"I don't know. Shall I? It's getting late."

"Don't be a fool. You're a man, aren't you? What if it is getting late? We lost our way."

It was still light and the westering sun streamed into the kitchen windows of the farm-house. Willi hesitated a moment. He was a little fellow, dark and thin-faced, a dress designer in civil life, and he didn't want Hans to think him a cissy. He got up and went towards the door through which Hans had come. When the woman saw what he was going to do she gave a shriek and sprang forwards.

"*Non. Non,*" she cried.

With one step Hans was in front of her. He seized her by the shoulders and flung her violently back. She tottered and fell. He took Willi's revolver.

253

"Stop still, both of you," he rasped in French, but with his guttural German accent. He nodded his head towards the door. "Go on. I'll look after them."

Willi went out, but in a moment was back again.

"She's unconscious."

"Well, what of it?"

"I can't. It's no good."

"Stupid, that's what you are. *Ein Weibchen*. A woman." Willi flushed.

"We'd better be getting on our way."

Hans shrugged a scornful shoulder.

"I'll just finish the bottle of wine and then we'll go."

He was feeling at ease and it would have been pleasant to linger. He had been on the job since morning and after so many hours on his motor-cycle his limbs ached. Luckily they hadn't far to go, only to Soissons—ten or fifteen kilometres. He wondered if he'd have the luck to get a bed to sleep in. Of course all this wouldn't have happened if the girl hadn't been a fool. They had lost their way, he and Willi, they had stopped a peasant working in a field and he had deliberately misled them, and they found themselves on a side road. When they came to the farm they stopped to ask for a direction. They'd asked very politely, for orders were to treat the French population well as long as they behaved themselves. The door was opened for them by the girl and she said she didn't know the way to Soissons, so they pushed in; then the woman, her mother, Hans guessed, told them. The three of them, the farmer, his wife and daughter, had just finished supper and there was a bottle of wine on the table. It reminded Hans that he was as thirsty as the devil. The day had been sweltering and he hadn't had a drink since noon. He asked them for a bottle of wine and Willi had added that they would pay them well for it. Willi was a good little chap, but soft. After all, they were the victors. Where was the French army? In headlong flight. And the

English, leaving everything behind, had scuttled like rabbits back to their island. The conquerors took what they wanted, didn't they? But Willi had worked at a Paris dressmaker's for two years. It's true he spoke French well, that's why he had his present job, but it had done something to him. A decadent people. It did a German no good to live among them.

The farmer's wife put a couple of bottles of wine on the table and Willi took twenty francs out of his pocket and gave it to her. She didn't even say thank you. Hans's French wasn't as good as Willi's, but he could make himself understood, and he and Willi spoke it together all the time. Willi corrected his mistakes. It was because Willi was so useful to him in this way that he had made him his friend, and he knew that Willi admired him. He admired him because he was so tall, slim and broad-shouldered, because his curly hair was so fair and his eyes so blue. He never lost an opportunity to practise his French, and he tried to talk now but those three French people wouldn't meet him half-way. He told them that he was a farmer's son himself and when the war was over was going back to the farm. He had been sent to school in Munich because his mother wanted him to go into business, but his heart wasn't in it, and so after matriculating he had gone to an agricultural college.

"You came here to ask your way and now you know it," said the girl. "Drink up your wine and go."

He had hardly looked at her before. She wasn't pretty, but she had fine dark eyes and a straight nose. Her face was very pale. She was plainly dressed, but somehow she didn't look quite like what she evidently was. There was a sort of distinction about her. Ever since the war started he'd heard fellows talk about the French girls. They had something the German girls hadn't. Chic, Willi said it was, but when he asked him just what he meant by that Willi could only say that you had to see it to understand. Of course he'd heard others say that they were mercenary and hard as nails. Well, they'd be in Paris in a week and he'd find out for himself. They said the High Command had already arranged for houses for the men to go to.

"Finish your wine and let's go," said Willi.

But Hans was feeling comfortable and didn't want to be hurried.

"You don't look like a farmer's daughter," he said to the girl.

"And so what?" she answered.

"She's a teacher," said her mother.

"Then you've had a good education." She shrugged her shoulders, but he went on good-humouredly in his bad French. "You ought to understand that this is the best thing that has ever happened to the French people. We didn't declare war. You declared war. And now we're going to make France a decent country. We're going to put order into it. We're going to teach you to work. You'll learn obedience and discipline."

She clenched her fists and looked at him, her eyes black with hatred. But she did not speak.

"You're drunk, Hans," said Willi.

"I'm as sober as a judge. I'm only telling them the truth and they may just as well know it at once."

"He's right," she cried out, unable any longer to contain herself. "You're drunk. Now go. Go."

"Oh, you understand German, do you? All right, I'll go. But you must give me a kiss first."

She took a step back to avoid him, but he seized her wrist.

"Father," she cried. "Father."

The farmer flung himself on the German. Hans let go of her and with all his might hit him in the face. He crumpled up on the floor. Then, before she could escape him, he caught the girl in his arms. She gave him a swinging blow on the cheek. . . . He chuckled grimly.

"Is that how you take it when a German soldier wants to kiss you? You'll pay for this."

With his great strength he pinioned her arms and was dragging her out of the door, but her mother rushed at him and catching him by the clothes tried to pull him away. With one arm holding the girl close to him, with the flat of his other hand he gave the woman a great push and she staggered back to the wall.

"Hans, Hans," cried Willi.

"Shut up, damn you."

He put his hands over the girl's mouth to stop her shrieking and carried her out of the room. That was how it had happened and you had to admit that she'd brought it on herself. She shouldn't have slapped him. If she'd given him the kiss he'd asked for he'd have gone away. He gave a glance at the farmer still lying where he had fallen and he could hardly help laughing at his funny face. There was a smile in his eyes when he looked at the woman cowering against the wall. Was she afraid it was her turn next? Not likely. He remembered a French proverb.

"*C'est le premier pas qui coûte.* There's nothing to cry about, old woman. It had to come sooner or later." He put his hand to his hip pocket and pulled out a wallet. "Look, here's a hundred francs so that mademoiselle can buy herself a new dress. There's not much left of that one." He placed the note on the table and put his helmet back on his head. "Let's go."

They slammed the door behind them and got on their motor-cycles. The woman went into the parlour. Her daughter was lying on the divan. She was lying as he had left her and she was weeping bitterly.

Three months later Hans found himself in Soissons again. He had been in Paris with the conquering army and had ridden through the Arc de Triomphe on his motor-cycle. He had advanced with the army first to Tours and then to Bordeaux. He'd seen very little fighting. The only French soldiers he'd seen were prisoners. The campaign had been the greatest spree he could ever have imagined. After the armistice he had spent a month in Paris. He'd sent picture postcards to his family in Bavaria and bought them all presents. Willi, because he knew the city like the palm of his hand, had stayed on, but he and the rest of his unit were sent to Soissons to join the force that was holding it. It was a nice little town and he was comfortably billeted. Plenty to eat and champagne for less than a mark a bottle in German money. When he was ordered to proceed there it had occurred to him that it would be fun to go and have a look at the girl he'd had. He'd take her a pair of silk stockings to show there was no ill-feeling. He had a good bump of locality and he thought he would be able to find the farm without difficulty. So one afternoon, when he had nothing to do, he put the silk stockings in his pocket and got on his machine. It was a lovely autumn day, with hardly a cloud in the sky, and it was pretty, undulating country that he rode through. It had been fine and dry for so long that, though it was September, not even the restless poplars gave sign that the summer was drawing to an end. He took one wrong turning, which delayed him, but for all that he got to the place he sought in less than half an hour. A mongrel dog barked at him as he walked up to the door. He did not knock, but turned the handle and stepped in. The girl was sitting at the table peeling potatoes. She sprang to her feet when she saw the uniformed man.

"What d'you want?" Then she recognised him. She backed to the wall, clutching the knife in her hands. "It's you. *Cochon.*"

"Don't get excited. I'm not going to hurt you. Look, I've brought you some silk stockings."

"Take them away and take yourself off with them."

"Don't be silly. Drop that knife. You'll only get hurt if you try to be nasty. You needn't be afraid of me."

"I'm not afraid of you," she said.

She let the knife fall to the floor. He took off his helmet and sat down. He reached out with his foot and drew the knife towards him.

"Shall I peel some of your potatoes for you?" She did not answer. He bent down for the knife and then took a potato out of the bowl and went to work on it. Her face hard, her eyes hostile, she stood against the wall and watched him. He smiled at her disarmingly. "Why do you look so cross? I didn't do you much harm, you know. I was excited, we all were, they'd talked of the invincible French army and the Maginot line . . ." he finished the sentence with a chuckle. "And the wine went to my head. You might have fared worse. Women have told me that I'm not a bad-looking fellow."

She looked him up and down scornfully.

"Get out of here."

"Not until I choose."

"If you don't go my father will go to Soissons and complain to the general."

"Much he'll care. Our orders are to make friends with the population. What's your name?"

"That's not your business."

There was a flush in her cheeks now and her angry eyes were blazing. She was prettier than he remembered her. He hadn't done so badly. She had a refinement that suggested the city dweller rather than the peasant. He remembered her mother saying she was a teacher. Because she was almost a lady it amused him to torment her. He felt strong and healthy. He passed his hand through his curly blond hair, and giggled when he thought that many girls would have jumped at the chance she had had. His face was so deeply tanned by the summer that his eyes were startlingly blue.

"Where are your father and mother?"

"Working in the fields."

"I'm hungry. Give me a bit of bread and cheese and a glass of wine. I'll pay."

9*

She gave a harsh laugh.

"We haven't seen cheese for three months. We haven't enough bread to stay our hunger. The French took our horses a year ago and now the Boches have taken our cows, our pigs, our chickens, everything."

"Well, they paid you for them."

"Can we eat the worthless paper they gave us?"

She began to cry.

"Are you hungry?"

"Oh, no," she answered bitterly, "we can eat like kings on potatoes and bread and turnip and lettuce. To-morrow my father's going to Soissons to see if he can buy some horse meat."

"Listen, Miss. I'm not a bad fellow. I'll bring you a cheese, and I think I can get hold of a bit of ham."

"I don't want your presents. I'll starve before I touch the food you swine have stolen from us."

"We'll see," he said good-humouredly.

He put on his hat, got up, and with an *au revoir, mademoiselle*, walked out.

He wasn't supposed to go joy-riding round the country and he had to wait to be sent on an errand before he was able to get to the farm again. It was ten days later. He walked in as unceremoniously as before and this time he found the farmer and his wife in the kitchen. It was round about noon and the woman was stirring a pot on the stove. The man was seated at table. They gave him a glance when he came in, but there was no surprise in it. Their daughter had evidently told them of his visit. They did not speak. The woman went on with her cooking, and the man, a surly look on his face, stared at the oil-cloth on the table. But it required more than this to disconcert the good-humoured Hans.

"*Bonjour, la compagnie*," he said cheerfully. "I've brought you a present."

He undid the package he had with him and set out a sizable piece of gruyère cheese, a piece of pork and a couple of tins of sardines. The woman turned round and he smiled when he saw the light of greed in her eyes. The man looked at the foodstuff sullenly. Hans gave him his sunny grin.

"I'm sorry we had a misunderstanding the first time I came here. But you shouldn't have interfered."

At that moment the girl came in.

"What are you doing here?" she cried harshly. Then her eyes fell on the things he had brought. She swept them together and flung them at him. "Take them away. Take them."

But her mother sprang forward.

"Annette, you're crazy."

"I won't take his presents."

"It's our own food that they've stolen from us. Look at the sardines. They're Bordeaux sardines."

She picked the things up. Hans looked at the girl with a mocking smile in his light blue eyes.

"Annette's your name, is it? A pretty name. Do you grudge your parents a little food? You said you hadn't had cheese for three months. I couldn't get any ham; I did the best I could."

The farmer's wife took the lump of meat in her hands and pressed it to her bosom. You felt that she could have kissed it. Tears ran down Annette's cheeks.

"The shame of it," she groaned.

"Oh, come now, there's no shame in a bit of gruyère and a piece of pork."

Hans sat down and lit a cigarette. Then he passed the packet over to the old man. The farmer hesitated for a moment, but the temptation was too strong for him; he took one and handed back the packet.

"Keep it," said Hans. "I can get plenty more." He inhaled the smoke and blew a cloud of it from his nostrils. "Why can't we be friends? What's done can't be undone. War is war, and well, you know what I mean. I know Annette's an educated girl and I want her to think well of me. I expect we shall be in Soissons for quite a while and I can bring you something now and then to help out. You know, we do all we can to make friends with the townspeople, but they won't let us. They won't even look at us when we pass them in the street. After all, it was an accident, what happened that time I came here with Willi. You needn't be afraid of me. I'll respect Annette as if she was my own sister."

"Why do you want to come here? Why can't you leave us alone?" asked Annette.

He really didn't know. He didn't like to say that he wanted a little human friendship. The silent hostility that surrounded them all at Soissons got on his nerves so that sometimes he wanted to go up to a Frenchman who looked at him as if he wasn't there and knock him down, and sometimes it affected him so that he was almost inclined to cry. It would be nice if he had some place to go where he was welcome. He spoke the truth when he said he had no desire for Annette. She wasn't the sort of woman he fancied. He liked women to be tall and full-breasted, blue-eyed and fair-haired like himself; he liked them to be strong and hefty and well-covered. That refinement which he couldn't account for, that thin fine nose and those dark eyes, the long pale face—there was something intimidating about the girl, so that if he hadn't been excited by the great victories of the German armies, if he hadn't been so tired and yet so elated, if he hadn't drunk all that wine on an empty stomach, it would never have crossed his mind that he could have anything to do with her.

For a fortnight after that Hans couldn't get away. He'd left the food at the farm and he had no doubt that the old people had wolfed it. He wondered if Annette had eaten it too; he wouldn't have been surprised to discover that the moment his back was turned she had set to with the others. These French people, they couldn't resist getting something for nothing. They were weak and decadent. She hated him, yes, God, how she hated him, but pork was pork and cheese was cheese. He thought of her quite a lot. It tantalised him that she should have such a loathing for him. He was used to being liked by women. It would be funny if one of these days she fell in love with him. He'd been her first lover and he'd heard the students at Munich over their beer saying that it was her first lover a woman loved, after that it was love. When he'd set his mind on getting a girl he'd never failed yet. Hans laughed to himself and a sly look came into his eyes.

At last he got his chance to go to the farm. He got hold of cheese and butter, sugar, a tin of sausages, and some coffee, and set off on his motor-cycle. But that time he didn't see Annette. She and her father were at work in the fields. The old woman was in the yard and her face lit up when she saw the parcel he was bringing. She led him into the kitchen. Her hands trembled a little as she untied the string and when she saw what he had brought her eyes filled with tears.

"You're very good," she said.

"May I sit down?" he asked politely.

"Of course." She looked out of the window and Hans guessed that she wanted to make sure that Annette was not coming. "Can I offer you a glass of wine?"

"I'd be glad of it."

He was sharp enough to see that her greed for food had made her, if not friendly to him, at least willing to come to terms with him. That look out of the window made them almost fellow conspirators.

"Did you like the pork?" he asked.

"It was a treat."

"I'll try to bring you some more next time I come. Did Annette like it?"

"She wouldn't touch a thing you'd left. She said she'd rather starve."

"Silly."

"That's what I said to her. As long as the food is there, I said, there's nothing to be gained by not eating it."

They chatted quite amicably while Hans sipped his wine. He discovered that she was called Madame Périer. He asked her whether there were any other members of the family. She sighed. No, they had a son, but he'd been mobilised at the beginning of the war and he'd died. He hadn't been killed, he'd got pneumonia and died in the hospital at Nancy.

"I'm sorry," said Hans.

"Perhaps he's better off than if he'd lived. He was like Annette in many ways. He could never have borne the shame of defeat." She sighed again. "Oh, my poor friend, we've been betrayed."

"Why did you want to fight for the Poles? What were they to you?"

"You're right. If we had let your Hitler take Poland he would have left us alone."

When Hans got up to go he said he would come again soon.

"I shan't forget the pork."

Then Hans had a lucky break; he was given a job that took him twice a week to a town in the vicinity so that he was able to get to the farm much oftener. He took care never to come without bringing something. But he made no headway with Annette. Seeking to ingratiate himself with her, he used the simple wiles that he had discovered went down with women; but they only excited her derision. Thin-lipped and hard, she looked at him as though he were dirt. On more than one occasion she made him so angry that he would have liked to take her by the shoulders and shake the life out of her. Once he found her alone, and when she got up to go he barred her passage.

"Stop where you are. I want to talk to you."

"Talk. I am a woman and defenceless."

"What I want to say is this: for all I know I may be here for a long time. Things aren't going to get easier for you French, they're going to get harder. I can be useful to you. Why don't you be reasonable like your father and mother?"

It was true that old Périer had come round. You couldn't say that he was cordial, he was indeed cold and gruff but he was civil. He had even asked Hans to bring him some tobacco, and when he wouldn't accept payment for it had thanked him. He was pleased to hear the news of Soissons and grabbed the paper that Hans brought him. Hans, a farmer's son, could talk about the farm as one who knew. It was a good farm, not too big and not too small, well watered, for a sizable brook ran through it, and well wooded, with arable land and pasture. Hans listened with understanding sympathy when the old man bewailed himself because without labour, without fertilisers, his stock taken from him, it was all going to rack and ruin.

"You ask me why I can't be reasonable like my father and mother," said Annette.

She pulled her dress tight and showed herself to him. He couldn't believe his eyes. What he saw caused such a convulsion to his soul as he had never known. The blood rushed to his cheeks.

"You're pregnant."

She sank back on her chair and leaning her head on her hands began to weep as though her heart would break.

"The shame of it. The shame."

He sprang towards her to take her in his arms.

"My sweet," he cried.

But she sprang to her feet and pushed him away.

"Don't touch me. Go away. Go away. Haven't you done me enough harm already?"

She flung out of the room. He waited by himself for a few

minutes. He was bewildered. His thoughts in a whirl, he rode slowly back to Soissons, and when he went to bed he couldn't get to sleep for hours. He could think of nothing but Annette and her swollen body. She had been unbearably pathetic as she sat there at the table crying her eyes out. It was his child she bore in her womb. He began to feel drowsy, and then with a start he was once more wide awake, for suddenly it came to him, it came to him with the shattering suddenness of gun-fire; he was in love with her. It was such a surprise, such a shock that he couldn't cope with it. Of course he'd thought of her a lot, but never in that way, he'd thought it would be a great joke if he made her fall in love with him, it would be a triumph if the time came when she offered what he had taken by force; but not for a moment had it occurred to him that she was anything to him but a woman like another. She wasn't his type. She wasn't very pretty. There was nothing to her. Why should he have all of a sudden this funny feeling for her? It wasn't a pleasant feeling either, it was a pain. But he knew what it was all right; it was love, and it made him feel happier than he had ever felt in his life. He wanted to take her in his arms, he wanted to pet her, he wanted to kiss those tear-stained eyes of hers. He didn't desire her, he thought, as a man desires a woman, he wanted to comfort her, he wanted her to smile at him—strange, he had never seen her smile, he wanted to see her eyes—fine eyes they were, beautiful eyes—soft with tenderness.

For three days he could not leave Soissons and for three days, three days and three nights, he thought of Annette and the child she would bear. Then he was able to go to the farm. He wanted to see Madame Périer by herself, and luck was with him, for he met her on the road some way from the house. She had been gathering sticks in the wood and was going home with a great bundle on her back. He stopped his motor-cycle. He knew that the friendliness she showed him was due only to the provisions he brought with him, but he didn't care; it was enough that she was mannerly, and that she was prepared to be so as long as she could get something out of him. He told her he wanted to talk to her and asked her to put her bundle down. She did as he bade. It was a grey, cloudy day, but not cold.

"I know about Annette," he said.

She stared.

"How did you find out? She was set on your not knowing."

"She told me."

"That was a pretty job of work you did that evening."

"I didn't know. Why didn't you tell me sooner?"

She began to talk, not bitterly, not blaming him even, but as though it were a misfortune of nature, like a cow dying in giving birth to a calf or a sharp spring frost nipping the fruit trees and ruining the crop, a misfortune that human kind must accept with resignation and humility. After that dreadful night Annette had been in bed for days with a high fever. They thought she was going out of her mind. She would scream for hours on end. There were no doctors to be got. The village doctor had been called to the colours. Even in Soissons there were only two doctors left, old men both of them, and how could they get to the farm even if it had been possible to send for them? They weren't allowed to leave the town. Even when the fever went down Annette was too ill to leave her bed, and when she got up she was so weak, so pale, it was pitiful. The shock had been terrible, and when a month went by, and another month, without her being unwell she paid no attention. She had always been irregular. It was Madame Périer who first suspected that something was wrong. She questioned Annette. They were terrified, both of them, but they weren't certain and they said nothing to Périer. When the third month came it was impossible to doubt any longer. Annette was pregnant.

They had an old Citroën in which before the war Madame Périer had taken the farm produce into the market at Soissons two mornings a week, but since the German occupation they had had nothing to sell that made the journey worth while. Petrol was almost unobtainable. But now they got it out and drove into town. The only cars to be seen were the military cars of the Germans. German soldiers lounged about. There were German signs in the streets, and on public buildings proclamations in French signed by the Officer Commanding. Many shops were closed. They went to the old doctor they knew, and he confirmed their suspicions. But he was a devout Catholic and would not help them. When they wept he shrugged his shoulders.

"You're not the only one," he said. "*Il faut souffrir.*"

They knew about the other doctor too and went to see him. They rang the bell and for a long time no one answered. At last the door was opened by a sad-faced woman in black, but when they asked to see the doctor she began to cry. He had been arrested by the Germans because he was a freemason, and was held as a hostage. A bomb had exploded in a café frequented by German officers and two had been killed and several wounded. If the guilty were not handed over before a certain date he was to be shot. The woman seemed kindly and Madame Périer told her of their trouble.

"The brutes," she said. She looked at Annette with compassion. "My poor child."

She gave them the address of a midwife in the town and told them to say that they had come from her. The midwife gave them some medicine. It made Annette so ill that she thought she was going to die, but it had no further effect. Annette was still pregnant.

That was the story that Madame Périer told Hans. For a while he was silent.

"It's Sunday to-morrow," he said then. "I shall have nothing to do. I'll come and we'll talk. I'll bring something nice."

"We have no needles. Can you bring some?"

"I'll try."

She hoisted the bundle of sticks on her back and trudged down the road. Hans went back to Soissons. He dared not use his motor-cycle, so next day he hired a push-bike. He tied his parcel of food on the carrier. It was a larger parcel than usual because he had put a bottle of champagne into it. He got to the farm when the gathering darkness made it certain that they would all be home from work. It was warm and cosy in the kitchen when he walked in. Madame Périer was cooking and her husband was reading a *Paris-Soir*. Annette was darning stockings.

"Look, I've brought you some needles," he said, as he undid his parcel. "And here's some material for you, Annette."

"I don't want it."

"Don't you?" he grinned. "You'll have to begin making things for the baby."

"That's true, Annette," said her mother, "and we have nothing." Annette did not look up from her sewing. Madame Périer's greedy eyes ran over the contents of the parcel. "A bottle of champagne."

Hans chuckled.

"I'll tell you what that's for presently. I've had an idea." He hesitated for a moment, then drew up a chair and sat down facing Annette. "I don't know quite how to begin. I'm sorry for what I did that night, Annette. It wasn't my fault, it was the circumstances. Can't you forgive me?"

She threw him a look of hatred.

"Never. Why don't you leave me alone? Isn't it enough that you've ruined my life?"

"Well, that's just it. Perhaps I haven't. When I knew you were going to have a baby it had a funny effect on me. It's all different now. It's made me so proud."

"Proud?" she flung at him viciously.

"I want you to have the baby, Annette. I'm glad you couldn't get rid of it."

"How dare you say that?"

"But listen to me. I've been thinking of nothing else since I knew. The war will be over in six months. We shall bring the English to their knees in the spring. They haven't got a chance. And then I shall be demobilised and I'll marry you."

"You? Why?"

He blushed under his tan. He could not bring himself to say it in French, so he said it in German. He knew she understood it.

"*Ich liebe dich.*"

"What does he say?" asked Madame Périer.

"He says he loves me."

Annette threw back her head and broke into a peal of harsh laughter. She laughed louder and louder and she couldn't stop and tears streamed from her eyes. Madame Périer slapped her sharply on both cheeks.

"Don't pay any attention," she said to Hans. "It's hysteria. Her condition, you know."

Annette gasped. She gained control over herself.

"I brought the bottle of champagne to celebrate our engagement," said Hans.

"That's the bitterest thing of all," said Annette, "that we were beaten by fools, by such fools."

Hans went on speaking in German.

"I didn't know I loved you till that day when I found out that you were going to have a baby. It came like a clap of thunder, but I think I've loved you all the time."

"What does he say?" asked Madame Périer.

"Nothing of importance."

He fell back into French. He wanted Annette's parents to hear what he had to say.

"I'd marry you now, only they wouldn't let me. And don't think I'm nothing at all. My father's well-to-do and we're well thought of in our commune. I'm the eldest son and you'd want for nothing."

"Are you a Catholic?" asked Madame Périer.

"Yes, I'm a Catholic."

"That's something."

"It's pretty the country where we live and the soil's good. There's not better farming land between Munich and Innsbrück, and it's our own. My grandfather bought it after the war of '70. And we've got a car and a radio, and we're on the telephone."

Annette turned to her father.

"He has all the tact in the world, this gentleman," she cried ironically. She eyed Hans. "It would be a nice position for me, the foreigner from the conquered country with a child born out of wedlock. It offers me a chance of happiness, doesn't it? A fine chance."

Périer, a man of few words, spoke for the first time.

"No. I don't deny that it's a fine gesture you're making. I went through the last war and we all did things we wouldn't have done in peace time. Human nature is human nature. But now that our son is dead, Annette is all we have. We can't let her go."

"I thought you might feel that way," said Hans, "and I've got my answer to that. I'll stay here."

Annette gave him a quick look.

"What do you mean?" asked Madame Périer.

"I've got another brother. He can stay and help my father. I like this country. With energy and initiative a man could make a good thing of your farm. When the war's over a lot of Germans will be settling here. It's well known that you haven't got enough men in France to work the land you've got. A fellow gave us a lecture the other day at Soissons. He said that a third of the farms were left uncultivated because there aren't the men to work them."

Périer and his wife exchanged glances and Annette saw that they were wavering. That was what they'd wanted since their son had died, a son-in-law who was strong and hefty and could take over when they grew too old to do more than potter about.

"That changes the case," said Madame Périer. "It's a proposition to consider."

"Hold your tongue," cried Annette roughly. She leant forward and fixed her burning eyes on the German. "I'm engaged to a teacher who worked in the boys' school in the town where I taught, we were to be married after the war. He's not strong and big like you or handsome; he's small and frail. His only beauty is the intelligence that shines in his face, his only strength is the greatness of his soul. He's not a barbarian, he's civilised: he has a thousand years of civilisation behind him. I love him. I love him with all my heart and soul."

Hans's face grew sullen. It had never occurred to him that Annette might care for anyone else.

"Where is he now?"

"Where do you suppose he is? In Germany. A prisoner and starving. While you eat the fat of our land. How many times have I got to tell you that I hate you? You ask me to forgive you. Never. You want to make reparation. You fool." She threw her head back and there was a look of intolerable anguish on her face. "Ruined. Oh, he'll forgive me. He's tender. But I'm tortured by the thought that one day the suspicion may come to him that perhaps I hadn't been forced—that perhaps I'd given myself to you for butter and cheese and silk stockings. I shouldn't be the only one. And what would our life be with that child between us, your child, a German child? Big like you, and blond like you, and blue-eyed like you. Oh, my God, why do I have to suffer this?"

She got up and went swiftly out of the kitchen. For a minute the three were left in silence. Hans looked ruefully at his bottle of champagne. He sighed and rose to his feet. When he went out Madame Périer accompanied him.

"Did you mean it when you said you would marry her?" she asked him, speaking in a low voice.

"Yes. Every word. I love her."

"And you wouldn't take her away? You'd stay here and work on the farm?"

"I promise you."

"Evidently my old man can't last for ever. At home you'd have to share with your brother. Here you'd share with nobody."

"There's that too."

"We never were in favour of Annette marrying that teacher, but our son was alive then and he said, if she wants to marry him, why shouldn't she? Annette was crazy about him. But now that our son's dead, poor boy, it's different. Even if she wanted to, how could she work the farm alone?"

"It would be a shame if it was sold. I know how one feels about one's own land."

They had reached the road. She took his hand and gave it a little squeeze.

"Come again soon."

Hans knew that she was on his side. It was a comfort to him to think that as he rode back to Soissons. It was a bother that Annette was in love with somebody else. Fortunately he was a prisoner; long before he was likely to be released the baby would be born. That might change her; you could never tell with a woman. Why, in his village there'd been a woman who was so much in love with her husband that it had been a joke, and then she had a baby and after that she couldn't bear the sight of him. Well, why shouldn't the contrary happen too? And now that he'd offered to marry her she must see that he was a decent sort of fellow. God, how pathetic she'd looked with her head flung back, and how well she'd spoken! What language! An actress on the stage couldn't have expressed herself better, and yet it had all sounded so natural. You had to admit that, these French people knew how to talk. Oh, she was clever. Even when she lashed him with that bitter tongue it was a joy to listen to her. He hadn't had a bad education himself, but he couldn't hold a candle to her. Culture, that's what she had.

"I'm a donkey," he said out loud as he rode along. She'd said he was big and strong and handsome. Would she have said that if it hadn't meant something to her? And she'd talked of the baby having fair hair and blue eyes like his own. If that didn't mean that his colouring had made an impression on her he was a Dutchman. He chuckled. "Give me time. Patience, and let nature go to work."

The weeks went by. The C.O. at Soissons was an elderly, easy-going fellow and in view of what the spring had in store for them he was content not to drive his men too hard. The German papers told them that England was being wrecked by the Luftwaffe and the people were in a panic. Submarines were sinking British ships by the score and the country was starving. Revolution was imminent. Before summer it would be all over and the Germans would be masters of the world. Hans wrote home and told his parents that he was going to marry a French girl and with her a fine farm. He proposed that his brother should borrow money to buy him out of his share of the family property so that he could increase the size of his own holding while land, owing to the war and the exchange, could still be bought for a song. He went over the farm with Périer. The old man listened quietly when Hans told him his ideas: the farm would have to be restocked and as a German he would have a pull; the motor tractor was old, he would get a fine new one from Germany, and a motor plough. To make a farm pay you had to take advantage of modern inventions. Madame Périer told him afterwards that her husband had said he wasn't a bad lad and seemed to know a lot. She was very friendly with him now and insisted that he should share their midday meal with them on Sundays. She translated his name into French and called him Jean. He was always ready to give a hand, and as time went on and Annette could do less and less it was useful to have a man about who didn't mind doing a job of work.

Annette remained fiercely hostile. She never spoke to him except to answer his direct questions and as soon as it was possible went to her own room. When it was so cold that she couldn't stay there she sat by the side of the kitchen stove, sewing or reading, and took no more notice of him than if he hadn't been there. She was in radiant health. There was colour in her cheeks and in Hans's eyes she was beautiful. Her approaching maternity had given her a strange dignity and he was filled with exultation when he gazed upon her. Then one day when he was on his way to the farm he saw Madame Périer in the road waving to him to stop. He put his brakes on hard.

"I've been waiting for an hour. I thought you'd never come. You must go back. Pierre is dead."

"Who's Pierre?"

"Pierre Gavin. The teacher Annette was going to marry."

Hans's heart leapt. What luck! Now he'd have his chance.

"Is she upset?"

"She's not crying. When I tried to say something she bit my head off. If she saw you to-day she's capable of sticking a knife into you."

"It's not my fault if he died. How did you hear?"

"A prisoner, a friend of his, escaped through Switzerland and he wrote to Annette. We got the letter this morning. There was a mutiny in the camp because they weren't given enough to eat and the ringleaders were shot. Pierre was one of them."

Hans was silent. He could only think it served the man right. What did they think that a prison camp was—the Ritz?

"Give her time to get over the shock," said Madame Périer.

"When she's calmer I'll talk to her. I'll write you a letter when you can come again."

"All right. You will help me, won't you?"

"You can be sure of that. My husband and I, we're agreed. We talked it over and we came to the conclusion that the only thing to do was to accept the situation. He's no fool, my husband, and he says the best chance for France now is to collaborate. And take it all in all I don't dislike you. I shouldn't wonder if you didn't make Annette a better husband than that teacher. And with the baby coming and all."

"I want it to be a boy," said Hans.

"It's going to be a boy. I know for certain. I've seen it in the coffee grounds and I've put out the cards. The answer is a boy every time."

"I almost forgot, here are some papers for you," said Hans, as he turned his cycle and prepared to mount.

He handed her three numbers of *Paris-Soir*. Old Périer read every evening. He read that the French must be realistic and accept the new order that Hitler was going to create in Europe. He read that the German submarines were sweeping the sea. He read that the General Staff had organised to the last detail the campaign that would bring England to her knees and that the Americans were too unprepared, too soft and too divided to come to her help. He read that France must take the heaven-sent opportunity and by loyal collaboration with the Reich regain her honoured position in the new Europe. And it wasn't Germans who wrote it all; it was Frenchmen. He nodded his head with approval when he read that the plutocrats and the Jews would be destroyed and the poor man in France would at last come into his own. They were quite right, the clever fellows who said that France was essentially an agricultural country and its backbone was its industrious farmers. Good sense that was.

One evening, when they were finishing their supper, ten days after the news had come of Pierre Gavin's death, Madame Périer, by arrangement with her husband, said to Annette:

"I wrote a letter to Jean a few days ago telling him to come here to-morrow."

"Thank you for the warning. I shall stay in my room."

"Oh, come, daughter, the time has passed for foolishness. You must be realistic. Pierre is dead. Jean loves you and wants to marry you. He's a fine-looking fellow. Any girl would be proud of him as a husband. How can we restock the farm without his help? He's going to buy a tractor and a plough with his own money. You must let bygones be bygones."

"You're wasting your breath, Mother. I earned my living before, I can earn my living again. I hate him. I hate his vanity and his arrogance. I could kill him: his death wouldn't satisfy me. I should like to torture him as he's tortured me. I think I should die happy if I could find a way to wound him as he's wounded me."

"You're being very silly, my poor child."

"Your mother's right, my girl," said Périer. "We've been defeated and we must accept the consequences. We've got to make the best arrangement we can with the conquerors. We're cleverer than they are and if we play our cards well we shall come out on top. France was rotten. It's the Jews and the plutocrats who ruined the country. Read the papers and you'll see for yourself!"

"Do you think I believe a word in that paper? Why do you think he brings it to you except that it's sold to the Germans? The men who write in it—traitors, traitors. Oh God, may I live to see them torn to pieces by the mob. Bought, bought every one of them—bought with German money. The swine."

Madame Périer was getting exasperated.

"What have you got against the boy? He took you by force —yes, he was drunk at the time. It's not the first time that's happened to a woman and it won't be the last time. He hit your father and he bled like a pig, but does your father bear him malice?"

"It was an unpleasant incident, but I've forgotten it," said Périer.

Annette burst into harsh laughter.

"You should have been a priest. You forgive injuries with a spirit truly Christian."

"And what is there wrong about that?" asked Madame Périer angrily. "Hasn't he done everything he could to make amends? Where would your father have got his tobacco all these months if it hadn't been for him? If we haven't gone hungry it's owing to him."

"If you'd had any pride, if you'd had any sense of decency, you'd have thrown his presents in his face."

"You've profited by them, haven't you?"

"Never. Never."

"It's a lie and you know it. You've refused to eat the cheese he brought and the butter and the sardines. But the soup you've eaten, you know I put the meat in it that he brought; and the salad you ate to-night, if you didn't have to eat it dry, it's because he brought me oil."

Annette sighed deeply. She passed her hand over her eyes.

"I know. I tried not to, I couldn't help myself, I was so hungry. Yes, I knew his meat went into the soup and I ate it. I knew the salad was made with his oil. I wanted to refuse it, I had such a longing for it, it wasn't I that ate it, it was a ravenous beast within me."

"That's neither here nor there. You ate it."

"With shame. With despair. They broke our strength first with their tanks and their planes, and now when we're defenceless they're breaking our spirit by starving us."

"You get nowhere by being theatrical, my girl. For an educated woman you have really no sense. Forget the past and give a father to your child, to say nothing of a good workman for the farm who'll be worth two hired men. That is sense."

Annette shrugged her shoulders wearily and they lapsed into silence. Next day Hans came. Annette gave him a sullen look, but neither spoke nor moved. Hans smiled.

"Thank you for not running away," he said.

"My parents asked you to come and they've gone down to the village. It suits me because I want to have a definitive talk with you. Sit down."

He took off his coat and his helmet and drew a chair to the table.

"My parents want me to marry you. You've been clever; with your presents, with your promises, you've got round them. They believe all they read in the papers you bring them. I want to tell you that I will never marry you. I wouldn't have thought it possible that I could hate a human being as I hate you."

"Let me speak in German. You understand enough to know what I'm saying."

"I ought to. I taught it. For two years I was governess to two little girls in Stuttgart."

He broke into German, but she went on speaking French.

"It's not only that I love you, I admire you. I admire your distinction and your grace. There's something about you I don't understand. I respect you. Oh, I can see that you don't want to marry me now even if it were possible. But Pierre is dead."

"Don't speak of him," she cried violently. "That would be the last straw."

"I only want to tell you that for your sake I'm sorry he died."

"Shot in cold blood by his German jailers."

"Perhaps in time you'll grieve for him less. You know, when someone you love dies, you think you'll never get over it, but you do. Won't it be better then to have a father for your child?"

"Even if there were nothing else do you think I could ever forget that you are a German and I'm a Frenchwoman? If you weren't as stupid as only a German can be you'd see that that child must be a reproach to me as long as I live. Do you think I have no friends? How could I ever look them in the face with the child I had with a German soldier? There's only one thing I ask you: leave me alone with my disgrace. Go, go—for God's sake go and never come again."

"But he's my child too. I want him."

"You?" she cried in astonishment. "What can a by-blow that you got in a moment of savage drunkenness mean to you?"

"You don't understand. I'm so proud and so happy. It was when I knew you were going to have a baby that I knew I loved you. At first I couldn't believe it; it was such a surprise to me. Don't you see what I mean? That child that's going to be born means everything in the world to me. Oh, I don't know how to put it; it's put feelings in my heart that I don't understand myself."

She looked at him intently and there was a strange gleam in her eyes. You would have said it was a look of triumph. She gave a short laugh.

"I don't know whether I more loathe the brutality of you Germans or despise your sentimentality."

He seemed not to have heard what she said.

"I think of him all the time."

"You've made up your mind it'll be a boy?"

"I know it'll be a boy. I want to hold him in my arms and I want to teach him to walk. And then when he grows older I'll teach him all I know. I'll teach him to ride and I'll teach him to shoot. Are there fish in your brook? I'll teach him to fish. I'm going to be the proudest father in the world."

She stared at him with hard, hard eyes. Her face was set and stern. An idea, a terrible idea was forming itself in her mind. He gave her a disarming smile.

"Perhaps when you see how much I love our boy, you'll come to love me too. I'll make you a good husband, my pretty."

She said nothing. She merely kept on gazing at him sullenly.

"Haven't you one kind word for me?" he said.

She flushed. She clasped her hands tightly together.

"Others may despise me. I will never do anything that can make me despise myself. You are my enemy and you will always be my enemy. I only live to see the deliverance of France. It'll come, perhaps not next year or the year after, perhaps not for thirty years, but it'll come. The rest of them can do what they like, I will never come to terms with the invaders of my country. I hate you and I hate this child that you've given me. Yes, we've been defeated. Before the end comes you'll see that we haven't been conquered. Now go. My mind's made up and nothing on God's earth can change it."

He was silent for a minute or two.

"Have you made arrangements for a doctor? I'll pay all the expenses."

"Do you suppose we want to spread our shame through the whole countryside? My mother will do all that's necessary."

"But supposing there's an accident?"

"And supposing you mind your own business!"

He sighed and rose to his feet. When he closed the door behind him she watched him walk down the pathway that led to the road. She realised with rage that some of the things he said had aroused in her heart a feeling that she had never felt for him before.

"O God, give me strength," she cried.

Then, as he walked along, the dog, an old dog they'd had for years, ran up to him barking angrily. He had tried for months to make friends with the dog, but it had never responded to his advances; when he tried to pat it, it backed away growling and showing its teeth. And now as the dog ran towards him, irritably giving way to his feeling of frustration, Hans gave it a savage, brutal kick and the dog was flung into the bushes and limped yelping away.

"The beast," she cried. "Lies, lies, lies. And I was weak enough to be almost sorry for him."

There was a looking-glass hanging by the side of the door and she looked at herself in it. She drew herself up and smiled at her reflection. But rather than a smile it was a fiendish grimace.

It was now March. There was a bustle of activity in the garrison at Soissons. There were inspections and there was intensive training. Rumour was rife. There was no doubt they were going somewhere, but the rank and file could only guess where. Some thought they were being got ready at last for the invasion of England, others were of opinion that they would be sent to the Balkans, and others again talked of the Ukraine. Hans was kept busy. It was not till the second Sunday afternoon that he was able to get out to the farm. It was a cold grey day, with sleet that looked as though it might turn to snow falling in sudden windy flurries. The country was grim and cheerless.

"You!" cried Madame Périer when he went in. "We thought you were dead."

"I couldn't come before. We're off any day now. We don't know when."

"The baby was born this morning. It's a boy."

Hans's heart gave a great leap in his breast. He flung his arms round the old woman and kissed her on both cheeks.

"A Sunday child, he ought to be lucky. Let's open the bottle of champagne. How's Annette?"

"She's as well as can be expected. She had a very easy time.

She began to have pains last night and by five o'clock this morning it was all over."

Old Périer was smoking his pipe sitting as near the stove as he could get. He smiled quietly at the boy's enthusiasm.

"One's first child, it has an effect on one," he said.

"He has quite a lot of hair and it's as fair as yours; and blue eyes just like you said he'd have," said Madame Périer. "I've never seen a lovelier baby. He'll be just like his papa."

"Oh, my God, I'm so happy," cried Hans. "How beautiful the world is! I want to see Annette."

"I don't know if she'll see you. I don't want to upset her on account of the milk."

"No, no, don't upset her on my account. If she doesn't want to see me it doesn't matter. But let me see the baby just for a minute."

"I'll see what I can do. I'll try to bring it down."

Madame Périer went out and they heard her heavy tread clumping up the stairs. But in a moment they heard her clattering down again. She burst into the kitchen.

"They're not there. She isn't in her room. The baby's gone."

Périer and Hans cried out and without thinking what they were doing all three of them scampered upstairs. The harsh light of the winter afternoon cast over the shabby furniture, the iron bed, the cheap wardrobe, the chest of drawers, a dismal squalor. There was no one in the room.

"Where is she?" screamed Madame Périer. She ran into the narrow passage, opening doors, and called the girl's name. "Annette, Annette. Oh, what madness!"

"Perhaps in the sitting-room."

They ran downstairs to the unused parlour. An icy air met them as they opened the door. They opened the door of a store-room.

"She's gone out. Something awful has happened."

"How could she have got out?" asked Hans sick with anxiety.

"Through the front door, you fool."

Périer went up to it and looked.

"That's right. The bolt's drawn back."

"Oh, my God, my God, what madness," cried Madame Périer. "It'll kill her."

"We must look for her," said Hans. Instinctively, because that was the way he always went in and out, he ran back into the kitchen and the others followed him. "Which way?"

"The brook," the old woman gasped.

He stopped as though turned to stone with horror. He stared at the old woman aghast.

"I'm frightened," she cried. "I'm frightened."

Hans flung open the door, and as he did so Annette walked in. She had nothing on but her nightdress and a flimsy rayon dressing-gown. It was pink, with pale blue flowers. She was soaked and her hair, dishevelled, clung damply to her head and hung down her shoulders in bedraggled wisps. She was deathly white. Madame Périer sprang towards her and took her in her arms.

"Where have you been? Oh, my poor child, you're wet through. What madness!"

But Annette pushed her away. She looked at Hans.

"You've come at the right moment, you."

"Where's the baby?" cried Madame Périer.

"I had to do it at once. I was afraid if I waited I shouldn't have the courage."

"Annette, what have you done?"

"I've done what I had to do. I took it down to the brook and held it under water till it was dead."

Hans gave a great cry, the cry of an animal wounded to death; he covered his face with his hand, and staggering like a drunken man flung out of the door. Annette sank into a chair, and leaning her forehead on her two fists burst into passionate weeping.

THE HAPPY MAN

IT is a dangerous thing to order the lives of others and I have often wondered at the self-confidence of politicians, reformers and such like who are prepared to force upon their fellows measures that must alter their manners, habits and points of view. I have always hesitated to give advice, for how can one advise another how to act unless one knows that other as well as one knows oneself? Heaven knows, I know little enough of myself: I know nothing of others. We can only guess at the thoughts and emotions of our neighbours. Each one of us is a prisoner in a solitary tower and he communicates with the other prisoners, who form mankind, by conventional signs that have not quite the same meaning for them as for himself. And life, unfortunately, is something that you can lead but once; mistakes are often irreparable, and who am I that I should tell this one and that how he should lead it? Life is a difficult business and I have found it hard enough to make my own a complete and rounded thing; I have not been tempted to teach my neighbour what he should do with his. But there are men who flounder at the journey's start, the way before them is confused and hazardous, and on occasion, however unwillingly, I have been forced to point the finger of fate. Sometimes men have said to me, what shall I do with my life? and I have seen myself for a moment wrapped in the dark cloak of Destiny.

Once I know that I advised well.

I was a young man and I lived in a modest apartment in London near Victoria Station. Late one afternoon, when I was beginning to think that I had worked enough for that day, I heard a ring at the bell. I opened the door to a total stranger. He asked me my name; I told him. He asked if he might come in.

"Certainly."

I led him into my sitting-room and begged him to sit down. He seemed a trifle embarrassed. I offered him a cigarette and he had some difficulty in lighting it without letting go of his hat. When he had satisfactorily achieved this feat I asked him if I should not put it on a chair for him. He quickly did this and while doing it dropped his umbrella.

"I hope you don't mind my coming to see you like this," he said. "My name is Stephens and I am a doctor. You're in the medical, I believe?"

"Yes, but I don't practise."

"No, I know. I've read a book of yours about Spain and I wanted to ask you about it."

"It's not a very good book, I'm afraid."

"The fact remains that you know something about Spain and there's no one else I know who does. And I thought perhaps you wouldn't mind giving me some information."

"I shall be very glad."

He was silent for a moment. He reached out for his hat and holding it in one hand absent-mindedly stroked it with the other. I surmised that it gave him confidence.

"I hope you won't think it very odd for a perfect stranger to talk to you like this." He gave an apologetic laugh. "I'm not going to tell you the story of my life."

When people say this to me I always know that it is precisely what they are going to do. I do not mind. In fact I rather like it.

"I was brought up by two old aunts. I've never been anywhere. I've never done anything. I've been married for six years. I have no children. I'm medical officer at the Camberwell Infirmary. I can't stick it any more."

There was something very striking in the short, sharp sentences he used. They had a forcible ring. I had not given him more than a cursory glance, but now I looked at him with curiosity. He was a little man, thick-set and stout, of thirty perhaps, with a round red face from which shone small, dark and very bright eyes. His black hair was cropped close to a bullet-shaped head. He was dressed in a blue suit a good deal the worse for wear. It was baggy at the knees and the pockets bulged untidily.

"You know what the duties are of a medical officer in an infirmary. One day is pretty much like another. And that's all I've got to look forward to for the rest of my life. Do you think it's worth it?"

"It's a means of livelihood," I answered.

"Yes, I know. The money's pretty good."

"I don't exactly know why you've come to me."

"Well, I wanted to know whether you thought there would be any chance for an English doctor in Spain?"

"Why Spain?"

"I don't know, I just have a fancy for it."

"It's not like Carmen, you know," I smiled.

"But there's sunshine there, and there's good wine, and there's colour, and there's air you can breathe. Let me say what I have to say straight out. I heard by accident that there was no English doctor in Seville. Do you think I could earn a living there? Is it madness to give up a good safe job for an uncertainty?"

"What does your wife think about it?"

"She's willing."

"It's a great risk."

"I know. But if you say take it, I will: if you say stay where you are, I'll stay."

He was looking at me intently with those bright dark eyes of his and I knew that he meant what he said. I reflected for a moment.

"Your whole future is concerned: you must decide for yourself. But this I can tell you: if you don't want money but are content to earn just enough to keep body and soul together, then go. For you will lead a wonderful life."

He left me, I thought about him for a day or two, and then forgot. The episode passed completely from my memory.

Many years later, fifteen at least, I happened to be in Seville and having some trifling indisposition asked the hotel porter whether there was an English doctor in the town. He said there was and gave me the address. I took a cab and as I drove up to the house a little fat man came out of it. He hesitated when he caught sight of me.

"Have you come to see me?" he said. "I'm the English doctor."

I explained my errand and he asked me to come in. He lived in an ordinary Spanish house, with a patio, and his consulting-room which led out of it was littered with papers, books, medical appliances, and lumber. The sight of it would have startled a squeamish patient. We did our business and then I asked the doctor what his fee was. He shook his head and smiled.

"There's no fee."

"Why on earth not?"

"Don't you remember me? Why, I'm here because of something you said to me. You changed my whole life for me. I'm Stephens."

I had not the least notion what he was talking about. He reminded me of our interview, he repeated to me what we had said, and gradually, out of the night, a dim recollection of the incident came back to me.

"I was wondering if I'd ever see you again," he said, "I was wondering if ever I'd have a chance of thanking you for all you've done for me."

"It's been a success then?"

I looked at him. He was very fat now and bald, but his eyes twinkled gaily and his fleshy, red face bore an expression of perfect good-humour. The clothes he wore, terribly shabby they were, had been made obviously by a Spanish tailor and his hat was the wide-brimmed sombrero of the Spaniard. He looked to me as though he knew a good bottle of wine when he saw it. He had a dissipated, though entirely sympathetic, appearance. You might have hesitated to let him remove your appendix, but you could not have imagined a more delightful creature to drink a glass of wine with.

"Surely you were married?" I said.

"Yes. My wife didn't like Spain, she went back to Camberwell, she was more at home there."

"Oh, I'm sorry for that."

His black eyes flashed a bacchanalian smile. He really had somewhat the look of a young Silenus.

"Life is full of compensations," he murmured.

The words were hardly out of his mouth when a Spanish woman, no longer in her first youth, but still boldly and voluptuously beautiful, appeared at the door. She spoke to him in Spanish, and I could not fail to perceive that she was the mistress of the house.

As he stood at the door to let me out he said to me:

"You told me when last I saw you that if I came here I should earn just enough money to keep body and soul together, but that I should lead a wonderful life. Well, I want to tell you that you were right. Poor I have been and poor I shall always be, but by heaven I've enjoyed myself. I wouldn't exchange the life I've had with that of any king in the world."

IN A STRANGE LAND

I AM of a roving disposition; but I travel not to see imposing monuments, which indeed somewhat bore me, nor beautiful scenery, of which I soon tire; I travel to see men. I avoid the great. I would not cross the road to meet a president or a king; I am content to know the writer in the pages of his book and the painter in his picture; but I have journeyed a hundred leagues to see a missionary of whom I had heard a strange story and I have spent a fortnight in a vile hotel in order to improve my acquaintance with a billiard-marker. I should be inclined to say that I am not surprised to meet any sort of person were it not that there is one sort that I am constantly running against and that never fails to give me a little shock of amused astonishment. This is the elderly Englishwoman, generally of adequate means, who is to be found living alone, up and down the world, in unexpected places. You do not wonder when you hear of her living in a villa on a hill outside a small Italian town, the only Englishwoman in the neighbourhood, and you are almost prepared for it when a lonely hacienda is pointed out to you in Andalusia and you are told that there has dwelt for many years an English lady. But it is more surprising when you hear that the only white person in a Chinese city is an Englishwoman, not a missionary, who lives there none knows why; and there is another who inhabits an island in the South Seas and a third who has a bungalow on the outskirts of a large village in the centre of Java. They live solitary lives, these women, without friends, and they do not welcome the stranger. Though they may not have seen one of their own race for months they will pass you on the road as though they did not see you, and if, presuming on your nationality, you should call, as likely as not they will decline to see you; but if they do, they will give you a cup of tea from a silver teapot and on a plate of Old Worcester you will find Scotch scones. They will talk to you politely, as though they were entertaining you in a Kentish vicarage, but when you take your leave will show no particular desire to continue the acquaintance. One wonders in vain what strange instinct it is that has driven them to separate themselves from their kith and kin and thus to live apart from all their natural interests in an alien land. Is it romance they have sought or freedom?

But of all these Englishwomen whom I have met or perhaps only heard of (for as I have said they are difficult of access) the one who remains most vividly in my memory is an elderly person who lived in Asia Minor. I had arrived after a tedious journey at a little town from which I proposed to make the ascent of a celebrated mountain and I was taken to a rambling hotel that stood at its foot. I arrived late at night and signed my name in the book. I went up to my room. It was cold and I shivered as I undressed, but in a moment there was a knock at the door and the dragoman came in.

"Signora Niccolini's compliments," he said.

To my astonishment he handed me a hot-water bottle. I took it with grateful hands.

"Who is Signora Niccolini?" I asked.

"She is the proprietor of this hotel," he answered.

I sent her my thanks and he withdrew. The last thing I expected in a scrubby hotel in Asia Minor kept by an old Italian woman was a beautiful hot-water bottle. There is nothing I like more (if we were not all sick to death of the war I would tell you the story of how six men risked their lives to fetch a hot-water bottle from a château in Flanders that was being bombarded); and next morning, so that I might thank her in person, I asked if I might see the Signora Niccolini. While I waited for her I racked my brains to think what hot-water bottle could possibly be in Italian. In a moment she came in. She was a little stout woman, not without dignity,

10*

and she wore a black apron trimmed with lace and a small black lace cap. She stood with her hands crossed. I was astonished at her appearance for she looked exactly like a housekeeper in a great English house.

"Did you wish to speak to me, sir?"

She was an Englishwoman and in those few words I surely recognised the trace of a Cockney accent.

"I wanted to thank you for the hot-water bottle," I replied in some confusion.

"I saw by the visitors' book that you were English, sir, and I always send up a 'ot-water bottle to English gentlemen."

"Believe me, it was very welcome."

"I was for many years in the service of the late Lord Ormskirk, sir. He always used to travel with a 'ot-water bottle. Is there anything else, sir?"

"Not at the moment, thank you."

She gave me a polite little nod and withdrew. I wondered how on earth it came about that a funny old Englishwoman like that should be the landlady of a hotel in Asia Minor. It was not easy to make her acquaintance, for she knew her place, as she would herself have put it, and she kept me at a distance. It was not for nothing that she had been in service in a noble English family. But I was persistent and I induced her at last to ask me to have a cup of tea in her own little parlour. I learnt that she had been lady's maid to a certain Lady Ormskirk, and Signor Niccolini (for she never alluded to her deceased husband in any other way) had been his lordship's chef. Signor Niccolini was a very handsome man and for some years there had been an "understanding" between them. When they had both saved a certain amount of money they were married, retired from service, and looked about for a hotel. They had bought this one on an advertisement because Signor Niccolini thought he would like to see something of the world. That was nearly thirty years ago and Signor Niccolini had been dead

for fifteen. His widow had not once been back to England. I
asked her if she was never homesick.

"I don't say as I wouldn't like to go back on a visit, though I
expect I'd find many changes. But my family didn't like the
idea of me marrying a foreigner and I 'aven't spoken to them
since. Of course there are many things here that are not the
same as what they 'ave at 'ome, but it's surprising what you get
used to. I see a lot of life. I don't know as I should care to live
the 'umdrum life they do in a place like London."

I smiled. For what she said was strangely incongruous with
her manner. She was a pattern of decorum. It was extraordinary that she could have lived for thirty years in this wild
and almost barbaric country without its having touched her.
Though I knew no Turkish and she spoke it with ease I was
convinced that she spoke it most incorrectly and with a
Cockney accent. I suppose she had remained the precise, prim
English lady's maid, knowing her place, through all these
vicissitudes because she had no faculty of surprise. She took
everything that came as a matter of course. She looked upon
everyone who wasn't English as a foreigner and therefore as
someone, almost imbecile, for whom allowances must be made.
She ruled her staff despotically—for did she not know how an
upper servant in a great house should exercise his authority
over the under servants—and everything about the hotel was
clean and neat.

"I do my best," she said, when I congratulated her on this,
standing, as always when she spoke to me, with her hands
respectfully crossed. "Of course one can't expect foreigners to
'ave the same ideas what we 'ave, but as his lordship used to say
to me, what we've got to do, Parker, he said to me, what we've
got to do in this life is to make the best of our raw material."

But she kept her greatest surprise for the eve of my departure.

"I'm glad you're not going before you've seen my two sons,
sir."

"I didn't know you had any."

"They've been away on business, but they've just come back. You'll be surprised when you've seen them. I've trained them with me own 'ands so to speak, and when I'm gone they'll carry on the 'otel between them."

In a moment two tall, swarthy, strapping young fellows entered the hall. Her eyes lit up with pleasure. They went up to her and took her in their arms and gave her resounding kisses.

"They don't speak English, sir, but they understand a little, and of course they speak Turkish like natives, and Greek and Italian."

I shook hands with the pair and then Signora Niccolini said something to them and they went away.

"They're handsome fellows, Signora," I said. "You must be very proud of them."

"I am, sir, and they're good boys, both of them. They've never give me a moment's trouble from the day they was born and they're the very image of Signor Niccolini."

"I must say no one would think they had an English mother."

"I'm not exactly their mother, sir. I've just sent them along to say 'ow do you do to 'er."

I dare say I looked a little confused.

"They're the sons that Signor Niccolini 'ad by a Greek girl that used to work in the 'otel, and 'aving no children of me own I adopted them."

I sought for some remark to make.

"I 'ope you don't think that there's any blame attaches to Signor Niccolini," she said, drawing herself up a little. "I shouldn't like you to think that, sir." She folded her hands again and with a mixture of pride, primness and satisfaction added the final words: "Signor Niccolini was a very full-blooded man."

THE LUNCHEON

I CAUGHT sight of her at the play and in answer to her beckoning I went over during the interval and sat down beside her. It was long since I had last seen her and if someone had not mentioned her name I hardly think I would have recognised her. She addressed me brightly.

"Well, it's many years since we first met. How time does fly! We're none of us getting any younger. Do you remember the first time I saw you? You asked me to luncheon."

Did I remember?

It was twenty years ago and I was living in Paris. I had a tiny apartment in the Latin Quarter overlooking a cemetery and I was earning barely enough money to keep body and soul together. She had read a book of mine and had written to me about it. I answered, thanking her, and presently I received from her another letter saying that she was passing through Paris and would like to have a chat with me; but her time was limited and the only free moment she had was on the following Thursday; she was spending the morning at the Luxembourg and would I give her a little luncheon at Foyot's afterwards? Foyot's is a restaurant at which the French senators eat and it was so far beyond my means that I had never even thought of going there. But I was flattered and I was too young to have learned to say no to a woman. (Few men, I may add, learn this until they are too old to make it of any consequence to a woman what they say.) I had eighty francs (gold francs) to last me the rest of the month and a modest luncheon should not cost more than fifteen. If I cut out coffee for the next two weeks I could manage well enough.

I answered that I would meet my friend—by correspondence —at Foyot's on Thursday at half-past twelve. She was not so young as I expected and in appearance imposing rather than attractive. She was in fact a woman of forty (a charming age, but not one that excites a sudden and devastating passion at first sight), and she gave me the impression of having more teeth, white and large and even, than were necessary for any practical purpose. She was talkative, but since she seemed inclined to talk about me I was prepared to be an attentive listener.

I was startled when the bill of fare was brought, for the prices were a great deal higher than I had anticipated. But she reassured me.

"I never eat anything for luncheon," she said.

"Oh, don't say that!" I answered generously.

"I never eat more than one thing. I think people eat far too much nowadays. A little fish, perhaps. I wonder if they have any salmon."

Well, it was early in the year for salmon and it was not on the bill of fare, but I asked the waiter if there was any. Yes, a beautiful salmon had just come in, it was the first they had had. I ordered it for my guest. The waiter asked her if she would have something while it was being cooked.

"No," she answered, "I never eat more than one thing. Unless you had a little caviare. I never mind caviare."

My heart sank a little. I knew I could not afford caviare, but I could not very well tell her that. I told the waiter by all means to bring caviare. For myself I chose the cheapest dish on the menu and that was a mutton chop.

"I think you're unwise to eat meat," she said. "I don't know how you can expect to work after eating heavy things like chops. I don't believe in overloading my stomach."

Then came the question of drink.

"I never drink anything for luncheon," she said.

"Neither do I," I answered promptly.

"Except white wine," she proceeded as though I had not

spoken. "These French white wines are so light. They're wonderful for the digestion."

"What would you like?" I asked, hospitable still, but not exactly effusive.

She gave me a bright and amicable flash of her white teeth.

"My doctor won't let me drink anything but champagne."

I fancy I turned a trifle pale. I ordered half a bottle. I mentioned casually that my doctor had absolutely forbidden me to drink champagne.

"What are you going to drink, then?"

"Water."

She ate the caviare and she ate the salmon. She talked gaily of art and literature and music. But I wondered what the bill would come to. When my mutton chop arrived she took me quite seriously to task.

"I see that you're in the habit of eating a heavy luncheon. I'm sure it's a mistake. Why don't you follow my example and just eat one thing? I'm sure you'd feel ever so much better for it."

"I *am* only going to eat one thing," I said, as the waiter came again with the bill of fare.

She waved him aside with an airy gesture.

"No, no, I never eat anything for luncheon. Just a bite, I never want more than that, and I eat that more as an excuse for conversation than anything else. I couldn't possibly eat anything more—unless they had some of those giant asparagus. I should be sorry to leave Paris without having some of them."

My heart sank. I had seen them in the shops and I knew that they were horribly expensive. My mouth had often watered at the sight of them.

"Madame wants to know if you have any of those giant asparagus," I asked the waiter.

I tried with all my might to will him to say no. A happy smile spread over his broad, priest-like face, and he assured me that they had some so large, so splendid, so tender, that it was a marvel.

"I'm not in the least hungry," my guest sighed, "but if you insist I don't mind having some asparagus."

I ordered them.

"Aren't you going to have any?"

"No, I never eat asparagus."

"I know there are people who don't like them. The fact is, you ruin your palate by all the meat you eat."

We waited for the asparagus to be cooked. Panic seized me. It was not a question now how much money I should have left over for the rest of the month, but whether I had enough to pay the bill. It would be mortifying to find myself ten francs short and be obliged to borrow from my guest. I could not bring myself to do that. I knew exactly how much I had and if the bill came to more I made up my mind that I would put my hand in my pocket and with a dramatic cry start up and say it had been picked. Of course it would be awkward if she had not money enough either to pay the bill. Then the only thing would be to leave my watch and say I would come back and pay later.

The asparagus appeared. They were enormous, succulent and appetising. The smell of the melted butter tickled my nostrils as the nostrils of Jehovah were tickled by the burned offerings of the virtuous Semites. I watched the abandoned woman thrust them down her throat in large voluptuous mouthfuls and in my polite way I discoursed on the condition of the drama in the Balkans. At last she finished.

"Coffee?" I said.

"Yes, just an ice-cream and coffee," she answered.

I was past caring now, so I ordered coffee for myself and an ice-cream and coffee for her.

"You know, there's one thing I thoroughly believe in," she

said, as she ate the ice-cream. "One should always get up from a meal feeling one could eat a little more."

"Are you still hungry?" I asked faintly.

"Oh, no, I'm not hungry; you see, I don't eat luncheon. I have a cup of coffee in the morning and then dinner, but I never eat more than one thing for luncheon. I was speaking for you."

"Oh, I see!"

Then a terrible thing happened. While we were waiting for the coffee, the head waiter, with an ingratiating smile on his false face, came up to us bearing a large basket full of huge peaches. They had the blush of an innocent girl; they had the rich tone of an Italian landscape. But surely peaches were not in season then? Lord knew what they cost. I knew too—a little later, for my guest, going on with her conversation, absent-mindedly took one.

"You see, you've filled your stomach with a lot of meat"—my one miserable little chop—"and you can't eat any more. But I've just had a snack and I shall enjoy a peach."

The bill came and when I paid it I found that I had only enough for a quite inadequate tip. Her eyes rested for an instant on the three francs I left for the waiter and I knew that she thought me mean. But when I walked out of the restaurant I had the whole month before me and not a penny in my pocket.

"Follow my example," she said as we shook hands, "and never eat more than one thing for luncheon."

"I'll do better than that," I retorted. "I'll eat nothing for dinner to-night."

"Humorist!" she cried gaily, jumping into a cab. "You're quite a humorist!"

But I have had my revenge at last. I do not believe that I am a vindictive man, but when the immortal gods take a hand in the matter it is pardonable to observe the result with complacency. To-day she weighs twenty-one stone.

I WONDER if I can do it.

I knew Salvatore first when he was a boy of fifteen with a pleasant, ugly face, a laughing mouth and care-free eyes. He used to spend the morning lying about the beach with next to nothing on and his brown body was as thin as a rail. He was full of grace. He was in and out of the sea all the time, swimming with the clumsy, effortless stroke common to the fisher boys. Scrambling up the jagged rocks on his hard feet, for except on Sundays he never wore shoes, he would throw himself into the deep water with a cry of delight. His father was a fisherman who owned his own little vineyard and Salvatore acted as nursemaid to his two younger brothers. He shouted to them to come in shore when they ventured out too far and made them dress when it was time to climb the hot, vineclad hill for the frugal midday meal.

But boys in those Southern parts grow apace and in a little while he was madly in love with a pretty girl who lived on the Grande Marina. She had eyes like forest pools and held herself like a daughter of the Cæsars. They were affianced, but they could not marry till Salvatore had done his military service, and when he left the island which he had never left in his life before, to become a sailor in the navy of King Victor Emmanuel, he wept like a child. It was hard for one who had never been less free than the birds to be at the beck and call of others; it was harder still to live in a battleship with strangers instead of in a little white cottage among the vines; and when he was ashore, to walk in noisy, friendless cities with streets so crowded that he was frightened to cross them, when he had been used to silent paths and the mountains and the sea. I suppose it had never struck him that Ischia, which he looked at every evening (it was like a fairy island in the sunset), to see what the weather would be like next day, or Vesuvius, pearly in the dawn, had anything to do with him at all; but when he ceased to have them before his eyes he realised in some dim fashion that they were as much part of him as his hands and his feet. He was dreadfully homesick. But it was hardest of all to be parted from the girl he loved with all his passionate young heart. He wrote to her (in his childlike handwriting) long, ill-spelt letters in which he told her how constantly he thought of her and how much he longed to be back. He was sent here and there, to Spezzia, to Venice, to Bari and finally to China. Here he fell ill of some mysterious ailment that kept him in hospital for months. He bore it with the mute and uncomprehending patience of a dog. When he learnt that it was a form of rheumatism that made him unfit for further service his heart exulted, for he could go home; and he did not bother, in fact he scarcely listened, when the doctors told him that he would never again be quite well. What did he care when he was going back to the little island he loved so well and the girl who was waiting for him?

When he got into the rowing-boat that met the steamer from Naples and was rowed ashore he saw his father and mother standing on the jetty and his two brothers, big boys now, and he waved to them. His eyes searched among the crowd that waited there, for the girl. He could not see her. There was a great deal of kissing when he jumped up the steps and they all, emotional creatures, cried a little as they exchanged their greetings. He asked where the girl was. His mother told him that she did not know; they had not seen her for two or three weeks; so in the evening when the moon was shining over the placid sea and the lights of Naples twinkled in the distance he walked down to the Grande Marina to her house. She was sitting on the doorstep with her mother. He was a little shy because he had not seen her for so long. He asked her if she had not received the letter that he had written to her to say that he was coming home. Yes, they had received a letter, and they had been told by another of the island boys that he was ill. Yes, that was why he was back; was it not a piece of luck? Oh, but they had heard that he would never be quite well again. The doctors talked a lot of nonsense, but he knew very well that now he was home again he would recover. They were silent for a little, and then the mother nudged the girl. She did not try to soften the blow. She told him straight out, with the blunt directness of her race, that she could not marry a man who would never be strong enough to work like a man. They had made up their minds, her mother and father and she, and her father would never give his consent.

When Salvatore went home he found that they all knew. The girl's father had been to tell them what they had decided, but they had lacked the courage to tell him themselves. He wept on his mother's bosom. He was terribly unhappy, but he did not blame the girl. A fisherman's life is hard and it needs strength and endurance. He knew very well that a girl could not afford to marry a man who might not be able to support her. His smile was very sad and his eyes had the look of a dog that has been beaten, but he did not complain, and he never said a word of the girl he had loved so well. Then, a few months later, when he had settled down to the common round, working in his father's vineyard and fishing, his mother told him that there was a young woman in the village who was willing to marry him. Her name was Assunta.

"She's as ugly as the devil," he said.

She was older than he, twenty-four or twenty-five, and she had been engaged to a man who, while doing his military service, had been killed in Africa. She had a little money of her own and if Salvatore married her she could buy him a boat of his own and they could take a vineyard that by a happy chance happened at that moment to be without a tenant. His mother told him that Assunta had seen him at the *festa* and had fallen in love with him. Salvatore smiled his sweet smile and said he would think about it. On the following Sunday, dressed in the stiff black clothes in which he looked so much less well than in the ragged shirt and trousers of every day, he went up to High Mass at the parish church and placed himself so that he could have a good look at the young woman. When he came down again he told his mother that he was willing.

Well, they were married and they settled down in a tiny white-washed house in the middle of a handsome vineyard. Salvatore was now a great big husky fellow, tall and broad, but still with that ingenuous smile and those trusting, kindly eyes that he had had as a boy. He had the most beautiful manners I have ever seen in my life. Assunta was a grim-visaged female, with decided features, and she looked old for her years. But she had a good heart and she was no fool. I used to be amused by the little smile of devotion that she gave her husband when he was being very masculine and masterful; she never ceased to be touched by his gentle sweetness. But she could not bear the girl who had thrown him over, and notwithstanding Salvatore's smiling expostulations she had nothing but harsh words for her. Presently children were born to them.

It was a hard enough life. All through the fishing season towards evening he set out in his boat with one of his brothers for the fishing grounds. It was a long pull of six or seven miles, and he spent the night catching the profitable cuttlefish. Then there was the long row back again in order to sell the catch in time for it to go on the early boat to Naples. At other times he was working in his vineyard from dawn till the heat drove him to rest and then again, when it was a trifle cooler, till dusk. Often his rheumatism prevented him from doing anything at all and then he would lie about the beach, smoking cigarettes, with a pleasant word for everyone notwithstanding the pain that racked his limbs. The foreigners who came down to bathe and saw him there said that these Italian fishermen were lazy devils.

Sometimes he used to bring his children down to give them a bath. They were both boys and at this time the elder was three and the younger less than two. They sprawled about at the water's edge stark naked and Salvatore, standing on a rock, would dip them in the water. The elder one bore it with stoicism, but the baby screamed lustily. Salvatore had enormous hands, like legs of mutton, coarse and hard from constant toil, but when he bathed his children, holding them so tenderly, drying them with delicate care, upon my word they were like flowers. He would seat the naked baby on the palm of his hand and hold him up, laughing a little at his smallness, and his laugh was like the laughter of an angel. His eyes then were as candid as his child's.

I started by saying that I wondered if I could do it and now I must tell you what it is that I have tried to do. I wanted to see whether I could hold your attention for a few pages while I drew for you the portrait of a man, just an ordinary Italian fisherman who possessed nothing in the world except a quality which is the rarest, the most precious and the loveliest that anyone can have. Heaven only knows why he should so strangely and unexpectedly have possessed it. All I know is that it shone in him with a radiance that, if it had not been so unconscious and so humble, would have been to the common run of men hardly bearable. And in case you have not guessed what the quality was, I will tell you. Goodness, just goodness.

HERE AND THERE

306

She was a good business woman and you had to get up very
early in the morning to beat her in a bargain. She was a
character. She combined ... ... good will with an
alert sense of the ridiculous.

HOME

THE farm lay in a hollow among the Somersetshire hills,
an old-fashioned stone house surrounded by barns and
pens and out-houses. Over the doorway the date when it was
built had been carved in the elegant figures of the period, 1673,
and the house, grey and weather-beaten, looked as much a part
of the landscape as the trees that sheltered it. An avenue of
splendid elms that would have been the pride of many a squire's
mansion led from the road to the trim garden. The people who
lived here were as stolid, sturdy and unpretentious as the
house; their only boast was that ever since it was built from
father to son in one unbroken line they had been born and died
in it. For three hundred years they had farmed the surrounding
land. George Meadows was now a man of fifty, and his wife
was a year or two younger. They were both fine, upstanding
people in the prime of life; and their children, two sons and
three girls, were handsome and strong. They had no new-
fangled notions about being gentlemen and ladies; they knew
their place and were proud of it. I have never seen a more
united household. They were merry, industrious and kindly.
Their life was patriarchal. It had a completeness that gave it a
beauty as definite as that of a symphony by Beethoven or a
picture by Titian. They were happy and they deserved their
happiness. But the master of the house was not George
Meadows (not by a long chalk, they said in the village); it was
his mother. She was twice the man her son was, they said. She
was a woman of seventy, tall, upright and dignified, with grey
hair, and though her face was much wrinkled, her eyes were
bright and shrewd. Her word was law in the house and on the
farm; but she had humour, and if her rule was despotic it was
also kindly. People laughed at her jokes and repeated them.

She was a good business woman and you had to get up very early in the morning to best her in a bargain. She was a character. She combined in a rare degree good will with an alert sense of the ridiculous.

One day Mrs. George stopped me on my way home. She was all in a flutter. (Her mother-in-law was the only Mrs. Meadows we knew: George's wife was only known as Mrs. George.)

"Whoever do you think is coming here to-day?" she asked me. "Uncle George Meadows. You know, him as was in China."

"Why, I thought he was dead."

"We all thought he was dead."

I had heard the story of Uncle George Meadows a dozen times, and it had amused me because it had the savour of an old ballad: it was oddly touching to come across it in real life. For Uncle George Meadows and Tom, his younger brother, had both courted Mrs. Meadows when she was Emily Green fifty years and more ago, and when she married Tom, George had gone away to sea.

They heard of him on the China coast. For twenty years now and then he sent them presents; then there was no more news of him; when Tom Meadows died his widow wrote and told him, but received no answer, and at last they came to the conclusion that he must be dead. But two or three days ago to their astonishment they had received a letter from the matron of the sailors' home at Portsmouth. It appeared that for the last ten years George Meadows, crippled with rheumatism, had been an inmate and now, feeling that he had not much longer to live, wanted to see once more the house in which he was born. Albert Meadows, his great-nephew, had gone over to Portsmouth in the Ford to fetch him and he was to arrive that afternoon.

"Just fancy," said Mrs. George, "he's not been here for

more than fifty years. He's never even seen my George, who's fifty-one next birthday."

"And what does Mrs. Meadows think of it?" I asked.

"Well, you know what she is. She sits there and smiles to herself. All she says is, 'he was a good-looking young fellow when he left, but not so steady as his brother.' That's why she chose my George's father. 'But he's probably quietened down by now,' she says."

Mrs. George asked me to look in and see him. With the simplicity of a country woman who had never been further from her home than London, she thought that because we had both been in China we must have something in common. Of course I accepted. I found the whole family assembled when I arrived; they were sitting in the great old kitchen, with its stone floor, Mrs. Meadows in her usual chair by the fire, very upright, and I was amused to see that she had put on her best silk dress, while her son and his wife sat at the table with their children. On the other side of the fireplace sat an old man, bunched up in a chair. He was very thin and his skin hung on his bones like an old suit much too large for him; his face was wrinkled and yellow and he had lost nearly all his teeth.

I shook hands with him.

"Well, I'm glad to see you've got here safely, Mr. Meadows," I said.

"Captain," he corrected.

"He walked here," Albert, his great-nephew, told me. "When he got to the gate he made me stop the car and said he wanted to walk."

"And mind you, I've not been out of my bed for two years. They carried me down and put me in the car. I thought I'd never walk again, but when I see them elm-trees, I remember my father set a lot of store by them elm-trees, I felt I could walk. I walked down that drive fifty-two years ago when I went away and now I've walked back again."

"Silly, I call it," said Mrs. Meadows.

"It's done me good. I feel better and stronger than I have for ten years. I'll see you out yet, Emily."

"Don't you be too sure," she answered.

I suppose no one had called Mrs. Meadows by her first name for a generation. It gave me a little shock, as though the old man were taking a liberty with her. She looked at him with a shrewd smile in her eyes and he, talking to her, grinned with his toothless gums. It was strange to look at them, these two old people who had not seen one another for half a century, and to think that all that long time ago he had loved her and she had loved another. I wondered if they remembered what they had felt then and what they had said to one another. I wondered if it seemed to him strange now that for that old woman he had left the home of his fathers, his lawful inheritance, and lived an exile's life.

"Have you ever been married, Captain Meadows?" I asked.

"Not me," he said, in his quavering voice, with a grin. "I know too much about women for that."

"That's what you say," retorted Mrs. Meadows. "If the truth was known I shouldn't be surprised to hear as how you'd had half a dozen black wives in your day."

"They're not black in China, Emily, you ought to know better than that, they're yellow."

"Perhaps that's why you've got so yellow yourself. When I saw you, I said to myself, why, he's got jaundice."

"I said I'd never marry anyone but you, Emily, and I never have."

He said this not with pathos or resentment, but as a mere statement of fact, as a man might say: "I said I'd walk twenty miles and I've done it." There was a trace of satisfaction in the speech.

"Well, you might have regretted it if you had," she answered.

I talked a little with the old man about China.

"There's not a port in China that I don't know better than you know your coat pocket. Where a ship can go I've been. I could keep you sitting here all day long for six months and not tell you half the things I've seen in my day."

"Well, one thing you've not done, George, as far as I can see," said Mrs. Meadows, the mocking but not unkindly smile still in her eyes, "and that's to make a fortune."

"I'm not one to save money. Make it and spend it, that's my motto. But one thing I can say for myself: if I had the chance of going through my life again I'd take it. And there's not many as'll say that."

"No, indeed," I said.

I looked at him with admiration and respect. He was a toothless, crippled, penniless old man, but he had made a success of life, for he had enjoyed it. When I left him he asked me to come and see him again next day. If I was interested in China he would tell me all the stories I wanted to hear.

Next morning I thought I would go and ask if the old man would like to see me. I strolled down the magnificent avenue of elm-trees and when I came to the garden saw Mrs. Meadows picking flowers. I bade her good morning and she raised herself. She had a huge armful of white flowers. I glanced at the house and I saw that the blinds were drawn: I was surprised, for Mrs. Meadows liked the sunshine.

"Time enough to live in the dark when you're buried," she always said.

"How's Captain Meadows?" I asked her.

"He always was a harum-scarum fellow," she answered. "When Lizzie took him in a cup of tea this morning she found he was dead."

"Dead?"

"Yes. Died in his sleep. I was just picking these flowers to put in the room. Well, I'm glad he died in that old house. It always means a lot to them Meadows to do that."

They had had a good deal of difficulty in persuading him to go to bed. He had talked to them of all the things that had happened to him in his long life. He was happy to be back in his old home. He was proud that he had walked up the drive without assistance, and he boasted that he would live for another twenty years. But fate had been kind: death had written the full-stop in the right place.

Mrs. Meadows smelt the white flowers that she held in her arms.

"Well, I'm glad he came back," she said. "After I married Tom Meadows and George went away, the fact is I was never quite sure that I'd married the right one."

THE END OF THE FLIGHT

I SHOOK hands with the skipper and he wished me luck. Then I went down to the lower deck crowded with passengers, Malays, Chinese and Dyaks, and made my way to the ladder. Looking over the ship's side I saw that my luggage was already in the boat. It was a large, clumsy-looking craft, with a great square sail of bamboo matting, and it was crammed full of gesticulating natives. I scrambled in and a place was made for me. We were about three miles from the shore and a stiff breeze was blowing. As we drew near I saw that the coconut trees in a green abundance grew to the water's edge, and among them I saw the brown roofs of the village. A Chinese who spoke English pointed out to me a white bungalow as the residence of the district officer. Though he did not know it, it was with him that I was going to stay. I had a letter of introduction to him in my pocket.

I felt somewhat forlorn when I landed and my bags were set down beside me on the glistening beach. This was a remote spot to find myself in, this little town on the north coast of Borneo, and I felt a trifle shy at the thought of presenting myself to a total stranger with the announcement that I was going to sleep under his roof, eat his food and drink his whisky, till another boat came in to take me to the port for which I was bound.

But I might have spared myself these misgivings, for the moment I reached the bungalow and sent in my letter he came out, a sturdy, ruddy, jovial man, of thirty-five perhaps, and greeted me with heartiness. While he held my hand he shouted to a boy to bring drinks and to another to look after my luggage. He cut short my apologies.

"Good God, man, you have no idea how glad I am to see you.

311

Don't think I'm doing anything for you in putting you up. The boot's on the other leg. And stay as long as you damned well like. Stay a year."

I laughed. He put away his day's work, assuring me that he had nothing to do that could not wait till the morrow, and threw himself into a long chair. We talked and drank and talked. When the heat of the day wore off we went for a long tramp in the jungle and came back wet to the skin. A bath and a change were very grateful, and then we dined. I was tired out and though my host was plainly willing to go on talking straight through the night I was obliged to beg him to allow me to go to bed.

"All right, I'll just come along to your room and see everything's all right."

It was a large room with verandas on two sides of it, sparsely furnished, but with a huge bed protected by mosquito netting.

"The bed is rather hard. Do you mind?"

"Not a bit. I shall sleep without rocking to-night."

My host looked at the bed reflectively.

"It was a Dutchman who slept in it last. Do you want to hear a funny story?"

I wanted chiefly to go to bed, but he *was* my host, and being at times somewhat of a humorist myself I know that it is hard to have an amusing story to tell and find no listener.

"He came on the boat that brought you, on its last journey along the coast, he came into my office and asked where the dak bungalow was. I told him there wasn't one, but if he hadn't anywhere to go I didn't mind putting him up. He jumped at the invitation. I told him to have his kit sent along."

" 'This is all I've got,' he said.

"He held out a little shiny black grip. It seemed a bit scanty, but it was no business of mine, so I told him to go along to the bungalow and I'd come as soon as I was through my work. While I was speaking the door of my office was opened and my clerk came in. The Dutchman had his back to the door and it may be that my clerk opened it a bit suddenly. Anyhow, the Dutchman gave a shout, he jumped about two feet into the air and whipped out a revolver.

" 'What the hell are you doing?' I said.

"When he saw it was the clerk he collapsed. He leaned against the desk, panting, and upon my word he was shaking as though he'd got fever.

" 'I beg your pardon,' he said. 'It's my nerves. My nerves are terrible.'

" 'It looks like it,' I said.

"I was rather short with him. To tell you the truth I wished I hadn't asked him to stop with me. He didn't look as though he'd been drinking a lot and I wondered if he was some fellow the police were after. If he were, I said to myself, he could hardly be such a fool as to walk right into the lion's den.

" 'You'd better go and lie down,' I said.

"He took himself off, and when I got back to my bungalow I found him sitting quite quietly, but bolt upright, on the veranda. He'd had a bath and shaved and put on clean things and he looked fairly presentable.

" 'Why are you sitting in the middle of the place like that?' I asked him. 'You'll be much more comfortable in one of the long chairs.'

" 'I prefer to sit up,' he said.

"Queer, I thought. But if a man in this heat would rather sit up than lie down it's his own look-out. He wasn't much to look at, tallish and heavily built, with a square head and close-cropped bristly hair. I should think he was about forty. The thing that chiefly struck me about him was his expression. There was a look in his eyes, blue eyes they were and rather small, that beat me altogether; and his face sagged as it were; it gave you the feeling he was going to cry. He had a way of looking quickly over his left shoulder as though he thought he heard something. By God, he was nervous. But we had a couple of drinks and he began to talk. He spoke English very well; except for a slight accent you'd never have known that he was a foreigner, and I'm bound to admit he was a good talker. He'd been everywhere and he'd read any amount. It was a treat to listen to him.

"We had three or four whiskies in the afternoon and a lot of gin pahits later on, so that when dinner came along we were by way of being rather hilarious and I'd come to the conclusion that he was a damned good fellow. Of course we had a lot of whisky at dinner and I happened to have a bottle of Benedictine, so we had some liqueurs afterwards. I can't help thinking we both got very tight.

"And at last he told me why he'd come. It was a rum story."

My host stopped and looked at me with his mouth slightly open as though, remembering it now, he was struck again with its rumness.

"He came from Sumatra, the Dutchman, and he'd done something to an Achinese and the Achinese had sworn to kill him. At first he made light of it, but the fellow tried two or three times and it began to be rather a nuisance, so he thought he'd better go away for a bit. He went over to Batavia and made up his mind to have a good time. But when he'd been there a week he saw the fellow slinking along a wall. By God, he'd followed him. It looked as though he meant business. The Dutchman began to think it was getting beyond a joke and he thought the best thing he could do would be to skip off to Soerabaya. Well, he was strolling about there one day, you know how crowded the streets are, when he happened to turn round and saw the Achinese walking quite quietly just behind him. It gave him a turn. It would give anyone a turn.

"The Dutchman went straight back to his hotel, packed his things, and took the next boat to Singapore. Of course he put up at the Van Wyck, all the Dutch stay there, and one day when he was having a drink in the courtyard in front of the hotel, the Achinese walked in as bold as brass, looked at him for a minute, and walked out again. The Dutchman told me he was just paralysed. The fellow could have stuck his kriss into him there and then and he wouldn't have been able to move a hand to defend himself. The Dutchman knew he was just biding his time, that damned native was going to kill him, he saw it in his eyes; and he went all to pieces."

"But why didn't he go to the police?" I asked.

"I don't know. I expect it wasn't a thing he wanted the police to be mixed up in."

"But what had he done to the man?"

"I don't know that either. He wouldn't tell me. But by the look he gave when I asked him, I expect it was something pretty rotten. I have an idea he knew he deserved whatever the Achinese could do."

My host lit a cigarette.

"Go on," I said.

"The skipper of the boat that runs between Singapore and Kuching lives at the Van Wyck between trips and the boat was starting at dawn. The Dutchman thought it a grand chance to give the fellow the slip; he left his luggage at the hotel and walked down to the ship with the skipper, as if he were just going to see him off, and stayed on her when she sailed. His nerves were all anyhow by then. He didn't care about anything but getting rid of the Achinese. He felt pretty safe at Kuching. He got a room at the rest-house and bought himself a couple of suits and some shirts in the Chinese shops. But he told me he couldn't sleep. He dreamt of that man and half a dozen times he awakened just as he thought a kriss was being drawn across his throat. By God, I felt quite sorry for him. He just shook as he talked to me and his voice was hoarse with terror. That was the meaning of the look I had noticed. You remember, I told

II

you he had a funny look on his face and I couldn't tell what it meant. Well, it was fear.

"And one day when he was in the club at Kuching he looked out of the window and saw the Achinese sitting there. Their eyes met. The Dutchman just crumpled up and fainted. When he came to, his first idea was to get out. Well, you know, there's not a hell of a lot of traffic at Kuching and this boat that brought you was the only one that gave him a chance to get away quickly. He got on her. He was positive the man was not on board."

"But what made him come here?"

"Well, the old tramp stops at a dozen places on the coast and the Achinese couldn't possibly guess he'd chosen this one because he only made up his mind to get off when he saw there was only one boat to take the passengers ashore, and there weren't more than a dozen people in it.

" 'I'm safe here for a bit at all events,' he said, 'and if I can only be quiet for a while I shall get my nerve back.'

" 'Stay as long as you like,' I said. 'You're all right here, at all events till the boat comes along next month, and if you like we'll watch the people who come off.'

"He was all over me. I could see what a relief it was to him.

"It was pretty late and I suggested to him that we should turn in. I took him to his room to see that it was all right. He locked the door of the bath-house and bolted the shutters, though I told him there was no risk, and when I left him I heard him lock the door I had just gone out of.

"Next morning when the boy brought me my tea I asked him if he'd called the Dutchman. He said he was just going to. I heard him knock and knock again. Funny, I thought. The boy hammered on the door, but there was no answer. I felt a little nervous, so I got up. I knocked too. We made enough noise to rouse the dead, but the Dutchman slept on. Then I broke down the door. The mosquito curtains were neatly tucked in round the bed. I pulled them apart. He was lying there on his back with his eyes wide open. He was as dead as mutton. A kriss lay across his throat, and say I'm a liar if you like, but I swear to God it's true, there wasn't a wound about him anywhere. The room was empty.

"Funny, wasn't it?"

"Well, that all depends on your idea of humour," I replied.

My host looked at me quickly.

"You don't mind sleeping in that bed, do you?"

"N-no. But I'd just as soon you'd told me the story to-morrow morning."

THE ANT AND THE GRASSHOPPER

WHEN I was a very small boy I was made to learn by heart certain of the fables of La Fontaine, and the moral of each was carefully explained to me. Among those I learnt was *The Ant and The Grasshopper* which is devised to bring home to the young the useful lesson that in an imperfect world industry is rewarded and giddiness punished. In this admirable fable (I apologise for telling something which everyone is politely, but inexactly, supposed to know) the ant spends a laborious summer gathering its winter store, while the grasshopper sits on a blade of grass singing to the sun. Winter comes and the ant is comfortably provided for, but the grasshopper has an empty larder: he goes to the ant and begs for a little food. Then the ant gives him her classic answer.

"What were you doing in the summer time?"

"Saving your presence, I sang, I sang all day, all night."

"You sang. Why, then go and dance."

I do not ascribe it to perversity on my part, but rather to the inconsequence of childhood, which is deficient in moral sense, that I could never quite reconcile myself to the lesson. My sympathies were with the grasshopper and for some time I never saw an ant without putting my foot on it. In this summary (and as I have discovered since, entirely human) fashion I sought to express my disapproval of prudence and common sense.

I could not help thinking of this fable when the other day I saw George Ramsay lunching by himself in a restaurant. I never saw anyone wear an expression of such deep gloom. He was staring into space. He looked as though the burden of the whole world sat on his shoulders. I was sorry for him. I suspected at once that his unfortunate brother had been causing trouble again. I went up to him and held out my hand.

"How are you?" I asked.

"I'm not in hilarious spirits," he answered.

"Is it Tom again?"

He sighed.

"Yes, it's Tom again."

"Why don't you chuck him? You've done everything in the world for him. You must know by now that he's quite hopeless."

I suppose every family has a black sheep. Tom had been a sore trial to his for twenty years. He had begun life decently enough: he went into business, married and had two children. The Ramsays were perfectly respectable people and there was every reason to suppose that Tom Ramsay would have a useful and honourable career. But one day, without warning, he announced that he didn't like work and that he wasn't suited for marriage. He wanted to enjoy himself. He would listen to no expostulations. He left his wife and his office. He had a little money and he spent two happy years in the various capitals of Europe. Rumours of his doings reached his relations from time to time and they were profoundly shocked. He certainly had a very good time. They shook their heads and asked what would happen when his money was spent. They soon found out: he borrowed. He was charming and unscrupulous. I have never met anyone to whom it was more difficult to refuse a loan. He made a steady income from his friends and he made friends easily. But he always said that the money you spent on necessities was boring; the money that was amusing to spend was the money you spent in luxuries. For this he depended on his brother George. He did not waste his charm on him. George was a serious man and insensible to such enticements. George was respectable. Once or twice he fell to Tom's promises of amendment and gave him considerable sums in order that he might make a fresh start. On these Tom bought a motor-car and some very nice jewellery. But when circumstances forced George to realise that his brother would never settle down and he washed his hands of him, Tom, without a qualm, began to blackmail him. It was not very nice for a respectable lawyer to find his brother shaking cocktails behind the bar of his favourite restaurant or to see him waiting on the box-seat of a taxi outside his club. Tom said that to serve in a bar or to drive a taxi was a perfectly decent occupation, but if George could oblige him with a couple of hundred pounds he didn't mind for the honour of the family giving it up. George paid.

Once Tom nearly went to prison. George was terribly upset. He went into the whole discreditable affair. Really Tom had gone too far. He had been wild, thoughtless and selfish, but he had never before done anything dishonest, by which George meant illegal; and if he were prosecuted he would assuredly be convicted. But you cannot allow your only brother to go to gaol. The man Tom had cheated, a man called Cronshaw, was vindictive. He was determined to take the matter into court; he said Tom was a scoundrel and should be punished. It cost George an infinite deal of trouble and five hundred pounds to settle the affair. I have never seen him in such a rage as when he heard that Tom and Cronshaw had gone off together to Monte Carlo the moment they cashed the cheque. They spent a happy month there.

For twenty years Tom raced and gambled, philandered with the prettiest girls, danced, ate in the most expensive restaurants, and dressed beautifully. He always looked as if he had just stepped out of a bandbox. Though he was forty-six you would never have taken him for more than thirty-five. He was a most amusing companion and though you knew he was perfectly worthless you could not but enjoy his society. He had high spirits, an unfailing gaiety and incredible charm. I never grudged the contributions he regularly levied on me for the necessities of his existence. I never lent him fifty pounds without feeling that I was in his debt. Tom Ramsay knew everyone and everyone knew Tom Ramsay. You could not approve of him, but you could not help liking him.

Poor George, only a year older than his scapegrace brother, looked sixty. He had never taken more than a fortnight's holiday in the year for a quarter of a century. He was in his office every morning at nine-thirty and never left it till six. He was honest, industrious and worthy. He had a good wife, to whom he had never been unfaithful even in thought, and four daughters to whom he was the best of fathers. He made a point of saving a third of his income and his plan was to retire at fifty-five to a little house in the country where he proposed to cultivate his garden and play golf. His life was blameless. He was glad that he was growing old because Tom was growing old too. He rubbed his hands and said:

"It was all very well when Tom was young and good-looking, but he's only a year younger than I am. In four years he'll be fifty. He won't find life so easy then. I shall have thirty thousand pounds by the time I'm fifty. For twenty-five years I've said that Tom would end in the gutter. And we shall see how he likes that. We shall see if it really pays best to work or be idle."

Poor George! I sympathised with him. I wondered now as I sat down beside him what infamous thing Tom had done. George was evidently very much upset.

"Do you know what's happened now?" he asked me.

I was prepared for the worst. I wondered if Tom had got into the hands of the police at last. George could hardly bring himself to speak.

"You're not going to deny that all my life I've been hard-working, decent, respectable and straightforward. After a life of industry and thrift I can look forward to retiring on a small income in gilt-edged securities. I've always done my duty in that state of life in which it has pleased Providence to place me."

"True."

"And you can't deny that Tom has been an idle, worthless, dissolute and dishonourable rogue. If there were any justice he'd be in the workhouse."

"True."

George grew red in the face.

"A few weeks ago he became engaged to a woman old enough to be his mother. And now she's died and left him everything she had. Half a million pounds, a yacht, a house in London and a house in the country."

George Ramsay beat his clenched fist on the table.

"It's not fair, I tell you, it's not fair. Damn it, it's not fair."

I could not help it. I burst into a shout of laughter as I looked at George's wrathful face, I rolled in my chair, I very nearly fell on the floor. George never forgave me. But Tom often asks me to excellent dinners in his charming house in Mayfair and if he occasionally borrows a trifle from me that is merely force of habit. It is never more than a sovereign.

THE MAN WITH THE SCAR

IT was on account of the scar that I first noticed him, for it ran, broad and red, in a great crescent from his temple to his chin. It must have been due to a formidable wound and I wondered whether this had been caused by a sabre or by a fragment of shell. It was unexpected on that round, fat and good-humoured face. He had small and undistinguished features, and his expression was artless. His face went oddly with his corpulent body. He was a powerful man of more than common height. I never saw him in anything but a very shabby grey suit, a khaki shirt and a battered sombrero. He was far from clean. He used to come into the Palace Hotel at Guatemala City every day at cocktail time and strolling leisurely round the bar offer lottery tickets for sale. If this was the way he made his living it must have been a poor one, for I never saw anyone buy, but now and then I saw him offered a drink. He never refused it. He threaded his way among the tables with a sort of rolling walk as though he were accustomed to traverse long distances on foot, paused at each table, with a little smile mentioned the numbers he had for sale and then, when no notice was taken of him, with the same smile passed on. I think he was for the most part a trifle the worse for liquor.

I was standing at the bar one evening, my foot on the rail, with an acquaintance—they make a very good dry Martini at the Palace Hotel in Guatemala City—when the man with the scar came up. I shook my head as for the twentieth time since my arrival he held out for my inspection his lottery tickets. But my companion nodded affably.

"*Qué tal, general?* How is life?"

"Not so bad. Business is none too good, but it might be worse."

"What will you have, general?"

"A brandy."

He tossed it down and put the glass back on the bar. He nodded to my acquaintance.

"*Gracias. Hasta luego.*"

Then he turned away and offered his tickets to the men who were standing next to us.

"Who is your friend?" I asked. "That's a terrific scar on his face."

"It doesn't add to his beauty, does it? He's an exile from Nicaragua. He's a ruffian of course and a bandit, but not a bad fellow. I give him a few *pesos* now and then. He was a revolutionary general, and if his ammunition hadn't given out he'd have upset the government and be minister of war now instead of selling lottery tickets in Guatemala. They captured him, along with his staff, such as it was, and tried him by court-martial. Such things are rather summary in these countries, you know, and he was sentenced to be shot at dawn. I guess he knew what was coming to him when he was caught. He spent the night in gaol and he and the others, there were five of them altogether, passed the time playing poker. They used matches for chips. He told me he'd never had such a run of bad luck in his life; they were playing with a short pack, Jacks to open, but he never held a card, he never improved more than half a dozen times in the whole sitting and no sooner did he buy a new stack than he lost it. When day broke and the soldiers came into the cell to fetch them for execution he had lost more matches than a reasonable man could use in a lifetime.

"They were led into the patio of the gaol and placed against a wall, the five of them side by side, with the firing party facing them. There was a pause and our friend asked the officer in charge of them what the devil they were keeping him waiting for. The officer said that the general commanding the govern-

ment troops wished to attend the execution and they awaited
his arrival.

" 'Then I have time to smoke another cigarette,' said our
friend. 'He was always unpunctual.'

"But he had barely lit it when the general—it was San
Ignacio, by the way: I don't know whether you ever met him—
followed by his A.D.C. came into the patio. The usual
formalities were performed and San Ignacio asked the condemned men whether there was anything they wished before
the execution took place. Four of the five shook their heads,
but our friend spoke.

" 'Yes, I should like to say good-bye to my wife.'

" '*Bueno*,' said the general, 'I have no objection to that.
Where is she?'

" 'She is waiting at the prison door.'

" 'Then it will not cause a delay of more than five minutes.'

" 'Hardly that, Señor General,' said our friend.

" 'Have him placed on one side.'

"Two soldiers advanced and between them the condemned
rebel walked to the spot indicated. The officer in command of
the firing squad on a nod from the general gave an order, there
was a ragged report, and the four men fell. They fell strangely,
not together, but one after the other, with movements that
were almost grotesque, as though they were puppets in a toy
theatre. The officer went up to them and into one who was still
alive emptied two barrels of his revolver. Our friend finished
his cigarette and threw away the stub.

"There was a little stir at the gateway. A woman came into
the patio, with quick steps, and then, her hand on her heart,
stopped suddenly. She gave a cry and with outstretched arms
ran forward.

" '*Caramba*,' said the general.

"She was in black, with a veil over her hair, and her face was
dead white. She was hardly more than a girl, a slim creature,

with little regular features and enormous eyes. But they were distraught with anguish. Her loveliness was such that as she ran, her mouth slightly open and the agony of her face beautiful, a gasp of surprise was wrung from those indifferent soldiers who looked at her.

"The rebel advanced a step or two to meet her. She flung herself into his arms and with a hoarse cry of passion: *alma de mi corazón*, soul of my heart, he pressed his lips to hers. And at the same moment he drew a knife from his ragged shirt—I haven't a notion how he managed to retain possession of it— and stabbed her in the neck. The blood spurted from the cut vein and dyed his shirt. Then he flung his arms round her and once more pressed his lips to hers.

"It happened so quickly that many did not know what had occurred, but from the others burst a cry of horror; they sprang forward and seized him. They loosened his gasp and the girl would have fallen if the A.D.C. had not caught her. She was unconscious. They laid her on the ground and with dismay on their faces stood round watching her. The rebel knew where he was striking and it was impossible to staunch the blood. In a moment the A.D.C. who had been kneeling by her side rose.

" 'She's dead,' he whispered.

"The rebel crossed himself.

" 'Why did you do it?' asked the general.

" 'I loved her.'

"A sort of sigh passed through those men crowded together and they looked with strange faces at the murderer. The general stared at him for a while in silence.

" 'It was a noble gesture,' he said at last. 'I cannot execute this man. Take my car and have him led to the frontier. Señor, I offer you the homage which is due from one brave man to another.'

"A murmur of approbation broke from those who listened.

The A.D.C. tapped the rebel on the shoulder, and between the two soldiers without a word he marched to the waiting car."

My friend stopped and for a little I was silent. I must explain that he was a Guatemalecan and spoke to me in Spanish. I have translated what he told me as well as I could, but I have made no attempt to tone down his rather high-flown language. To tell the truth I think it suits the story.

"But how then did he get the scar?" I asked at length.

"Oh, that was due to a bottle that burst when he was opening it. A bottle of ginger ale."

"I never liked it," said I.

LOUISE

ICOULD never understand why Louise bothered with me. She disliked me and I knew that behind my back, in that gentle way of hers, she seldom lost the opportunity of saying a disagreeable thing about me. She had too much delicacy ever to make a direct statement, but with a hint and a sigh and a little flutter of her beautiful hands she was able to make her meaning plain. She was a mistress of cold praise. It was true that we had known one another almost intimately, for five-and-twenty years, but it was impossible for me to believe that she could be affected by the claims of old association. She thought me a coarse, brutal, cynical and vulgar fellow. I was puzzled at her not taking the obvious course and dropping me. She did nothing of the kind; indeed, she would not leave me alone; she was constantly asking me to lunch and dine with her and once or twice a year invited me to spend a week-end at her house in the country. At last I thought that I had discovered her motive. She had an uneasy suspicion that I did not believe in her; and if that was why she did not like me, it was also why she sought my acquaintance: it galled her that I alone should look upon her as a comic figure and she could not rest till I acknowledged myself mistaken and defeated. Perhaps she had an inkling that I saw the face behind the mask and because I alone held out was determined that sooner or later I too should take the mask for the face. I was never quite certain that she was a complete humbug. I wondered whether she fooled herself as thoroughly as she fooled the world or whether there was some spark of humour at the bottom of her heart. If there was it might be that she was attracted to me, as a pair of crooks might be attracted to one another, by the knowledge that we shared a secret that was hidden from everybody else.

I knew Louise before she married. She was then a frail, delicate girl with large and melancholy eyes. Her father and mother worshipped her with an anxious adoration, for some illness, scarlet fever I think, had left her with a weak heart and she had to take the greatest care of herself. When Tom Maitland proposed to her they were dismayed, for they were convinced that she was much too delicate for the strenuous state of marriage. But they were not too well off and Tom Maitland was rich. He promised to do everything in the world for Louise and finally they entrusted her to him as a sacred charge. Tom Maitland was a big, husky fellow, very good-looking and a fine athlete. He doted on Louise. With her weak heart he could not hope to keep her with him long and he made up his mind to do everything he could to make her few years on earth happy. He gave up the games he excelled in, not because she wished him to, she was glad that he should play golf and hunt, but because by a coincidence she had a heart attack whenever he proposed to leave her for a day. If they had a difference of opinion she gave in to him at once, for she was the most submissive wife a man could have, but her heart failed her and she would be laid up, sweet and uncomplaining, for a week. He could not be such a brute as to cross her. Then they would have quite a little tussle about which should yield and it was only with difficulty that at last he persuaded her to have her own way. On one occasion seeing her walk eight miles on an expedition that she particularly wanted to make, I suggested to Tom Maitland that she was stronger than one would have thought. He shook his head and sighed.

"No, no, she's dreadfully delicate. She's been to all the best heart specialists in the world and they all say that her life hangs on a thread. But she has an unconquerable spirit."

He told her that I had remarked on her endurance.

"I shall pay for it to-morrow," she said to me in her plaintive way. "I shall be at death's door."

"I sometimes think that you're quite strong enough to do the things you want to," I murmured.

I had noticed that if a party was amusing she could dance till five in the morning, but if it was dull she felt very poorly and Tom had to take her home early. I am afraid she did not like my reply, for though she gave me a pathetic little smile I saw no amusement in her large blue eyes.

"You can't very well expect me to fall down dead just to please you," she answered.

Louise outlived her husband. He caught his death of cold one day when they were sailing and Louise needed all the rugs there were to keep her warm. He left her a comfortable fortune and a daughter. Louise was inconsolable. It was wonderful that she managed to survive the shock. Her friends expected her speedily to follow poor Tom Maitland to the grave. Indeed they already felt dreadfully sorry for Iris, her daughter, who would be left an orphan. They redoubled their attentions towards Louise. They would not let her stir a finger; they insisted on doing everything in the world to save her trouble. They had to, because if she was called upon to do anything tiresome or inconvenient her heart went back on her and there she was at death's door. She was entirely lost without a man to take care of her, she said, and she did not know how, with her delicate health, she was going to bring up her dear Iris. Her friends asked why she did not marry again. Oh, with her heart it was out of the question, though of course she knew that dear Tom would have wished her to, and perhaps it would be the best thing for Iris if she did; but who would want to be bothered with a wretched invalid like herself? Oddly enough more than one young man showed himself quite ready to undertake the charge and a year after Tom's death she allowed George Hobhouse to lead her to the altar. He was a fine, upstanding fellow and he was not at all badly off. I never saw anyone so grateful as he for the privilege of being allowed to take care of this frail little thing.

"I shan't live to trouble you long," she said.

He was a soldier and an ambitious one, but he resigned his commission. Louise's health forced her to spend the winter at Monte Carlo and the summer at Deauville. He hesitated a little at throwing up his career, and Louise at first would not hear of it, but at last she yielded as she always yielded, and he prepared to make his wife's last few years as happy as might be.

"It can't be very long now," she said. "I'll try not to be troublesome."

For the next two or three years Louise managed, notwithstanding her weak heart, to go beautifully dressed to all the most lively parties, to gamble very heavily, to dance and even to flirt with tall slim young men. But George Hobhouse had not the stamina of Louise's first husband and he had to brace himself now and then with a stiff drink for his day's work as Louise's second husband. It is possible that the habit would have grown on him, which Louise would not have liked at all, but very fortunately (for her) the war broke out. He rejoined his regiment and three months later was killed. It was a great shock to Louise. She felt, however, that in such a crisis she must not give way to a private grief, and if she had a heart attack nobody heard of it. In order to distract her mind she turned her villa at Monte Carlo into a hospital for convalescent officers. Her friends told her that she would never survive the strain.

"Of course it will kill me," she said, "I know that. But what does it matter? I must do my bit."

It didn't kill her. She had the time of her life. There was no convalescent home in France that was more popular. I met her by chance in Paris. She was lunching at the Ritz with a tall and very handsome young Frenchman. She explained that she was there on business connected with the hospital. She told me that the officers were too charming to her. They knew how delicate she was and they wouldn't let her do a single thing. They took care of her, well—as though they were all her husbands. She sighed.

"Poor George, who would ever have thought that I with my heart should survive him?"

"And poor Tom!" I said.

I don't know why she didn't like my saying that. She gave me her plaintive smile and her beautiful eyes filled with tears.

"You always speak as though you grudged me the few years that I can expect to live."

"By the way, your heart's much better, isn't it?"

"It'll never be better. I saw a specialist this morning and he said I must be prepared for the worst."

"Oh, well, you've been prepared for that for nearly twenty years now, haven't you?"

When the war came to an end Louise settled in London. She was now a woman of over forty, thin and frail still, with large eyes and pale cheeks, but she did not look a day more than twenty-five. Iris, who had been at school and was now grown up, came to live with her.

"She'll take care of me," said Louise. "Of course it'll be hard on her to live with such a great invalid as I am, but it can only be for such a little while, I'm sure she won't mind."

Iris was a nice girl. She had been brought up with the knowledge that her mother's health was precarious. As a child she had never been allowed to make a noise. She had always realised that her mother must on no account be upset. And though Louise told her now that she would not hear of her sacrificing herself for a tiresome old woman the girl simply would not listen. It wasn't a question of sacrificing herself, it was a happiness to do what she could for her poor dear mother. With a sigh her mother let her do a great deal.

"It pleases the child to think she's making herself useful," she said.

"Don't you think she ought to go out and about more?" I asked.

"That's what I'm always telling her. I can't get her to enjoy herself. Heaven knows, I never want anyone to put themselves out on my account."

And Iris, when I remonstrated with her, said: "Poor dear mother, she wants me to go and stay with friends and go to parties, but the moment I start off anywhere she has one of her heart attacks, so I much prefer to stay at home."

But presently she fell in love. A young friend of mine, a very good lad, asked her to marry him and she consented. I liked the child and was glad that she was to be given at last the chance to lead a life of her own. She had never seemed to suspect that such a thing was possible. But one day the young man came to me in great distress and told me that his marriage was indefinitely postponed. Iris felt that she could not desert her mother. Of course it was really no business of mine, but I made the opportunity to go and see Louise. She was always glad to receive her friends at tea-time and now that she was older she cultivated the society of painters and writers.

"Well, I hear that Iris isn't going to be married," I said after a little.

"I don't know about that. She's not going to be married quite as soon as I could have wished. I've begged her on my bended knees not to consider me, but she absolutely refuses to leave me."

"Don't you think it's rather hard on her?"

"Dreadfully. Of course it can only be for a few months, but I hate the thought of anyone sacrificing themselves for me."

"My dear Louise, you've buried two husbands, I can't see the least reason why you shouldn't bury at least two more."

"Do you think that's funny?" she asked me in a tone that she made as offensive as she could.

"I suppose it's never struck you as strange that you're

always strong enough to do anything you want to and that your weak heart only prevents you from doing things that bore you?"

"Oh, I know, I know what you've always thought of me. You've never believed that I had anything the matter with me, have you?"

I looked at her full and square.

"Never. I think you've carried out for twenty-five years a stupendous bluff. I think you're the most selfish and monstrous woman I have ever known. You ruined the lives of those two wretched men you married and now you're going to ruin the life of your daughter."

I should not have been surprised if Louise had had a heart attack then. I fully expected her to fly into a passion. She merely gave me a gentle smile.

"My poor friend, one of these days you'll be so dreadfully sorry you said this to me."

"Have you quite determined that Iris shall not marry this boy?"

"I've begged her to marry him. I know it'll kill me, but I don't mind. Nobody cares for me. I'm just a burden to everybody."

"Did you tell her it would kill you?"

"She made me."

"As if anyone ever made you do anything that you were not yourself quite determined to do."

"She can marry her young man to-morrow if she likes. If it kills me, it kills me."

"Well, let's risk it, shall we?"

"Haven't you got any compassion for me?"

"One can't pity anyone who amuses one as much as you amuse me," I answered.

A faint spot of colour appeared on Louise's pale cheeks and though she smiled still her eyes were hard and angry.

"Iris shall marry in a month's time," she said, "and if anything happens to me I hope you and she will be able to forgive yourselves."

Louise was as good as her word. A date was fixed, a trousseau of great magnificence was ordered, and invitations were issued. Iris and the very good lad were radiant. On the wedding-day, at ten o'clock in the morning, Louise, that devilish woman, had one of her heart attacks—and died. She died gently forgiving Iris for having killed her.

A STRING OF BEADS

"WHAT a bit of luck that I'm placed next to you," said Laura, as we sat down to dinner.

"For me," I replied politely.

"That remains to be seen. I particularly wanted to have the chance of talking to you. I've got a story to tell you."

At this my heart sank a little.

"I'd sooner you talked about yourself," I answered. "Or even about me."

"Oh, but I must tell you the story. I think you'll be able to use it."

"If you must, you must. But let's look at the menu first."

"Don't you want me to?" she said, somewhat aggrieved. "I thought you'd be pleased."

"I am. You might have written a play and wanted to read me that."

"It happened to some friends of mine. It's perfectly true."

"That's no recommendation. A true story is never quite so true as an invented one."

"What does that mean?"

"Nothing very much," I admitted. "But I thought it sounded well."

"I wish you'd let me get on with it."

"I'm all attention. I'm not going to eat the soup. It's fattening."

She gave me a pinched look and then glanced at the menu. She uttered a little sigh.

"Oh, well, if you're going to deny yourself I suppose I must too. Heaven knows, I can't afford to take liberties with my figure."

"And yet is there any soup more heavenly than the sort

336

of soup in which you put a great dollop of cream?"

"Bortsch," she sighed. "It's the only soup I really like."

"Never mind. Tell me your story and we'll forget about food till the fish comes."

"Well, I was actually there when it happened. I was dining with the Livingstones. Do you know the Livingstones?"

"No, I don't think I do."

"Well, you can ask them and they'll confirm every word I say. They'd asked their governess to come in to dinner because some woman had thrown them over at the last moment—you know how inconsiderate people are—and they would have been thirteen at table. Their governess was a Miss Robinson, quite a nice girl, young, you know, twenty or twenty-one, and rather pretty. Personally I would never engage a governess who was young and pretty. One never knows."

"But one hopes for the best."

Laura paid no attention to my remark.

"The chances are that she'll be thinking of young men instead of attending to her duties and then, just when she's got used to your ways, she'll want to go and get married. But Miss Robinson had excellent references, and I must allow that she was a very nice, respectable person. I believe in point of fact she was a clergyman's daughter.

"There was a man at dinner whom I don't suppose you've ever heard of, but who's quite a celebrity in his way. He's a Count Borselli and he knows more about precious stones than anyone in the world. He was sitting next to Mary Lyngate, who rather fancies herself on her pearls, and in the course of conversation she asked him what he thought of the string she was wearing. He said it was very pretty. She was rather piqued at this and told him it was valued at eight thousand pounds.

" 'Yes, it's worth that,' he said.

"Miss Robinson was sitting opposite to him. She was

looking rather nice that evening. Of course I recognised her dress, it was one of Sophie's old ones; but if you hadn't known Miss Robinson was the governess you would never have suspected it.

" 'That's a very beautiful necklace that young lady has on,' said Borselli.

" 'Oh, but that's Mrs. Livingstone's governess,' said Mary Lyngate.

" 'I can't help that,' he said. 'She's wearing one of the finest strings of pearls for its size that I've ever seen in my life. It must be worth fifty thousand pounds.'

" 'Nonsense.'

" 'I give you my word it is.'

"Mary Lyngate leant over. She has rather a shrill voice.

" 'Miss Robinson, do you know what Count Borselli says?' she exclaimed. 'He says that string of pearls you're wearing is worth fifty thousand pounds.'

"Just at that moment there was a sort of pause in the conversation so that everybody heard. We all turned and looked at Miss Robinson. She flushed a little and laughed.

" 'Well, I made a very good bargain,' she said, 'because I paid fifteen shillings for it.'

" 'You certainly did.'

"We all laughed. It was of course absurd. We've all heard of wives palming off on their husbands as false a string of pearls that was real and expensive. That story is as old as the hills."

"Thank you," I said, thinking of a little narrative of my own.

"But it was too ridiculous to suppose that a governess would remain a governess if she owned a string of pearls worth fifty thousand pounds. It was obvious that the Count had made a bloomer. Then an extraordinary thing happened. The long arm of coincidence came in."

"It shouldn't," I retorted. "It's had too much exercise. Haven't you seen that charming book called *A Dictionary of English Usage?*"

"I wish you wouldn't interrupt just when I'm really getting to the exciting point."

But l had to do so again, for just then a young grilled salmon was insinuated round my left elbow.

"Mrs. Livingstone is giving us a heavenly dinner," I said.

"Is salmon fattening?" asked Laura.

"Very," I answered as I took a large helping.

"Bunk," she said.

"Go on," I begged her. "The long arm of coincidence was about to make a gesture."

"Well, at that very moment the butler bent over Miss Robinson and whispered something in her ear. I thought she turned a trifle pale. It's such a mistake not to wear rouge; you never know what tricks nature will play on you. She certainly looked startled. She leant forwards.

" 'Mrs. Livingstone, Dawson says there are two men in the hall who want to speak to me at once.'

" 'Well, you'd better go,' said Sophie Livingstone.

"Miss Robinson got up and left the room. Of course the same thought flashed through all our minds, but I said it first.

" 'I hope they haven't come to arrest her,' I said to Sophie. 'It would be too dreadful for you, my dear.'

" 'Are you sure it was a real necklace, Borselli?' she asked.

" 'Oh, quite.'

" 'She could hardly have had the nerve to wear it to-night if it were stolen,' I said.

"Sophie Livingstone turned as pale as death under her make-up, and I saw she was wondering if everything was all right in her jewel case. I only had on a little chain of diamonds, but instinctively I put my hand up to my neck to feel if it was still there.

" 'Don't talk nonsense," said Mr. Livingstone. 'How on earth would Miss Robinson have had the chance of sneaking a valuable string of pearls?'

" 'She may be a receiver,' I said.

" 'Oh, but she had such wonderful references,' said Sophie.

" 'They always do,' I said."

I was positively forced to interrupt Laura once more.

"You don't seem to have been determined to take a very bright view of the case," I remarked.

"Of course I knew nothing against Miss Robinson, and I had every reason to think her a very nice girl, but it would have been rather thrilling to find out that she was a notorious thief and a well-known member of a gang of international crooks."

"Just like a film. I'm dreadfully afraid that it's only in films that exciting things like that happen."

"Well, we waited in breathless suspense. There was not a sound. I expected to hear a scuffle in the hall or at least a smothered shriek. I thought the silence was ominous. Then the door opened and Miss Robinson walked in. I noticed at once that the necklace was gone. I could see that she was pale and excited. She came back to the table, sat down and with a smile threw on it . . ."

"On what?"

"On the table, you fool. A string of pearls."

" 'There's my necklace,' she said.

"Count Borselli leant forwards.

" 'Oh, but those are false,' he said.

" 'I told you they were,' she laughed.

" 'That's not the same string that you had on a few moments ago,' he said.

"She shook her head and smiled mysteriously. We were all intrigued. I don't know that Sophie Livingstone was so very much pleased at her governess making herself the centre of interest like that and I thought there was a suspicion of tartness in her manner when she suggested that Miss Robinson had better explain. Well, Miss Robinson said that when she went into the hall she found two men who said they'd come from Jarrot's Stores. She'd bought her string there, as she said, for fifteen shillings, and she'd taken it back because the clasp was loose and had only fetched it that afternoon. The men said they had given her the wrong string. Someone had left a string of real pearls to be re-strung and the assistant had made a mistake. Of course I can't understand how anyone could be so stupid as to take a really valuable string to Jarrot's, they aren't used to dealing with that sort of thing, and they wouldn't know real pearls from false; but you know what fools some women are. Anyhow, it was the string Miss Robinson was wearing, and it was valued at fifty thousand pounds. She naturally gave it back to them—she couldn't do anything else, I suppose, though it must have been a wrench—and they returned her own string to her; then they said that although of course they were under no obligation—you know the silly, pompous way men talk when they're trying to be businesslike— they were instructed, as a solatium or whatever you call it, to offer her a cheque for three hundred pounds. Miss Robinson actually showed it to us. She was as pleased as Punch."

"Well, it was a piece of luck, wasn't it?"

"You'd have thought so. As it turned out it was the ruin of her."

"Oh, how was that?"

"Well, when the time came for her to go on her holiday she told Sophie Livingstone that she'd made up her mind to go to Deauville for a month and blue the whole three hundred pounds. Of course Sophie tried to dissuade her, and begged her to put the money in the savings bank, but she wouldn't hear of it. She said she'd never had such a chance before and would never have it again and she meant for at least four weeks to live like a duchess. Sophie couldn't really do anything,

and so she gave way. She sold Miss Robinson a lot of clothes
that she didn't want; she'd been wearing them all through the
season and was sick to death of them; she says she gave them to
her, but I don't suppose she quite did that—I dare say she sold
them very cheap—and Miss Robinson started off, entirely
alone, for Deauville. What do you think happened then?"

"I haven't a notion," I replied. "I hope she had the time of
her life."

"Well, a week before she was due to come back she wrote to
Sophie and said that she'd changed her plans and had entered
another profession, and hoped that Mrs. Livingstone would
forgive her if she didn't return. Of course poor Sophie was
furious. What had actually happened was that Miss Robinson
had picked up a rich Argentine in Deauville and had gone off to
Paris with him. She's been in Paris ever since. I've seen her
myself at Florence's, with bracelets right up to her elbow and
ropes of pearls round her neck. Of course I cut her dead. They
say she has a house in the Bois de Boulogne and I know she has
a Rolls. She threw over the Argentine in a few months and
then got hold of a Greek; I don't know who she's with now,
but the long and short of it is that she's far and away the
smartest cocotte in Paris."

"When you say she was ruined you use the word in a
purely technical sense, I conclude," said I.

"I don't know what you mean by that," said Laura. "But
don't you think you could make a story out of it?"

"Unfortunately I've already written a story about a pearl
necklace. One can't go on writing stories about pearl neck-
laces."

"I've got half a mind to write it myself. Only, of course, I
should change the end."

"Oh, how would you end it?"

"Well, I should have had her engaged to a bank clerk who
had been badly knocked about in the war, with only one leg,

say, or half his face shot away; and they'd be dreadfully poor
and there would be no prospect of their marriage for years, and
he would be putting all his savings into buying a little house in
the suburbs, and they'd have arranged to marry when he had
saved the last instalment. And then she takes him the three
hundred pounds and they can hardly believe it, they're so
happy, and he cries on her shoulder. He just cries like a child.
And they get the little house in the suburbs and they marry,
and they have his old mother to live with them, and he goes to
the bank every day, and if she's careful not to have babies she
can still go out as a daily governess, and he's often ill—with his
wound, you know—and she nurses him, and it's all very
pathetic and sweet and lovely."

"It sounds rather dull to me," I ventured.

"Yes, but moral," said Laura.

THE VERGER

THERE had been a christening that afternoon at St.
Peter's, Neville Square, and Albert Edward Foreman
still wore his verger's gown. He kept his new one, its folds as
full and stiff as though it were made not of alpaca but of
perennial bronze, for funerals and weddings (St. Peter's,
Neville Square, was a church much favoured by the fashionable
for these ceremonies) and now he wore only his second-best.
He wore it with complacence, for it was the dignified symbol of
his office, and without it (when he took it off to go home) he
had the disconcerting sensation of being somewhat insufficiently
clad. He took pains with it; he pressed it and ironed it himself.
During the sixteen years he had been verger of this church he
had had a succession of such gowns, but he had never been
able to throw them away when they were worn out and the
complete series, neatly wrapped up in brown paper, lay in the
bottom drawer of the wardrobe in his bedroom.

The verger busied himself quietly, replacing the painted
wooden cover on the marble font, taking away a chair that had
been brought for an infirm old lady, and waited for the vicar
to have finished in the vestry so that he could tidy up in there
and go home. Presently he saw him walk across the chancel,
genuflect in front of the high altar and come down the aisle;
but he still wore his cassock.

"What's he 'anging about for?" the verger said to himself.
"Don't 'e know I want my tea?"

The vicar had been but recently appointed, a red-faced
energetic man in the early forties, and Albert Edward still
regretted his predecessor, a clergyman of the old school who
preached leisurely sermons in a silvery voice and dined out a
great deal with his more aristocratic parishioners. He liked

things in church to be just so, but he never fussed; he was not like this new man who wanted to have his finger in every pie. But Albert Edward was tolerant. St. Peter's was in a very good neighbourhood and the parishioners were a very nice class of people. The new vicar had come from the East End and he couldn't be expected to fall in all at once with the discreet ways of his fashionable congregation.

"All this 'ustle," said Albert Edward. "But give 'im time, he'll learn."

When the vicar had walked down the aisle so far that he could address the verger without raising his voice more than was becoming in a place of worship he stopped.

"Foreman, will you come into the vestry for a minute. I have something to say to you."

"Very good, sir."

The vicar waited for him to come up and they walked up the church together.

"A very nice christening, I thought, sir. Funny 'ow the baby stopped cryin' the moment you took him."

"I've noticed they very often do," said the vicar, with a little smile. "After all I've had a good deal of practice with them."

It was a source of subdued pride to him that he could nearly always quiet a whimpering infant by the manner in which he held it and he was not unconscious of the amused admiration with which mothers and nurses watched him settle the baby in the crook of his surpliced arm. The verger knew that it pleased him to be complimented on his talent.

The vicar preceded Albert Edward into the vestry. Albert Edward was a trifle surprised to find the two churchwardens there. He had not seen them come in. They gave him pleasant nods.

"Good afternoon, my lord. Good afternoon, sir," he said to one after the other.

They were elderly men, both of them, and they had been

churchwardens almost as long as Albert Edward had been verger. They were sitting now at a handsome refectory table that the old vicar had brought many years before from Italy and the vicar sat down in the vacant chair between them. Albert Edward faced them, the table between him and them, and wondered with slight uneasiness what was the matter. He remembered still the occasion on which the organist had got into trouble and the bother they had all had to hush things up. In a church like St. Peter's, Neville Square, they couldn't afford a scandal. On the vicar's red face was a look of resolute benignity, but the others bore an expression that was slightly troubled.

"He's been naggin' them, he 'as," said the verger to himself. "He's jockeyed them into doin' something, but they don't 'alf like it. That's what it is, you mark my words."

But his thoughts did not appear on Albert Edward's clean-cut and distinguished features. He stood in a respectful but not obsequious attitude. He had been in service before he was appointed to his ecclesiastical office, but only in very good houses, and his deportment was irreproachable. Starting as a page-boy in the household of a merchant-prince, he had risen by due degrees from the position of fourth to first footman, for a year he had been single-handed butler to a widowed peeress and till the vacancy occurred at St. Peter's, butler with two men under him in the house of a retired ambassador. He was tall, spare, grave and dignified. He looked, if not like a duke, at least like an actor of the old school who specialised in dukes' parts. He had tact, firmness, and self-assurance. His character was unimpeachable.

The vicar began briskly.

"Foreman, we've got something rather unpleasant to say to you. You've been here a great many years and I think his lordship and the general agree with me that you've fulfilled the duties of your office to the satisfaction of everybody concerned."

The two churchwardens nodded.

"But a most extraordinary circumstance came to my knowledge the other day and I felt it my duty to impart it to the churchwardens. I discovered to my astonishment that you could neither read nor write."

The verger's face betrayed no sign of embarrassment.

"The last vicar knew that, sir," he replied. "He said it didn't make no difference. He always said there was a great deal too much education in the world for 'is taste."

"It's the most amazing thing I ever heard," cried the general. "Do you mean to say that you've been verger of this church for sixteen years and never learned to read or write?"

"I went into service when I was twelve, sir. The cook in the first place tried to teach me once, but I didn't seem to 'ave the knack for it, and then what with one thing and another I never seemed to 'ave the time. I've never really found the want of it. I think a lot of these young fellows waste a rare lot of time readin' when they might be doin' something useful."

"But don't you want to know the news?" said the other churchwarden. "Don't you ever want to write a letter?"

"No, me lord, I seem to manage very well without. And of late years now they've all these pictures in the papers I get to know what's goin' on pretty well. Me wife's quite a scholar and if I want to write a letter she writes it for me. It's not as if I was a bettin' man."

The two churchwardens gave the vicar a troubled glance and then looked down at the table.

"Well, Foreman, I've talked the matter over with these gentlemen and they quite agree with me that the situation is impossible. At a church like St. Peter's, Neville Square, we cannot have a verger who can neither read nor write."

Albert Edward's thin, sallow face reddened and he moved uneasily on his feet, but he made no reply.

"Understand me, Foreman, I have no complaint to make

12

against you. You do your work quite satisfactorily; I have the highest opinion both of your character and of your capacity, but we haven't the right to take the risk of some accident that might happen owing to your lamentable ignorance. It's a matter of prudence as well as of principle."

"But couldn't you learn, Foreman?" asked the general.

"No, sir, I'm afraid I couldn't, not now. You see I'm not as young as I was and if I couldn't seem able to get the letters in me 'ead when I was a nipper I don't think there's much chance of it now."

"We don't want to be harsh with you, Foreman," said the vicar. "But the churchwardens and I have quite made up our minds. We'll give you three months and if at the end of that time you cannot read and write I'm afraid you'll have to go."

Albert Edward had never liked the new vicar. He'd said from the beginning that they'd made a mistake when they gave him St. Peter's. He wasn't the type of man they wanted with a classy congregation like that. And now he straightened himself a little. He knew his value and he wasn't going to allow himself to be put upon.

"I'm very sorry, sir, I'm afraid it's no good. I'm too old a dog to learn new tricks. I've lived a good many years without knowin' 'ow to read and write and without wishin' to praise myself, self-praise is no recommendation, I don't mind sayin' I've done my duty in that state of life in which it 'as pleased a merciful providence to place me, and if I *could* learn now I don't know as I'd want to."

"In that case, Foreman, I'm afraid you must go."

"Yes, sir, I quite understand. I shall be 'appy to 'and in my resignation as soon as you've found somebody to take my place."

But when Albert Edward with his usual politeness had closed the church door behind the vicar and the two churchwardens he could not sustain the air of unruffled dignity with which he had borne the blow inflicted upon him and his lips quivered. He walked slowly back to the vestry and hung up on its proper peg his verger's gown. He sighed as he thought of all the grand funerals and smart weddings it had seen. He tidied everything up, put on his coat, and hat in hand walked down the aisle. He locked the church door behind him. He strolled across the square, but deep in his sad thoughts he did not take the street that led him home, where a nice strong cup of tea awaited him; he took the wrong turning. He walked slowly along. His heart was heavy. He did not know what he should do with himself. He did not fancy the notion of going back to domestic service; after being his own master for so many years, for the vicar and churchwardens could say what they liked, it was he that had run St. Peter's, Neville Square, he could scarcely demean himself by accepting a situation. He had saved a tidy sum, but not enough to live on without doing something, and life seemed to cost more every year. He had never thought to be troubled with such questions. The vergers of St. Peter's, like the popes of Rome, were there for life. He had often thought of the pleasant reference the vicar would make in his sermon at evensong the first Sunday after his death to the long and faithful service, and the exemplary character of their late verger, Albert Edward Foreman. He sighed deeply. Albert Edward was a non-smoker and a total abstainer, but with a certain latitude; that is to say he liked a glass of beer with his dinner and when he was tired he enjoyed a cigarette. It occurred to him now that one would comfort him and since he did not carry them he looked about him for a shop where he could buy a packet of Gold Flakes. He did not at once see one and walked on a little. It was a long street, with all sorts of shops in it, but there was not a single one where you could buy cigarettes.

"That's strange," said Albert Edward.

To make sure he walked right up the street again. No, there

was no doubt about it. He stopped and looked reflectively up and down.

"I can't be the only man as walks along this street and wants a fag," he said. "I shouldn't wonder but what a fellow might do very well with a little shop here. Tobacco and sweets, you know."

He gave a sudden start.

"That's an idea," he said. "Strange 'ow things come to you when you least expect it."

He turned, walked home, and had his tea.

"You're very silent this afternoon, Albert," his wife remarked.

"I'm thinkin'," he said.

He considered the matter from every point of view and next day he went along the street and by good luck found a little shop to let that looked as though it would exactly suit him. Twenty-four hours later he had taken it and when a month after that he left St. Peter's, Neville Square, for ever, Albert Edward Foreman set up in business as a tobacconist and newsagent. His wife said it was a dreadful come-down after being verger of St. Peter's, but he answered that you had to move with the times, the church wasn't what it was, and 'enceforward he was going to render unto Cæsar what was Cæsar's. Albert Edward did very well. He did so well that in a year or so it struck him that he might take a second shop and put a manager in. He looked for another long street that hadn't got a tobacconist in it and when he found it, and a shop to let, took it and stocked it. This was a success too. Then it occurred to him that if he could run two he could run half a dozen, so he began walking about London, and whenever he found a long street that had no tobacconist and a shop to let he took it. In the course of ten years he had acquired no less than ten shops and he was making money hand over fist. He went round to all of them himself every

Monday, collected the week's takings and took them to the bank.

One morning when he was there paying in a bundle of notes and a heavy bag of silver the cashier told him that the manager would like to see him. He was shown into an office and the manager shook hands with him.

"Mr. Foreman, I wanted to have a talk to you about the money you've got on deposit with us. D'you know exactly how much it is?"

"Not within a pound or two, sir, but I've got a pretty rough idea."

"Apart from what you paid in this morning it's a little over thirty thousand pounds. That's a very large sum to have on deposit and I should have thought you'd do better to invest it."

"I wouldn't want to take no risk, sir. I know it's safe in the bank."

"You needn't have the least anxiety. We'll make you out a list of absolutely gilt-edged securities. They'll bring you in a better rate of interest than we can possibly afford to give you."

A troubled look settled on Mr. Foreman's distinguished face. "I've never 'ad anything to do with stocks and shares and I'd 'ave to leave it all in your 'ands," he said.

The manager smiled. "We'll do everything. All you'll have to do next time you come in is just to sign the transfers."

"I could do that all right," said Albert uncertainly. "But 'ow should I know what I was signin'?"

"I suppose you can read," said the manager a trifle sharply.

Mr. Foreman gave him a disarming smile.

"Well, sir, that's just it. I can't. I know it sounds funny like, but there it is, I can't read or write, only me name, an' I only learnt to do that when I went into business."

The manager was so surprised that he jumped up from his chair.

"That's the most extraordinary thing I ever heard."

"You see, it's like this, sir, I never 'ad the opportunity until it was too late and then some'ow I wouldn't. I got obstinate like."

The manager stared at him as though he were a prehistoric monster.

"And do you mean to say that you've built up this important business and amassed a fortune of thirty thousand pounds without being able to read or write? Good God, man, what would you be now if you had been able to?"

"I can tell you that, sir," said Mr. Foreman, a little smile on his still aristocratic features. "I'd be verger of St. Peter's, Neville Square."

THE SOCIAL SENSE

I DO not like long-standing engagements. How can you tell whether on a certain day three or four weeks ahead you will wish to dine with a certain person? The chances are that in the interval something will turn up that you would much sooner do and so long a notice presages a large and formal party. But what help is there? The date has been fixed thus far away so that the guests bidden may be certainly disengaged and it needs a very adequate excuse to prevent your refusal from seeming churlish. You accept, and for a month the engagement hangs over you with gloomy menace. It interferes with your cherished plans. It disorganises your life. There is really only one way to cope with the situation and that is to put yourself off at the last moment. But it is one that I have never had the courage or the want of scruple to adopt.

It was with a faint sense of resentment then that one June evening towards half-past eight I left my lodging in Half Moon Street to walk round the corner to dine with the Macdonalds. I liked them. Many years ago I made up my mind not to eat the food of persons I disliked or despised, and though I have on this account enjoyed the hospitality of far fewer people than I otherwise should have done I still think the rule a good one. The Macdonalds were nice, but their parties were a toss-up. They suffered from the delusion that if they asked six persons to dine with them who had nothing in the world to say to one another the party would be a failure, but if they multiplied it by three and asked eighteen it must be a success. I arrived a little late, which is almost inevitable when you live so near the house you are going to that it is not worth while to take a taxi, and the room into which I was shown was filled with people. I knew few of them and my heart sank as I saw myself laboriously

353

making conversation through a long dinner with two total strangers. It was a relief to me when I saw Thomas and Mary Warton come in and an unexpected pleasure when I found on going in to dinner that I had been placed next to Mary.

Thomas Warton was a portrait-painter who at one time had had considerable success, but he had never fulfilled the promise of his youth and had long ceased to be taken seriously by the critics. He made an adequate income, but at the Private View of the Royal Academy no one gave more than a passing glance at the dull but conscientious portraits of fox-hunting squires and prosperous merchants which with unfailing regularity he sent to the annual exhibition. One would have liked to admire his work because he was an amiable and kindly man. If you happened to be a writer he was so genuinely enthusiastic over anything you had done, so charmed with any success you might have had, that you wished your conscience would allow you to speak with decent warmth of his own productions. It was impossible and you were driven to the last refuge of the portrait-painter's friend.

"It looks as if it were a marvellous likeness," you said.

Mary Warton had been in her day a well-known concert singer and she had still the remains of a lovely voice. She must in her youth have been very handsome. Now, at fifty-three, she had a haggard look. Her features were rather mannish and her skin was weather-beaten; but her short grey hair was thick and curly and her fine eyes were bright with intelligence. She dressed picturesquely rather than fashionably and she had a weakness for strings of beads and fantastic ear-rings. She had a blunt manner, a quick sense of human folly and a sharp tongue, so that many people did not like her. But no one could deny that she was clever. She was not only an accomplished musician, but she was a great reader and she was passionately interested in painting. She had a very rare feeling for art. She liked the modern, not from pose but from natural inclination, and she had bought for next to nothing the pictures of unknown painters who later became famous. You heard at her house the most recent and difficult music and no poet or novelist in Europe could offer the world something new and strange without her being ready to fight on his behalf the good fight against the Philistines. You might say she was a highbrow; she was; but her taste was almost faultless, her judgment sound and her enthusiasm honest.

No one admired her more than Thomas Warton. He had fallen in love with her when she was still a singer and had pestered her to marry him. She had refused him half a dozen times and I had a notion that she had married him in the end with hesitation. She thought that he would become a great painter and when he turned out to be no more than a decent craftsman, without originality or imagination, she felt that she had been cheated. She was mortified by the contempt with which the connoisseurs regarded him. Thomas Warton loved his wife. He had the greatest respect for her judgment and would sooner have had a word of praise from her than columns of eulogy in all the papers in London. She was too honest to say what she did not think. It wounded him bitterly that she held his work in such poor esteem, and though he pretended to make a joke of it you could see that at heart he resented her outspoken comments. Sometimes his long, horse-like face grew red with the anger he tried to control and his eyes dark with hatred. It was notorious among their friends that the couple did not get on. They had the distressing habit of fripping in public. Warton never spoke to others of Mary but with admiration, but she was less discreet and her confidants knew how exasperating she found him. She admitted his goodness, his generosity, his unselfishness; she admitted them ungrudgingly; but his defects were of the sort that make a man hard to live with, for he was narrow, argumentative and conceited. He was not an artist and Mary Warton cared more for art than for anything in the world. It was a matter on which she could not compromise. It blinded her to the fact that the faults in Warton that maddened her were due in large part to his hurt feelings. She wounded him continually and he was dogmatic and intolerant in self-protection. There cannot be anything much worse than to be despised by the one person whose approval is all in all to you; and though Thomas Warton was intolerable it was impossible not to feel sorry for him. But if I have given the impression that Mary was a discontented, rather tiresome, pretentious woman I have been unjust to her. She was a loyal friend and a delightful companion. You could talk to her of any subject under the sun. Her conversation was humorous and witty. Her vitality was immense.

She was sitting now on the left hand of her host and the talk around her was general. I was occupied with my next-door neighbour, but I guessed by the laughter with which Mary's sallies were greeted that she was at her brilliant best. When she was in the vein no one could approach her.

"You're in great form to-night," I remarked, when at last she turned to me.

"Does it surprise you?"

"No, it's what I expect of you. No wonder people tumble over one another to get you to their houses. You have the inestimable gift of making a party go."

"I do my little best to earn my dinner."

"By the way, how's Manson? Someone told me the other day that he was going into a nursing home for an operation. I hope it's nothing serious."

Mary paused for a moment before answering, but she still smiled brightly.

"Haven't you seen the paper to-night?"

"No, I've been playing golf. I only got home in time to jump into a bath and change."

"He died at two o'clock this afternoon." I was about to make an exclamation of horrified surprise, but she stopped me. "Take care. Tom is watching me like a lynx. They're all watching me. They all know I adored him, but they none of them know for certain if he was my lover, even Tom doesn't know; they want to see how I'm taking it. Try to look as if you were talking of the Russian Ballet."

At that moment someone addressed her from the other side of the table, and throwing back her head a little with a gesture that was habitual with her, a smile on her large mouth, she flung at the speaker so quick and apt an answer that everyone round her burst out laughing. The talk once more became general and I was left to my consternation.

I knew, everyone knew, that for five and twenty years there had existed between Gerrard Manson and Mary Warton a passionate attachment. It had lasted so long that even the more strait-laced of their friends, if ever they had been shocked by it, had long since learnt to accept it with tolerance. They were middle-aged people, Manson was sixty and Mary not much younger, and it was absurd that at their age they should not do what they liked. You met them sometimes sitting in a retired corner of an obscure restaurant or walking together in the Zoo and you wondered why they still took care to conceal an affair that was nobody's business but their own. But of course there was Thomas. He was insanely jealous of Mary. He made many violent scenes and indeed, at the end of one tempestuous period, not so very long ago, he forced her to promise never to see Manson again. Of course she broke the promise, and though she knew that Thomas suspected this, she took precautions to prevent him from discovering it for a fact.

It was hard on Thomas. I think he and Mary would have jogged on well enough together and she would have resigned herself to the fact that he was a second-rate painter if her intercourse with Manson had not embittered her judgment.

The contrast between her husband's mediocrity and her lover's brilliance was too galling.

"With Tom I feel as if I were stifling in a closed room full of dusty knick-knacks," she told me. "With Gerrard I breathe the pure air of the mountain tops."

"Is it possible for a woman to fall in love with a man's mind?" I asked in a pure spirit of enquiry.

"What else is there in Gerrard?"

That, I admit, was a poser. For my part I thought, nothing; but the sex is extraordinary and I was quite ready to believe that Mary saw in Gerrard Manson a charm and a physical attractiveness to which most people were blind. He was a shrivelled little man, with a pale intellectual face, faded blue eyes behind his spectacles, and a high dome of shiny bald head. He had none of the appearance cf a romantic lover. On the other hand he was certainly a very subtle critic and a felicitous essayist. I resented somewhat his contemptuous attitude towards English writers unless they were safely dead and buried; but this was only to his credit with the intelligentsia, who are ever ready to believe that there can be no good in what is produced in their own country, and with them his influence was great. On one occasion I told him that one had only to put a commonplace in French for him to mistake it for an epigram and he had thought well enough of the joke to use it as his own in one of his essays. He reserved such praise as he was willing to accord his contemporaries to those who wrote in a foreign tongue. The exasperating thin; was that no one could deny that he was himself a brilliant writer. His style was exquisite. His knowledge was vast. He could be profound without pomposity, amusing without frivolity, and polished without affectation. His slightest article was readable. His essays were little masterpieces. For my part I did not find him a very agreeable companion. Perhaps I did not get the best out of him. Though I knew him a great many years I never heard him say an amusing thing. He was not talkative and when he made a remark it was oracular. The prospect of spending an evening alone would have filled me with dismay. It never ceased to puzzle me that this dull and mannered little man should be able to write with so much grace, wit and gaiety.

It puzzled me even more than that a gallant and vivacious creature like Mary Warton should have cherished for him so consuming a passion. These things are inexplicable and there was evidently something in that odd, crabbed, irascible creature that appealed to women. His wife adored him. She was a fat, frowzy, boring person. She had led Gerrard a dog's life, but had always refused to give him his freedom. She swore to kill herself if he left her and since she was unbalanced and hysterical he was never quite certain that she would not carry out her threat. One day, when I was having tea with Mary, I saw that she was distraught and nervous and when I asked her what was the matter she burst into tears. She had been lunching with Manson and had found him shattered after a terrific scene with his wife.

"We can't go on like this," Mary cried. "It's ruining his life. It's ruining all our lives."

"Why don't you take the plunge?"

"What do you mean?"

"You've been lovers so long, you know the best and the worst of one another by now; you're getting old and you can't count on many more years of life; it seems a pity to waste a love that has endured so long. What good are you doing to Mrs. Manson or to Tom? Are they happy because you two are making yourselves miserable?"

"No."

"Then why don't you chuck everything and just go off together and let come what may?"

Mary shook her head.

"We've talked that over endlessly. We've talked it over for a quarter of a century. It's impossible. For years Gerrard couldn't on account of his daughters. Mrs. Manson may have been a very fond mother, but she was a very bad one, and there was no one to see the girls were properly brought up but Gerrard. And now that they're married off he's set in his habits. What should we do? Go to France or Italy? I couldn't tear Gerrard away from his surroundings. He'd be wretched. He's too old to make a fresh start. And besides, though Thomas nags me and makes scenes and we frip and get on one another's nerves, he loves me. When it came to the point I simply shouldn't have the heart to leave him. He'd be lost without me."

"It's a situation without an issue. I'm dreadfully sorry for you."

On a sudden Mary's haggard, weather-beaten face was lit by a smile that broke on her large red mouth; and upon my word at that moment she was beautiful.

"You need not be. I was rather low a little while ago, but now I've had a good cry I feel better. Notwithstanding all the pain, all the unhappiness this affair has caused me, I wouldn't have missed it for all the world. For those few moments of ecstasy my love has brought me I would be willing to live all my life over again. And I think he'd tell you the same thing. Oh, it's been so infinitely worth while."

I could not help but be moved.

"There's no doubt about it," I said. "That's love all right."

"Yes, it's love, and we've just got to go through with it. There's no way out."

And now with this tragic suddenness the way out had come. I turned a little to look at Mary and she, feeling my eyes upon her, turned too. There was a smile on her lips.

"Why did you come here to-night? It must be awful for you."

She shrugged her shoulders.

"What could I do? I read the news in the evening paper while I was dressing. He'd asked me not to ring up the nursing-home on account of his wife. It's death to me. Death. I had to come. We'd been engaged for a month. What excuse could I give Tom? I'm not supposed to have seen Gerrard for two years. Do you know that for twenty years we've written to one another every day?" Her lower lip trembled a little, but she bit it and for a moment her face was twisted to a strange grimace; then with a smile she pulled herself together. "He was everything I had in the world, but I couldn't let the party down, could I? He always said I had a social sense."

"Happily we shall break up early and you can go home."

"I don't want to go home. I don't want to be alone. I daren't cry because my eyes will get red and swollen, and we've got a lot of people lunching with us to-morrow. Will you come, by the way? I want an extra man. I must be in good form; Tom expects to get a commission for a portrait out of it."

"By George, you've got courage."

"D'you think so? I'm heartbroken, you know. I suppose that's what makes it easier for me. Gerrard would have liked me to put a good face on it. He would have appreciated the irony of the situation. It's the sort of thing he always thought the French novelists described so well."